The Stars
On My Arm

Tekla Series

Leigh Jarrett

Published by Steambath Press (self-published)

Paperback 1st edition published July 2012
ISBN-13: 978-0987964090
ISBN-10: 0987964097

Paperback 2nd edition published October 2017
ISBN-13: 978-1-927553-43-5

*To all three of my children, whose diverse group of friends
provided me with some of the most incredible character studies I
ever could have imagined possible.*

*And to my children's friends, thank you for being
unapologetically original, and often deliciously and
extravagantly eccentric.*

Chapter One

The beach was clearing out after what had been another typically hot summer day in the waterfront community. The smell of suntan lotion and fries was still heavy in the air, and the flock of gulls that had been circling overhead since late afternoon had finally decided to make a landing, and see what scraps of food were left behind.

Joel Carrigan and his girlfriend, Erica, had spent the entire day soaking up the sun and were starting to pack up their things when a car full of Joel's friends showed up to take an evening swim in an attempt to cool off. This summer had been one of the hottest on record, and even though it was the last week of summer holidays before school started again, the stifling hot days were unrelenting, and close proximity to the water was one of the benefits Joel and his friends enjoyed.

He had lived in a few different houses throughout his life, but they had always been in the same neighborhood by the beach. His current home had a swimming pool, but access to the sandy beaches was only a few doors away from his house, so he tended to spend his time there instead. His best friend, Ryan, lived right on the beach, but spent most of his time indoors playing video games, and tended to only venture out at night when things cooled off.

Joel watched as his friends piled out of Ryan's convertible with their towels and the inevitable cooler.

"I guess we won't be going back to your place for a while," said Erica as she stuffed their towels into her beach bag. She handed the bag to Joel before pulling her shorts on and digging around in the sand to retrieve her flip-flops. She finally found them, dusted them off, and slipped them on her feet.

"We'll just hang out with them for a few minutes and then head out." Joel ran his hand up Erica's arm and kissed her softly on the lips. "I promise we won't stay long."

"It's not often your whole family is out of town," Erica added, and then pulled him back close to her lips. "They'll have left by now."

"Mm ...this is true." Joel looked over his shoulder at his friends frantically digging a hole to put the cooler in before the next police patrol passed through. Most of the time it was a pointless exercise; the police knew to check the drink containers of every teenager on the beach at this time of day. After even one was found to contain alcohol, they would be asked to get up and move their towels.

Ryan stopped digging and motioned for Joel to join them. "Hey, Joel," he shouted. "Do you want a beer before we sink this thing?"

"Sure thing, Ryan," answered Joel, and then laced his fingers with Erica's and led her reluctantly over to sit with his friends. Ryan handed him a pop bottle full of beer, and then went back to smoothing out the sand around the cooler before throwing a towel over the entire buried affair.

"Hey," Ryan said to Joel. "We went by your house to see if you and Erica were there, and someone is moving into that gigantic freakin' mansion next door."

"Finally," replied Joel. "It sold like …the beginning of summer. My mom was getting all freaked out, thinking the house was going to be used for a marijuana grow op."

"It wouldn't be the first one on your street." Erica pulled one of the towels back out of her beach bag. She stretched out on the sand and put her sunglasses on; the sun was setting, and it was absolutely brutal on the eyes. She settled in and listened to the boys talking about their usual stuff. Sports, girls, any upcoming parties, and then sports again.

Closing her eyes, Erica thought about her and Joel's plans for the final few days of their summer holidays. His family was going to be away the entire time so they would have the house to themselves. They were entering their final year at Tekla Senior High and had been together since the middle of grade ten, and they'd spent much of the summer discussing their university applications so they wouldn't be separated after high school graduation.

Erica opened her eyes when she felt Joel sit down beside her, and smiled as he began running his fingers through her hair.

"That feels nice," she said as she gazed up at him. Joel was an attentive and extremely attractive boyfriend; with his sun-bleached blond hair, tanned skin, and soft brown eyes that made her heart melt each time she saw him. He was quite a bit taller than she was, standing at least five foot eleven, and he kept fit by working out regularly in Ryan's home gym. It still gave her shivers when he wrapped her up in his strong arms. Joel's personality had always been a bit unusual in comparison to his friends and the other guys at school. He was what her mom referred to as an *old soul*, as he was always trying to impart pieces of his own spiritual understanding to others. It had been one of the things that had initially intrigued her about him.

Joel licked his lips. "I'm going to finish this beer, and then I think we should take off back to my house, and find some other things to do that feel nice." He threw back the remainder of the beer and then leaned over and kissed her. He shivered and laughed as Erica made soft purring noises in response.

Erica packed up her towel again and waited while Joel told his friends they were leaving, and then headed out through the parking lot with him toward his house. The cool evening breezes coming off the water were being funneled straight down his street, and they felt wonderful against her sun-warmed skin.

"It's getting dark earlier," she said. "What time is it anyway?"

"It's only eight thirty."

They slowed at the end of Joel's driveway, curious to see who was moving in next door. A large moving truck was parked outside the house, and a group of men were bringing in pieces of furniture and cartloads of boxes. All the furniture they saw going in was large and ornate with elaborate wooden carvings and had either red, purple or black upholstery. A massive black headboard with posts stylized to look like crazed, leering gargoyles caught Erica's eye.

"Someone has interesting stuff," Erica commented and then turned to Joel. "Maybe after they get settled, I can introduce myself and get a tour around the place."

"Yeah, like that wouldn't be too weird."

"People like to show off their homes, Joel."

"I'll have to take your word for that." Joel typed in the code on the garage door and waited for it to open, and as the interior was revealed, he was relieved to see his parents' car was gone. He pulled his keys out of his pocket and unlocked the interior door before closing the garage door back down behind them.

"So, what's first on our agenda?" Erica threw the beach bag down on the bench in the laundry room as they passed through it, and smiled, ripe with excitement, as Joel doubled back and caught her up in his arms, spinning her to him.

"I'm afraid I only have one thing planned for the entire agenda," Joel answered. "And it could become tiresome."

Erica giggled in anticipation.

Joel took her mouth, caressing her lips with his own, and deftly worked the knots of her bikini top loose. He let it fall to the floor before lifting his own shirt off over his head.

"I think we should go for a swim." Erica grabbed both of Joel's hands and led him through to the family room. She let his hands drop as they reached the sliding glass door that led out to the back yard, and removed her shorts and the bottom half of her bikini.

Catching the glint in Joel's eyes, Erica took off squealing through the patio door, and out across the pool deck, and into the pool, as he chased her. Joel struggled with the knot of his bathing suit but finally managed to pull the unwanted clothing off. He threw it onto one of the lounges and dove into the pool after her.

"You're so bad …," Joel said as he swam up to her. But Erica kept swimming away, just out of his reach, so he dove under the water and came up behind her, and wrapped his arms around her waist. The scent of her tanning lotion filled his senses as he kissed the back of her neck and ran his lips along the back of her shoulders.

Erica sighed from deep within, as Joel moved his body closer to hers, and reached back for him as he brought them together and pushed into her gently. She tipped her head back, and their mouths met while rocking her hips and clinging to the edge of the pool.

She shivered as she felt Joel crest deep within her much sooner than what she had been anticipating.

She turned and wrapped her arms around his neck "You've been holding that in," she said, and then kissed him.

"Sorry, I've been thinking about it all day," Joel replied. "Apparently, I have no control whatsoever."

Erica looked at Joel and rolled her eyes.

"After dinner, everything will work nice and slow," Joel said as he winked at her. "I promise."

"Mm …I should make dinner then." Erica ruffled his hair and carefully pulled herself out of the pool, using one of the ladders, and headed back toward the house.

Joel decided to stay in the pool and enjoy the cooling effect of the water on his bare skin, and the relaxing euphoria he always felt after having sex. He counted himself lucky to have found someone like Erica so early on in his life. She was a beautiful girl with dark brown hair and intense green eyes. Her figure was petite and toned, and she had a sexuality about her that had attracted him to her from the first day he'd set eyes on her. He drifted contentedly around in the water, thinking about Erica and their future together.

A male voice, with a distinctly British accent, spoke from the other side of the short fence that ran the perimeter of his back yard.

"Nice night," the voice commented.

It was dark at that side of the yard because of the dense trees, and all Joel could see was the lit end of a cigarette. He swam to the edge of the pool and tried to adjust his eyes to see the figure standing there. But he couldn't see anyone.

"It was a bit hot today," Joel answered, "but it's cooled down nicely now." He kicked off from the edge and drifted to the middle of the pool. He still couldn't see whom he was talking to, but the figure in the darkness sounded like he might be about the same age.

He peered into the darkness. "Where are you from?"

"London mostly …but we move around a bit."

"Are you in high school or …"

"Yeah. Your equivalent of grade eleven. You?"

"Grade twelve. Finally."

Joel jumped when he heard the fence rattle and saw his new neighbor land in his yard.

"Name's Ethan." Ethan walked over to the edge of the pool and stared down at Joel as he continued to smoke his cigarette.

The first thing Joel noticed about Ethan was his ominous stature. He wasn't particularly broad, but he was very tall, and would easily dwarf him and any of his friends. The second thing he noticed about Ethan was his clothes; he was dressed entirely in black. Black jeans supported by a silver studded black belt, a loosely tucked black t-shirt, and heavy black combat boots.

"Hey, I'm Joel." Joel swam over to the far edge of the pool, not sure how much of his nudity could be seen below the surface of the water because of the in-pool lighting. He wanted to gain some distance, just in case.

"So, what is there to do around here?" Ethan asked as he tossed his cigarette down on the pool deck and crushed it out.

"We tend to go to the beach every day."

"Beaches aren't my thing." Ethan walked across the pool deck and sat down on one of the lounges. He picked up Joel's bathing suit and tossed it onto the next one over. "What else is there to do?"

"There will probably be a few parties happening before school goes back next week. I could let you know if I hear anything."

Joel continued looking Ethan over nervously while clinging to the edge of the pool, not sure what to make of him. Ethan's hair was straight and black, hanging down past his shoulders, and he had black smudged liner circling his eyes, making him look like a few musicians Joel had seen in older music videos. As Ethan tucked a strand of hair behind his ear, the setting sun lit up Ethan's profile, and Joel could see a plethora of tattoos literally covering Ethan's arms and hands ...and a staggering amount of facial piercings. The overall visual effect was quite disturbing.

Joel's gut twisted a little, and his breath caught short in his chest.

"I saw your parents pack up and leave a few hours ago," Ethan said as he untied his boots. He pulled them off, threw them on the pool deck, and stuffed his removed socks into them. "Are you going to have a party while they're gone?" He walked over to Joel's side of the pool and rolled up his pant legs, and then sat down at the edge of the pool next to Joel, and dropped his feet into the water.

"No, I'm not having a party," Joel answered as he moved further away from Ethan as he lit up another cigarette, not wanting to breathe in any of the smoke.

"Why not?"

"I don't need the hassle from my parents if they find out."

"Plus you'll have your hands full shaggin' that girlfriend."

"How do you know about her?" Joel swam over to the side of the pool closest to the house and looked anxiously back at Ethan. "How long have you been standing out here?"

"Long enough." Ethan pulled his feet out of the water and walked over to where Joel was gripping the pool edge. "Maybe I should go introduce myself." He started toward the house and smiled when he heard Joel lift himself out of the water.

"I think you should leave now," Joel demanded.

Ethan slowed his pace and turned to face him. "Yeah …I don't think so, sunshine." He approached Joel and circled around him, staring at him. "You're looking frightfully cold, beach boy. Do you want a towel or something?"

The patio door opened behind Ethan, and he turned slowly to face it, and upon seeing Erica, made a theatrical bow. "My lady—"

Erica eyed Ethan nervously. "Is everything all right out here?"

"Everything is ship shape on the pool deck, captain," Ethan said and began circling Joel again. "I was just asking Joel here if he needed a towel to cover himself …the cold seems to be affecting him adversely." He took a final draw off his cigarette and then threw it down on the ground, crushing it out with his bare foot.

"And what is your name, my dear?" he asked.

"Um …Joel. Could I get you to help me in the kitchen?" Erica asked with apparent fear in her eyes.

Joel, fearing what his new neighbor might do next, skirted around Ethan, and ran into the house, at which point Erica slammed the sliding glass door behind him and locked it.

"What the hell?" Erica cried. "Is that your new neighbor?"

"Yeah. Lucky me. I think it would've been better to have a grow op next door. That guy is seriously scary."

Joel closed the curtains over the window of the patio door and grabbed a towel to dry off. After he'd thrown it in the laundry, he went to his room to grab some clothes, and then returned to the family room, where he found Erica standing by the window.

"Should we be calling the police?" Erica asked as she peered out through the curtains into the darkness. She couldn't see Ethan anywhere.

"No, he's probably gone home." Joel touched Erica's arm and led her away from the window. "What are we having for dinner?"

"Your mom left some spaghetti sauce defrosting in the fridge for us. I'll heat that up if you can get some water boiling." Erica turned back to the kitchen and shrieked with joy as Joel wrapped her up in his arms and kissed the back of her neck.

"I love it when my family goes away," Joel said, "and we can pretend this is our house, and do all the everyday stuff together."

"Like laundry, washing dishes …taking out the garbage—" Erica laughed when Joel turned her to face him, but then she screamed; Ethan was peering in through a kitchen window.

"What the fuck?" Joel said when he turned and saw Ethan.

"That's it, I'm calling the police," Erica said.

Joel finished pulling his shirt on over his head as Erica headed to his bedroom to get her cell phone. He walked over to the kitchen window and pushed it open. "My girlfriend is calling the police."

"I'll be gone by the time they get here." Ethan lit up a cigarette and took a long draw as he looked past Joel into the house. "How long have you been shaggin' that?"

"That is none of your fucking business."

"Fine, be like that." Ethan blew smoke in through the window into Joel's face. "I'll see you around, neighbor."

Then he winked and took off at a jog, headed for the fence. He pulled himself over and walked sedately back into his house.

The moving men were bringing in the last of the boxes and Ethan directed them to leave everything in the living room and go. The day had been too long already, and he just wanted it to be over; he followed the men to the door and pressed it closed behind them.

Ethan wandered into the kitchen and pulled open the fridge to peruse through the paltry selection of things he'd picked up from the shops near the airport that afternoon. He would need to head out as soon as his car arrived to buy more food. His cook wasn't scheduled to arrive until sometime next week. He would have to fend for himself until she got there.

He lifted a beer from the door and pulled out his cell phone, found the nearest pizza place, and placed an order.

He didn't feel like cooking.

Chapter Two

The breakfast dishes had been cleared away, and the floor swept, but Joel had put off taking the garbage out the night before, and it had spilled out into the cupboard under the sink, prompting an emergency evacuation and clean up.

"Are you sure you still like this domestic stuff?" Erica asked.

Joel sighed and rolled his eyes at her. "It has to be done, but it's a royal pain," he said, and then swore as he fumbled with the tie on the bag.

"You're so cute when you're flustered." Erica collected her purse and keys off the kitchen counter and turned back to Joel. "I have to leave for work. Are you going to be all right by yourself for the entire day?"

"I'll probably head over to Ryan's for a few hours …and then a nap is next on the list," Joel said as he washed his hands. He dried them off and gathered Erica up in his arms, and gave her a long kiss before saying good-bye to her at the door.

Joel watched Erica pull out of the driveway and then wandered into his bathroom to start up the water for a shower, and after grabbing a towel and throwing it onto the counter, he stepped in with the intention of enjoying the refreshing feel of it on his skin.

With his eyes closed, Joel let the water rush over his face and thought about the night he'd spent with Erica. They'd made love a few times before falling asleep in each other's arms. The scent and feel of her were so familiar and comforting that he'd had one of the best night's sleep in a long time.

He'd only just finished up, stepped out of the shower, and wrapped the towel around his waist when he heard the doorbell ring. Thinking it was probably someone trying to sell something, he reluctantly went to answer it and was surprised to see it was Ethan.

"Hiya," Ethan said casually. He looked Joel up and down, smirked, then cocked an eyebrow in amusement. "Boy, you really don't like wearing clothes much do you?"

"I just got out of the shower. What the fuck do you want?"

"I saw your slapper leave a few minutes ago."

"My what?" Joel shook his head, not actually wanting to know. "Never mind. Why are you here?"

"I was hoping you could help me out. I've run clean out of fags and beer, and I don't know where the nearest shops are at."

Joel kicked roughly at the doorframe, trying to decide whether he should just slam the door in Ethan's face.

"There are some stores not far from here," he said finally. "But you have to be nineteen to buy that stuff."

"Bollocks." Ethan pulled his wallet out of his pocket and flipped through some of the cards in it. "Will this get me through?"

"Crazy looking driver's license, but probably." Joel looked it over then handed it back. "It says you're twenty-one. How old are you really?"

"Eighteen." Ethan grinned at Joel and put his wallet back. "There must've been some weird time shift when I jumped the pond."

"How on earth did you get a fake driver's license?"

"My dad got it for me." Ethan winked at Joel. "Now, these shops I'm looking for. How do I get to them? Keeping in mind, I'll be leggin' it. My car hasn't arrived yet."

"Wait ...your dad got it for you?" Joel said then exhaled in exasperation. Some people had all the luck when it came to parents.

"If you follow the path at the end of the street there," he said. "It'll take you through a field and out onto the main road, and then you'll be able to see them off to the left."

"Did you want to be coming with me, Joel?" Ethan shifted his weight and chewed anxiously on his thumbnail. "Hurry up and decide though," he said, releasing his thumb. "Because if I don't get some fags soon, I'm going to have no fuckin' nails left."

Joel studied Ethan, trying to judge what his motivation was for inviting him along. He didn't look nearly as intimidating as what he had the night before. He was still wearing the black jeans, but he hadn't smudged the black eyeliner, and he'd had enough sense to put on a sleeveless shirt and a pair of flip-flops ...even though it was obvious his feet hadn't seen sunlight in years.

His attention wandered. The extent of Ethan's piercings was actually quite fascinating. Both of Ethan's eyebrows had mini curved barbells capped with silver pointed spikes, and he had a series of six balls running along the sides of his nose directly between his eyes.

Joel blinked, not able to tear his attention away. Ethan's nose had a circular barbell through his septum that hung down almost as far as his top lip, and he had a ring through each nostril. There were three rings through his lower lip, the center one having a small ball attached to it, and then there were two small silver balls running down the center of his chin.

He let his gaze wander away from Ethan's face to the massive holes he'd stretched in his ears and adorned with black gauged earrings with silver rims, and the assortment of spikes, balls and other holes around them. His attention drifted to the series of black crescent moons tattooed all along Ethan's collarbone, then downwards. The tightness of Ethan's shirt made it evident that his nipples were pierced and decorated with some fairly significant rings.

Joel tipped his head sideways and tried to make out the images depicted in the tattoos on both of Ethan's arms and hands, but without looking at them straight on, he couldn't get the full effect of them.

Ethan continued to chew on his thumbnail as he waited for Joel to finish looking him over. He was used to people staring at him. It was one of the reasons he loved body modification; he liked the reaction he got from people. But more importantly, he liked the way it looked. He viewed his body as a canvas he could alter to express his personality. The overall effect made some people uncomfortable and even frightened, and some just curious.

Joel seemed to be falling squarely in the curious camp.

He watched as Joel made eye contact with him again.

"Didn't some of those hurt?" asked Joel.

"The worst ones were these ones here." Ethan flicked at his nipples. "Surprisingly, the least painful ones were down here." He patted the front of his pants. "And this one just about made me throw up." He lifted his shirt to show the surface piercing that sat just below his belly button. "The rest made me tear up a bit, but they weren't too bad. Except for my tongue." He stuck it out, and Joel cringed as he saw the size of the black ball on it. "It didn't hurt too much, but it totally swelled up. I could barely talk for days."

He dropped his hands to his hips and stared at Joel. "So, are you coming with me or what?"

"Only if you buy me some beer." Joel motioned for Ethan to come into the house and closed the door. "Just let me get dressed."

Ethan sat down on the bench in the front hall and looked around. It was a nice enough house; nothing like his though. It was a strange neighborhood, the way the different classes of people were so mixed together. It was completely different back home where everyone was boxed away nicely in their appointed neighborhoods.

He turned when he heard Joel coming down the hall.

"Finally," he said. "I get to see you with some clothes on." Ethan patted Joel's arm lightly and opened the front door.

"I'm not too sure about your style though, preppy pastel boy."

"At least I won't boil to death, like you." Joel led Ethan down the road sticking to the shady side of the street. "Don't you own a pair of shorts or anything?"

"I thought I did pretty good digging these flippy floppy things out of a box," Ethan replied. "And I destroyed one of my shirts." He pulled disgustedly at the edge of his cut-off sleeve.

They reached the end of the road and squeezed through an opening in the fence. The field on the other side was thick with tall grass and full of crickets that, much to his embarrassment, made Ethan jump every time one of them leaped across his path. They emerged at the edge of a busy road and turned to walk a couple of blocks to a small strip mall. Ethan immediately headed for the cold beer and wine store and was about to go in when Joel stopped him.

"Hey, you promised to get me some beer," Joel said.

"I will. Come in and tell me what you want."

"I can't go in there. I have to be nineteen."

"Are you fuckin' with me?" Ethan looked around behind him and saw the woman working the till inside. "She's not going to bust my balls about buying for you, is she?"

"I think she's probably going to be too preoccupied with your overall look and the age on your driver's license to be worrying about me standing out here, waiting for you."

"Good. So, what do you want?"

"Just grab me a case of that Canadian stuff there in the blue box at the bottom of the cooler."

Joel sat down on the curb and pretended to be texting someone on his cell phone, making it look like he had a reason for sitting there. It wasn't long before Ethan came back out with four cases of beer, two bottles of rum, and a carton of cigarettes.

Ethan handed Joel two of the cases and the bag with the bottles in it and started walking back down the street. "That should hold me until I have a chance to get to the shops," he said and laughed shortly. "My staff won't be showing up until next week, so I'm kind of winging it over at my place."

"You have staff? What does your dad do for work?"

"Funny thing that. I don't actually know." Ethan sat down at the edge of the field, ripped open the carton of cigarettes, and passed the remnants to Joel to put in the bag with the rum. He pulled open a package and quickly had a cigarette lit. "Sit. I want to have at least two of these before we go any further."

Ethan leaned toward Joel and took one of the rum bottles out of the bag and opened it. He took a long swig and passed it to Joel, motioning for him to have some.

"It's a bit early for that, isn't it?" Joel said.

"Time is relative," Ethan said, and then smiled as Joel took a long draw off the bottle. "See. You didn't burst into flames or anything."

"Amazing!" Joel grinned and shoved Ethan lightly.

Ethan studied Joel for a second then crushed out his first cigarette to start on his second.

"So, you have no idea what your dad does?" Joel asked, curious as to how Ethan could be oblivious to something like that.

"Not a clue."

"Whatever he does, he must make a lot of money doing it to be able to afford that house of yours. Is he at work now?"

"I don't know. I rarely see my dad. I tend to live pretty much on my own." Ethan stood and tossed his cigarette off to one side, whereby Joel leaped up, scrambling past him to stomp it out.

"Ethan, man, you can't do that," Joel said. "This place is like a fucking tinder box at this time of year."

"Sorry. I'm not used to this kind of heat." Ethan picked up his stuff, headed out across the field, and tried not to jump every time a cricket crossed his path. "It rains a lot back home."

"We don't get much of that around here." Joel held back and studied Ethan, taking in some of the finer details of his overall demeanor. It was possible he wasn't a psychopath after all.

"Hey, did you want to hang out at my place?" Ethan slowed to let Joel catch up with him. "The decorators and organizers are all over the place inside, but we could sit out in the back garden. It's pretty cool and shady out there."

Joel stopped and leaned the cases of beer against the fence. He took another mouthful of rum and passed the bottle to Ethan. "Sure, why not?" he replied. "My eyeballs are already floating. I might as well make a day of it."

Ethan grinned, pleased with Joel's response. He needed to start making friends. "Sounds like a plan, preppy boy."

They took their time making their way back down the street, talking and stopping every so often to cool off. The trees were providing plenty of shade, but even this early in the day, the air moving across them was like opening an oven.

"Hey, do you have a pool in your yard?" Joel asked as they approached Ethan's front door.

Ethan pushed the unlatched door open with his foot and strode inside. The decorators had been ferrying things in and out through the door and weren't bothering to close it. Fortunately, the air conditioning was cranked up full, compensating for their negligence.

"Yeah, it's all set up and ready to go," Ethan answered as he led the way into an expansive foyer with black marble floors that felt wonderful and cool on Joel's bare feet.

Joel followed Ethan through to the back of the house and into the kitchen, where he set everything down on the counter, looking on with concern as Ethan lit up yet another cigarette while putting the beer into the fridge.

"How many of those do you smoke a day?" Joel ripped open his case of beer, took two cans out, and poured them into the massive, chilled beer glass Ethan handed to him.

"Too many. I've tried to quit, but it's a bit of a comfort thing for me …being alone so much and all."

"Where's your mom?"

"She died when I was five. My dad has remarried a few times, but it never lasts long."

"I'm sorry."

Joel grabbed his glass and followed Ethan through a few more rooms until they ended up on a large patio off a casual family type room. The patio was in full shade, and there were a series of large bamboo fans moving the air around over their heads. He could see the pool stretching out at the bottom of the steps, but it was currently in full sunlight, meaning they would have to wait for a while before venturing into the water for a swim.

He stretched out on a lounge chair and shivered as the ice-cold beer made its way down his throat.

"This is the life, isn't it?" Ethan flicked his shoes to one side of the patio, pulled his shirt off over his head, and dropped down on the lounge next to Joel's. "I could stretch out here all day."

"Enjoy it while it's like this. The winters can be brutal here sometimes." Joel turned and looked at Ethan, and couldn't help perusing the artwork tattooed across Ethan's chest and down his arms. The images, patterns, and colors gracing Ethan's smooth skin were beyond fascinating.

Joel swallowed heavy into his chest as his gaze landed on the nipple rings. They were heavy and …incredible.

"Do you ski or snowboard?" he asked when he finally managed to peel his eyes away from the rings of cool metal.

"No, not much snow where I come from. My dad was never around long enough to take a trip to the Alps."

"That's too bad," Joel replied. "My friends and I do a lot of snowboarding. Maybe we can get you up to the local mountain during winter break. You could get your dad to rent a place, and then we wouldn't have to take the bus up every day."

"Yeah, we'll see. Do you have a lot of friends around here?"

"I've lived here my whole life, so I pretty much know everybody. But I have two close friends, Ryan and Max, and my girlfriend, Erica …who you've met."

Ethan sat up and caught Joel's eye. "Yeah, about last night. I have a nasty habit of trying to fuck with people for my own amusement. I'm sorry."

"It's not a big deal …but how long were you standing there? Did you see us in the pool?"

"No, I just heard you talking. I didn't see anything."

"All right …good. Because that would be really creepy."

Joel closed his eyes and tried to clear his mind of that incident, and the other bizarre thoughts he was having. By late afternoon, they'd finished one of the bottles of rum and half a case of beer. After talking with Ethan for a few hours, Joel was feeling extremely comfortable in Ethan's company—maybe more than he should.

The sun finally moved toward the horizon, prompting Ethan to pull himself off the lounge and take the steps down to the pool to test the water with his foot.

Joel sat straight up.

Two angel's wings, intricate and delicate with subtle shading of white and gray, fanned up from Ethan's slim waist and extending, outstretched—in sharp contrast to Ethan's overall appearance.

Joel threw back the last of his beer and headed for the pool, which was now partially shaded by the massive trees that blanketed the back of the property. He pulled off and tossed his shirt onto the grass, and dove into the deep end of the pool.

The cool water felt glorious.

When he resurfaced, Ethan was sitting at the edge of the pool with his feet dangling in the water.

"Aren't you coming in?" Joel made for the edge of the pool after realizing he'd had far too much to drink to be swimming around.

"Yeah, but I want to take these jeans off," Ethan replied. "So, you have to promise not to laugh."

"Laugh at what?" Joel pushed off from the edge, drifted into the center of the pool, then headed back again.

Ethan undid the buttons of his jeans, hauled them off, and stood at the edge of the pool. Just above the band of his underwear, a little to the left of his right hip, the top portion of a tattoo in the shape of a big, pink heart was visible.

"I got it for an ex. It's kind of pathetic." Ethan stepped cautiously into the water and let himself sink until the water had only just cleared his shoulders. "I keep meaning to incorporate it into something else ...or fill it in with a different color. I just haven't got round to it."

"There's no way I would let my girlfriend talk me into something like that." Joel laughed and dove beneath the water, then resurfaced and made his way down toward the shallow end. "What's your excuse for the wings?"

"No excuse. Those were my idea." Ethan drifted back over to the steps and pulled himself out of the water. "They're sentimental."

Joel gazed up at Ethan's body, taking in the overall effect of what he was seeing. Most of the tattooed images were intricately detailed and dark in nature, but some of them were surprisingly colorful and somewhat artsy. "You're like a walking piece of art."

"That's the general idea behind it." Ethan wrung his hair out and pulled his jeans back on loosely, not bothering with the buttons.

"What does *cupido* mean?" Joel asked.

"It's Latin—" Ethan answered then turned around, laughing, to face Joel, who was pulling himself out of the water using one of the ladders. "Were you checking out my ass?"

"Fuck off! You walked up out of the water right in front of me. It would've been difficult to miss a word tattooed across your lower back …not your ass."

"Yeah, well, there's a long story behind that one." Ethan crossed his arms and smirked at Joel.

"What?"

"Nothing. Did you want to grab another beer?"

"No. I think I'm going to snag a nap before Erica comes home from work." Joel retrieved his shirt off the grass and pulled it back on before making his way over to the fence. "I'll grab the rest of my beer off you later. Thanks for that by the way."

"Sure thing, but before you go ...where's the best place to pick up a few party favors? Do you have a number for someone?"

"No," Joel replied, shaking his head. "I'm not really into that shit. There's a guy that deals in the beach parking lot down the street. He's there around two in the morning or so. Nasty guy though. You'd be safer to head downtown and ask around."

"There's no one from school?"

"There are a few guys, but they're all on holidays right now ...as far as I know. I'm afraid you're stuck with the downtown crowd until school starts." Joel pulled himself up on the fence and jumped over. "I'll give you a shout later tonight and get that beer off you."

"I'll be here." Ethan watched Joel until he was out of sight, then turned back toward his house to get out of the heat. He headed straight for the kitchen to get a glass of water and a couple of aspirin. He hadn't drunk that much in a long time, and it was making him feel nauseous.

After knocking them back, he lay down on the sofa in the small den attached to the kitchen and closed his eyes.

Ethan groaned, rolling, and tucked further into the sofa, shielding his eyes from the setting sun. He was getting tired of moving around so much. It was incredibly stressful setting himself up in an entirely new area, trying to meet up with the local kids and figure out who was who, and how they fit in with the social structure of the school. His patience for the entire thing was starting to wear thin, and he wasn't sure how much longer he'd be able to keep it up.

Chapter Three

Erica threw her purse down on the counter and hauled open the freezer. She had come home to find Joel passed out on the sofa, completely wasted. He was supposed to have cooked dinner tonight, but that possibility was unlikely now.

"I can't believe you spent the entire day hanging out and drinking with that creep next door," Erica said, her frustration apparent.

"Ethan's an interesting guy. He was just fucking with us last night. And you should see some of the tattoos he has …and the piercings." Joel shifted over to face her. "Get this. Ethan was telling me he even has piercings in his dick. He says some of them make sex better."

"All right, that's just disgusting," Erica replied. "I don't want to hear any more about him or his perverse piercings." She shook her head as she turned the oven on. "We're having cod for dinner, all right?"

"I don't know if I can eat anything. The heat and the alcohol have done me in. I'm getting a vicious headache." Joel pulled himself off the sofa and headed for the medicine cabinet in the kitchen. He lifted out an assortment of bottles, but couldn't find what he was looking for. "Do you have any aspirin in your purse?"

"No. You know I don't get headaches." Erica took overlooking in the cabinet but didn't find anything. "I could drive over to my house. I'm sure my mom has something that would help."

"That's all right. I'll go next door and ask Ethan. I have to pick up the rest of my beer anyway. And I left my shoes over there."

Erica propped a hand on her hip.

"Just be careful," she said. "The guy scares me."

"There's nothing to worry about. I won't be long."

Joel staggered out through the front door, breathing in the cool breeze that was coming off the water now that the sun had gone down behind the hills. He stepped up to Ethan's door, noting it had been left open again, knocked lightly, and let himself in.

The decorators had definitely been busy while they'd been out in the backyard. Joel barely recognized the rooms he moved through on his way to the kitchen. The whole house appeared to have been done up to look like a bizarre, gothic castle from the medieval ages.

Joel smirked, hearing a string of obscenities coming from the kitchen, so he continued in that direction. He stepped into the kitchen just as a pan was being dropped onto the floor, spraying hot grease everywhere.

"Bloody hell—" Ethan threw the oven mitts off and jogged over to the sink, flicking on the water.

"Hiya," he said, peering over his shoulder. "Hey, you don't know anything about cooking do you, Joel?"

Then hissed sharp, as the water rolled over his arm.

"Not unless you can put it in the microwave." Joel stepped cautiously around the grease and looked in at Ethan's arm.

"That's what I'm investing in tomorrow. Microwave food." Ethan shut the water off and cringed as the air swept over his arm. "Do you have a first aid kit at your house?"

"I do ...I'll trade you for some pain meds. I've got a nasty headache after drinking in the heat all day."

"I've got some aspirin," Ethan replied.

"I was hoping for something stronger than that. This feels like a trip to the emergency room coming on."

"I might have some Oxy. Are you all right with that?"

"The stronger, the better. My head feels like someone's trying to remove it from my body while forcing my eyeballs out through their sockets ...and exploding my brain up through the top of my head."

"Kudos on the imagery." Ethan grabbed a clean tea towel and wrapped it gently around his arm. "Come on upstairs to my room. I've got my pharmacy up there."

Ethan's bedroom was in what should've been the master suite, but as he'd told Joel, his dad wasn't around very often, so Joel didn't think too much of it. The massive ornate bed that he and Erica had seen being moved into the house was set up in there, along with a lot of very unusual furniture. The dark gothic motif was prevalent in Ethan's bedroom, more so than in the rest of the house.

Joel followed Ethan into the ensuite bathroom and watched him root around in the cabinet under the sink, eventually pulling out a small box and setting it on the counter.

"Please tell me you have relief in there," Joel said and stepped closer, looking at an impressive selection of prescription bottles.

"Here ..." Ethan handed Joel a bottle and filled up a glass of water for him. "Take two. You don't want your headache to only be half gone. Just watch yourself tonight. No swimming, driving, or anything stupid. You're going to be completely stoned in about twenty minutes." He took the bottle back off Joel and dumped out three pills for himself before putting the box away.

Joel swallowed the pills and sat down on the edge of the tub, while Ethan ran his arm under the cold water and dabbed it with a cloth. He considered getting up, but decided to stay put and wait for Ethan to finish up; his mind was feeling a bit fuzzy.

By the time Ethan stepped out of a small room at one end of the bathroom, Joel wasn't sure if he was going to be able to stand up.

Ethan leaned against the counter and washed back the three pills he had set aside for himself.

"Does your arm really hurt?" Joel asked.

"Fuck, yeah." Ethan lifted the towel to check on it again and cringed at the sight of his reddened skin. "Let's head over to your house and get this bandaged up."

"Hold on," Joel said. "My legs feel funny."

"Already?" Ethan laughed with amusement. "Maybe you should sit down in my room for a minute. I don't want you falling off that tub edge and cracking your head open."

Ethan led Joel back out to the bedroom and had him sit down in a high backed chair by the window.

"Have you had the whoosh thing happen yet?" he asked Joel.

Joel ran his hands over the zebra-striped upholstery of the chair, taking in the directional texture of it, and marveling at the smoothness of the twisted horns the chair was constructed from, letting his fingers wander all over the piece.

"I'm not sure," he answered. "I just feel all floaty. My headache is still there, but I don't really care about it anymore." He paused. "Where did you get this chair from? It feels so nice."

"I picked it up in Africa." Ethan looked around the room, trying to figure out a way to protect his arm so he could help Joel down the stairs and over to his house—but he didn't see anything.

"I don't know how I'm going to get you home," he said.

"Leave me here …get Erica …she can sit with me." Joel slid down further in the seat. "She's making fish …cod …that could be your dinner …she's an excellent cook …don't forget the first aid kit …how's your arm?" Then he snorted and slipped off the chair, landing on the floor, his head lolling to one side.

"Fuck, you're stoned," Ethan said, grinning, and rechecked his arm. "I can't just leave you here. You're liable to fall down the stairs trying to follow me."

"Phone her …here." Joel handed Ethan his cell phone and closed his eyes. "Her number is …there."

"All right. If you think that's wise." Ethan scrolled through the contacts, found Erica, and waited for her to answer.

"Joel, what's taking you so long?" Erica answered.

"It's Ethan. His neighbor?"

"What ...what have you done with Joel?"

"Nothing. Joel is off in his own little world at the moment, and he wants you to come babysit him until he comes down."

"Comes down from what?"

"The pain meds I gave him for his headache."

"Are you fucking with me?"

Ethan grinned. "There's only one way to find out."

"Can't you bring him back here?"

"No, I burned my arm." Ethan waited out the silence and smirked as he heard Erica sigh. "Could you bring a first aid kit with you?"

"I'll be right there."

Erica arrived and became extremely annoyed when Ethan didn't answer the door—even after she'd rung the bell multiple times. She finally decided to let herself in and called out for Joel.

"We're upstairs in my bedroom," Ethan answered. "Double doors at the end of the hall." He crossed the room and swung the doors open before returning to Joel's side. He'd managed to lift Joel up onto the bed, but Joel kept rolling around sporadically and was liable to fall off the edge, so Ethan was keeping a close eye on him.

"What the hell did you give him?" Erica pushed the first aid kit at Ethan and went to check on Joel.

"Obviously, too much of a good thing," Ethan replied. "On the bright side, his headache is gone, and he's providing me with some classic entertainment." He flipped open the first aid kit and fished around until he found a roll of tape and a gauze bandage big enough to cover his arm.

"Could you help me with this, please?" Ethan asked Erica.

Erica turned around and visibly cringed at the sight of Ethan. He was one of the scariest looking guys she had ever come across, and the freaky motif of his bedroom was making her nervous.

Ethan held out the medical tape for Erica to take and she snapped it out of his hand, tore off strips with her teeth, and haphazardly stuck them down, barely holding the gauze in place on Ethan's arm.

"Go see a doctor tomorrow and get that looked at," she said.

"Sure thing, Nurse Ratched," Ethan answered as he tried to reapply the edges of the tape. "What are we going to do about Joel? I don't think he'd make it down the stairs without falling."

"I don't know," Erica replied. "Maybe it will wear off soon, and he can walk home on his own." She turned back to face Joel, who had started laughing hysterically. "What is so funny?" She looked up to what Joel was pointing at; a massive gothic framed mirror mounted on the ceiling over the bed—she turned on Ethan.

"You're fucking repulsive, do you know that?" she shouted. "I don't care what Joel says about you. I want you and your disgusting mind to stay away from him."

Ethan pulled his shirt off over his head, causing Erica to step back in fear. "That's kind of his choice, isn't it?" He headed to his closet, flipped through the racks of clothing and lifted out a long sleeved shirt. "And I don't need fuckin' tight ass bitches, like you, treating me like shit, and telling me what to do in my own house."

Ethan pulled the shirt on with the utmost of care and tested the sensitivity of his burned arm through the material.

It would have to do.

He surged toward Erica, stopping short before veering past her toward the bed. "I'm going to carry Joel home."

Hoisting Joel into his arms, Ethan carried him effortlessly down the stairs. He swore when he realized the front door was closed. Once Erica had it open, Ethan pushed past her and used his long strides to keep ahead of her. At Joel's house, he kicked mercilessly at the gate to the backyard until it crashed open. He jogged the short distance to the deck and cleared the two steps leading up to it, pushed one of the lounges closer to the house, and carefully set Joel down.

"Hey," Joel said, reaching for Ethan's sleeve. "Thanks for getting me home."

"No problem, preppy boy. I'll see you tomorrow."

Then Ethan took off at a run toward the short fence separating the properties, and was quickly over it, into his own yard.

Chapter Four

Joel was feeling pretty good the next morning. Ethan had slipped an extra pill into his hand when he'd brought him home the night before. The pain in his head had started up again a bit before sunrise, so Joel had taken it, and now the bedroom was taking on all sorts of fabulous colors as the sun shone through the window.

He sighed in disappointment when Erica closed the curtains.

"It's going to get too hot in here if we leave the curtains open," Erica said. "Your air conditioner is on full, but the house is still heating up. This has got to be one of the hottest summers ever." She flopped down on the bed beside Joel and tucked herself in against him, resting her head on his chest.

Joel turned and kissed her on the head. "I love you."

"I love you too." Erica lifted her head and kissed Joel back. "Can you believe this is our last year of high school? I'm so excited about getting finished. I've had enough."

"It'll be nice to finally get out of there." Joel rubbed his hand across his eyes, trying to regain some focus. "Hey, do I smell coffee?" He pulled away from Erica and attempted to get out of bed, but his head swooned. "Fuck, those pills are something else."

"They should've worn off by now." Sitting up, Erica rubbed Joel's back as he sat at the edge of the bed.

"Ethan gave me an extra one in case the headache came back."

Before Erica could comment, Joel dragged himself onto his feet and wandered into the ensuite bathroom. He dropped himself down on the toilet and rested his face in his hands. The colors were back, thankfully, and were taking the edge off the developing hangover.

"Joel?" Erica stepped into the bathroom. "How long were you planning on sitting on that toilet. You've been in here for almost half an hour." She had to keep herself from laughing when Joel looked up at her; he was barely managing to keep himself upright.

"Yeah, I think I fell asleep," Joel replied then wiped the drool from his chin and motioned for Erica to leave the bathroom.

Standing just outside the door, Erica listened for any signs that he was having trouble getting organized. Joel's phone buzzed on the bedside table, and she went to check the text message; it was from Ethan. She quickly deleted it and threw the phone on the bed.

"I have to leave for work," Erica said as she checked her makeup in the large mirror over the dresser. "Should I ask Ryan to come over in a few hours and make sure you're all right?"

"No, I'm fine." Joel walked out of the bathroom, headed straight for the bed and crashed back onto it. "I'm going to sleep for a while longer." He rolled over and grabbed his phone. "I thought I heard my phone."

"I didn't hear it." Erica leaned over and kissed him. "I'll see you tonight. Please remember to make dinner."

Joel grunted and tucked himself up, and pulled the pillow over his head. He didn't hear Erica leave, but a few hours later, he heard someone knocking on his bedroom window. He reluctantly pulled himself out of bed and let Ethan into the house.

"What are you doing here so early?" Joel asked in irritation.

"It's almost two in the afternoon, sunshine," Ethan answered as he ruffled Joel's hair. "What do you have planned for today?"

"My only plan is nursing a hangover."

"Have you had any coffee yet?" Ethan motioned for Joel to sit at the kitchen table, and within a few minutes, he set a cup of coffee and a few pieces of toast in front of him.

"Hey, thanks," Joel said.

"Lucky for you, I've mastered the technique of pouring coffee and making toast. It's one of the few cooking skills I have." Ethan picked up Joel's cell phone and scanned through the messages. "Didn't you get my text this morning?"

"Maybe. Erica probably deleted it while I was in the bathroom. She really doesn't like you."

"But I've been so charming ..." Ethan tidied away the toaster and rinsed out the empty coffee pot before turning back to Joel. "Finish up. I'm getting really bored ...and that is never a good thing."

"What did you want to do?"

"I need to see a doctor and get my arm bandaged properly. Your girlfriend's lackluster attempt fell off halfway through the night."

"Let me finish up here, and I'll give you a lift."

"Priceless. Thank you." Ethan patted Joel on the back and headed down the hall to Joel's bedroom. While Joel was finishing his breakfast, Ethan set about rifling through Joel's closet. He scrutinized a few items of clothing and picked out a pair of shorts and a t-shirt.

Joel caught the clothes that Ethan threw at him and quickly got dressed. He stuffed the last piece of toast in his mouth, finished up the coffee, and motioned for Ethan to follow him.

"Your car still hasn't shown up?" Joel asked as he pushed a huge pile of dirty laundry out of the way with his foot on their way through the laundry room to the garage.

"The shipping company rang this morning." Ethan grinned and clapped his hands together excitedly. "It's coming tomorrow."

"Why didn't your dad just buy you a new car?"

"And leave my baby behind? Never." Ethan followed Joel out to the garage. "You don't mind, do you? I'll pay for the petrol."

"No, but I think you should drive. My head is all floaty."

Joel threw the keys to Ethan and slid into the passenger seat.

"You know, I've rarely driven on the wrong side of the road," Ethan said as he perused the interior of the vehicle, relieved to see it was an automatic at least.

"The wrong side?" Joel laughed. "You'll be fine."

Ethan backed out of the garage and up the driveway, laughing at himself for shoulder checking on the wrong side. He took off along their street and stopped at the intersection that would have them join the main road.

"Fuck, I'm completely confused already," Ethan said as he waited past a few openings before finally turning left.

Joel directed him to the nearest walk-in clinic, and they were soon making their way inside. The receptionist behind the counter was visibly shaken as Ethan stepped up to give his information, and eyed him anxiously as she directed him to take a seat in the waiting room.

When they found some seats, a few people with small children decided they wanted to sit on the other side of the office from them.

Joel watched as nervous mothers gathered up their children and all their toys, and carried them across the room.

"Do you get this a lot?" Joel asked, annoyed by the reaction.

"Yeah, all the time." Ethan leaned back and started chewing on his thumbnail. "I went into it, the modifications, knowing it was going to scare some people …so I can't exactly get upset when it does."

Ethan tucked his feet in as a woman with a stroller tried to push her way past, to move away from him. The wheels became stuck on the chair across the aisle, and the whole thing started to tip. He was on his feet so fast, Joel didn't even have time to react.

Ethan righted the stroller and helped the woman get it safely to the other side of the room before sitting back down.

"But there's a big difference between being scared or upset and downright abusive though," continued Ethan. "Sometimes I get that from people, and that really pisses me off. I'm still a human being." He looked around at the number of people sitting in the waiting room. "How long is this going to take? I really need to have a smoke."

"Welcome to the Canadian healthcare system. We could be here awhile. You may as well get comfortable." Joel tucked his arms across his chest and closed his eyes, grateful for the opportunity to sleep a while longer.

Once they got into an examination room, the visit went reasonably quick. Ethan's arm was correctly bandaged and he was given a prescription for anti-inflammatory medication. As was his habit, Ethan made sure to thank the doctor and the receptionist on the way out, because if there was one thing he liked better than fucking with people, it was proving them wrong in their assumptions about him.

"I guess you still need groceries," Joel said as they left the doctor's office. "There's a store not too far from here where you can fill the prescription and get stocked up on microwavable food. I'll drive."

"That would be great." Ethan slid into the passenger seat, relieved to be out of the driver's seat. "Do you mind if I smoke in the car?"

"No, go for it," Joel replied, then unlatched his seatbelt and reached across Ethan's body, and rolled Ethan's window down slightly. "I'll just crack the window a bit."

Ethan held his breath as Joel moved back across him.

"Thanks," Ethan said, eyeing Joel suspiciously. He lit up his cigarette, took a long draw, and let the calming effect take over. He hated waiting around. It made him anxious.

Joel pulled into the parking lot of the local grocery store. His head wasn't all floaty anymore, and Ethan had readily passed the keys and the driving over to him. They weren't in the store for long, but Joel was disappointed by the way people treated Ethan. He'd never realized just how judgmental people really were because he'd always hung out with people that were essentially *normal*.

By the time they left the store, he was disgusted by what he'd seen and heard. But Ethan seemed to be completely unaffected. They decided to sit in the car for a minute before continuing on so they could finish the cold drinks they'd picked up in the store.

"I need some shorts or something," Ethan said as he finished the last of a cigarette and snubbed it out on the metal frame of the car, making sure it was completely out, before throwing it out the window. "These jeans are deadly in this heat."

"There's a board shop around the corner that sells shorts at this time of year. It's expensive though." Joel laughed when Ethan raised an eyebrow at him. "I guess that's not an issue for you, is it?"

"Never has been. Never will be. My dad is loaded."

"Must be nice," Joel said. "My parents won't even let me work, because I need to keep my grades up for university." He checked for traffic and pulled out onto the road, and then immediately turned into the next entrance. "I tried to get a summer job, but work is pretty scarce. I never seem to have any money."

"Did you want me to buy you something from here?" Ethan closed the car door and followed Joel across the parking lot.

Joel paused and looked back at Ethan.

"No. Thanks though," Joel answered, mystified by the offer. He'd only known the guy for two days. He stepped back as Ethan held the door open for him, and went in ahead, immediately busying himself with the racks at the front of the store, searching through the shorts to find anything that Ethan wouldn't find too offensive.

He jumped when Ethan stepped up behind him.

"What about these?" Ethan asked as he circled around to be in front of Joel, and held up a pair of white, pink, and yellow shorts.

Joel raised an eyebrow at him and burst out laughing. Ethan grinned and tossed the shorts back at the rack.

"I was thinking more in terms of black," Joel said. "Or gray on black. Or black on gray. Or shades of gray on black."

"Some fashion consultant you turned out to be."

Joel released a loud shriek as Ethan poked him in the ribs.

"All right, what about these?" Joel said once he'd caught his breath. "Purple with black checks." He passed them to Ethan and dove back into the garment racks to see what else he could find. By the time they finished at the store and drove home, Erica's car was already sitting in the driveway.

Joel checked his phone.

"Are you in trouble?" Ethan asked.

"Yeah, my phone is dead. I forgot to charge it. Erica's probably been calling. I was supposed to make dinner tonight."

Ethan pulled out his phone and dialed a number. "I should put these guys on speed dial." He covered the mouthpiece. "What kind of pizza do you want? My treat."

"Hawaiian would be great, thanks." Joel laughed when Ethan made a face at him. "I take it you're not a fruit on your pizza guy."

"It's unnatural." Ethan turned his attention back to his phone and began placing Joel's order for delivery, his accent echoing throughout the small car. Joel unlatched his seatbelt and settled into his seat to wait for Ethan to finish on the phone. He dropped his gaze and looked away when Ethan caught his eye and smiled at him. He'd never felt as comfortable around anyone in his life, but at the same time, Ethan made him incredibly nervous.

"Here's the cash, plus some for …gas." Ethan flipped open his wallet and gave a few bills to Joel. "I'll just grab my stuff from the back." He threw his door open and shoved Joel affectionately. "Thanks again by the way. I appreciate it."

"Aren't you going to eat with us?"

"No, I don't think your girlfriend would be too thrilled with that idea. I have enough food now. I'll be fine." Ethan hauled himself out of his seat and peered back in the door to speak to Joel. "Are you going to be around tomorrow?"

"Yeah, I'll come by when Erica goes to work."

Ethan nodded his head and reached through into the back seat to get his bags. He reluctantly withdrew himself from the car and pushed the door closed with his foot, wishing his house wasn't so empty. He headed toward it.

When Joel stepped in through the front door of his own house, Erica was standing by the window with her cell phone to her ear. She ended the call and set it on the kitchen table.

"Where have you been?" Erica asked. "I've been phoning and sending you text messages for over an hour."

"I was running errands with Ethan. My phone died."

"And what kind of errands does someone like Ethan have? A trip to the tattoo parlor. An afternoon of frightening old ladies. Maybe a few drug deals to cap off the day."

Joel rolled his shoulders and crossed his arms.

"That's really uncalled for," he said. "We went to the doctor's office and bought groceries and shorts. Scary stuff." Then Joel threw his keys on the counter and went to sit in the family room.

Erica followed him into the room and stood with her hands on her hips, glaring at him, but Joel just flicked the television on and tucked himself into the sofa. He wasn't about to give her the satisfaction of drawing him out.

"What about dinner?" Erica asked finally. "You were supposed to make it. Remember?"

"It'll be here in twenty minutes." Joel changed channels and tried to ignore her. "Ethan bought us a pizza because he kept me from getting home on time."

"Did he now?" Erica dropped herself down on the sofa beside Joel and cuddled up to him. "I'm sorry. Maybe he's not all bad."

"He really isn't. People sure give him a hard time though. I can't imagine putting up with that every day."

"He did it to himself." Erica looked up at Joel and smiled as he moved in to kiss her.

"And he's fully aware of that …but it's important to him." Joel kissed Erica and then turned his attention back to the television. "What do you want to watch tonight?"

"Maybe …now that we don't have to cook and clean dishes, we could spend some extra time together."

Joel smiled over at Erica and gave her a slow sensuous kiss, and then touched her lightly on the nose. "Mm …that sounds like a wonderful plan." He retook her mouth, hoping the pizza would get there soon—he was starving.

Ethan read the instructions on the microwaveable meal he had in his hands before ripping it open. He pulled the frozen bag out of the box and just stared at it. It looked disgusting. He whipped out his cell phone and ordered some chicken wings and pizza instead.

While he was waiting for the order to arrive, Ethan stepped out onto his back patio for a smoke. He took a seat in the chair he had set up at the far end of the patio, specifically positioned to see into Joel's backyard. He finished his cigarette and lifted the chair back to the table where it belonged. He'd decided it wasn't going to be necessary to watch Joel.

The house phone in the kitchen rang, causing Ethan to sprint in through the door, just making it in time to pick it up.

"Hello?"

"Ethan, my boy. How's the new house?"

"It's brilliant, Dad. It's really fuckin' hot here though."

"Can't be helped. One has to go where one's needed."

"Am I going to see you anytime soon?"

"Probably not. I'm a bit tied up. Maybe I'll see you at Christmas. Can't promise anything though."

"Don't stress about it, Dad. I'm doing fine."

"Call me if you need anything, all right?"

"Sure thing. I've got you on speed dial."

"I love you, son."

"I love you too, Dad. Talk to you soon."

Ethan hung up the phone and started chewing on his thumbnail. He looked through the tourist pamphlets he'd picked up in anticipation of his dad's visit. He'd grabbed ones with the locations of walking and biking trails, and all the local wineries and vineyards.

He pushed the lot into the garbage and lit another cigarette.

Chapter Five

As soon as Erica left for work the next morning, Joel made his way next door. A large truck was parked in Ethan's driveway, and it was unloading what turned out to be Ethan's car.

"Hiya, Joel." Ethan paced nervously as the driver backed his car down the ramp of the truck, and drove it over toward the garage. "I'm so excited. My baby has finally arrived."

Joel walked around the car, looking it over. From what little he knew …it was *so* Ethan. It was one of those small cars you saw in British television shows driving narrow roads through green fields covered in grazing sheep. It was painted bright red with the exception of the roof; it had a rendition of the *Union Jack* flag over its entire surface.

He peered inside and saw it was right-hand drive as he'd expected it would be, and the interior was done out in black velvet covered in skulls and gothic crosses. He grinned. From the rear view mirror hung, what Joel could only guess, was some kind of large intimate piercing ring or attachment.

"It's something else, Ethan," Joel said. "It's very you."

"Did you want to go for a ride? I made sure they filled her up before bringing her out to me." Ethan took the keys off the truck driver and slid into the driver's seat of his car. "Are there any country type roads around here where I can have a bit of fun?"

"Yeah," Joel replied. "If we head into the southeast area, there are lots of winding narrow roads with loads of hills and dips." He popped open the door and dropped into the passenger seat, marveling at the fact Ethan could actually fit inside the car. It seemed so small from the outside.

"Sounds perfect." Ethan started up the car and fired it out of his driveway. "This is going to be even more stressful than driving your car for a bit. Totally wonky."

"You think that's weird. I'm cruising down the middle of the road without a freakin' steering wheel." Joel cringed as a succession of cars flew past his window. "Please keep an eye on the centerline."

He breathed a sigh of relief when Ethan turned off the main road and headed toward the less traveled rural area.

Ethan was thrilled to have his car back. It was one of the few constant things in his life. No matter where he ended up, his car was something that always went with him. He drove through a series of turns and hills and soaked in the exhilaration of its familiarity.

"Did you want to stop for ice cream or something?" Joel turned in his seat. "There's a little gas station over to the right there—" He hung on as Ethan veered into the parking lot.

"Do you think they sell fags as well?" Ethan asked.

"I'm sure they do," Joel followed Ethan into the store and rooted through the freezer while Ethan bought cigarettes.

"Grab me an orange iced-lolly," Ethan said.

"A whosy-whatsy?" Joel laughed as he pulled two popsicles from the freezer. "Never mind. I know what you mean." He slid in beside Ethan, nudging him on purpose, and tossed the popsicles on the counter. The clerk behind the counter was eyeing Ethan anxiously.

"Oh, for fuck's sake," Joel said and spun off toward the door.

Ethan reached for him and grabbed his arm. "Let it go, Joel."

"Fuck that." Joel pulled Ethan's hand off his arm and stormed out of the store to wait for him.

"I appreciate the sentiment, but try not to get so stressed out." Ethan tossed Joel his Popsicle and took a seat at the picnic bench outside the store. He leaned back against the table and looked out at the orchard across the road. "It's nice out here. My dad should've bought an acreage."

Joel sighed with fake resignation. "I don't know, Ethan. There would be very few neighbors out here for you to fuck with. Big negative." He grinned at Ethan and laughed when he received a smack in the back of the head.

"It would be fun to bomb around on a couple of dirt bikes though, wouldn't it?" Ethan collected up the wrappers and sticks and threw them in the garbage. "I have a couple of bikes back home. Road bikes. They're wicked."

"If your dad is never around, why did you have to move away from home? Couldn't you just stay in Britain?"

"It's not that easy. There are other factors. I really don't get a say in where I live." Ethan spun the keys around on his finger and watched the limited traffic coming up and down the road. "My dad phoned last night."

"Is he going to be here soon?"

"No, he's going to try for Christmas though."

"That's a ways off …but that'll be nice, right?"

"I'm not going to hold my breath on that one. My dad hasn't spent Christmas with me in over three years." Ethan unlocked the car and slid behind the wheel.

"Jeez, I'm sorry, Ethan. If it doesn't look like he's coming, I want you to spend Christmas at my house, all right?"

"Thanks, Joel." Ethan sat and studied Joel for a second before starting up the car and taking off back toward home. After parking the car in Ethan's driveway, they headed over to Joel's house.

They had quite a few hours before Erica would be coming home, so they grabbed Joel's laptop and went to sit in the family room to pass some time. Ethan searched up a few things on the internet and showed Joel where two of his houses were, some pictures of his last high school, and the websites for his favorite places throughout Europe. Then he perused through Joel's downloaded music folder and picked out a few to move to his player, and uploaded some of his own he thought Joel would like.

They talked about their favorite actors and movies and discovered they had similar tastes in both, so they found a movie they both liked on the internet and settled in to watch it. During the movie, they managed to work their way through two bags of salt and vinegar chips and an entire case of beer. Ethan ended up in hysterics because the chips had caused Joel's tongue to swell up so much Joel was having trouble speaking properly.

Ethan's solution was more beer and Joel had readily agreed.

By mid-afternoon, the heat and the beer had worn them out, and they'd stretched out at opposite ends of the sofa and fallen asleep.

An hour later, Joel rolled over and checked the time on his phone, and sighed with resignation.

"I need to start dinner," Joel said as he threw a cushion at Ethan's head to make sure he was awake.

"Did you want help? I can take directions well." Ethan sat up and rubbed his eyes, pulled a cigarette out of his pack, and put it in his mouth. He was about to light it, but then remembered where he was, and tucked it behind his ear.

"I'll start the chicken, and you can help me with the potatoes," Joel said. "You know how to peel potatoes, don't you?"

"I'm part Irish. I can peel potatoes." Ethan pulled himself off the sofa and followed Joel into the kitchen.

The next half hour passed quickly as they worked to get the dinner started. Joel's kitchen was much smaller than Ethan's and wasn't meant for two people to be moving around in, which led to some near misses with knives and handfuls of potato peelings and chicken skin. They washed up what dishes they'd used in the preparation, and once finished, cracked open another couple of beers and pulled themselves up on the kitchen counter to wait.

"So, where were you living last?" Joel asked.

"A flat in the middle of London. It was brilliant."

"Did you have a lot of friends there?"

"Yeah. Some. I don't tend to make friends easily." Ethan raised his hand to his mouth and started chewing on his nails.

"Did you want to sit outside and have a smoke?"

"Is it that obvious?" Ethan jumped off the counter and made a run for the patio door. As soon as he was outside, he lit up a cigarette and stretched out on a lounge, breathing easier.

"Jeez, it's still hot." Joel stripped off his shirt and dropped down into a patio chair, and put his feet up on a planter box.

Ethan looked over at Joel and flicked aggressively at his cigarette, and then lay back and closed his eyes.

"So, did you leave behind a girlfriend back home?" Joel asked.

"Nah. My last girlfriend and I broke up over two years ago. I've been keeping things on a casual basis since then. I hate being tied down by someone like that." Ethan glanced over at Joel. "Not that there's anything wrong with it for some people."

Joel abandoned his chair and stepped across the patio to lay down on the lounge beside Ethan's. "I got lucky with Erica. She doesn't make me feel tied down, most of the time." Then he laughed and snorted. "Who am I kidding? Sometimes it's like we're married already."

"You're planning on marrying her?"

"Yeah, after we finish university." Joel's eyebrows wrinkled up, and he exhaled slowly through tight lips. "We've been together for almost two years now. I love her. We'll be good together."

"You don't sound convinced."

"I don't know. Sometimes I wonder."

"About what?"

"It's just …she doesn't get me most of the time, you know? I spend a lot of time thinking about …stuff. She listens to me when I share my ideas with her, but then she discards them because she thinks I'm not being realistic." Joel sighed heavily and turned to Ethan. "I can't help it. It's just the way I'm wired. What do you think I should do?"

"I think you've had too much to drink if you think I'm going to have any insight, whatsoever, into something like that." Ethan crushed out his cigarette. "But, in the interest of reviving the disappearing art of introspection, here goes anyway. In my humble opinion, if Erica doesn't get you after two years of dating, she's never going to be able to relate to you in any meaningful way."

"That's what I was afraid of." Joel looked down at his phone and leaped out of his seat. "We need to check on things inside."

Back in the kitchen, Joel pulled open the fridge and starting hauling vegetables out to make a salad. He grabbed a large bowl out of the cupboard and slipped the cutting board out from beside the microwave. After ripping up the lettuce, he set about cutting up some tomatoes.

"How does the chicken look in there?" Joel checked behind him, but couldn't see what was happening in the oven.

"I don't know," Ethan replied peering into the oven. "It's not blowing up anyway. That's a start. It's still got another twenty-five minutes left." He stood up and poked at the potatoes on the stove with a knife. "Did you want to mash these, because I think they've gone past the point where we can do anything else with them?"

"Can you do that for me?" Joel dug around in one of the drawers then handed Ethan a potato masher.

"Do you have milk?"

"There should be some in the fridge." Joel pulled the fridge open and slid a few things around. "Damn it. I was supposed to pick some up today. Erica's going to kill me."

"I've got some at my house." Ethan smacked Joel on the ass and started for the door. "You owe me for this by the way. Cooking for a girlfriend is not something I've ever done before. Nor is it something I will ever attempt to do again."

"I appreciate you helping me out. Three nights in a row of not cooking dinner was going to land me in a serious dog house."

"After all this effort, I sincerely hope you see a little action tonight." Ethan winked at Joel then dashed out the door.

The chicken came out perfect, and Erica was impressed with the entire meal, particularly the fluffiness of the mashed potatoes. Joel decided against telling her that Ethan had made them, or that he'd had any hand in the preparation of dinner, thinking that would probably ruin her enjoyment factor.

"You made a lovely dinner tonight," Erica said. "Funny though. I'm sure I used the last of the milk this morning, and I don't see any new stuff in the fridge." She turned and studied Joel's face.

"You're too fucking observant, you know that?" Joel retorted. "I borrowed some milk from Ethan."

"So ...you were hanging out with him again today?"

"Yeah, we went for a drive in his car." Joel looked at her with a chastised expression. "It just arrived today. We had to take it out."

"I really wish you wouldn't spend so much time with him. I can only imagine what kind of friends he's going to attract at school." Erica grabbed the television remote and reached for the movies on the coffee table. "Which one do you want to watch?" She held the selection up for Joel to look at.

"Is there another choice?" Joel flipped through the three movies Erica had brought home; they were all romantic comedies.

"No. Let's watch this one." Erica put one in the player and settled in against Joel's shoulder.

Joel discreetly pulled out his cell phone and texted Ethan with a message that read *HELP*. He immediately received a response in the form of a line of question marks. He typed back *chick flick* and almost shrieked aloud in hysterics at the picture Ethan sent him of himself screaming in horror.

He saved the picture and stuffed the phone back in his pocket.

Chapter Six

The bedroom was already starting to heat up, and the sheets were wrapped so tightly around Joel's legs that the combination was causing him to overheat. He rolled over to unravel himself and ran straight into Erica's sleeping body. He checked the clock, and seeing it was ten in the morning, shook Erica awake.

"Hey," Joel said. "You're supposed to be at work."

"I phoned in," Erica replied. "I'm not feeling well. I told them I'd go in at one. I just need some more sleep."

Joel shifted away from her. "Do you mind if I take off? I promised Ethan a swimming lesson before it gets too hot out."

"A swimming lesson? Are you serious?" Erica rubbed her eyes and rolled closer to Joel, pinning him in place. "Won't he sink with all that metal hanging off his body?"

"Ha ...very funny."

"Why don't you stay here with me ...see if you can make me feel better?" Erica kissed Joel's chest then playfully flicked at his nipple with her tongue.

"Mm ...tempting, but I promised I'd be over there by now." Joel kissed her dismissively and patted her head. "We'll have plenty of time together tonight." He rolled himself out of bed, picked his swimsuit off the floor, and pulled it on. "I'll see you later."

"Will I see you for lunch before I go to work?"

"No," Joel said, shaking his head. Erica reached for him, but he backed away, running his hand through his hair. "Ethan has a chef coming in to make us lunch today. He's tired of delivery food."

Erica rolled her eyes.

"It must be nice," she said, tracking Joel's retreat from her second attempt to reach for him. "Get tired of delivery food …hire someone to cook …because heaven forbid he'd have to cook for himself."

Joel took a deep breath, refusing to take the bait. A fight with Erica meant he'd be delayed, and the stirring inside his gut to get moving was already overwhelming him.

He clenched his jaw to keep from responding to Erica's demands for him to answer and took off for Ethan's.

The water was the perfect temperature, and the sun was only shining on one half of the pool. Unfortunately, it was the shallow end, so Joel had the task of trying to convince Ethan that he wasn't going to let him drown if he ventured into the deep end.

"This is stupid," Ethan said as he clung to the edge of the pool, his fingers digging into the concrete coping. "I'm going to sink like a fuckin' stone."

"Not if you do what I say. I've been swimming my whole life." Joel grabbed hold of Ethan's arm and pulled him away from the edge, using his legs to keep them both above water. "The first thing you need to learn is how to tread water. It's what's going to keep you afloat when you're not actually swimming around."

"Maybe I shouldn't be swimming around," Ethan replied.

"If you're going to live here, you need to learn how to swim. Where's your sense of adventure?"

"Firmly planted on terra firma."

Ethan copied the movements Joel was making with his arms and legs and was surprised to find it came quite naturally to keep himself afloat that way. But every once in a while, he would panic and grab onto Joel's shoulders, dunking Joel under.

After such a dunking, Joel emerged and shook his hair out. "Again ...try not to drown the swimming instructor." He wiped the water off his face and watched Ethan for a second. "You're definitely getting it."

"Great. Then can we stop for a while? I need a smoke."

Ethan tried unsuccessfully to swim toward the edge and was thankful when Joel shoved him the rest of the way. He climbed out and grabbed a towel off one of the lounges, dried himself off, and reached for his cigarettes, quickly lighting one.

Joel wrapped a towel around his own shoulders and sat down beside Ethan. He picked up the empty cigarette package and held it to his nose, inhaling the scent, then crumpled it up. "I think it's actually starting to cool down a bit." He looked toward the house as he saw some lights come on. "Hey, I think your lunch guy is here."

"Brilliant." Ethan crushed out his cigarette, shoved Joel aside, and sprinted toward the house. Once inside, he slowed down, wandering nonchalantly into the kitchen, and posed himself seductively in a doorway to watch an attractive, young woman cruising around the kitchen, setting out trays of food, and lighting the indoor grill.

"No one answered," the woman said. "So I let myself in. I hope that's all right?" She smiled over at Ethan and went back to what she was doing. "I've got carrot and butterbean soup to start, and your father says you've become partial to pheasant of late, so I've prepared a pheasant salad with beetroot and watercress." She peered up toward Ethan again and grinned mischievously. "Is everything to your satisfaction, Master Cooke?"

"Nancy, my sweet," Ethan replied. "I'm just so thrilled to see real food for a change." Moving away from the doorway, he studied the spread, circling around until he was beside Joel. He placed an arm around Joel's shoulders. "What do you think, Joel?"

"You call this *real* food?" Joel perused the selection, laughing, and grabbed a stick of celery off the vegetable tray on the nearest counter. "Remind me to eat at your house more often."

"What lovely delicacies have you prepared for dessert?" Ethan moved through the kitchen and lifted the covers off some of the containers, trying to find the one with the dessert in it.

"Honey-roasted plums with thyme and crème fraiche," Nancy replied. "Or ...I've also made your favorite chocolate mousse."

"Oh my god! Please marry me." Ethan bumped Nancy playfully with his hip and then headed for the hallway. "After I get changed, of course." He winked and lingered at the door momentarily before making a run to his bedroom.

Joel retrieved his t-shirt from the sofa where he'd tossed it, pulling it on, and took a seat at the island. "This all looks great."

Nancy nodded. "Thank you."

Joel picked through a bunch of grapes and popped a few into his mouth. "I'm Joel, by the way."

Nancy nodded again. "Nice to meet you."

Joel tipped his head. "You're from Britain as well?"

"Mm …hm. I've worked for Ethan many times back home." Nancy looked out toward the foyer then returned her attention to Joel. "It's nice to see Ethan enjoying himself for a change."

"I guess swimming agrees with him."

"Yeah …I suppose that could be it." Nancy smiled at Joel and went back to cutting up the ingredients for the salad. Then she smiled. She'd caught a glimpse of Ethan sneaking up behind her out of the corner of her eye, and managed to side step him in time to avoid the embrace he was about to wrap her in.

"You've got eyes in the back of your head," Ethan said.

"And yet you never stop trying." Nancy grabbed a grape and flicked it at Ethan, squealing and struggling when he ducked away from it and pulled her into his arms.

"Now what are you going to do?" Ethan stood nose to nose with Nancy, gazing into her eyes, letting his breath roll across her lips.

"I'm going to call your father if you don't let me go." Nancy smiled wickedly at Ethan and kissed him on the nose before extracting herself from his arms. "Let me finish making your lunch. Go ...scoot."

"You're no fun at all." Ethan left the kitchen and flopped down on the sofa in the den, and lit up a cigarette. He shoved over, crossing his legs when Joel sat down beside him.

"So, is Nancy a special friend of yours?" Joel asked, attempting to whisper under his breath, without making it too obvious.

"No, she's not my type." Ethan looked back at Nancy and blew her a kiss. "I just like to tease her." He leaned in close to Joel. "She's always a good sport about it, and she's one of the few people that can see through my crap."

"Crap? What crap? Who said you had crap?" Joel made a stupid face and flicked one of Ethan's nose rings. He barely managed to get off the sofa ahead of Ethan, sensing an assault, but lost footing on the slippery marble floor and ended up in a headlock on the ground.

Ethan was laughing so hard, he was having trouble keeping Joel restrained, eventually giving up and crawling back across the floor on his hands and knees to the sofa, with Joel right behind him.

Nancy watched them for a minute, smiling to herself, and then completed her lunch preparation. She set everything out for them on the outdoor patio and headed back inside to tidy up.

Once they'd finished lunch, Ethan and Joel stretched out on the lounges, enjoying the afternoon heat. But the weather was definitely changing. It was still warm during the day, but it was beginning to get really cold at night. The feeling of a cool breeze blowing across his chest alerted Joel to the fact he and Ethan had fallen asleep.

And it was now quite late in the day.

"Hey, sleepyhead." Joel leaned over and poked Ethan in the ribs. "I think either your chef drugged us, or we ate way too much for our own good."

"Nancy's cooking always puts you into a food coma. It's a lovely feeling, isn't it?" Ethan rolled onto his side and yawned. "I had her do up a plate for Erica since you probably won't feel like cooking dinner for her tonight."

"Hey, thanks. What time is it anyway?" Joel pulled out his phone and groaned. "Ten missed calls and …twenty two text messages. Impressive, even for her." He pulled himself off the lounge and stuck the phone back in his pocket. "Erica has the day off tomorrow, so I won't be seeing you again until first day back at school."

"Yeah, about that." Ethan scratched his head. "Just a head's up. School is *not* my favorite place to be, and I have a tendency to be a bit, shall we say …rebellious."

"You, rebellious? Who would've suspected." Joel patted Ethan on the back on his way past into the house. "See you at school."

"See ya." Ethan lay back down and closed his eyes. He was not looking forward to yet another year at high school.

"So, guys. Last day of summer holidays." Ryan flipped his shoes off and dug his toes into the sand.

Max pulled open the cooler and grabbed a cola. "It's hard to believe this is our last year of high school." He pulled, hard, sloppy, and rough on the tab and ended up spraying cola all over Erica and her friend, Angela.

"Jeez, Max," Angela said as she jumped up and shook the cola from her hair. "Now I'm going to have to go into those disgusting washrooms to get cleaned up."

"Just wash up out in the water." Joel picked up Angela's cola sprayed towel and flipped it over before putting it back on the sand.

Erica busied herself brushing the beading cola off her sweater, which had been lying beside her. "It's too cold out there." She gave it a final shake and put it back in her bag. She looked over at Angela. "You're fine. But if it's really bugging you, we can head back to Joel's. You can grab a shower."

"No, I'm fine." Angela settled onto her towel and looked around indignantly. "Why are guys such assholes?"

Erica lay down beside her. "It's a recurring genetic defect."

"That's hardly fair to those of us that are perfect gentlemen," Ryan said, and then burped loudly.

"My point exactly." Erica looked up at Joel when he walked back from the cooler and sat down beside her. "I'm lucky to have found someone like Joel."

Joel beamed as he leaned over and kissed her.

Ryan dropped down beside Joel and bashed him roughly in the shoulder. "So, this new neighbor of yours. According to Erica, he's some kind of gothic Satan worshipper."

"Ethan is not a Satan worshipper." Joel looked at Erica. "Seriously? That's what you're telling people?"

"The way he dresses and acts. And the décor of his house," Erica said. "He's got something strange going on."

Joel shook his head and turned back to Ryan. "Ethan is a little different. He's from Britain, and he's a bit eccentric when it comes to the way he presents himself."

"Is that a polite way of saying he's a freak?" Max asked.

Angela snorted. "Freak or not. Is he hot?"

"No, he's fucking scary." Erica smacked Angela on the arm and then rolled over onto her stomach. She laid her head down on her arm and closed her eyes.

"Are you still feeling sick?" Joel asked as he placed his hand on Erica's back and began rubbing circles. "Maybe I should take you back to the house."

"I think I might phone my mom to come get me," Erica said. "Your parents should be home by now, and I don't feel like doing the whole chatting thing."

Erica tucked her head further into her arm and attempted to quell the nausea rising in her throat, but the heat of the day was making things worse. "Joel, could you phone my mom, please?" she asked frantically. The nausea was overwhelming. She felt certain she was going to throw up and wanted to get out of there and back to her own home as soon as possible.

Joel completed the call, and within a few minutes, Erica and Angela were being picked up. As soon as they were out of sight, Max leaped up and high fived Ryan.

"Yes—" Max exclaimed happily. "A girl free beach day."

"So, did you manage to snag any beverages?" Ryan asked Joel.

Joel reached into his bag and pulled out the bottle of rum Ethan had picked up for him the day before.

"Awesome! You came through," Ryan said. "Who'd you get to boot for you?" He unscrewed the cap and took a long swallow.

"Ethan grabbed it for me. He's got a fake driver's license." Joel reached back into his bag, pulled out a package of cigarettes, and put on his best British accent. "Would anyone care for a packet of fags?" Then rolled over and laughed, and threw them at Ryan.

Ryan ripped open the pack and caught the lighter Joel tossed to him. He looked it over and tipped it up to examine the pictures on it. "Did you get this from Ethan? It looks like it's from Britain. It's got pictures of that Big Ben clock and those crazy buses."

"Yeah, that's his favorite one," Joel said. "I'm surprised he put it in the bag for me. Be careful with it."

"You should've invited him to hang out with us," Max said as he grabbed the bottle from Ryan.

Joel supported himself on his elbows and looked at the water. "Lying on the beach like this would constitute his worst nightmare." He drew a long drink off the bottle. "I had enough trouble getting him into the pool yesterday." He raised the bottle toward the guys. "Here's to our final year at high school. Let it be easy and somewhat interesting." The other two agreed.

The sun started going down a lot sooner than they would've liked, and it was getting cold. A wind had whipped up, howling down from the north, making it particularly uncomfortable to stay outside any longer. Joel packed up his bag and waved to the guys as they headed out on foot in the opposite direction from him. He zipped up his sweater and slowly made his way back home.

As he opened the garage door, Joel was only moderately pleased to see that his parents were home. It meant he wouldn't have to wash the mountain of laundry that had piled up in the laundry room, and he wouldn't have to cook dinner …but he would be subjected to the twenty questions game his parents unconsciously put him through every time he came home.

"Hey, I'm home," Joel said and braced himself.

"Joel, sweetheart." His mom rushed into the miraculously tidy laundry room and pulled him into her arms. "We missed you so much. How was your week? Did you and Erica have a nice time?"

"It was all right, Carol," Joel replied sedately. His parents fancied themselves as being progressive, which was the furthest thing from the truth in Joel's opinion, but they insisted their children call them by their first names. "Erica hasn't been feeling well for the past two days," he added.

"And she worked the whole time. So, it was just all right." He hugged his mom back. "I missed you guys."

"Even me?" Joel's little sister, Jocelyn, stepped into the room and leaned against the doorway. She was only three years younger than he was, but she was intrinsically immature when it came to her mouth. Joel had been embarrassed more than a few times when she had spoken out of turn for her own amusement or lack of couth.

"I'm sorry. And who are you?" Joel said as he threw his wet towel are his sister. "Carol, I think we have an intruder in the house. I'm going to need to throw her out." He raced at Jocelyn and hoisted her up onto his shoulder and carried her out to the family room, and dropped her onto the sofa.

"You're drunk," Jocelyn stated obstinately.

"And you're short," Joel replied as he smacked her in the head. He turned and raised his eyebrows at his dad, who was sitting in a chair across from the sofa. "And you're burned, Arthur."

Arthur replied, "Yeah, I got a little too much sun."

"You were in Vancouver …how is that even possible?" Joel sat down beside his sister and deliberately breathed heavily on her.

"That's disgusting," Jocelyn said. "Arthur, Joel is really drunk, and he stinks." She pushed her brother away and took off for the kitchen to see what was for dinner.

"Where did you get the alcohol from, Joel?" Carol stared at her son with her hands on her hips. She'd overheard the conversation from the kitchen. She did not look pleased.

"Leave him alone, Carol." Arthur waved her off and crossed his legs. "I see someone has finally moved in next door. Have you had a chance to meet them yet?"

Joel let himself fall over on the sofa. He pulled his feet up and tucked a cushion under his head. "It's just one person. His name is Ethan Cooke. He's eighteen."

"And he lives there on his own?" Carol was back in the family room, and she was fretting with her apron. "Who does his cooking and his laundry? That poor boy. He can't live there on his own."

"He usually has staff," Joel said. "But they haven't arrived yet."

Arthur leaned forward in his chair. "What's he doing for his dinner tonight?"

"I took him to the grocery store for microwaveable food a couple of days ago." Joel rolled over, so his face was against the back of the sofa. He'd had far too much to drink again, and the more he moved, the more it felt like he was going to throw up.

"That's ridiculous. Joel, phone him." Carol held out the house phone to him. "Tell him to come over for dinner."

"I have his number in my cell phone," Joel replied. "And I'll *ask* him if he wants to come over for dinner." He slid his phone open and typed a quick message. He had to wait for longer than expected for an answer, but eventually, Ethan texted back, saying he would be right over.

"What did he say?" Jocelyn bounced down on the sofa making Joel feel queasy. "Is he coming? Is he hot?"

"Yes, he's coming, and why does everyone want to know if he's hot? How the hell would I know?" Joel pulled himself into a sitting position. "He's British. He's eccentric. He's totally gothic. And he's a really nice guy." He fell back over and curled himself up. "Oh …and he has enough metal on his body to sink a small ship."

"What does gothic mean?" Carol sat down and clutched her hands in her lap. "That sounds like a bad thing."

"It just means he likes things all dark and creepy," Jocelyn said and then smiled knowingly. "Does he have tattoos?"

"Loads. But please don't ask to see them." Joel peered at Jocelyn. "Promise me you won't embarrass him."

"We'll see," Jocelyn replied. "There's the door!" She jumped up and ran to open the door.

Joel smiled when he heard a small squeak come out of his sister as she opened the door for Ethan. He hadn't mentioned that Ethan was a big guy and that most of the metal was on his face.

"Hiya, Joel." Ethan stepped shyly into the room and nodded to Joel before turning to Joel's dad. "Mr. Carrigan." He held out his hand and met Arthur's shaky grip.

"Call me Arthur." Arthur gulped and sat back down.

"Mrs. Carrigan." Ethan accepted Carol's hand, but then lifted it and laid his lips to it.

"Please. Carol is fine," Carol said as she dropped her gaze, and then pulled Jocelyn out from behind her, where she was hiding. "And this is our daughter, Jocelyn."

"It's a pleasure, Jocelyn." Ethan bowed and then stepped back to make his way over to the sofa. He kicked Joel with his foot to get him to move over. "Drinking in the heat again?"

"You'd think I'd learn." Joel dropped his head against Ethan's shoulder, leaning into him, and tried to keep his head from spinning. He looked over toward the kitchen.

"Carol," Joel asked. "Did you take the headache medication with you when you went away?"

"Yes, dear, but it's back in the box now," Carol replied. "Did you want some?" She pulled the box out, turned to set it on the counter, and jumped when she backed straight into Ethan.

"Sorry," Ethan said. "I'm unusually stealthy for a guy my size." He smiled at her, then stepped past to get a glass of water for Joel. "I'll bring it to him." He grabbed the bottle and headed back to the sofa, and tapped Joel with his foot.

"What?" Joel said with annoyance.

"Joel, get with it," Ethan demanded. "Sit up."

Joel reluctantly let Ethan pull him back into a sitting position. He took the pills offered and drank the entire glass of water at Ethan's urging. He wasn't, however, as cooperative when Ethan brought his dinner over for him. He couldn't imagine it would stay down.

Ethan sat on the sofa beside Joel and finished his dinner first before trying to get Joel to eat anything. After much coercion and a few threats, he finally managed to get Joel to eat the bread and a few slices of roast beef. His mission complete, Ethan threw his feet up and leaned back, and noticed that Jocelyn was staring at him.

"What did you want to know?" Ethan asked Jocelyn.

Jocelyn looked around behind her, and then her eyes popped open as she realized he was talking to her. "Um …"

"My sister at a loss for words," Joel said. "That has got to be a first." He sat up and settled himself into the corner of the sofa, tucking his freezing cold toes under Ethan's thigh. "Carol, write this date down on the calendar. Jocelyn was tongue-tied."

Ethan smiled at Jocelyn then went to stand by the patio door.

"If you'll excuse me for a minute," he said to no one in particular. "I have a bad habit I need to feed." Ethan stepped outside and closed the door. He'd left his favorite jacket at home, not wanting to make a bad first impression, but now he was freezing. He lit up a cigarette and cursed having to smoke outside in other people's homes.

Carol watched Ethan through the window as she started cleaning up the dinner dishes. "He seems like a perfectly pleasant, young man." She dropped the dishcloth on the counter. "But why did he have to go and put all that stuff on his face? And why does he wear all that dark clothing?"

She stared at Joel, expecting an answer.

"Because he likes it," Joel replied. "It's a form of self-expression."

He turned and gazed out the window, watching Ethan. He smiled when he caught Ethan's eye and stuck his tongue out at him. He was rewarded with what he'd discovered was Ethan's signature tongue move. Ethan had a freakishly long tongue that he manipulated at will, and the ball seemingly perched in the center of it added to the overall depraved look when he stuck it out.

"Well, that is one of the scariest things I've ever seen," Arthur said as he leaned back, watching Ethan through the patio door.

"He's perfectly harmless." Joel pulled himself up to help his mom carry the desserts into the family room. He knocked on the window of the patio door and held a cup of coffee up to it.

Ethan crushed out his cigarette when he heard Joel at the window. He was anxious to get back inside and introduce the coffee to his chilled insides. Overall, he felt dinner with Joel's family had gone relatively well. They hadn't immediately thrown him out. No one had screamed at the sight of him. And he'd managed to remember his manners. All in all—it was a good night.

He relaxed in the relative calm of Joel's house. Tomorrow at school was going to be another scenario entirely. He smiled to himself. He had to admit he had fun at school. It wasn't all bad.

Chapter Seven

It was the first day back at Tekla Senior High, and the crowds were finally starting to clear away from the front doors of the school, as everyone met up with their friends and headed inside.

Joel had walked to school with Ryan that morning, because Ethan had headed in early to finish his registration, and Erica still wasn't feeling well and was staying home.

He'd stopped by to see Erica on the way to school, but her mother had told him to come by in the afternoon instead. They had just turned down the main hallway of the school when Ryan laid his hand on Joel's arm to stop his progress down the hall.

"What …the fuck …is that?" Ryan asked.

Most of the traffic in the hallway had slowed to a crawl, and some people were turning back, attempting to figure out a different way to their homeroom class. Joel looked down the hallway to see what all the fuss was about and choked back a laugh.

"Crazy fucker …," Joel whispered, smiling.

Ethan was leaning nonchalantly against the lockers and soaking in the spoils of the commotion he was causing. He easily stood six foot five already, but the huge boots he was wearing were adding another three inches at least. In addition to his usual black jeans and t-shirt, he was wearing a black leather jacket covered in chains and metal spikes. He'd donned his black eyeliner, smudged, but today he was also wearing black eyeshadow and black lipstick. A few girls were trying to sneak past him, but they shrieked and turned back when he made rude gestures at them with his hips.

"That would be an Ethan," Joel said, beaming. He waved down the hall and headed off toward him. Ryan stayed where he was.

Ethan stuck his tongue out at Joel and shoved him playfully. "I wasn't sure if you were going to pretend to not know me once you saw me in full *Ethan* mode." He pounded a heavy hand on Joel's shoulder. "I was gearing up for a solo flight."

"That would definitely be gentler on my reputation, but not nearly as much fun." Joel turned around, motioned for Ryan to join them, and then turned back. "What did you do to your hair?" He ran his fingers up through Ethan's hair and lifted it with his hand. Ethan had cut it much shorter and shaved everything off except for a three-inch swath right down the middle.

"It's a Mohawk, preppie boy," Ethan replied. "I didn't bother doing it up full today. Didn't want to freak people out. It adds an extra four inches to my height." He laughed and then peered around Joel as Ryan approached.

"Hiya," Ethan said. "You must be Ryan."

Ryan extended his hand, cringing when Ethan took it. "Joel told me you were different ...but holy fuck. Is this a British thing?"

"It's definitely more common there. But I'm an original."
Ethan stepped away from the two and leered at a group of
cheerleaders that were trying to make their way past. "Hey
there, chickadees." He stuck his tongue out, making
grotesque licking motions, then licked his lips. "Want to
play with my spike?"

Joel reached out and grabbed onto Ethan's arm, and
pulled him back across the hall away from the girls. "Ethan,
you should probably tone it down a bit, or you're going to
end up spending your first day in the office in detention."

"Yeah, I doubt that." Ethan grinned. "Teachers love me."

"More like they're scared shitless of you."

"That could be it too." Ethan pulled a crumpled piece of
paper from his jean pocket and tried to smooth it out.
"Where's my homeroom? I can't figure this fuckin' thing
out."

"I'm going to head out," Ryan said. "See you later, Joel,
and um …unusual pleasure meeting you, Ethan." He
nodded and then jogged off down the hallway.

"I thought you said you were in grade eleven." Joel took
the sheet off Ethan and tried to decipher the smudged ink.

"The transcripts from my old school showed up, and
they promoted me to grade twelve after looking at them."

"You've got a lot of art classes. That's all you'll be doing
most days. Did you do all your sciences and stuff already?"
Joel handed the sheet back and motioned for Ethan to
follow him.

"I was in all sorts of advanced placement classes the past
couple of years. Realistically, I should be in university

already, but my dad didn't want me to 'socially isolate myself further by moving away from my age appropriate peers.'"

"How's that working for you?" Joel asked, grinning.

"Peachy. I'm thinking of joining the glee club in addition to volunteering as a peer counselor." Ethan snorted and followed Joel into the art department.

"Your homeroom and your first class are both in here. Mr. Carmilan is a pretty cool guy. Try not to freak him out too much. He's a good person to have on your side."

"Hey, I have a lot of respect for art teachers. I'll play nice."

"Will I see you at lunch?" Joel headed out through the door but turned back to hear Ethan's response.

"Yeah. No." Ethan smiled and shook his head. "No offense, but I'm not looking to hang out with a bunch of people. The solitary persona at school works for me." He looked over his shoulder as the bell rung and stepped closer to Joel. "I'd like to hang out with you after school though if that's all right."

"I'm not sure what I'm doing after school yet. We'll see."

"Right. Well ...I'll be at home." Stuffing his hands into his pockets, Ethan ducked into the classroom.

Joel grinned to himself as he slung his backpack onto his shoulder and made a dash for his own homeroom. Ethan's idea of being rebellious was going to be something unprecedented at the school. He hoped the administration was ready for him.

Joel's first class after homeroom was physics. Not his favorite, but he needed it for university. He planned to get a degree in environmental engineering so he could work with environmental groups and the government to study and monitor the effects of piping oil from the prairies to the coast for export to the states.

He briefly scanned the room and found Ryan, who was saving a seat for him. Ryan was only taking the course because he found physics easy and needed the credits to graduate. His father owned a large flooring company in town, and Ryan had already been working there every weekend and summers for years. Ryan wasn't going to be attending university, because he would be working for the family business full time once he graduated.

"Our very last science class ever." Ryan rubbed away some mock tears and pretended to look sad.

"Speak for yourself. I still have another six years after I'm finished here." Joel pulled his binder out and scanned through the textbook that had been passed back to him.

"Don't envy you there." Ryan flipped through the textbook and rolled his eyes. "This is going to be so boring."

Joel made a sound of agreement and pulled out his cell phone when he felt it buzz. It was a text message from Ethan. He wanted to know what Ryan's phone number was. Joel typed in a line of question marks and sent the message to Ethan.

"Ethan just asked me for your phone number," Joel said.

"Yeah," Ryan said. "I ran into him in the hall on the way here but didn't have time to give him my number. He's looking for the names and numbers of our local contacts. I told him I could help him out."

In reality, Ethan had descended, aggressively, on him and his friends, sending most of them scurrying off to class early. He'd been too shell-shocked by Ethan's approach to verbalize his phone number and had just nodded his head when Ethan asked if he knew the names and phone numbers of the guys in school that dealt drugs.

"I'll give you his number, and then you can text him yourself." Joel took Ryan's phone and added Ethan as a contact.

"Yeah, sure. Thanks."

The teacher started the lesson, and Joel began writing down notes on what was being said. He looked over at Ryan and sighed in exasperation. Ryan never needed to make notes. He just remembered everything that he'd ever heard or read. It was completely unfair.

Joel hunched over the desk and kept writing.

After school, the plan was to go and see Erica, and then head to Joel's house to start in on the homework they'd been assigned already. They were halfway home when Erica phoned Joel and asked him not to bother coming around. She still wasn't feeling well. They were about to head down Joel's driveway when Joel changed his mind and motioned for Ryan to follow him over to Ethan's house instead.

Joel knocked lightly on Ethan's door, waited a few seconds, and then let himself in.

"Are you sure we should just let ourselves in like this?" Ryan stepped into the foyer after Joel, and stopped, staring, open-mouthed.

"Yeah," Joel replied. "Ethan never answers his door." He spun around taking in the full effect of the foyer. "Wow, looks like the painters showed up yesterday after all. Not sure if I like dark burgundy walls. Kind of creepy. Reminds me of blood."

"Fuck, Joel. How well do you know this guy?"

"Don't be such a chicken ...speaking of which. Do you smell food cooking?" Joel led the way through to the kitchen and stepped around a stout, middle-aged woman pulling pans out of the oven.

"Hiya, guys." Ethan jumped up from the sofa he was stretched out on in the den. "This here is Sophie. She's been cooking and cleaning for me since I was like ten." He smiled at Sophie, then gave her the finger when she turned away from him.

"She hates me," he whispered.

"The pizza place is going to feel the pinch with you not ordering from them every day," Joel said.

"Yeah, I may still order from them. Sophie is currently on a health kick. And she thinks I should be too. The bitch won't even buy me any bacon." Ethan sneered at Sophie when she turned and glared at him. "Not the same as Nancy ...at all." He dug around in his pocket, pulled out a pack of cigarettes, and lit one up.

"So, your staff showed up," said Joel.

"Yeah, finally." Ethan blew out a ring of smoke. "I think Edgar is floating around here somewhere. I'm not entirely sure what he does. But then, I don't pay attention when things are running smoothly. And they usually are. So he must be doing something."

Ethan took a seat back on the sofa and motioned for Joel and Ryan to join him in the den. Ryan lingered, and Joel waved Ethan off and headed for the fridge to grab a couple of beers first. Ethan already had one started, so he brought one for himself and Ryan.

Joel dropped down beside Ethan and settled in. "I can't believe how quickly it's cooled off outside."

"How cold does it get here?" Ethan leaned back and took a long draw off his cigarette.

"Sometimes, we can drop down as low as minus twenty-five Celsius," Joel replied. "It doesn't last long though."

"I didn't need to hear that. We rarely hit zero back home."

Ryan took a seat and listened in silence while he downed his beer. He was having difficulty getting past Ethan's appearance and demeanor. Even though now that he was at home, Ethan was behaving reasonably normal. Stories of his outrageous behavior and frightening outbursts throughout the day had been flying rampant around the school, and Ryan was becoming increasingly concerned about Joel hanging out with him.

"It's not actually that bad unless it's windy at the same time." Joel finished his beer and set the empty down on a side table.

"Hey, how's Erica feeling? I heard she missed school today." Ethan leaned forward and crushed his cigarette out in an ashtray on the coffee table, and then lit up another one.

"She's been throwing up for days," Joel said.

"In the morning?" Ethan looked over at Ryan, then winked at him, making Ryan jump. "Ryan. Another beer?"

Ryan just nodded.

"Yeah, mostly in the morning," Joel replied. "You thinking the same thing I am?" He waited for Ethan to return, then turned to face him, praying Ethan would have another explanation.

"Afraid so. Do you think Erica has done a test yet?" Ethan handed Ryan his beer and then resumed his place beside Joel.

"I don't know." Joel raised his eyebrows when he saw Ethan hadn't brought one for him as well. He motioned for Ethan's beer and took a long swig before passing it back.

"You think Erica might be pregnant?" Ryan shifted in his seat and leaned forward. "Has she not said anything to you?"

"Nothing," Joel answered.

"Jeez. What are you going to do?" Ryan pushed his beer across the coffee table to Joel and then settled back in his chair.

"I think you should wait until she says something to you," Ethan said. "She probably wants to decide what she's going to do before telling you." He leaned back and blew smoke rings into the air. "Hell of a situation to be in for the final year of high school."

"I guess I don't get a say in what happens, do I?" Joel asked.

"Nope." Ethan laid his hand on Joel's shoulder. "Hey, Joel ...I want to apologize for the whole friend, solitary persona thing today." He ruffled Joel's hair. "But my intimidation factor would plummet if I hung out with a sissy boy like you during school."

"Wow ...burn!" Ryan said, and then laughed nervously, not sure if he should've commented.

Joel crossed his arms and let a grin spread across his face as he studied Ethan.

"Don't take it the wrong way," Ethan said, and then smirked at Joel's expression. "You know I have a comfort zone that includes fuckin' with people. And I can't do that with you around ...beach blond baby." He pushed Joel's leg roughly with his knee and then held up his hands as Joel tried to jab at him. "It's not like we can't talk to each other. I just don't want to hang out with you at lunch and stuff. You'll kill my badass reputation."

Ethan shrieked and covered his head as Joel started smacking him playfully and trying to pin him to the sofa.

Ryan stood and ran his hands down his jeans, feeling the growing discomfort of the possibility his best friend was being pulled away from him. "I'm going to go," he said, not even sure anyone was even listening to him. "I've got a lot of math homework I need to get started on." He pulled out his phone and then tucked it back in his pocket.

Ethan groaned through a breath as Joel finally released him.

"Sorry, Ryan ...you were saying?" he asked.

"Nothing," Ryan said. "I just have to get going. And I have those numbers you were looking for today. I'll text them to you."

"Great. Could you do that as soon as you get home? I'm running a bit short on supplies." Ethan struggled to his feet, shook Ryan's hand, and then dropped back onto the sofa — right into Joel's lap.

He laughed when Joel groaned in pain beneath him.

"Edgar!" Ethan checked around over his shoulder, looking for him. "Bloody hell, where is he? Sophie, could you see Ryan out?"

"That's all right," Ryan said. "I can find my own way out."

He raised his eyebrows at Joel, making Joel laugh aloud as he peered out from behind Ethan's body.

"See you tomorrow, Ryan," Joel said and shoved Ethan off his legs. He slid down further in his seat and waggled his empty beer can in Ethan's face, and bumped him repeatedly with his knee until Ethan got up to get him a new one.

The next morning Joel arrived at school over an hour late. He'd stopped by Erica's on the way, and it had taken longer than expected.

She still wasn't feeling well, and she'd told him she had a doctor's appointment later in the day, and she'd phone him once she knew what was going on. The whole conversation had stressed Joel out to the point where he'd almost turned back toward his house. Then he'd decided he needed the distraction school would provide, and he really needed to talk to Ryan about the real possibility of Erica being pregnant. She had confessed she thought she was pregnant, and they'd talked about what her options were if she was.

He wandered into the school parking lot and took note of a group of students standing at the smoke pit. Amongst them were the usual suspects, with one new addition. Ethan was standing with them, the full extent of his Mohawk causing him to tower over the rest. They were packed tightly together, and there was an open exchange of money and small bags of drugs changing hands. Joel lowered his gaze when Ethan lifted his head and made eye contact with him.

Shaking his head in disbelief, Joel jogged off toward the school, just managing to make it in time for the last couple of minutes of first break. He located Ryan at his locker and pulled him off into an empty classroom.

"I went to see Erica this morning," Joel said. "She's still throwing up. We were right yesterday. She thinks she's pregnant."

Ryan sighed heavily. "When will she know for sure?"

"She's going to the doctor's today."

"Fuck, I'm sorry, Joel. I know this isn't what the two of you were planning ...but you love each other. You'll get through it."

Joel groaned when he heard the bell ring.

"I know," he said. "I'll talk to you more at lunch." He patted Ryan on the back and took off out through the door. His class was all the way on the other side of the school, which meant he was going to be late getting there. He picked up his pace as the last of the students cleared the hallways—and ran straight into Ethan.

"Hiya, Joel," Ethan said. "You're running a bit late all over the place today." He shrugged. "I'm having the same problem."

"Ethan, what were you doing with those guys out there? They're trouble, and you're going to land yourself in it with them."

"Have you seen me lately?" Ethan stepped back, opening his arms dramatically. "Look carefully. I'm as much or more trouble than those guys will ever be."

"That's bullshit, and you know it." Joel leaned heavily against the lockers then sank down onto the ground. "Erica is going to the doctor's today. She thinks she's pregnant."

"Fuck. So, we were right. I'm sorry."

"What am I going to do?"

"There's really not much you can do. You have to wait until Erica makes a decision ...and then do your best to support her."

"She's going to phone me with the results this afternoon."

"I want you to text me as soon as you know, all right?" Ethan kicked Joel's knee lightly with his foot. "You can call me anytime you want to talk about this. Day or night. And you're right, you know. I'm actually a big pushover."

"Then why are you hanging out with those guys?"

"It's who people expect me to hang out with. And I do a lot of drugs ...so it works for me." Ethan held out his hand to Joel. "Come on. Up you get. You're already late for class."

"Are you headed my way?"

"Nah, I got called to the office. Something about setting fire to rolls of toilet paper in the girl's washroom?" Ethan shrugged his shoulders and laughed. "Should be a fun filled day with my new best friend, *Mr. Principal*."

"Ethan …this is only your second day."

"I know, isn't it brilliant. I haven't had this much fun since …well, since my last school year."

"You're going to get yourself expelled."

"Never." Ethan smiled at Joel and then started laughing.

Joel jumped back in surprise when Ethan started bopping around and pogoing up and down the hallway.

"What the hell are you doing?" Joel asked, entertained.

"I love this song!" Ethan shouted, and then stopped dancing when he caught Joel looking at him in surprise. "Right, you can't hear it, can you?" He fished around in his jacket and pulled out a small speaker, plugged his player into it, and set it on the floor. The music came through quite loud and filled the hallway. "Dancing is the best stress reliever ever. Come on, blondie. Let's see your moves."

Joel burst out laughing. Ethan kept bashing into him, eventually prompting Joel to join him in dancing around.

He doubled over, breathless and snorting with amusement when Ethan started singing at top volume. Then surprised himself by joining in, singing and leaping around, shaking off the stress. They were launching into the next song when the classroom doors up and down the hallway began to open, and someone called the office.

"You got detention for dancing in the hallway?" Erica looked at Joel in disbelief. "You …were dancing?"

"And singing. Don't forget I was singing too." Joel fell back on her bed and pulled her to him. "It was exhilarating."

"That's the last thing I'd expect you to be doing after the conversation we had this morning." Erica pulled away from Joel's arms and sat up. "And why am I not surprised it was Ethan's fault. I really wish you wouldn't hang out with him."

She brushed Joel's hands off her leg. "You need to grow up. This is serious stuff we're dealing with. I'm pregnant."

"I'm pretty sure my dancing around and having a bit of fun with Ethan isn't going to change that. You'll still be pregnant ...and I'll still be screwed." Joel hauled himself off the bed and went to stand by the window in an attempt to control his temper.

"Is that what you think? Seriously, Joel! You are getting off easy at this point. You're not pregnant. You're not the one who has to decide what to do about this."

"And why is that?" Joel asked. "Why don't I get a say? I thought we were in this together." Turning back to face her, Joel held Erica by the shoulders. "I love you. And we were planning on getting married and having a family together. We've talked about it so often. The timing is a little messed up ...but it'll work."

"I love you too, Joel. And I want to believe it'll work. But I need to think this through for myself. I'm the one that has to be pregnant throughout my entire grade twelve year."

Joel turned away from her in frustration, reached into his pocket and pulled out his phone. It had buzzed. He'd texted Ethan as soon as Erica had phoned him. But hadn't heard back from him yet. Ethan had been kept after school for vandalizing school property and hadn't been able to get back to him until right then.

He smiled at the picture Ethan had just sent him. It was a moderately artistic rendition, depicting one of Ethan's more intimate piercings, spray-painted on the wall of the school gym. The text message read he was walking home and wanted to know where Joel was so he could meet up with him. Joel responded, saying he was at Erica's, but that he desperately needed to be rescued.

He stuffed his phone back in his pocket and sat down beside Erica, wondering what kind of rescue Ethan would launch. He felt a bit let down when he heard the doorbell ring and listened to Erica's brother speaking quietly to someone, but then Joel heard a string of obscenities echoing down the hall, and he grinned.

Ethan popped his head into Erica's bedroom, ducking a good foot, to even clear the door with his hair.

"Hiya. Fuckin' hobbit house this one is, eh?" Ethan said, remaining crouched down.

"What the hell is he doing here?" Erica looked at Joel in disgust and then used her feet to kick him off the bed.

"Right. Well. It's nice to see you too." Ethan cocked his eyebrow at Joel and rolled his eyes toward Erica.

"I asked him to come by," Joel replied.

"Why on earth would you do that?" Erica glared at Joel and crossed her arms.

"Here's the thing, twist," Ethan began. "Your boy here is afraid of the dark, and I'm here to escort him home." He leaned heavily against Erica's dresser and began playing with the perfume bottles and other knick-knacks.

"What?" Erica asked incredulously.

"Yeah, sure. Didn't you know?" Ethan threw on his best Irish brogue. "Aye, my boy Joel. He's deathly afraid of them there shadows and creepy crawlies of the night. It's a horrible thing really." He rippled a shiver up his spine. "It sends him into frightful fits that can only be calmed by copious amounts of rum." He pulled a brown paper bag out from behind his back. "Oh, now, would you looky here. We're in luck." He winked at Joel. "All right, boyo. Let's get you home before them fits start."

Joel laughed under his breath and pushed Ethan toward the door before turning back to Erica. "Do you think you'll be coming to school tomorrow?" He laid a kiss on Erica's lips when she nodded in agreement. "I'll pick you up, all right?"

"Yeah, all right." Erica smiled, relaxing. "I love you, Joel."

"I love you too." Joel kissed her again, and then followed Ethan out of the house, wondering what Ethan had in store. They headed down the street toward home but took a detour through the beach parking lot. Ethan attempted to sit on a security chain strung between two cement posts but fell off when Joel joined him.

"Thanks a lot," Ethan said as he laid down flat on his back and passed Joel the bottle of rum.

"You've completely fucked up your hair now," Joel replied, then grinned as he undid the cap, and took a swig.

"It's a new look." Ethan pushed himself up on his elbows and took the bottle back. "So, the girlfriend is definitely pregnant."

"Yup." Joel motioned for the bottle and took three consecutive swallows, ending in a fit of coughing as it burned his throat.

"That sucks." Ethan pulled himself off the ground and tried to fix the hair at the back of his head, eventually giving up. He couldn't see what he was doing.

"Here." Joel motioned for Ethan to move closer and used his hands to smooth out the damaged section of hair. "So, tell me. What's with you and this psychopathic persona at school?" He shoved Ethan away with his foot so he could get a better look at what he'd done with his hair. It was a bit better.

"What can I say?" Ethan replied. "I hate school, and I view it as an opportunity to live out my childhood dream of being a lascivious, gothic giant." He took off at a run for a short distance and then turned back to face Joel. "Life is too short not to have a bit of fun."

"So, does this all fall into the fucking with people agenda?"

"Precisely." Ethan stopped and waited for Joel to find his feet after getting up. "You can't get away with this shit as an adult."

"Is it really necessary to lay it on so thick?" Joel followed Ethan down the street toward his house, remembering some of the incredible stories he'd heard throughout the day about Ethan—and wishing he'd witnessed even half of them.

"Thick? You haven't seen anything yet. I'm just getting the full-blown *Ethan* persona warmed up." Ethan smirked as Joel groaned. "If it gets too hot, I'll understand if you bail."

"Not a fucking chance."

"Good, because I kind of like having you around." Ethan smiled at Joel and passed him back the bottle. "When are you going to tell the parental units about Erica?"

"Her parents already know. Her mom went with her to the doctor appointment today. I'll talk to my parents tonight."

"You must be freaking out a bit."

"Nothing a bit more of this won't calm." Joel took another long swallow of the rum and then screwed the cap back on. They wandered into Ethan's house and headed straight for the den to take up their regular spots on the sofa.

Ethan lit up a cigarette. "Isn't Erica going to go with you?"

"No, she's already had to endure enough today. I'll talk to my parents on my own." Joel checked the time on his cell phone and pushed it back in his pocket. "It's getting late already." He looked over at Ethan. "Could you come with me?"

"Sure. If you want. Did you want to go now?" Ethan bumped Joel with his elbow. "The sooner you get it over with, the better."

Ethan stood and hauled Joel onto his feet.

"Ugh. Fuck my life," Joel said and went to unscrew the cap on the rum, but Ethan stopped him.

"You don't want to be completely plastered when you're talking to your parents about something as serious as this. It sends a bad message." Ethan grinned and clapped Joel on the back. "Come on." He pushed Joel out his front door and down Joel's driveway.

Standing outside his door, Joel shook out his body and rolled his head to try to relieve some of the stress in his shoulders. He took a deep breath and opened his front door.

"Hey, I'm home!" Joel shouted to no one in particular.

Carol stepped into the front hall, her face creased up in a concerned and teary expression. "Joel, I'm glad you're finally home. I was going to call you. We need to talk."

Joel grabbed Ethan's sleeve and dragged him along into the living room. He was only moderately surprised to see Erica's parents sitting there with his dad.

"So, you already know," Joel said and looked at each of his parents. They seemed completely distraught. There was no available seating, so he was left to stand awkwardly beside Ethan while being scrutinized by the two sets of parents.

Joel glanced around and decided to grab a chair from the dining room. He motioned for Ethan to get one too.

"I think Ethan should go home," Arthur said. "We need to have a serious discussion about you and Erica."

Ethan set his chair beside Joel's and sat down. "I promised Joel I'd stay with him." He leaned back and crossed his arms. "But I'll leave if he wants me to." He looked over at Joel, who grabbed his sleeve and shook his head *no.*

"Fine," Arthur said. "I take it you know already anyway."

"He does," Joel said. "And quite honestly, I'm not sure what we need to discuss at this point. Everyone knows Erica is pregnant. And that it's mine. And that she's the only one who gets to decide what happens next. What else is there?"

"I think Larry and Cindy are looking for assurances that you're going to be around for Erica," Carol said. "That you're not going to abandon her over this."

"That isn't my intention," Joel replied. "We've always talked about having kids someday. Why would I break up with her over it?"

"If Erica decides to keep the baby," Arthur continued, "her parents want to know that you'll do the right thing by her."

"Of course I will. I love her." Joel stood up. "Is that it? Because until Erica decides what's happening with the baby, we really don't have much else to talk about." He waited until his dad waved him off, then headed off to his room, with Ethan in tow.

"Thank God they knew already," Joel said as he flopped down on his bed. He stuffed an extra pillow behind his head and threw a couple over to the other side of the bed for Ethan.

"Yeah, that was relatively quick and painless, considering."

Ethan lay down, squirmed until he was comfortable, and joined Joel in staring at the ceiling.

"Tip of the iceberg, I'm sure." Joel scrubbed his face. "Do the right thing by her—" He blew air out past his lips, reverberating them. "I'm too young to get married."

"You were old enough to do the crime." Ethan reached over and shoved Joel's head. "You're old enough to do the time."

"Thanks a lot."

"You really love Erica, don't you?"

"Yeah, I do." Joel rolled over on his side and watched the increasingly familiar expressions and movements of Ethan's face when he was deep in thought.

"How do you know it's love?" Ethan asked.

"Hm …I suppose I'm only speculating …based on my perceived emotional response. I fell content when she's with me, and I miss her when she's not." Joel sighed when he saw creases forming around Ethan's eyes and mouth. "I'm concerned for her welfare on par with what I feel for my family. And I'm going to assume, for argument's sake, that I love them."

"Joel, you sound like a fuckin' droid. And what you're describing, that's not love, that's familiarity." Ethan turned and faced Joel. "What do you feel deep in your gut when you think about her?" He began chewing aggressively on his thumbnail. "If I was to tell you, you couldn't see Erica or speak to her for an entire year, what would that do to your heart?"

"How can I possibly associate something as subjective as love to my physical body parts?" Joel answered.

"Wrong answer."

"You don't honestly believe you can feel the effects of an emotion such as love in your physical body?" Joel held up his hand to keep Ethan from answering while he gave it some more thought. "To love someone so much it hurts. To feel the pain of heartache." He rolled onto his back. "I suppose sayings like those came from somewhere. People must be capable of feeling that kind of pain, or they wouldn't keep using them."

"And then on top of love," Ethan said, "there's a whole other level of emotional connection that can happen between two people. Things like passion, undying devotion, and …desperation."

Joel nodded his head.

"The full effect would be an exhilarating rush of painful joy and serene desperation, deep within your physical soul."

"Nice. I like that." Ethan pulled a pillow out from behind his neck and smacked Joel in the face with it.

"Oh, no you didn't." Joel leaped up, grabbed his pillow, and smoked Ethan in the side of the head.

"You little bugger."

Joel screamed when Ethan came at him, knocking him off the bed. He tried to continue his retaliation, but he was no match for Ethan's size and strength, and soon had to throw his hands up in defeat.

Ethan pulled himself off the floor and fell back onto the bed. He leaned against the headboard and motioned for Joel to open the window before he lit up a cigarette.

"Are you going to be all right tonight?" Ethan asked.

Joel reached under his bed and pulled out the small bowl Ethan had used as an ashtray the last time he'd been in his room.

"I hate being alone when my mind is racing like this," Joel replied. "But I'm about ready to pass out, I'm so tired."

"Then go to sleep." Ethan tapped his cigarette over the bowl and peered over at Joel's bedside table. "Throw me that book, there." He took the novel Joel passed to him and looked it over. "I've actually been meaning to read this" He opened it up, crossed his legs, and got comfortable. "If you wake up, I'll be here to talk. Just give me a good jab if I'm asleep."

Joel's face screwed up, aghast.

"You're not seriously going to stay?" he asked.

"Yeah," said Ethan, shooing Joel away with his hand. "You roll over and go to sleep. I'm good."

"Thanks, Ethan." Joel pulled a blanket over his shoulders and watched the smoke drifting around Ethan's face. He shifted closer, steadied his breathing, and closed his eyes.

"Ethan ...," he whispered.

"Shh," Ethan interrupted. "I'm reading. Go to sleep."

Chapter Eight

Joel and Erica managed to get through the first month of school as a couple without any drama, but Erica was definitely starting to show, and rumors were beginning to circulate around the school. Joel was running late for lunch break, and Erica was alone at her locker, trying to find her biology textbook, when a group of girls approached and surrounded her. One of the girls, Erica recognized as Jessica spoke.

"Erica …true love waits," she stated bluntly.

Erica turned to face Jessica. "Really? Is that so?"

"Sex before marriage is a sin," Jessica spouted. "If Joel really loved you, he would've waited until you were married."

"Leave me alone," replied Erica.

"Can we pray for you and your baby?"

"I said leave me alone!" Erica tried to push past, but they were standing firm, waiting for a more positive response from her.

"Hiya. What's up with all this?" Ethan stepped up, crowding in beside Erica, and leered at the girls. "I'd love to spend some time showing you strumpets what I know about the bible. I'm an expert on Sodom and Gomorrah." Then he set into a full-on, graphic description of what he'd like to do to them, that had Erica cringing, and the girls running for the office.

"You're seriously disturbed," Erica said to Ethan, pushing him away. "And you're fucking disgusting."

She slammed her locker shut and took off down the hall.

"You've got that right! I love a good disgusting fuck!" Ethan shouted at full volume down the hall, and hooted, clapping his hands when people turned toward him in shock. He peered over his shoulder when he heard his friends howling behind him, and made his way back to them. "Fuckin' bitch has no sense of humor, whatsoever." He clapped his hands together. "What do we have on the menu this afternoon? I could really use a flight into oblivion."

Ethan followed along to one of the fields at the far end of the school property. He stuffed his hands in his pockets, wholly annoyed with what had transpired. He knew his methods were unconventional, but he had only been trying to help her.

He took the pill passed to him, pretended to take it, pocketing it instead. He rolled his shoulders. He had no choice but to actually participate when someone lit up a joint. His thumbnail went straight to his mouth. He thought back to his lewd outburst in the hallway and shook his head at his own unrelenting immaturity.

Ethan took a long toke off the joint. The stress relieving properties of the weed was definitely going to be welcome today.

It was going to be a very long day.

Erica finally caught up with Joel in the cafeteria and slammed her textbooks down on the table beside him.

"Ethan is a disgusting pig!"

Joel opened his lunch and traded off his sandwich with Ryan, refusing to jump at Erica's outburst.

"What did he do to piss you off this time?" he asked.

"Jessica and her *do rights* were harassing me about the sins of sex before marriage, and he walks up and starts telling them all the nasty stuff he would do to them if he got them alone."

"Did they leave you alone after that?" Joel asked.

"Well, yeah. They took off running for the office."

"Erica, he was trying to help you in his own bizarre and twisted way." Joel took a bite of his apple. "Did you think of that?"

"Why do you always have to take his side?" Erica grabbed the apple from Joel's hand and started eating it. "He embarrassed me."

Joel cradled Erica's face and kissed her. "You need to lighten up a little bit. Ethan's not a bad guy. He's just somewhat gregarious and undisciplined when he's at school."

"Somewhat undisciplined?" Ryan laughed. "He's got all the students, and the faculty, scared to death of him. He smokes in the hallways. Skips most of his classes. Swears, yells, and makes lewd gestures at practically everyone. And no one stops him, because they're too afraid to confront him. Even the police liaison officer won't interfere with him."

"Ryan is right," Max agreed. "Ethan is out of control. I don't think you should be hanging out with him."

"And I think you need to mind your own business," Joel replied.

Ryan crossed his arms, concerned.

"What exactly do you guys do every day?" he asked Joel. "You're not doing drugs with him, are you?"

"Joel?" Erica said. "You wouldn't do drugs, would you?"

"No!" Joel answered emphatically. "You guys know I'm not into that crap." He crumpled up his lunch bag and pitched it at the garbage can. "Believe it or not …Ethan and I have a lot in common. I can't talk to any of you morons about philosophical stuff, but Ethan is totally into it, and he has some pretty impressive insights."

Erica burst out laughing. "You're joking, right?" she asked in belief. "I'm sorry, but I can't picture you and Ethan sitting around having deep philosophical discussions."

"Believe what you want," Joel said. "But that's exactly what we do most of the time. Or we watch old horror movies …or drink ourselves stocious. Usually, but not necessarily, in that order."

"Why don't you take a break from him?" Max asked. "We're all headed to Ryan's tonight to play video games."

"You know I hate video games, Max," Joel said. "But I'll come by to keep you guys from harassing me." He smiled at Erica. "And you …try to chill out. Life's too short to let people annoy you."

After lunch, Joel headed straight for the office with Ryan and peered in through the windows, along with masses of other people. Rumor had it that a massive drug bust had been made on school property over the lunch hour and that Ethan and five of his friends had been hauled into the office for questioning by the police.

Joel scanned the interior and saw Ethan sitting in a chair in the principal's office. Ethan was waiting for someone to come and speak with him. When he turned and saw Joel peering in at him, Ethan grinned and gave Joel two emphatic thumbs up.

Joel smiled at him. "Ethan seems to be having fun."

"Joel, the guy is a lunatic." Ryan rearranged the books in his arms to make sure he didn't drop any onto the floor.

"He gets bored easily. This qualifies as entertainment."

Ryan just rolled his eyes.

"I'm going to class," he said. "What about you?"

"I'm going to wait for Ethan."

Ryan's sigh was audible.

"You're not planning on coming to my place tonight, are you?"

"Yeah, I don't think so. We'll see." Joel shrugged when Ryan shook his head in disappointment. Then he went to sit in the office.

It was almost three when Ethan was eventually let go, and he was visibly pleased to see Joel waiting for him.

"Hiya. What are you doing here?" Ethan asked.

"Waiting for my criminally insane friend."

"Well, I'm free to fly another day." Ethan turned and gave the principal the finger on the way out the door. "They've got nothing on me, as usual. I'm as smooth as silk."

"What about the other guys."

"Those losers. They're all getting arrested."

"I thought they were friends of yours." Joel followed Ethan out into the hall. "You hang with them every day."

"They're hardly friend material." Ethan stopped and turned to Joel. "Small problem though. I'm going to need a new dealer. Can you let me know if you hear who's stepping in after these guys?"

"Yeah …sure."

"Ethan, could I have another word with you?" The police liaison officer stepped into the hallway outside the office and waited for Ethan to make his way back to her.

Joel waited and watched them speaking quietly with each other. They were deep in conversation for a few minutes, and then the officer shook Ethan's hand before turning back toward the office.

"What was all that about?" Joel asked.

"She's under the impression I'm going to help her." Ethan took off down the hallway and made a jump for a banner hanging across its width. He tore it down and pulled out his lighter.

"What are you doing?" Joel asked as he held back.

"Do you want the rest of the day off?" Ethan grinned as he set the banner on fire and held it up to a smoke detector. Then he waited for the inevitable fire alarm, and stomped out the flaming paper, before high tailing it back down the hallway.

He grabbed Joel by the arm and hauled him out of the school.

Joel was out of breath when they finally stopped running. He could hear the fire engines in the distance. He and Ethan had covered at least eight blocks and were hiding in some bushes by the time the police started combing the area for them.

"You're fucking insane, you know that?" Joel said.

"You know you love it. Quite the rush, wasn't it?" Ethan pulled out his cell phone and breathlessly speed dialed a number. "Hiya. Yeah …right …sorry." He laughed and ended the call. "Forgot to phone my dad again. I have to check in every once in a while, so he knows I'm still alive, and staying out of trouble."

"He really doesn't know you very well, does he?"

Ethan poked his head out of the bushes and scanned up and down the street. He grabbed hold of Joel's sleeve and pulled him in the direction of their road. "My dad trusts my judgment. He knows I'll never take things to an unreasonable level." He bent down, picked up a stone off the road, and chucked it as hard as he could down the street. "We have a good relationship that way. He stays out of my way, and allows me to do my thing."

"You're lucky. My parents have me pretty nailed down. This thing with Erica has really tipped their boat."

"What's the latest?" Ethan threw his arm around Joel's shoulder and pulled him in—then released him.

"I'm so stressed out. Erica still hasn't decided what she wants to do with the baby. If she decides to have an abortion at this stage …I'm going to have to break up with her."

"Yeah, I'm with you on that." Ethan looked over at Joel and studied him intently. "The little guy or girl deserves a chance." He pounded Joel on the back. "I know just the thing you need. Party at my house Saturday night?"

"Yes! That would be awesome!" Joel bumped Ethan with his shoulder and then took off at a run toward Ethan's house.

Trucks of equipment started showing up at Ethan's house very early on Saturday morning. Joel was woken up by the sound of the trucks' reversing indicators, and men shouting back and forth to each other. His mom had planned on going shopping that morning, but very soon after leaving, she'd come back into the house complaining she wasn't able to reverse out of their driveway.

Joel pulled on some clothes and grabbed a heavy coat before heading outside. October was a funny month. It often started out not too cold, but by Halloween, it could drop below zero.

He walked to the end of his driveway and stood dumbfounded at the number of men moving cartloads of equipment into Ethan's house. He watched as a truck with a massive generator pulled itself in tight against the edge of the house across the street, and men started running thick electrical cables out to it.

Not wanting to get in the way, but wanting to talk to Ethan, he pulled out his cell phone and called him.

"Hiya, Joel," Ethan answered.

"What the fuck kind of party are you throwing?"

"Too much?" Ethan laughed through the phone. "It's going to be the party of the century. I wanted to make sure the baby was the last thing on your mind. Oops, I used the *b*-word."

"You're unbelievable. What time does this thing start?"

"My permit has it running from seven until seven."

"You took out a permit?"

"I told you. Party of the century. I'll see you tonight."

Joel dropped his phone back in his pocket, pulled his coat tightly around himself, and watched as a few more trucks started showing up. He whipped his cell phone right back out again, and phoned Ryan when the equipment trucks for one of the biggest DJ's in the world began pulling into Ethan's driveway.

By eight that evening, there was a line up halfway down the street, and the ground was shaking rhythmically from the intensity of the speakers. The entire neighborhood was lit up by massive panning exterior spotlights and the flashing, colored strobe lights finding their way out through all the windows of Ethan's house.

Joel bypassed the line up with Ryan in tow and was immediately let in by the bouncers at the door.

The inside of Ethan's house was absolute mayhem. The far end of the massive living room had an impressive stage set up with huge screens of flashing images behind three men working different boards of equipment. In front of the stage was a sea of dancing people, stretching out in every direction. The music was heavy electronic dance, and the DJ behind the main board was shouting and singing, and working the crowd into a pulsing frenzy.

Joel and Ryan were taking it all in when Ethan pogoed up behind Joel and swept him onto the dance floor.

"Hey, blondie, you're late," Ethan shouted.

Joel laughed. "What?"

Ethan gripped Joel's shoulders from behind and angled him into the crowd, protecting Joel from the crowd of surging bodies as they all got into the music, jumping up and down, arms pumping and singing along at top volume.

Once Joel got over the initial inhibition, he found himself singing and jumping as much as everybody else. He was utterly worn out by the time the DJ took a break and switched over to house music. He followed Ethan out of the living room and into the family room down the hall, where a fully stocked and attended bar was set up.

"So, what do you think?" Ethan yelled. He'd had the entire house wired with speakers, making it very difficult to hear anything. The house looked and felt like one gigantic, gothic nightclub.

He motioned for the bartender to hand him a bottle of rum and pulled Joel off in the direction of the office down the hall. He removed a set of keys from his pocket and unlocked the door, slipping inside with Joel then locking the door again.

"That is something else out there." Joel fell down in the chair behind the desk and accepted the bottle from Ethan. He took a long swig before passing it back. "Good idea locking off some of the rooms like this." He leaned forward and picked up the set of keys Ethan slid toward him, questioning Ethan with his eyes.

"Those are yours," Ethan said. "There's a key on there for the front door as well." He slumped down into the large overstuffed chair in front of the desk. "The entire upstairs is locked down, so you'll need those if you want to stay over. I had a big gate installed at the top of the stairs. One can't be too careful." He tipped back the bottle. "And my garage is filled with portable toilets …disgusting, but necessary."

"It's almost like you've done this before." Joel winked at Ethan and took the bottle he offered.

"My friends and I used to head to Berlin a lot. Ultimate dance clubs of all time in that city." Ethan hummed happily, remembering. "Sometimes we would try and set up a similar kind of experience at home." He lit a cigarette, inhaling deeply, then manipulated the smoke into pooling about his lips as he exhaled.

"I wasn't sure if I'd be able to pull it off here," he continued. "I had to fly a lot of these guys in from Europe. Luckily this DJ was already in America with his equipment, and one of the film studios in Vancouver came in pretty handy." He waved his hand in the air. "All in all, not a bad job."

"Not a bad job? It's fucking unbelievable."

Ethan checked the time on his phone. "Right, break's over. Time for round two." He took another swig of rum, grabbed Joel's arm, and hauled him back out to the living room.

By seven the next morning, Joel was hoarse, exhausted, and completely elated. He'd convinced Ryan to stay the night at Ethan's, after much coercion, and they'd flaked out in one of the guest rooms just after eight in the morning. By the time they emerged, it was almost seven thirty in the evening, and they were famished.

After wandering down to the kitchen, Joel unlocked the gate protecting it with the keys Ethan had given him the night before and headed straight for the fridge. He grinned eagerly, as he saw it was overflowing with pre-made food. Sophie could be a bitch sometimes, but she certainly knew how to stock a fridge.

"This place looks even more like a medieval castle with all these gates everywhere," Ryan said.

"Do you blame him? How many people do you think were in here last night?" Joel pulled out the coffee maker and started it going before looking through the pastries he'd just uncovered. Sophie was apparently off her health kick.

"I don't know. Like three hundred." Ryan grabbed an orange, and a chocolate filled croissant and went to sit at the island.

Joel took two cups from the cupboard and filled them with coffee, giving one to Ryan before sitting down beside him.

"It's so weird being in his house," Ryan said.

"What do you mean?"

"Joel, maybe you haven't noticed, but Ethan is one seriously scary guy. And this house. It's like something out of a horror movie." He took a sip of his coffee and glanced anxiously around the room. "You two have become pretty close though, haven't you?"

"Yeah, we spend a lot of time together. Although, he's been taking off to Vancouver every weekend recently, which works out great because I like to spend all weekend with Erica." Joel looked at Ryan over his cup. "You're still my best friend."

"No, it's all right. I'm working every spare minute I have anyway. But I wish you'd found someone else to hang out with …besides Ethan." Ryan popped the last of the croissant in his mouth. "When do you think he's going to get up?"

"Who knows? Ethan's not much of a morning person, and it sounded like he was having his own private party in his bedroom after everyone left. So, I'm assuming he'll emerge sometime after we hear someone sneaking out the front door."

"Unless I insisted they sneak out the back door." Ethan swept into the kitchen and headed straight for the coffee. He settled in with a cup at the island and lit a cigarette. "So, is everyone in one piece today? Is my house in one piece today?"

"We're both intact, and the house doesn't look too bad." Joel wandered around the island and fingered the sleeve of the lavish, purple kimono Ethan was wearing. "Silk …very nice." He smirked as he caught Ethan's eye. "I didn't think you owned any clothing that wasn't black. Especially something so …provocative." He circled around Ethan, barely able to contain his amusement. "Are you wearing anything under there, sweetheart?"

Joel laughed when Ethan smacked him in the back of the head.

"Why on earth would I do that?" Ethan said as he stood up. "I simply adore the feel of silk on my bare arse." He grinned and blew smoke in Joel's face, pausing to study Joel's expression. He blinked and looked away, then crushed out his cigarette and went to grab another cup of coffee. "I'm going back to bed. I've been in it all day, but haven't managed to get any sleep …lucky me."

Then he winked bawdily at Joel and left the kitchen.

The next few weeks were uneventful. Ethan continued to be hauled into the office for all sorts of bizarre infractions, some of which had Joel thinking that someone was making them up. And Joel continued to wait for Ethan to be released from the office every day after school. He used his time to do homework and study for tests and found that the one or two hours at the end of each day were making a big difference to his marks.

Today was a half-day at school because of parent-teacher meetings, and Ethan hadn't been called into the office for a change. Joel's parents were attending the meetings as usual but had agreed it wasn't necessary for him to go with them, so he'd taken off with Ethan to his house. It was great to have the rest of the day off, but the plans he and Ethan had for the afternoon were making Joel extremely nervous.

"Do you have any more of those nacho chips?" Joel dug around in the cupboard before heading over to the larder to have a look there. "Ethan. Does Sophie have a shopping list I can add stuff to?"

Joel jumped when Ethan step up behind him. "Please don't sneak up on me," he said. "My nerves are on edge."

"Did you look in the drawer here?" Ethan leaned over and pulled open a drawer full of canned goods. "Maybe not that one."

"I've looked everywhere. Are you sure Sophie knows you like those lime ones?" Joel pushed past Ethan to get out of the larder.

"She knows I like them all right," replied Ethan. "Why do you think she stopped buying them?"

"What did you do to piss her off this time?"

"I don't know. I breathed?"

"Fuck. I need something to eat. My stomach is going nuts on me. Are you sure you know what you're doing?"

"I told you. I've been tattooing for years." Ethan grabbed Joel by the shoulders, guided him down the hallway, and opened the door to a room Joel had never been in before, leading him into what turned out to be a small tattoo studio, complete with all the equipment.

"What the …," Joel started.

"As soon as I finish getting everything organized," Ethan said, "I'll ask my dad to get me a business license, and then I'll start advertising …pick up some legit clients."

"I didn't realize you were actually a pro at it." Joel sat down on the edge of the table and watched Ethan fussing around at a counter on the other side of the room.

"I just finished setting up the last of the equipment yesterday. I wanted to surprise you." Ethan flipped open a binder and turned back to Joel. "Did your mom sign that consent form?"

"Yeah, here." Joel handed a piece of paper to Ethan when he came over to get it. "I guess the official-looking consent form should've been my first clue that you weren't playing around."

"Mm ...hm." Ethan clipped the paper into his binder and went back to Joel with a stencil he'd sketched up earlier in the day. He directed Joel to lay down. "This is going to be fairly quick. I'm only doing five stars for now. You can add more later if you decide you want more."

"We'll see how this goes first." Joel shifted, trying to get comfortable while Ethan laid the stencil along his forearm.

"Just try and relax." Ethan leaned in and transferred the pattern. "I'm only going to fill in two of them today." He lifted Joel's arm and showed it to him. "How's that?"

"Looks good." Joel laughed nervously and grabbed onto Ethan's arm. "Be honest. How much is this going to hurt?"

"You'll be fine. Just remember to breath. And like I said, I'll be done fairly quickly." Ethan studied Joel's eyes. "Let me know when you're ready." He adjusted his gloves, grabbed the gun and waited for Joel to nod his approval, and then started.

"Fuck!" Joel said, cringing. "That burns."

"Just stay still." Ethan rapidly sketched the outlines and then stopped to let Joel catch his breath. He changed his gun and set back at it, filling in two of the stars. Once they were done, Ethan wiped them off and held Joel's arm up so he could see.

"Hey, I really like that," Joel said. "Can I get another one?"

"I think that's enough for today." Ethan took his equipment back across the room, disposing of the needles and throwing everything else in the autoclave. He carefully put his inks away and grabbed a spray bottle to disinfect the table. "But I'll do as many as you want. Take a look through my book and pick out what you want. Or if you have something different in mind, I'll sketch it up for you."

"Is that why you take so many art classes?" Joel flipped the book open and perused through it with one hand while Ethan attached a loose dressing to his other arm.

"Yeah," Ethan replied. "I've always wanted my own studio. I apprenticed with a guy back home for a couple of years."

"What's all that stuff?" Joel left the book and wandered over to a reclining chair with a bank of clear drawers full of metal objects.

"Piercings." Ethan grinned and pulled out a sealed package containing a clamp and needle. "You want to give that a try too?"

"Jeez, what the hell are those?"

"They look more ominous than they actually are." Ethan threw them back in the drawer and closed it up. "Some other time?"

"Yeah, a very long time from now." Joel stepped back over to the book. "Can I think on what else I want?"

"Sure, it's definitely not something you want to rush into. Some people believe each tattoo should mean something to you."

"Yeah? So why did you pick the stars for me?"

"Maybe I'll tell you someday." Ethan flicked the lights off, threw his arm around Joel's shoulders, and led him from the room.

Chapter Nine

"I'm glad you understand this crap," Joel said. "Math has never been my best subject, but I need it for physics." He flipped open his textbook and dropped down onto the sofa beside Ethan.

"You don't need to completely understand everything yet," Ethan said. "You just need to memorize the formulas and recognize a few things." He grabbed a stack of blank paper and deftly wrote out the formulas they would be using, entirely from memory.

"How the hell did you do that?" Joel asked, stunned.

"Repetition. I've done this math before, plus I'm a bit of a freak when it comes to remembering things."

"Not you too." Joel sat back. "Ryan is like that, and it drives me crazy. The only two people I know that aren't going to university are fucking geniuses. It's not fair."

"Maybe that says something." Ethan laughed and shook his head when Joel glared at him. "Just copy this sheet out until you can do it without looking. When you go into the test, you write it out on the back of the exam paper and voila—legal cheat sheet." He shoved the paper and a pencil at him. "Go ahead, get started."

"I hate this." Joel set to work copying and re-copying the formulas until they were starting to stick in his head. Ethan watched him carefully, waiting to see if it was sinking in. He couldn't understand what Joel was complaining about. Judging by what he was seeing, he was more competent than he gave himself credit for.

"All right, you're getting somewhere." Ethan reached behind Joel and grabbed the television remote. "Fifteen-minute break and then we'll work on figuring out which formulas need to be applied to what and why. A little bit of understanding is necessary."

"You're cruel, but I appreciate it." Joel pulled himself off the sofa and headed for the kitchen. He was pleased to see that his mom had replenished the cupboard over the fridge with chips. He grabbed a bag of salt and vinegar and headed back to the sofa. "What are we watching for our fifteen-minute window?"

"We have a choice of news, news, or more news ...no wait, there's a kid's show on this channel. Why don't you have proper channels at your house?" Ethan turned the television off and threw the remote down on the coffee table before grabbing a handful of chips and stuffing them into his mouth.

"Did you want to go back to your house instead?" Joel asked.

"No, I was kind of hoping your mom would come home soon and make dinner for us. That lasagna last night was amazing."

"You're out of luck. My mom and dad are at a Christmas party tonight with my sister. We'll have to go bug Sophie if we want someone to cook dinner for us."

"She's being a bitch today. I'm not eating any of her fuckin' food until she smartens up." Ethan took another handful of chips and settled into the cushions with the bag.

Joel watched Ethan stuff handful after handful into his mouth.

"Did you want something to drink with those," he asked, snatching the bag from Ethan. "Before you choke on them?"

"No, but let's get this math done before I drift into a coma from boredom." Ethan turned a few pages over in the textbook. "Do these questions first, and then I'll help you through the next section."

"So much for my fifteen-minute break."

"Stop whining and start working." Ethan sat back and watched Joel work through the problems. He shifted uncomfortably when his attention became focused on the movements of Joel's hands turning the pages and occasionally touching his mouth when he was deep in thought. Ethan took a sharp breath and looked up at the ceiling. "I need a smoke. Are you all right on your own for a minute?"

"Sure, yeah."

Grabbing his heavy jacket, Ethan slipped his shoes on and stepped out on the back patio. He took the steps down onto the grassy area between the house and the pool. There was a small jut out along the side of the house, and he headed for that before lighting up a cigarette.

He leaned against the wall and rubbed his hand across the back of his neck. The stress was starting to get to him. He'd never been in a situation like this before, and he wasn't sure what to do about it—if anything. He took a few long steady breaths to clear his head.

Ethan looked up when he heard the patio door open.

"Ethan, I need your help," Joel called from the door.

"I'll be right in." Ethan finished his cigarette, headed back into the house, and took up his spot beside Joel.

He looked over the question Joel was having a problem with.

"I'm pretty sure I messed it up." Joel wrote down a few numbers and then erased them.

"Yeah, this part here," Ethan said. "You used the wrong formula. If you look carefully at the diagram with this question you can tell what they're looking for ..." He stopped when he realized Joel was staring at him. "What?"

"I'm not an expert on tutoring in Britain, but I'm pretty sure holding my leg and stroking it with your thumb isn't going to help me ...or maybe it would. I don't know."

Ethan snatched his hand away. "Jeez, Joel, I'm sorry. I wasn't—fuck!" He scrubbed his hand through his hair. "I wasn't thinking. I was just ...I was ...never mind. I'm sorry."

"Hm, that doesn't explain much at all." Joel grinned and went back to scanning through his work. "It's not the first time you've done that tonight, you know?" He flipped to the back of the book to check his answer before turning to face Ethan.

"I hadn't realized," Ethan replied. "I'm sorry."

"You don't need to keep apologizing. If it were really pissing me off, I would've beaten the crap out of you by now."

Ethan laughed and pushed Joel. "I'd like to see you try."

"Some other time maybe. So, what's going on?" Joel leaned back in his seat and watched the expression on Ethan's face change.

"What do you mean?"

"This past couple of weeks, you've been acting differently around me. You've been touching my arm when you're speaking to me. Sitting closer when we're watching movies. Stuff like that."

"Please, Joel. Don't make a big deal out of this."

"Come on, we're friends. You can talk to me."

"I know I can talk to you." Ethan sat back and crossed his arms tightly across his chest. "It's nothing. We've gotten closer this past couple of weeks. You're like the best friend I've ever had. I feel comfortable with you. And I come from an affectionate family. The touching, the closeness …it just comes naturally to me."

"And that's it?"

"Yeah, that's it."

"There's no other reason you'd be acting like this."

"No, of course not."

"Hm—" Joel closed the math book and set it down on the coffee table. "I happened to look up *cupido* on the internet the other day." He chewed on his pencil and watched the anxiety rising in Ethan's eyes. "*Cupido* is Latin for desire, with Cupid being the god of desire, affection, and erotic love. Mm …sounds kinky." He smiled at Ethan's obvious discomfort. "I also read that lower back tattoos like the one you have are generally worn by women."

"What's your point?"

"My point is you've been keeping something from me." Joel tapped Ethan lightly on the knee with his pencil. "Something significant that you should've shared with me ages ago. So, I'm going to go out on a limb here, Ethan." He stopped tapping and poked Ethan in the arm with the pencil. "You're gay, aren't you?"

Ethan exhaled the breath he'd been holding and nodded his head. "I wanted to tell you, Joel, really I did, but I was worried it would make you feel uncomfortable."

"Why would you think that?"

"We spend a lot of time together. I didn't want you getting the wrong idea about my motivation for that."

"You were worried that I'd think you were only hanging out with me ...because you were attracted to me?"

"Something like that."

"Ethan, we hang out all the time because we get on really well, and we have a lot of fun together. We both know that."

"I know. I was just worried."

"All right, well, don't worry about it. We're all good." Joel's face lit up with a devious smile. "And sorry for torturing you. I've actually known you were gay for months." His eyebrows rose in anticipation when Ethan looked on in disbelief.

"You little bugger—" Ethan pinned a shrieking Joel to the sofa and mercilessly tickled him until Joel complained he was going to wet himself if Ethan didn't stop.

Gasping for breath, Ethan relented, climbed off, and grabbed the bag of chips. "Why didn't you say something?"

"I'm sorry. I didn't know how to bring it up," Joel replied as he pulled the chips away from Ethan and scooped a handful. "It had nothing to do with the tattoo by the way. I made that up. I figured out you were gay when I saw a guy going into your bedroom after the party. The noises after that were pretty self-explanatory."

"Fuck, that's embarrassing. I'm not used to having other people stay overnight at my house. Were we really that loud?"

Joel smirked. "Yeah, kind of."

"Did Ryan hear anything?"

"Are you kidding me? He was passed out cold. That boy is a lightweight when it comes to hard alcohol." Joel stood up from the sofa and walked to the far side of the coffee table. "I, on the other hand, was sober enough to be thoroughly entertained by the symphony of your activities." He was halfway out the patio door before Ethan even managed to get off the sofa. "And I found it to be very educational!" He rounded the corner of the house and just managed to slip out of Ethan's grasp. "Although, I'm a bit confused as to what needed to be fucked harder!" He flew in through the front door and barricaded himself behind a chair in the dining room.

Ethan skidded to a stop in front of him, panting. "Are you done?" He coughed and then smiled at Joel.

"That's all I have for now," Joel said as he stepped out from behind his barricade and skirted around Ethan to close the front door. "I'll just toss them out there as I think of them." He pulled off his wet socks, threw them onto the carpet, and dropped down onto the sofa and set the math books back on his lap.

Ethan shoved Joel over and sat down. "Don't you dare or I'll throttle you. I mean it. Now, get back to work."

Joel grinned at him and picked up his pencil.

They worked through every question in the chapter and Ethan made up a few questions of his own that turned out to be harder than those in the textbook. Once Joel had finished them, he slammed his book shut and threw it onto the coffee table.

"That's it. No more," Joel said. "My head is going to fucking explode." He flicked the pencil across the room and stood up, stretching himself out before walking to the kitchen. "Do you want a drink of something?"

"Anything with alcohol would be brilliant." Ethan pulled himself off the sofa and crossed the room to join Joel. He waited to see what Joel was pulling out of the liquor cabinet before opening the freezer and taking the ice cubes out. "Make mine neat with ice."

"So, is your dad coming for Christmas?" Joel asked.

"I don't know yet."

"You never told me. When was the last time you saw your dad?" Joel handed Ethan his glass and turned to pour his own.

"No joke. About two years ago."

"Two years ago? You weren't exaggerating about living on your own. That must be tough."

"It's not a big deal. I'm used to it. I've been living on my own for most of my life. But speaking of tough …" Ethan swirled the ice cubes in his glass. "How are you holding up this week?"

"I'm managing. The doctor says the baby is doing really well, and Erica isn't feeling sick anymore, so that's progress."

"Is she getting excited about the baby?"

"Yeah, she's picking out names and everything. And yesterday, she came over with a big bag of baby clothes that a friend gave her." Joel rubbed his nose. "It was a strange experience holding up those little clothes and knowing that in five months, I'm going to have a baby to fill them."

"Try not to get too anxious about it. You're going to make a great dad." Ethan patted Joel on the shoulder and added some more ice to his drink. "Did you get the wedding date sorted out?"

"Yeah. January fifteenth."

"That's only a month from now." Ethan grabbed the bottle and motioned for Joel to head back over to the sofa.

"I think Erica's parents are thinking the sooner, the better, in case I try to escape. I'll let you know the details about the whole groomsman thing when I know more." As Joel settled in, he finished what was in his glass and reached across the coffee table for the bottle. "But enough about my romantic life. I'd like to hear about some of your escapades."

"Who says I had escapades?" Ethan replied.

"The pink heart …the ex? What happened there?"

"I don't know, Joel. I feel weird talking to you about it."

"Why? We talk about all sorts of personal stuff. You know I won't judge you." Joel smiled at Ethan. "Come on, spill."

"Fine. His name was Lucien Dubois. He was a guy I met in Paris while I was there on summer break year before last." Ethan closed his eyes and sat quietly for a second before continuing. "It's really sappy. I fell in love with him, but he didn't feel the same way about me. I had the heart done when I got home to remember him by."

"Jeez, Ethan. That's really sad."

"It is what it is." Ethan reached for the bottle and refilled his glass. "I got the wings done a few months after that on the anniversary of my mom's death. My parents were madly in love with each other when she died. I thought I'd found that kind of love with Lucien." He took a long drink. "I know my mom is up in heaven somewhere watching over me, and I'm sure she has angel's wings. I just wanted a matching pair."

He smiled, listening to Joel laughing softly.

"That's really nice," Joel said. "What about *cupido*?"

"No story there actually. I lied. It's simply a visual for the pitching party. Similar to the star on my ass."

"Pitching?" Joel crunched up his face in confusion. "Oh, right. Never mind …gotcha." He paused in thought. "Hey, I'm sorry it didn't work out for you with Lucien." He held his glass up and nodded for Ethan to top it up. "You said you had a girlfriend at one time?"

"I did."

"What happened with her?"

"She was a girl I grew up with. A really fun girl. Maybe too much fun." Ethan laughed to himself. "We went our separate ways, and I never went back after that."

"To girls?"

"Yeah. It wasn't anything she did exactly." Ethan sipped long on his drink. "But indirectly, I came to understand myself better, and now I know I could never be happy in a relationship with anyone but a guy."

"Is it a sex thing? Do you like fucking guys better?"

"Joel!" Ethan laughed in shock.

"I'm serious. Is it just a physical attraction thing?"

"No." Ethan shook his head emphatically. "The physical aspect is definitely a must, and I find guys seriously hot, but the intellectual and emotional connection is the main thing I'm looking for. And I've only ever experienced that with guys." He looked at Joel with uncertainty. "It's really girly, and it might be an unattainable dream, but I want to find that special guy out there someday and fall in love. Like real forever love."

"There hasn't been anyone since Lucien?"

"No, not really. I'm an unusual guy. Trying to find someone that in your words *gets me* …is going to be difficult."

"What about the guy at the party?"

"Um, …he's what's affectionately referred to as a *fuck buddy*. I met him in Vancouver. We usually hook up when I go down there on weekends. He decided he didn't want to miss a weekend, so he drove up to check out the party."

"You're not interested in having a relationship with him?"

"No!" Ethan laughed sharp. "He's actually straight."

"Are you serious?"

"Yeah, it was strictly about sex." Ethan paused. "We were just having a bit of fun." He looked back at Joel. "I broke things off with him last weekend though. I don't want my life all cluttered up with meaningless relationships right now."

"The whole thing sounds complicated." Joel took a long drink and laid his head back on the sofa. "But at least you know what you're looking for in a guy. I had no idea what I wanted in a girlfriend when I asked Erica out."

"And look how complicated that's become."

"Fuck, I know. I think my mind was totally preoccupied with the physical aspects of having a girlfriend. And look where that got me." Joel sat back up, watching Ethan. "What you were saying before. I totally agree with you."

"About what?"

"If I had to do it all over again, I'd put all my focus on finding someone that connects with me intellectually and emotionally." Joel crunched on an ice cube and studied the shifting patterns in Ethan's eyes. "I'd want to find someone that completes me on more of a holistic and spiritual level."

"Maybe it's not too late."

"Ethan, my girlfriend is pregnant, and I'm getting married in a month." Joel's face twisted in defeat and he shook his head. "It's too late for everything, including my ultimate happiness, and even worse ...my sense of inner peace. I've completely fucked up."

Ethan shifted in his seat. "No, you haven't."

"I'm so fucking stressed out." Joel dropped his head into his hand and ran it up through his hair in exasperation. "For someone that spends as much time as I do contemplating life, I'm awfully fucking stupid when it comes to relationships."

"You're too hard on yourself. Here, hand me your glass. And don't take this the wrong way. I'm not coming on to you."

Ethan took the glass from Joel, set it down on the coffee table, and turned Joel away from him to begin massaging his shoulders.

"God, that feels good." Joel dropped his head forward, sighing as Ethan worked the stress out of his shoulders. He closed his eyes and tried to direct his attention away from Erica and the baby, and the life that was rapidly closing in on him—but he couldn't.

A small sound of anguish and regret escaped from Joel's throat as his body began to shake, and then the tears started to flow.

Ethan stopped rubbing Joel's shoulders, leaned his head against Joel's neck, and fought to hold back his own tears.

"Jeez, Joel," he said. "You're killing me. Please don't fall apart like this."

A shiver ran up Joel's spine as Ethan's hot breath rolled across his shoulders. He steadied his breathing. He had seen the answers he was looking for in Ethan's eyes as he'd questioned him.

He reached back for Ethan's leg and let his thumb brush softly across the surface of Ethan's jeans.

"Ethan, I'm scared," Joel whispered.

"I know." Ethan hesitated while he tried to decipher the subtle signals Joel might be sending.

He leaned in and kissed Joel on the back of the neck while continuing to massage his shoulders, waiting for Joel to object, but he didn't. "We'll get through this together, all right?"

Joel sighed softly, nodded, and tried to collect his thoughts.

Emboldened by Joel's acceptance of the kiss, Ethan brushed his lips along the back of Joel's ear, attempting to keep his breathing even. "You mean so fuckin' much to me, Joel. I'm here for you no matter what, all right?" He let his lips linger, taking in the enticing energy radiating from Joel's body.

"I know you are," Joel answered quietly.

Ethan gazed up at the ceiling, searching his mind for guidance, as he pressed deeper with his fingers until the tight muscles in Joel's shoulders finally began to relax. "How's that feel?"

"Amazing ..."

Joel closed his eyes, the feel of Ethan's lips, and tentative nature of Ethan's breath against his ear still fresh in his memory. Things had definitely changed between them in the past couple of weeks.

His heart raced as he focused on the warmth of Ethan's body behind him, wondering how Ethan was going to react. He leaned back against Ethan's chest and shuddered with excitement as Ethan pulled him in tight against his body.

"Joel ...," was all Ethan whispered, then he held Joel in place and kissed and sucked at the skin of Joel's neck, working his way down along his shoulder by forcefully pulling Joel's shirt away.

Joel heard the stitches of his shirt popping as he was consumed by Ethan's power drawing at him—but he didn't want him to stop. His whole body was shivering with emotion and need as Ethan pulled him even closer into his arms and aggressively bit and licked at his jawline. Then Ethan began to move away. Joel wrapped his arm around the back of Ethan's neck and held him in place.

"I don't want you to stop," Joel said.

"We need to stop." Ethan's breathing was heavy as he bit playfully at Joel's ear. "Your girlfriend will kill me if I break you."

He ran his hand along Joel's neck, caressing his skin.

"Fuck, I'm sorry," Ethan said. "I think I might have marked you up."

"Don't be. I knew it was happening. I could've stopped you."

"Why didn't you?"

"It felt so good that I didn't want you to stop." Joel smiled when he felt Ethan laughing behind him. "Do it again, but on this side this time." He tipped his head to one side and held his breath, waiting for a response. His whole body shook as Ethan's mouth dropped down onto the other side of his neck, licking and sucking.

He tried to sit still but found that his body wanted to press itself closer to Ethan each time he set his mouth down in a new spot. He reached back and ran his hand up into Ethan's hair.

Then Joel's eyes flew open. Ethan's hand had found its way up under his shirt, and was running across the surface of his chest, caressing his body into a new rush of heated desire.

His gut clawed at him to act, but Ethan pulled away before he had a chance. The disappointment churned in Joel's stomach. He'd been prepared to go so much further than that.

"Ethan ...," he started.

Ethan hummed against the side of Joel's neck. "You have some serious love bites up and down both sides of your neck." He licked at Joel's earlobe and then took it into his mouth, sucking on it.

"Ethan ...," Joel began again, and turned toward Ethan, gripping Ethan's shoulders, prepared to push him over—wanting more.

"Fuck, don't be doing that!" Ethan shoved Joel away from his body with far more force than necessary.

"Don't be doing what?" Joel whipped back around to face Ethan and watched Ethan's gaze dart up and down his neck.

"I shouldn't have done that to you," Ethan said.

Joel's face flushed. "It's not a big deal." He covered up his neck with his hands and tried to avoid Ethan's gaze. "We were just goofing around and got a bit carried away. It doesn't mean anything."

"But it does." Ethan ran his hand through his hair and closed his eyes. "It does mean something to me." He opened them again and looked at Joel. "I have feelings for you, all right?" He crossed his arms defensively. "Are you happy now? You got it out of me."

Joel's eyebrows creased up, confused.

"No," he said. "I'm not happy now. Because you're all pissed off about something that should be making you happy. Which has pissed me off because now you're making it impossible for me to be happy about the thing I suspected and hoped you'd be happy about."

Ethan just stared at Joel.

"What?" Ethan replied finally, and then snorted and started laughing. "Fuck, you're more insane than I am." He shoved Joel affectionately in the shoulder and dropped his gaze.

"So," he said. "Is it safe to assume that you're happy about the thing I told you, that pissed me off, but I should be happy about?"

"Yes, that would be a safe assumption," Joel replied.

"Can I also assume you feel the same way?"

"Again within the realms of safe assumptions."

"Good. I'm glad we cleared that up." Ethan tilted his head so he could check out Joel's neck again. "How the fuck are we going to cover those up?" He ran his fingers along the marks and then looked up into Joel's eyes. "Hey, isn't Erica coming over tonight?"

"Fuck! She's going to be here any minute." Joel leaped up and made a run down the hallway to his bedroom with Ethan close behind. "I've got a turtleneck in here somewhere that I use for snowboarding."

Panicking, he tore through his cupboard while Ethan started rummaging through his dresser drawers.

"This crazy looking thing?" Ethan disdainfully held up a striped, multi-colored shirt and threw it at Joel's head.

"Snowboarding clothes are really colorful." Joel pulled his shirt off and pulled the turtleneck on.

"In that case, I may have to rethink joining you on the slopes during winter break." Ethan stared at Joel. "That looks fuckin' ridiculous. She's going to know something's up if you're wearing that around for the next week or so."

"Great," Joel said, thinking. "All right, here's the story. You and I went to a party last night. I got drunk, and you found me making out with some crazy, aggressive girl, and pulled me away. But not before she had totally marked me up." He pulled the turtleneck off and went to put the other shirt back on, but seeing that it was ripped at the neck, he grabbed a new one instead. "She'll be mad at me, but telling her the truth would be way worse."

"I'm with you on that." Crossing his legs, Ethan chewed nervously on his thumbnail. "What is the truth exactly?"

Joel looked up when he heard the doorbell ring. "I'm not sure."

Ethan pulled himself off the floor, and followed after Joel to let Erica in and hopefully explain Joel's neck to her satisfaction.

The math test was easier than Joel had expected thanks to Ethan's help. He'd impressed himself with the amount of information he'd managed to retain from their tutoring session, considering what had happened at the end of it. Joel gathered up his books as the bell rung and left to find Erica, but ran straight into Ethan, who'd been hovering outside his classroom door.

"Hiya, babe. How'd it go?" Ethan asked.

"Ethan, what are you doing out here?" Joel moved away from the doorway so the rest of the students could get out of the classroom without having to come too close to Ethan. "Shouldn't you be headed for the smoke pit with the rest of your cronies?"

"I wanted to find out how you did on your test." Ethan tucked his thumb into his mouth and started chewing on his nail.

"I did really well, thanks to you." Joel shrugged and smiled. "I think I might've got a 'B' at least."

"That's amazing, babe." Ethan crossed his arms and moved closer to Joel. "I'm really proud of you."

"Thanks, Ethan," Joel said, then placed a hand on Ethan's chest, keeping him at a distance. "Um …what's with the *babe* thing?"

"It's nothing." Ethan studied Joel's face and then let his attention wander over the marks on Joel's neck. "It's just you're like a babe in the woods hooking up with the likes of me."

"The likes of you?" Joel grinned. "Seriously? You can't fool me with this getup of yours, and you know it." He waved his hand around at Ethan's outfit. "The Ethan I know. Is not all this." He winked at Ethan, and then leaned against the lockers, dropping his gaze shyly.

"Will I be seeing you again tonight?" he asked.

"No, I'm heading off to Vancouver after school today. I'm staying for the rest of the week." Ethan checked the hall to make sure no one was looking and then gripped Joel's wrist with his fingers. "My dad has me looking into something for him, but I'll be back on Monday in plenty of time to head up the mountain with you and your friends."

He touched Joel's chin. "I wouldn't miss it."

Joel looked up at Ethan, his disappointment obvious, and crossed his arms. "I guess I'll see you on Monday then."

Ethan lingered and ran his hand along Joel's arm to the inner joint of his elbow. He gazed into Joel's eyes as he brushed his thumb there and then dropped his hand. Without saying another word, he smiled, bumped Joel with his hip, and took off down the hallway.

"What did he want?" Erica asked as she pushed up beside Joel and tucked her arm through his, completely startling him.

"He wanted to see how I did on my math test." Joel turned and kissed her. "How's Mommy doing today?"

"Before or after I had to endure the additional ridicule of supposedly giving you all those hickeys."

"Before please."

"Feeling rather large. I know it's going to get much worse than this, but none of my clothes fit anymore." Erica dropped her hand into Joel's as they made their way down to the cafeteria.

"Did you want to go shopping this week?" Joel asked. "We could venture into the maternity shops. There might be something that's not too hideous." He raised his eyebrows at Erica and tried to keep a straight face, but ended up creasing up and falling against the lockers as he tried to catch his breath.

"Thanks a lot." Erica smiled at Joel and brought his hand to her lips. "Seriously, I think they sell jeans at those stores.

I'll grab a pair ...with my mom." She laughed as Joel sighed in relief. "But you're coming with me to the doctor's appointment next month."

"Only because I love you." Joel kissed her and then cupped Erica's pregnant belly in his hands. "And little peanut here."

Chapter Ten

The road up to the local mountain started off mundane enough with a weather-beaten highway and typical foliage, but as they drove closer, Ethan could see that the trees were gradually becoming shorter and sparser, and a little snow was dusting the side of the road.

The car slowed right down, and Joel steered through a winding portion that looped back and forth, as it made its way up the steep hill. At each bend in the road, the snow became deeper, and as they reached a crest and sped up along a straight piece of road, the snow appeared to be more than a meter deep in places.

"So, what do you think?" Joel pulled into a parking lot and turned in his seat, speaking to Ethan, who appeared to be awestruck by what he was seeing. The chalets he'd first spotted had become denser, and by the time they'd turned into the parking lot, they were surrounded by luxury chalets, lofty ski lifts, and swarms of walking, skiing, and snowboarding people.

"I had no idea this was up here," Ethan answered.

"Pretty incredible, hey?" Joel climbed out of his car and starting pulling their bags out of the back. "We need to cart this stuff up in the gondola to the main concourse. I don't want to drive up there. This is actually easier."

"Sure thing." Ethan grabbed what was handed to him, and followed Joel and his friends onto the gondola. Once they reached the check-in desk, Ethan stepped ahead of the rest of them and paid for the chalet he was renting for the week. He'd planned on backing out so he could fly to Amsterdam and party with a few friends, but his recent encounter with Joel had caused him to reconsider. Although he wasn't entirely sure what he was expecting to happen. Especially with Erica and Joel's friends with them. He just knew he wanted to be where Joel was, even if that meant just being his friend.

They traipsed through the village and arrived at a sizeable picturesque chalet situated in the village square, very close to the main lodge, where many of the shops and restaurants were located. Joel had thought it was overkill renting such an expensive place, but Ethan had figured that if he was going to spend an entire week at a ski resort, he wanted the full experience.

The chalet slept fifteen, but there were only five of them, so there was going to be plenty of room for people to have their own space. Once everyone had picked out a room, they all met back in the living room to discuss further plans, and to grab a drink.

"Where do you guys want to go for dinner?" Max inquired as he looked through a restaurant pamphlet sitting by the phone.

Ryan stretched out on the sofa and pulled on a beer. "I thought we could order pizza."

"We should've brought more food with us from home," Erica said as she fussed about in the kitchen, trying to put away what few supplies they'd brought with them. "We need to pick up some milk and a few other things for the morning."

"I think we need more beer," Joel chimed in, and then gave Ryan a high five as he passed by him. "Who needs food?"

"The baby needs food." Erica glared at Joel from the kitchen, as Joel rolled his eyes and threw back the last of his beer.

"I'll grab you some groceries from the store we passed in the village," Ethan said as he walked into the kitchen. "Could you write me up a list of what you want, Erica?" He leaned against the kitchen counter, waiting as Erica scrutinized him.

"Fine," Erica said and wrote out what she wanted.

Ethan tucked the list into his pocket and squeezed Joel's shoulder on his way out through the door to the village square.

There was silence for a few seconds after the door closed behind Ethan, and then Max stood up in the middle of the room and placed his hands on his hips. "All right. Does anyone else find it weird having Ethan freakin' Cooke here with us?"

"Max. Do I need to remind you …Ethan is footing the entire bill for this unbelievable chalet?" Ryan held his beer up in mock salute. "He's all right in my books. For this week anyway."

"But that's the problem," Max said. "We're going to be living with him for an entire week. Who knows what kind of trouble he's going to get into. We'll probably all be arrested on suspicion of drug trafficking before the week is out."

"Shut the fuck up, Max." Joel dropped down onto one of the sofas by the fire and looked over at Erica for support.

"Sorry, Joel," Erica said. "I'm with Max on this one."

"You guys are fucking pathetic." Joel set his beer down, jumped to his feet, and grabbed his coat. Then he pulled out his cell phone and dialed a number. "Hey. Where are you?" He stared at Erica as he did up his coat, and then stepped outside. "I'll be right there."

Joel looked down the center of the village square and could see Ethan standing outside one of the stores with a smoke in his hand. He waved, catching Ethan's attention, and jogged toward him.

"Hiya, babe." Ethan waited until Joel was on him before turning down one of the side streets. "I'm feeling a bit out of place."

"Why? The coat looks really good on you," Joel replied. He'd convinced Ethan to buy something that wasn't completely black when he'd gone with him to shop for winter clothes. The small splashes of color were not mirroring Ethan's current mood though.

"That's not what I meant." Ethan took a long drag off his cigarette. "Your friends don't want me here."

"I want you here. What they want doesn't matter."

Ethan pulled Joel along the side street a bit further by the sleeve and then slowed by the side of an underpass used mainly by pedestrians and the occasional snowboarder. He slowed beneath it and pushed Joel against the wall just inside the tunnel.

"Why do you want me here?" Ethan gazed with intent into Joel's eyes and tried to judge the possible response from them.

"You're my best friend." Joel dropped his gaze and then looked up again, witnessing disappointment cross Ethan's face.

He waited while Ethan finished his cigarette, noting there weren't many people passing through at this time of night.

"How was Vancouver?" Joel asked, trying to make conversation that didn't revolve around their relationship. Ethan looked at him and sighed, pinching at the bridge of his nose.

"Boring without you there," Ethan replied.

Joel grabbed hold of Ethan's coat as a rush of warmth pulsed through his chest, and he pulled Ethan closer to his body. "You need to be careful you don't get run over, standing out that far."

He ran his hand down the front of Ethan's coat pretending to smooth out the fasteners. "I wouldn't want you to get hurt." He looked up into Ethan's face and licked his lips—he couldn't stop himself. The need was coursing through him, overtaking any feelings of being found out. Even the guilt he felt, betraying Erica—buried itself deep when he was with Ethan. "I'd feel better if you stayed close to me."

"Yeah?" Ethan replied, pressing Joel's body firm to the wall.

"Mm…hm."

Ethan sighed and shuffled his feet nervously. "Babe, those stars I tattooed on your arm—"

"I know what they mean." Joel pulled up the sleeve of his coat and looked at them. "After my tutoring session …" He smiled. "I was lying in bed looking at them, and I figured it out."

"You did?"

"They symbolize your feelings for me, don't they?"

"Yeah." Ethan took Joel's arm and brushed his thumb over the tattoo of the stars. "I should've said something to you before I went and did something so permanent. I'm sorry."

"No. It was your own unique way of expressing your feelings. That makes them special. They mean a lot to me."

"I'd like to add more stars. If you'd let me."

Joel shut his eyes and shivered. He opened them again and felt his heart hammering as Ethan gazed down at him. "We need to get the groceries before Erica comes looking for us." He pulled lightly on the bottom of Ethan's coat. "I'd let you add more."

The next morning, the sun reflecting off the snow outside the window was absolutely blinding. Ethan rolled over and pulled a pillow over his head. He reached out to the bedside table, grabbed his cell phone, and brought it under the pillow with him. There were only four text messages, but they were all from Joel. The first one was informing him that he was leaving to hit the *park*. The second was a picture of Joel on a snowboard in what Ethan assumed was the *park*. The third was a picture of Joel stuck in a snowbank, and the fourth was a message telling him to, "Get the fuck up."

Ethan saved the pictures and rolled out of bed.

The chalet was quiet, and there was a faint smell of coffee, so Ethan headed for that first. He hadn't bothered to pull on any clothes, other than his underwear, thinking everyone was out snowboarding anyway; completely forgetting that Erica wouldn't be risking the slopes, because of the baby.

He made his way to the kitchen, turned on the oven to preheat it, and opened the fridge, pulling out the cinnamon buns Sophie had done up for him. He just needed to bake them for thirty minutes at three seventy-five as per her written instructions. He uncovered the pan, set it on top of the stove, and poured himself a coffee, then turned to face the living room, and was met by Erica glaring at him.

"What?" Ethan took a sip of his coffee. "Can't a guy bake a few cinnamon buns and get a cup of coffee around here without bringing down the wrath of Lilith."

He wandered into the living room and made a point of scratching and adjusting his *package* before he sat down directly in front of a very irate and irritated Erica.

"Why are you here?" Erica demanded.

"I don't know how to snowboard, and the pubs aren't open yet?" Ethan slurped noisily at his coffee and pretended to be absentmindedly playing with one of his nipple rings.

"Mm …that's not what you meant is it?" he asked.

"I don't want you hanging out with Joel anymore."

"Funny. I think we've had this conversation already."

Not wanting to engage Erica further, Ethan stood and headed back to the kitchen. Thankfully, the oven had reached its preheat temperature. He lifted the pan off the stove, placed it in the oven, and set the timer. Then leaned against the counter and dumped the remainder of his coffee into the sink. There was no way he was going back into the living room with Erica.

He headed to the bathroom to get cleaned up instead.

Once in the shower, Ethan stood perfectly still, letting the hot water run over him, as he stared at the ceiling. He thought about the conversation he'd had with Joel the night before, and rubbed his eyes, letting the tears streak his face and join the water going down the drain. The timing was so off. But if he waited, it would be too late. Joel would be married.

The sound of the bathroom door opening had Ethan catching his breath, wondering who it was.

"Hey, Ethan, sorry," Joel said, stepping into the bathroom. "But Erica said you'd been in here a long time. The oven timer went off, so I took your cinnamon buns out of the oven." He closed the door behind him and stood quietly by the sink, leaning against the counter. "Are you all right?"

"Yeah, babe." Ethan clutched at his stomach and tried to control his breathing. "I'm good."

"Are you sure?" Joel pulled the edge of the shower curtain open, peering inside.

Ethan shuddered and cowered into one corner of the small shower enclosure.

"Ethan …" Joel touched Ethan's shoulder and let his hand drift down the entire length of one of the wings, lingering tenderly at the small of Ethan's back.

"Babe, don't." Ethan pushed Joel's hand away, but Joel stepped closer and kissed Ethan on the shoulder.

"Ethan …"

"Joel, please. Don't touch me."

Ethan waited until he heard the door close before he sunk down onto the floor, folded his arms over his head, and dissolved into tears. It was an agonizing decision, but he needed to put a stop to things before anything happened between them. He couldn't risk a potential physical encounter with Joel. It was just too dangerous.

The water began to run cold, so Ethan reached up and reluctantly turned it off. He pulled himself to his feet, stepped out of the shower, and cleaned the steam off the mirror so he could look at himself.

There was absolutely nothing redeeming about his appearance, and it was only made worse by what he'd done to himself. The idea that someone as beautiful as Joel could look at him and see past all of that, to what was underneath, was unfathomable in his opinion.

He studied his reflection. Regardless, when Joel looked at him, his focus was set much deeper than the surface of his skin. Joel was one of the few people that had ever *got* him.

Joel was the one—he knew it.

Ethan gripped the edge of the sink.

But it couldn't be.

He finished up in the bathroom and headed out to the kitchen to grab another coffee and a cigarette. The cinnamon buns smelled amazing, but his stomach was too knotted up to even contemplate eating anything. So he covered them up, set them to one side, and headed into the living room. Joel and Erica were sitting together on the sofa in front of the fire, and Erica was curled up under Joel's arm with her hands running up through Joel's hair as she kissed him.

Ethan stood and watched them for a second, the knot in his gut twisting mercilessly, sending waves of anguish clear through to his extremities. He cleared his throat and sat down in a chair close to them. He waited and then cleared his throat louder.

Pulling away from Erica, Joel attempted to straighten out his clothes and hair. He looked up and felt his heart shudder and wrench violently in his chest when he saw the look in Ethan's eyes.

Joel was shaken as he realized—he'd actually felt the pain.

He gently pushed Erica away.

"Sorry, Ethan," Joel said. "I didn't hear you come in."

"It's all good." Ethan pulled out a cigarette and lit it up.

"Excuse me! I'm pregnant!" Erica jumped up and made a grab at the cigarette in Ethan's mouth.

Ethan waved her hand away and tossed the cigarette into his coffee, extinguishing it. He pushed her clear of his path and headed for the deck. "I'm sorry. I wasn't thinking."

He stepped out through the door and slammed it behind him.

Joel immediately turned on Erica. "What the fuck was that?"

"He can't smoke in here." Erica crossed her arms defensively, turned away, and headed for the kitchen.

"You could've given him a chance to put it out before you went all ape shit on him. Look, I know you don't like him, but the least you could do is treat him with a little respect."

Joel turned when he heard the door to the deck open again.

"Joel, I think I'm going to head home," Ethan said. "I don't like all this snow after all." He stuffed his package of cigarettes into his pocket and headed off toward his bedroom.

Joel ran to catch up with him. "Ethan, please. You can't go. Erica can be a bit of a bitch sometimes, but she doesn't mean anything by it. She just doesn't think most of the time."

"It's not that." Ethan closed the door behind them and leaned heavily against it. "Seeing you two together like that." He exhaled, exhausted. "I'm not strong enough to shut that out." He crossed the room, pulled out his bag, and started throwing clothes into it.

"It won't happen again. I can promise you that." Joel walked up behind Ethan and ran his hands across Ethan's shoulders. "I felt something out there just now. And it wasn't for her."

He wrapped his arms around Ethan's waist and kissed the center of Ethan's back. "Ethan, I actually felt it. Just like we talked about." He tucked his face into Ethan's back and rubbed his cheek softly against it. "I don't want you to go. I want you to stay here with me."

"Joel, we can't do this." Ethan pulled away, ripping free of Joel's embrace, and turned to face him. "I'm going home, and we're going to forget about all this between us, all right? Let's just go back to the way things were before." He patted Joel affectionately on the shoulder and headed for the door. "I'll see you back at home."

He paused before he opened the door and caught the look of distress on Joel's face. "Jeez Joel. Don't look at me like that." He sighed. "Look. I still have feelings for you. But we can't be doing this *thing* between us. We just can't."

"Ethan," Joel replied. "This whole *thing* has been tough for me to wrap my head around. I've never felt this strongly about anyone before, especially a guy, and it's confusing the hell out of me."

Joel paused, considering how far he wanted to take this *thing*. "I want us to do this. I want us to be together." He approached Ethan and tentatively reached out to hold Ethan's face in his hands. "I'll go out there right now and tell Erica it's over between her and me. I'll tell her that I want to be with you. I'm that serious about what I'm feeling." He brushed his thumb across Ethan's lips and searched his eyes. "Just say the word, and I'll be yours."

Ethan dropped his head. "Babe, I don't know what to say. I want to be with you too." He took one of Joel's hands, kissed it softly, and held it to his cheek. "But I can't. I'm sorry."

Joel yanked his hand out of Ethan's grasp.

"Are you fucking kidding me, Ethan?"

"Joel, please ..."

"No. What changed from last week? Hell, what changed from last night even?"

"Nothing changed. But I can't do this with you."

"Why? Why can't you?"

"I just can't."

"Is there someone else?"

"No, it's nothing like that. I just can't."

"That's it. You just can't." Joel pushed Ethan out of the way and hauled the door open. "Fuck you! These stars on my arm don't wash off, you know?" He took off down the hall to his own bedroom and slammed the door. Ethan contemplated going to Joel's bedroom to talk to him, but decided against it, knowing that if he did, he would be running the risk of changing his mind. He went to the kitchen to grab his stuff but had to wait for Erica, who was moving stuff around in the fridge, before he could get past her to collect everything.

"Did you two break up?" Erica asked.

"What?" Ethan grabbed the carton of cigarettes off the counter and stuffed it into his bag. He looked at the tray of cinnamon buns but decided to leave it. Sophie would have his head, but he didn't want to hang around to clean the pan. He'd buy her a new one.

"The way he stormed off and slammed the door," Erica said, "I thought maybe you two had a fight." She opened a drawer and pulled out a knife to cut up the apple she'd pulled from the fridge.

"He's just pissed that I'm taking off." Ethan stole a couple of apple slices and stuffed them in his mouth. "Tell him to call me when he gets home."

Erica smiled sweetly at him, turned back to what she was doing, and didn't answer him.

"Never mind. I'll text him," Ethan said and left the kitchen. He pushed open the door and headed for the lodge to call for a taxi to take him back into town. While he was waiting, he received a text from Joel in the form of a row of stars. There were ten of them; five more than currently on Joel's arm. Ethan groaned, clutching his stomach. It was undeniable.

Joel knew what his heart was longing for, despite his rejecting him. Ethan ran his fingers over the screen of his cell phone. Under different circumstances, he would've been gearing up to cover Joel's entire body in stars by now, but it wasn't to be.

He placed his phone back in his pocket and pinched the bridge of his nose. The number of tears he'd shed in the past couple of days was unprecedented. Second only to when Lucien had told him he didn't love him.

He pulled his phone back out and called his dad.

It was almost midnight on Christmas Eve, and Joel was up a ladder helping his mom put the last of the Christmas decorations on the tree. For some reason, she always left it to the last possible moment, because she wanted it to be a special family thing. But inevitably, Arthur would find something that needed attending to in the garage, and Jocelyn would make such a mess of things that Carol would ask her to stop and watch a movie or something instead, and Joel would be left to help his mom on his own.

Joel hadn't spoken to Ethan since their argument at the chalet the week before, and it was eating at him. He needed to know why Ethan had put an abrupt stop to things when he'd been so obviously interested the night before. He climbed down off the ladder and sank onto the sofa. He missed him.

"What's the matter, Joel?" Carol asked. "You've been sulking around here for days?"

"Ethan and I had a fight."

"I wondered why I hadn't seen him. But I was trying to keep my nose out of it." Carol sat down beside Joel and rubbed his back. "What did you fight about?"

"I'd rather not talk about it." Joel turned to face his mom. "Do you think some people just click for a reason?"

"Are we talking about Ethan or Erica now?"

"Both, I suppose."

"I believe there are people out there that mesh with us so well that we may as well be one person. Your dad and I have that kind of relationship, and I hope you and Erica do as well." Carol held Joel's face in both hands. "And to some extent, good friends like Ethan can be like that too. It's important to hang on to those relationships because they make us feel whole."

"I guess that's why I'm feeling so shattered." Joel pulled out his phone. "If he's still talking to me, do you mind if Ethan stays overnight, so he's here for Christmas morning?"

"I think that would be lovely. I was concerned I wasn't going to see him, and I was trying to figure out how I was going to give him his present and stocking before morning."

"You did him up a stocking?" Joel grinned at his mom as he texted a message to Ethan.

"What's wrong with that?"

"Nothing. He's going to love it."

Joel waited anxiously. Ethan was taking a long time to answer. He knew he was answering texts, because he had responded to his original, "Hey" message. He received an answer of, "Overnight" with a row of question marks. Joel replied that he could sleep on the sofa no matter how vehemently his mom insisted that she set up a bed in his room—and that he promised to leave him alone.

When Ethan arrived, Joel was sitting on the makeshift bed on the sofa watching a movie, so Ethan sat down beside him.

"How have you been?" Ethan asked.

"Miserable. You?"

"Same." Ethan turned to face Joel. "I'm sorry about what I said at the chalet. I know we can't go back to the way things were."

"You took me by surprise. Turning me down like that."

"I know. I'm sorry. I'm just so confused."

"You're confused? I thought I knew what my life was going to look like with Erica, but then you came along, and threw a huge question mark into that." Joel sighed and rested his hand on Ethan's leg. "I have all these intense feelings for you." He brushed his fingers softly across the fabric of Ethan's jeans. "I want to be with you."

"I want to be with you, too." Ethan took Joel's hand and held it tightly in his own. "More than you can imagine."

"Then let's just do it. My parents will freak out, but they might come around. Eventually. My friends already make cracks about you being my boyfriend anyway so they won't be surprised. And Erica. She'll be upset. But she wants me to be happy."

"Babe, we wouldn't be able to tell anyone."

Joel shifted his position. "What? Why not?"

"I'm sorry. I wish I could tell you why."

"That wouldn't work, Ethan. What would I tell Erica? She's expecting to get married next month. And my parents. What would I say to them? How would I explain backing out like that?"

"Fuck, I don't know." Ethan tried to pull his hand away, but Joel gripped it tighter. "Let's just forget about it. Maybe we shouldn't be starting anything."

"Ethan, I'm totally confused. I'd rather be with you, but you're making it sound like that's never going to happen." Joel looked intently into Ethan's eyes, searching them for an answer. "Should I be marrying Erica, or not?"

"You and Erica have a baby on the way. I think you should marry her, Joel." Ethan's breath caught. "It's the right thing to do."

"So, you don't really want me."

"Babe, I want you so bad it's agonizing."

"Fuck! You're making me crazy." Joel pulled his hand away and crossed his arms. "If that's what you want …to be with me. Why do you keep pushing me away?"

"My life is complicated right now," Ethan replied. "I want to be with you, I really do, but I can't. Not the way you want me to …because of other circumstances. I know it's not much of an explanation, but that's why I keep changing my mind."

"Ethan, regardless of your circumstances, I need you to decide one way or the other, so I can figure out what I'm doing with Erica." Joel leaned into Ethan's side, soaking in the warmth of him. "I'm going to bed. Please spend some time thinking about us and how amazing we'd be together." He stood up and faced Ethan. "I'll be thinking about you tonight." Gazing down into Ethan's eyes, Joel watched them change. "I'll see you in the morning."

Christmas morning turned out to be quite emotional for Ethan. He'd never been given a stocking before. And was finding the realization that Carol had spent a significant amount of time picking out all the little, personalized items in it, a bit overwhelming. Then he'd opened his wrapped present to find that Carol had hand knit him a black sweater with tiny, white gothic crosses on it, and he'd had to leave the room to collect his emotions.

Joel followed Ethan into his bedroom and closed the door.

"Are you all right?" Joel asked.

"Your mom went to a lot of bother for me." Ethan traced a finger over some of the tiny crosses in his sweater, and then noticed she had also embroidered his name and the year along the bottom edge.

"My parents really like you. You're like one of the family around here." Joel motioned for the sweater. "Take your other one off, so you try this on."

Ethan pulled his old sweater off over his head, practically taking his shirt with it and producing a lot of static electricity.

Joel managed to get seriously zapped handing him the new sweater, which amused Ethan immensely.

The new sweater hung loose and long, just the way Ethan liked it. Joel smiled. That had taken a lot of willpower on his mom's part to make the sweater the way Ethan would want it, rather than the way she thought it should be.

Joel reached up and tried to calm Ethan's statically charged hair with his hands, which didn't work at all and only managed to facilitate his hands finding their way onto Ethan's face.

"Ethan, I need you."

"I know, babe." Ethan tucked his face into Joel's hand. "I need you too." He grasped onto Joel's wrist and laid a kiss in his palm.

"So, are we doing this?"

Ethan nodded and pulled Joel in. He was about to kiss him when Erica opened the door directly into the back of them.

"What are you guys doing standing right behind the door like that?" Erica asked as she pushed into the room.

"Ethan was trying on his new sweater and didn't want Jocelyn walking in on him," Joel answered, moving away from Ethan and running an awkward hand through his hair.

"It's not like he has to get naked to try on a sweater." Erica stepped further into the room, wrapped her arms around Joel's neck, and attempted to kiss him, but Joel pulled away and held her by the shoulders. "What's wrong?" she asked.

"Nothing," Joel replied and kissed her forehead dismissively. "Could you tell Carol we'll be out for lunch in just a second?"

"Sure, I'll see you out there," Erica replied and left the room.

Joel turned his attention back to Ethan.

"How do you want to do this?" he asked.

"Babe, forget it. I can't—" Ethan closed the door and stroked his fingers down the side of Joel's face. "I want to. But I can't do this with you."

Joel knocked Ethan's hand away.

"For fuck's sake, Ethan. Are you serious?"

"I'm sorry."

"You keep changing your mind every two seconds."

"I know. I'm sorry."

"But I thought—" Joel dropped his voice. "Ethan, if it were up to me, I'd be breaking up with Erica right now." He pushed past Ethan and yanked the door open. "But apparently, this is entirely up to you. So …after you have some Christmas lunch, I think you should go home and give some serious thought as to what *you* really want."

Chapter Eleven

First day back after winter break was always bittersweet. Joel was excited to see the friends he hadn't managed to catch up with over break, but it also meant the end of semester one was drawing near, and he needed to prepare for final exams.

Joel wasn't particularly concerned about the exams though. He had other things on his mind. The first day back to school this year also meant his wedding was less than ten days away.

But right now, he was struggling to help Erica put stuff in her locker and find the books she needed for her first class. They'd arrived early to ensure enough time to collect up everything she needed, but there was a bit of digging involved.

"Make sure you grab that small book down at the bottom there," Erica said. "We're supposed to have read it by now, but I've been a bit preoccupied."

"What could possibly be on your mind?" Joel dipped Erica into his arms and kissed her.

"Careful," Erica said, dismissing his attempt. "I'm getting so big. You're going to drop me one of these days." She laughed and cupped Joel's face affectionately. Ever since New Year's Eve, Joel had become extremely attentive. And in the past week, he'd expressed how excited he was about the wedding. She'd been concerned about him for a few weeks before that. He'd become frighteningly distant and almost reluctant to go ahead with the wedding. But now, everything appeared to be back to normal between them.

"You're in a good mood," Erica commented.

"I must have the same affliction as you." Joel took Erica's hand and walked with her to her first class. "I think it's incurable."

"Speaking of which …I don't have my flu shot yet. Could you take me down to the clinic today after school?"

"Your wish is my command." Joel handed Erica her books and kissed her. "I'll come get you after class. Wait for me."

Joel turned away, started toward his classroom, and happened to look down the hall to where Ethan was standing with a bunch of his friends. Ethan was wearing his usual black jeans and the sweater that Carol had knit for him, but there was no sign of his leather jacket, his hair wasn't done up, and he wasn't wearing any eyeliner or other makeup. Joel's heart sunk painfully, as he realized Ethan's posture and entire demeanor were uncharacteristically subdued.

Ethan looked up, caught Joel watching him, and his eyes lit up briefly until he realized Joel had no intention of walking down the hall to see him. He stuffed his hands into his pockets and headed off in the opposite direction.

"What's wrong with Ethan?" Ryan asked as he came up behind Joel, observing Ethan's unusual behavior.

"I think he's depressed." Joel grabbed Ryan and turned him toward the classroom they were headed for.

"Why would he be depressed?"

"Because. We had another big fight, and we're taking a break from each other for a while."

"You two kill me sometimes with all your fights and breaks and everything. Are you sure he's not your boyfriend?"

"Very funny. Ethan certainly knows how to piss me off far worse than even Erica could manage to do."

"What are you fighting about this time?"

"His indecisiveness and innate ability to waffle endlessly."

"I'm sorry I asked," Ryan replied. "I was thinking more in terms of him stealing your beer, hogging the remote. Stuff like that."

"I wish it was that simple. God, he drives me insane." Joel pulled open the classroom door and followed Ryan to their seats. "Yesterday, he sent me a text saying he wasn't sure if he'd be able to attend the wedding. Can you believe that?"

"He's a groomsman. He can't just back out like that. I'm sure he doesn't mean it."

"I know. But it hurt that he would even say it."

Joel flipped open his binder, started taking notes, and tried to put the sight of Ethan in the hallway out of his mind. It had been a difficult decision to make, to forget about the possibility of pursuing a deeper relationship with him. He'd sent Ethan a text on Boxing Day, stating that he really needed to hear from him by New Year's Eve, so he'd have enough time to cancel the wedding. He'd waited anxiously for a call or text from Ethan right up until midnight admitting he'd been an idiot and desperately wanted to be with him.

But none had come, so Joel had gathered up his feelings and boxed them away. He needed to concentrate on Erica and the baby, and his upcoming wedding. He'd resigned himself to living a *normal life* and was planning to make every effort to make it work.

It was the right thing to do.

For the middle of January, the weather was co-operating beautifully with a crisp sunny day. It was always a gamble at this time of year. There was very little precipitation in the valley, but during the winter, the chances of seeing some were much higher, and that would mean snow. Some had fallen the night before, and it had been sparingly cleared away from the roadways, leaving behind a postcard backdrop to the picturesque Victorian chapel.

The interior of the church was done up in delicate pink roses, ivy, and sprigs of baby's breath that Erica had painstakingly spent hours binding together herself. Joel took a walk through the church on his way to the vestibule at the front, trying to come to terms with what the day held for him. He looked up and could see Ryan and Max watching him anxiously. They had arrived at the church with him, but it was getting late, and they were still waiting for Ethan.

Ryan came out of the vestibule, grabbed Joel, and pulled him the rest of the way down the aisle to the room at the front of the church reserved for the groom.

"Maybe he's not coming after all," Ryan said.

"He wouldn't do that to me," Joel replied. "He promised me he'd always be there for me. No matter what."

He looked in the mirror and tried to straighten out his tie for the fiftieth time. His gaze caught the door as it opened behind him, and he almost passed out. It was Ethan, finally, but Joel felt like he wouldn't have recognized him if he'd passed him on the street.

Ethan had spent the past two days getting ready. His first stop had been a piercing studio downtown. He'd had one of the staff there remove all of the piercings from his face and ears. Technically, he could've done it himself, but the idea of removing his identity like that had stressed him out, and he'd decided a steady hand would be preferable. He'd been pleased to see most of the holes weren't too visible. His next stop had been the hairdressers, where he'd almost had an anxiety attack as they'd cut his hair to a respectable length. He'd already grown out the shaved portions of his Mohawk in anticipation of Joel's wedding, but the new cut looked like something his dad would've approved of. He was going to have to wear a toque for months until his hair grew back. The suit was easier to don as he had been forced to wear similar outfits his entire life with the constant flow of dignitaries that used to come to his house for dinner. Then he'd spent the morning digging around in his bedroom until he'd found the cufflinks and watch his dad had bought him years ago.

Ethan walked into the room and saw Joel fixing his tie in the mirror. The look on Joel's face was one of absolute shock.

"Jeez, who the fuck are you?" Joel whipped around and approached him, placing his hands on Ethan's shoulders. "Guys, could I talk to Ethan, alone, for a minute?" He looked over his shoulder and motioned for Ryan to leave the room with Max. He waited until he saw the door close before turning back to Ethan.

"Hey, Joel." Ethan fixed Joel's tie with an expert hand and gazed intently into his eyes. "How are you holding up?"

"I'm coping." Joel couldn't take his attention away from Ethan's face. "Fuck, I'm sorry. I'm still in shock." He ran his fingers over the areas of Ethan's face that would normally be covered in metal, letting them trail longingly. "I always knew you were hot under all that stuff. But damn. I had no idea just how right I was."

"You're delusional." Ethan brushed a few strands of hair from Joel's eyes and then lowered his hand. "You, on the other hand, are absolutely gorgeous."

Ethan hesitated, sighing, and then raised his hand to cup Joel's face.

Joel's breath caught, escaping in short gasps.

"I was starting to think you weren't coming," he whispered and then laid a soft kiss in Ethan's palm, and watched as Ethan's eyes softened, tears collecting along the edges.

"I told you we'd get through this together, and I meant it. I'm here for you …as your best friend." Ethan wiped the tears from his face, pulled Joel into his arms, and held him. "It's better this way."

Joel clung to Ethan in what he hoped wouldn't be their last meaningful embrace, and then reluctantly released him. He held Ethan's face and looked deep into his eyes. They were already soft and comforting, and the emotion swimming in them was in sharp contrast to Ethan's words, making Joel's heart surge with uncertainty as to the strength of Ethan's resolve.

He brought his mouth to within a hair's breadth of Ethan's and basked in the warmth of Ethan's breath as it rolled seductively over his lips. He knew he could spend a lifetime in Ethan's embrace.

"Goddammit, Ethan …"

Ethan dropped his gaze. "I know, babe."

The sound of a door at the far end of the room opening had them stepping away from each other, as the pastor moved into the room and tried to make sense of what little he had seen.

Joel went back to the mirror to straighten out his hair and wipe the tears from his cheeks. Checking behind him, he caught the pastor staring at him and averted his gaze as Ethan opened the other door and let Ryan and Max back in.

"We're all set to begin in a few minutes," the pastor said. "Everyone has been seated. So, if you gentlemen would like to follow me, we'll get you in position."

Joel followed Ryan to the door, but looked over his shoulder at Ethan, checking one last time, to make sure Ethan wasn't going to change his mind again. He would've abandoned the wedding and run off with him in a second if Ethan had asked him to.

He dropped his head in resignation and stepped through the door when Ethan turned his back to him.

As he stood at the altar with Erica, Joel felt as though his soul was being torn apart, overcome by deep, unrelenting, and excruciating anguish. It took all of his strength to keep from crying out.

Chapter Twelve

The doctor's office wasn't very crowded, which made Joel feel slightly better about being there. Erica had convinced him to come along with her to a prenatal appointment because she wanted him to meet the obstetrician that would be delivering the baby. He had managed to get out of all the previous appointments, but now that they were married and Erica was living with him, he'd been unable to escape her insistence that he go along. It made him feel like an asshole, not being there for her, but his heart just wasn't in it.

Joel sighed and looked around at the other pregnant women, and couldn't help the overwhelming feeling that he wasn't ready for this.

"See, this isn't so bad," Erica said.

"Are you serious?" Joel shifted uncomfortably in his seat and pretended to be looking through some of the magazines on the table, but they were all about babies and childbirth options, and he was beginning to feel sick.

"Joel!" Erica said as she tugged at his sleeve.

"What?"

"They just called us."

Erica pulled Joel to his feet and held his hand as they made their way into one of the examination rooms. She was scheduled for an ultrasound today, but she hadn't told him. She wanted it to be a surprise. Joel had become disturbingly sullen and depressed since the wedding, and she was hoping that seeing the baby might bring him back to her. She squeezed his hand. No amount of self-assurances could convince her that he wasn't slipping away from her.

By the time they left the doctor's office, Joel felt as if his legs were about to go out from under him. He asked Erica to drive home. He couldn't focus on anything other than the ultrasound pictures he was clutching in his hand. When they pulled into his driveway, he handed them to her.

"I'm going to Ethan's," Joel said.

"Joel, please. I thought we could have a nice dinner with your parents and show them the pictures."

"No. I'm not staying home tonight. I need to get away from anything baby related for a night, and I haven't seen Ethan since the wedding." Joel fought to undo his seatbelt, but he was so flustered, he was having difficulty with it. It finally relented, and he threw his door open. "I've spent the past two weeks moving you into my room and setting up the baby's nursery. I need some guy time."

"All right," Erica agreed. "What time will you be home?"

"I don't know!" Joel stared at her, frustration tensing his body. The next part just slipped out. "There have been times when I haven't come home from Ethan's for days."

He held up his hands as Erica made to object.

"Obviously, I'm not going to do that," he said. "But I don't want you waiting up for me. You need your sleep, for the baby."

"I'll see you in the morning then." Erica leaned over, reaching for Joel, but he retreated from her. She persisted and kissed Joel's cheek, then pulled herself out of the car.

"See you—bye."

Joel climbed out of the car, jogged back up his driveway and down Ethan's. He let himself into Ethan's house and made his way into the den, where he knew he would likely find Ethan at this time of day.

"Hiya, Joel!" Ethan said as he looked over his shoulder. "I was starting to think you'd forgotten about me. How's married life treating you?" He shut the television off and turned in his chair to get a better look at Joel.

"Don't start. You know exactly how it's treating me." Joel wandered into the den, leaned against the back of Ethan's chair, hanging over it, and pulled affectionately at Ethan's short hair. "I want you to take me out tonight."

"Sure. What's up?"

"I just need to get away from everything."

"Where do you want to go?" Ethan lifted himself out of his chair and circled around behind Joel to set some dishes in the kitchen.

"I feel like doing some serious dancing. Could you take me to one of your clubs down in Vancouver?"

Ethan turned to face Joel. "Are you sure you want to do that?"

"I'm sure." Joel lifted his arm to run his hand down the front of Ethan's shirt, but stopped himself, and looked up into Ethan's face instead. He was pleased to see Ethan had put all his piercings back. He studied Ethan's face further and looked into his eyes; they were registering a comforting revelation.

"All right. Let's get geared up," Ethan said. "I've got some clothes upstairs that might fit you."

Ethan dressed himself in what would be considered his uniform at this point, and then pulled out a few items of clothing for Joel to put on, making it look like they belonged together somewhat.

The drive to Vancouver took a lot longer than what Joel had been expecting because of the snow. He had never been to the coast before and wasn't sure what one of Ethan's clubs was going to look like, or what kind of people were going to be there, but he knew it was where he needed to be tonight. He tucked into the passenger seat, deciding not to engage in any serious conversation with Ethan while he was driving. Once in the heart of Vancouver, Ethan parked the car and led the way down the street toward a lineup of people outside a brightly lit club with pounding bass bursting through its doors.

Joel stared in astonishment at the attire of some of the men making their way inside. Growing up in a small town had sheltered him somewhat, and he almost tripped over his own feet when Ethan unexpectedly stopped to speak to him.

"Joel, you need to stay right with me," said Ethan. Then he fished around in his pocket and unraveled one of the chains from his jacket. He clipped the end onto the collar he had insisted Joel wear around his neck. "That should make it easier." He grinned at Joel and motioned for him to be

THE STARS ON MY ARM

silent. They walked past the lineup of people straight to the door. A very large Hawaiian looking bouncer grinned happily and extended his hand to Ethan.

"Hey, Ethan, my man," the bouncer said. "I haven't seen you down this way in a few weeks."

"I've been keeping myself busy, Matt." Ethan opened his coat, turning side to side, and Matt nodded at him.

"You working tonight?"

"Always. I brought a *boy toy* prop. Is that cool?"

"Yeah, whatever works for you, buddy." Matt stepped out of the way and let Ethan and Joel in. Once inside, Ethan pulled roughly on Joel's chain and hauled him over to the far side of the room. He set Joel down at a table and attached the chain to his chair.

Ethan laughed when Joel raised an eyebrow at him.

"Give me your coat," he said and helped Joel slip out of it, hanging it on the back of his chair.

"Can I speak now?" Joel asked.

"That depends on what you want to say. You were awfully quiet on the trip down."

"I didn't want to distract you while you were driving."

"Mm …" Ethan leaned in against the table and ran Joel's chain through his fingers. "Did you want something to drink?"

"Yeah, sure," Joel said and grabbed Ethan's arm as he turned to leave. "Why does he think you're working? You're not one of *those* guys they have down here, are you?"

Ethan pounded the table, laughing loudly, and ruffled Joel's hair before turning toward the bar to get them some drinks. When he returned to the table, he leaned in close to Joel's ear.

"I'm not a rentboy or an escort or anything like that," he said. "But there are some parts of my life, especially when I'm down here that I prefer to keep to myself ...for now."

"Fair enough," Joel replied. "But do you care to explain why my drink is just soda." He held it up and looked at Ethan with skepticism.

"You're not nineteen. You're not even supposed to be in here. I don't want to push it by buying you alcohol."

"Ethan—" Then Joel shook his head in resigned acceptance. "I'm not even going to ask." He directed his attention back toward the dance floor, enthralled by the gyration of male bodies moving to the music. But it was the subtle motion beside him that had his stomach fluttering in a wave of anticipation.

Ethan moved his chair closer to Joel's and simply watched him for a few minutes. He went to lift his hand, but then set it back down on his lap. His breathing was uneven as his nerves continued to get the better of him. He took a sip of his drink and tried to clear his head. He'd been thinking about Joel a lot in the two weeks they'd been apart but had decided to wait and see if Joel came to him. Now here he was. Joel had come to him, and he was obviously still interested.

"How are you doing?" Ethan asked.

"Great. The music is great." Joel looked over his shoulder pleased to see that Ethan was sitting close beside him. He leaned in, so his shoulder was resting against Ethan's arm, and then shifted his body, so his hand came to rest lightly on Ethan's leg. He sighed with relief when Ethan reached for his hand and took it in his own.

"God, I missed you," Ethan said.

"I missed you too." Joel squeezed Ethan's hand and brought it up to meet his lips. "I tried to forget about you. I really did. But I can't do it. I honestly can't live without you."

"But, what about Erica? You're married to her now."

"No, I'm not. Not really. Not where it counts." Joel leaned hard into Ethan's shoulder. "It's a lie …a horrible, heart-wrenching lie. I want us to be together now more than ever." He tucked his head in and kissed Ethan's cheek, whispering in his ear. "Ethan, I want us to be together so bad it hurts. Actually physically hurts. It's horrible."

He smiled when Ethan chuckled against him. "And I know you want that too," he added." I can see it in your eyes."

"Babe," Ethan whispered into Joel's ear as he tucked himself up closer. "I do want that. Without hesitation." He bit playfully at Joel's earlobe and kissed his cheek.

"And I won't be changing my mind this time," he said.

"You're sure?"

"Absolutely." Ethan ran his thumb across Joel's cheek, sending Joel's pulse quickening with anticipation.

Joel moaned in pent up exhilaration when Ethan took his mouth for the very first time, the warmth of Ethan's lips combined with the cool ridges of the rings feeling more incredible than what he'd been expecting. He met Ethan's demands with hunger and began a quest to seek out the piercing in Ethan's tongue. His whole body shivered when he found it and responded with urgency each time the metal ball slid over his tongue.

Joel stopped and gripped Ethan's shoulders, tucking his head against Ethan's chest as he tried to catch his breath.

"You're positive this time," Joel said.

Ethan grinned, hugging him closer. "Yes, babe, I'm sure."

"All right. But we need to keep this between us for now," Joel said, fully aware of the absurdity of the request, considering what he'd put Ethan through when Ethan had insisted on secrecy.

Ethan wrapped Joel up in his arms and backed him in close to his chest, and nuzzled his face against the back of Joel's neck.

"Fine by me," he said. "But in here, no one knows us, and I really need to keep you close to me tonight—boyfriend of mine."

"Mm …that sounds nice." Joel reached back and brushed his hand down Ethan's face. "Do you want to dance?"

"Absolutely."

Ethan unhooked the chain from Joel's collar, grabbed his hand, and pulled him onto the dance floor. He smiled wickedly at Joel then pushed up behind him, wrapping Joel up in his arms, so he could move him to the music, pressed tightly against Joel's body.

Joel forgot his life back home, allowing Ethan to hold him and guide his body through song after song, reveling in the emotion invoked each time Ethan's warm breath graced the back of his neck.

The following afternoon, Ethan was lying in bed—alone, staring up at the ceiling. He and Joel had stayed at the club until closing and hadn't returned home until almost eight-thirty that morning. It had been agonizing watching Joel get out of his car, and take off down the driveway to his own house. He would've given anything to have been able to take Joel home to his bed.

He closed his eyes and remembered the taste of Joel's mouth and the feel of his body pressed against him as they'd danced, and felt a shiver run through his entire existence.

Dropping his arm over his eyes, Ethan tried unsuccessfully to stop the tears from starting again. His relationship with Joel had the potential to tear his carefully constructed life apart, and he couldn't stop himself from letting it happen.

Joel cringed and hid his face when Erica threw the curtains open. He hadn't had nearly enough sleep, but despite the exhaustion, he rolled over and grinned into his pillow, remembering Ethan laughing at his attempt to sing along to some of Ethan's heavy metal music on the stereo. Joel hummed to himself, grinding against the sheets, replaying the memory of Ethan's body pressed up behind him on the dance floor, moving with him.

He sighed ...and of Ethan's powerful mouth as it explored his in the driveway this morning before he'd reluctantly pulled himself away, at Ethan's insistence.

"Joel, wake up!" Erica demanded. "It's almost dinner time, and you smell like a stinking brewery. You need a shower."

Joel tucked himself up, preferring to remain in the memory of the night before. "I'll get up in a second."

"No, you're going to get up now, because as soon as I leave the room, you're going to fall back asleep." Erica grabbed the blankets and hauled them off. "What the hell are you wearing?"

"Yeah, long story that." Joel's hands flew to his neck, and he sighed with relief when he found the collar was no longer there. Ethan must've slipped it off him while devouring him the car, but the rest of his outfit from the night before was still intact.

Ethan had found a pair of black leather pants in his closet that fit Joel perfectly, and a sleeveless, black, see-thru mesh shirt. Then Ethan had done up Joel's eyes up with black eyeliner, and his cheeks with a touch of glitter, because, what the hell …they were having fun.

Joel vaguely remembered Ethan trying to convince him to come back to his place to get changed into his own clothes, but he'd vehemently opposed the idea, not trusting himself to be in Ethan's bedroom in any state of undress.

"This should be interesting," Erica said. "My husband goes next door to drink with a buddy, and comes home looking like he's spent the night in a gay bar."

"There you go …not such a long story after all." Joel rolled away from Erica's glare and pulled a pillow over his head. "Ethan is gay. He wanted to go clubbing in Vancouver. I went with him."

"Ethan's gay?" Erica pulled the pillow off Joel's head and hit him with it. "You drove all the way to Vancouver, in the snow, so he could go dancing?" She sat down on the edge of the bed. "I don't know what's more ludicrous. His being gay or the driving."

"Believe me. The driving was the most ludicrous part." Joel reached below the covers, unzipped his pants, and struggled out of them. "That and some of the things that were going on in the washroom of that club. Bit of an eye opener, let me tell you."

"Jeez, Joel. Is this something you and Ethan do often?" Erica rubbed at his face, trying to remove the glitter off his cheeks.

"No, we usually just bop around at his house. But I would definitely go again. It was a rush."

"You're insane."

"That's a distinct possibility." Joel smiled at her and made a production of twirling his pants around over his head before throwing them across the room. "How's our martial arts expert today?" He motioned for Erica to lay down and lifted her shirt so he could place his hands on her bare belly. He placed his lips there as well and started singing, making Erica giggle. He was rewarded with a good solid thump. "Oh! Field goal!"

"It's so nice to see you in a good mood for a change." Erica watched Joel's expression and gently brushed her fingers through his hair. "I love you, so much, Joel."

"Jeez, you're right. I stink—" Joel replied, kissed Erica's hand, and headed off for a shower.

The beach parking lot was completely vacant, and the wind was trying its best to remove Ethan's coat from his body. He reluctantly pulled it closed, opting for comfort over appearance, doing up the zipper at the front, and then tucked his body up against the hedge running down one side of the beach. It was a ridiculous time of night to be out, and he cursed the moron that had broken the last of the lights. It was absolutely pitch black.

In the distance, he could hear the sound of someone walking toward him. He listened carefully and could tell that the person approaching was accompanied by a large dog; it was the guy he'd been waiting over an hour for.

Ethan stepped out of the shadows and jogged toward the parking lot, smirking when the dog skittered back in surprise.

"Hiya, Syd," Ethan said.

"Fuck, Ethan. I swear to God, one of these days, Butch is going to have a go at you." Syd shortened up the leash and pulled the dog in tight against his leg. "And I'm not going to be able to stop him. He's fucking insane. You know that."

"And that, Syd, would be Butch's last day on earth." Ethan made a production of retracting his knife's switchblade and then tucked it back in his pocket. "What have you got for me?"

"I tried, but I couldn't get you a full kilo."

Ethan stepped up in Syd's face, ignoring the low rumbling growl coming from Butch. He gripped the trigger of the gun in his pocket carefully, not wanting to shoot the dog accidentally. "Why not?"

"I need more time to talk to my supplier. I don't have that kind of inventory just lying around." Syd backed away from Ethan and anxiously scrubbed his hand across his mouth.

"Week after week of the same fuckin' crap. I'm disappointed in you, Syd." Ethan pushed Syd hard in the chest, making Butch snarl and snap. "Maybe I should be talking to your supplier directly."

"That's not possible."

"Really?" Ethan sneered at Syd, took the gun out of his pocket, and pointed it at the dog's head. "Get him on the phone ...now! And Butch here might live to see another day."

"Fuck, don't hurt him. I'm sorry, man. I'm doing my best."

Syd fumbled with his phone and considered dropping the leash, but Butch would be more inclined to go after Ethan, rather than take off for safety, so he hung on tight.

Ethan sighed with impatience as he waited for Syd to finish talking to his supplier, and then motioned for the phone. He almost laughed aloud when he recognized the voice at the other end. This was going to be easier than he thought. He chatted with the guy briefly, ended the call mid-sentence, then turned the gun on Syd.

"What are you doing?" Syd asked.

"Shut up." Using Syd's phone, Ethan sent a text message, then threw the phone onto the ground, using his heel to break it apart, and pulled out his own cell phone.

"Jeez, what the fuck are you doing?" Syd ran his hand through his hair. "Ethan, think about what you're doing. You've completely lost it. I told you that shit would fuck you up." He held his hands out in front of him and tried to back away slowly. "How about you let Butch and me go now?"

"Shut the fuck up, Syd." Ethan sent a text from his own phone and stuffed it back in his pocket, keeping his gun trained on Syd.

"Fucking crackheads," Syd said under his breath. "Turn your back on them for one second, and they go out and buy a fucking gun."

"Syd, I swear. One more word out of you and I'll kill your fuckin' dog." Ethan reached into his inside coat pocket and pulled out a wad of cash. "Give me what you've got. All of it. This should cover it." He held out the money, letting Syd take it, and snatched back the plastic bag Syd handed him.

Ethan's head whipped around when he heard a squad of police cars descending on them, and took off at a run toward the water. He got out as far as his waist when he heard an officer on the beach telling him to stop, drop his weapon, and put his hands on his head.

Valentine's Day had come up rather suddenly, putting Joel in an unusual situation. He had only been together with Ethan for a few weeks, but he felt as though they should be doing something to celebrate, considering it had taken them so long to get to that place in their relationship. He'd planned to take Erica out for a nice lunch so he would have all evening to spend with Ethan, but Erica had been called into work, and he hadn't been able to contact Ethan, so he was effectively alone on what should've been a busy day for him. He checked his phone again. It was unusual for Ethan to be out of communication for so long. He hadn't seen him around in almost three days and had assumed Ethan had taken off to Vancouver on business for his dad. He read the last text he'd received from Ethan two nights ago, stating he'd run into a problem and would be delayed for a few days, and not to worry.

Letting himself into Ethan's house, Joel made his way to the den and flicked the television on. He turned, peering over the back of the sofa when he heard someone enter the kitchen, then sighed with disappointment when he saw it was Sophie.

"Hey, Sophie," Joel said. "Do you know where Ethan is? I've been trying to contact him for days, but he's not returning any of my calls or texts."

"Master Cooke is off on private business, but we're expecting him home this evening." Sophie stepped into the den. "He asked me to ascertain whether or not you're available for dinner tonight."

"Yeah, I am. Erica has to work tonight." Joel stood and approached Sophie. "You're able to reach Ethan?"

Sophie shifted uncomfortably and folded her hands together over her apron. "No. I have no way of contacting Master Cooke directly. He called me this morning, and I was instructed to prepare a romantic dinner if you were available."

"Well, …at least he's all right." Joel circled back around the sofa and lay down. "I guess I'll wait for him here."

As the hours passed, Joel watched a movie and a couple of other shows and then flicked the television off and closed his eyes. The past few weeks with Ethan had been more than amazing. They had been spending as much time as possible together without arousing suspicion, and Joel couldn't imagine being happier in anyone's company than what he was with Ethan. He settled into the familiar folds of the sofa and recalled the night in the club when Ethan had first kissed him, and let the emotion and desire wash over him.

"What are you smiling at?" Ethan leaned over the back of the sofa and grinned as Joel opened his eyes.

"I was remembering our first kiss." Joel reached up and grabbed hold of Ethan's collar, then pulled him down just far enough to kiss him. "Where have you been?" he asked after releasing him.

"You wouldn't believe me if I told you." Ethan stepped away from the sofa and headed back out through the kitchen.

Joel vaulted over the back of the sofa and caught up with Ethan in the front foyer, skidding to a stop in shock.

"What the fuck happened to you?" Joel inquired, dramatically waving his arms in Ethan's direction. "Look at you!" He crossed his arms as Ethan turned around to face him, and took a step back. Ethan's pants were covered in mud, and his favorite leather jacket was severely water damaged, and it was obvious he hadn't showered in days.

Joel scrubbed a hand across his face, then looked toward the front door where Ethan's boots lay, completely trashed.

"Seriously," he said. "Where have you been?"

"I got arrested a few days ago," answered Ethan, "while trying to make a swim for it. You would've been proud of me. Except, I didn't get out deep enough to actually start treading water, not that I could've anyway. I lost all feeling in my limbs within seconds. That lake is fuckin' cold at this time of year."

Joel's expression hardened, and he wrapped his arms tighter across his chest. "Arrested for what exactly?"

"Mistaken identity really. But it took the police a few days to sort it all out. I wasn't carrying any identification." Ethan shrugged at Joel. "I didn't do anything. I promise."

Joel shifted his weight from one foot to the other, then headed across the foyer toward Ethan.

"Ethan," he said. "People don't get chased into the lake by the police for no reason." Joel placed his hand on Ethan's back and walked with him up the stairs. "You know how I feel about you dealing drugs, and the people you associate with to get those drugs. You're going to get hurt someday."

Ethan leaned up against the door to his bedroom and stroked Joel's face, attempting to calm him. "I know you worry about me, but I can take care of myself. I'm tougher than I look."

He smiled when Joel grinned, laughed, and lowered his gaze.

"Let me get a shower," Ethan said, "and then you and I can spend some time together …my gorgeous valentine."

Joel kissed Ethan's lips and shook his head in resignation. "I knew that swimming lesson was going to come back and bite me in the ass someday." He slapped Ethan on the ass playfully, and then turned and headed back down the stairs. "Make it quick. I'm hungry."

Ethan sighed to himself and shut the door. He leaned wearily against it and covered his face, and tried to contain the rapid state of his breathing. He hated lying to Joel. It was excruciating keeping the truth from him, especially because Joel was always so forgiving and non-judgmental about the situations he was seemingly getting himself in to. But for the time being, he had no other choice. He was almost finished, and then he wouldn't be taking any new jobs.

Chapter Thirteen

It was Friday morning, and Joel was feeling ecstatic. He rolled over reveling in the fact there was no school today. There was definitely something to be said for teacher's professional days.

Joel kicked his feet frantically under the covers and screamed as loud as he could. Erica had already left for work, and no one else was home, so he didn't need to worry about anyone thinking he'd gone insane. It just felt so good to let loose and let his emotions bubble to the surface, exploding like fireworks from his soul.

Having days off school like this was amazing because it meant he could spend the entire day with Ethan. His feelings for Ethan were growing exponentially, and they felt more real and truthful than any he had ever experienced before—and it was becoming increasingly difficult to justify keeping their relationship a secret. He hated the fact they couldn't go out in public as the couple he knew they'd become. When they did go out, they spent a lot of time just hanging out at the mall, dining at a few casual restaurants to avoid suspicion, and more recently, since it had warmed up a bit, sitting on the park benches at the beach, talking. But due to the restrictions, they preferred staying home. When they were at Ethan's house, they spent most of their time curled up on the sofa together watching movies, sharing ideas, and holding each other ...and making out.

Joel smiled to himself. They had been doing a lot of the latter, but on Ethan's insistence, Joel had reluctantly agreed they should take things slow to see how their emotional relationship developed before taking any steps toward a serious, physical one.

Ethan had set some strict limits on how far they could go with each other for now, because he thought there was too much at stake with Joel's marriage to rush into things.

Truth be told. It was infuriatingly difficult.

Joel didn't bother to have breakfast, because he knew Sophie would already have something set out on the table at Ethan's house, and he wanted to get over there as soon as possible. When he arrived, Joel let himself in and headed for the kitchen. He was taken aback when he walked in to see that Ethan wasn't alone.

"Hiya ...Joel," Ethan said, rapidly clearing away some papers that were laid out on his kitchen island, then frantically stuffing them into an envelope. A look of concern streaked across Joel's face.

"Hey, Ethan ...who's this?" Joel asked and flicked his head toward the guy standing beside Ethan.

"Um ...yeah," Ethan said. "This is Karl. We've known each other for a bit. He's only just moved back in with me." He ran his hand up Karl's arm and patted him on the shoulder, whereby Karl wrapped his arm around Ethan's waist, kissed him on the cheek, and then turned his back on Joel, completing the process of putting the papers away.

"Ethan. A word please?" Joel hovered at the doorway of the kitchen and motioned for Ethan to follow him down the hall. He looked back at Karl before heading out of the kitchen. He was the same height as Ethan and had a very similar style of dress, but he was much older, and Joel could see through his short growth of hair, a tattoo of a swastika on the back of his head.

"I can explain, babe." Ethan pushed Joel into the office, closed the door, and leaned against it. He pulled out his cigarettes and lit one, but his hands were shaking.

"Explain?" Joel said. "How could you possibly explain that?"

"Karl just showed up kind of unexpectedly. I would've told you if I'd known he was coming." Ethan tucked an arm against his chest and bit aggressively at his thumbnail, between inhalations of his cigarette.

"I promise you," he said. "It's not what it looks like …at all."

"It's not what it looks like? What the fuck does that mean?" Joel jammed his hands into his pockets and kicked aggressively at the leg of the desk. "I can't believe you would do something like this to me. After everything we've been through to be together."

"You need to trust me on this." Ethan moved to touch Joel's shoulder, but Joel pulled away from him. "Babe, please."

"Don't you fucking touch me." Joel pushed past Ethan and stormed back out through the front door, unimpeded.

Ethan ran his hands over his face and went back to the kitchen.

"Who was that?" Karl asked as he pulled the papers back out from the envelope and reorganized them.

"Just some kid from the school. He lives next door." Ethan took the documents Karl handed him and attempted to read them over. "He has a bad habit of wandering in here whenever he wants." He flipped over the page, read through the paragraph and tried to focus, but the words were like lines of insignificant letters dancing before his eyes. He took a deep breath. "He stormed out of here pissed because I told him off about it." Grabbing a pen from his pocket, Ethan started signing the pages Karl was directing him to. He would have to read them later.

"Is everything all right?" Karl asked. "You seemed a bit nervous when he walked in here. He's not one of them, is he?"

"Fuck, no. Furthest thing from it."

"You'd tell me if there was a problem, wouldn't you?"

"Of course. When have I ever kept anything from you?"

Karl stood back and crossed his arms. "Let's keep it that way."

Ethan's face flushed as he tried to fill in the next set of sheets correctly, but he felt sure he was going to throw up. Karl had arrived without warning to check in on him and would be staying at the house for the next couple of days so he could monitor Ethan's progress. Ethan's gut rolled. He would have to text Joel with an explanation as soon as he had a chance, but first, he needed to figure out what he was going to tell him—the truth wasn't an option.

Joel ran all the way from Ethan's house to Ryan's doorstep, his body shaking violently. He was short of breath and in tears by the time Ryan opened the door.

"What's wrong?" Ryan asked, his mind filling with fear and gruesome images. "Did something happen to Erica? Is the baby all right?" He pulled Joel inside and had him sit down in the living room. "Tell me. What's happened?"

"Erica is fine. The baby is fine." Joel heaved and gasped for breath as he fought back the steady flow of tears.

"Then what the hell is wrong with you?" Ryan sat down on the coffee table in front of Joel and tried to get Joel to make eye contact with him. After a few minutes, Joel took a few deep breaths and finally managed to regain his composure.

"Ethan's old boyfriend just moved back in with him. I didn't even know the guy existed until today."

"All right. Well. I didn't know Ethan was gay, so that's news in itself." Ryan pulled himself up and wandered into the kitchen to get a glass of water for Joel. "Why are you so upset about Ethan's boyfriend?" He set the glass on the coffee table and sat back down. "Was the guy an asshole to you?"

"Don't be thick, Ryan. I spend every spare moment I have with Ethan. Why do you think I'm upset about his boyfriend?"

Ryan shrugged.

"I don't know."

"God, Ryan." Joel smacked Ryan in the side of the head. "I spend all that time with Ethan …because I like him."

"Of course you like him. He's your friend." Ryan paused for a second. "Oh. You mean you like him, like him."

"Thank you."

Ryan scrubbed his face aggressively, then stood and began pacing the room. "All right, here's what I'm thinking. You're under a lot of stress …and here's this guy, Ethan, that doesn't appear to have a care in the world. He's exciting, impulsive, and completely reckless. All the things you can't be because you have a responsibility to Erica and the baby." He turned to face Joel and clapped his hands together.

"The way I see it," he said. "It's not that you like him. You like the idea of him. You want to be like him."

"I wish it was that abstract." Joel took a drink of water and set the glass back down on the table. "Remember before Christmas, I went to that party, and that girl seriously marked up my neck."

"Yeah, that was fucking hilarious." Ryan laughed to himself and moved to sit down beside Joel. "I've never seen that many hickeys on a person in my life."

"There was no party, and there was no girl. That was Ethan."

Ryan shoved Joel with both hands. "Are you fucking with me?"

"No. Ethan was helping me study. We got talking, and it just happened. It was pretty intense."

Joel closed his eyes for a second, hoping Ryan wouldn't judge him too harshly, and would actually be there for him like he always had been in the past.

"I'm sorry," Ryan said. "But you let a guy suck on your neck?"

"It wasn't just a guy. It was Ethan." Joel jumped up from the sofa and ran his hands through his hair as he stood staring out the window. "Our relationship had changed." He traced the shape of a star with his finger on the glass. "Our feelings for each other had gone way beyond friendship." He added a heart around the outside of the star before reluctantly wiping it out with his palm.

"But in the end," he said. "Ethan decided he didn't want to go through with a relationship, so I married Erica."

"You would've blown off your wedding? For Ethan?"

"Mm …absolutely." Joel continued to stare out the window, trying to make sense of the world. "I'm not in love with Erica. I know that now. Actually, I suspected it before I married her."

"Then why did you marry her?"

"It seemed like the right thing to do, because of the baby. And we get on all right together." Joel twisted the wedding ring around on his finger, and then pulled it off and shoved it in his pocket. He watched the steady formation of some white clouds off in the distance that reminded him of snow and sighed. "Ethan took me to Vancouver, and we went to one of those clubs …you know, where we could really dance together as guys. As a couple."

He leaned heavily against the windowsill and placed his forehead on the glass, grateful for its cold surface. "It was amazing, Ryan. Ethan held me against him all night as we danced, and it felt so right. I never thought I'd feel that strongly about anyone."

"That makes two of us." Ryan sighed in confusion. "When was that? When did Ethan take you to Vancouver?"

"About a month ago." Joel clutched at his stomach, remembering. "Ethan told me he wanted to be with me, without hesitation. That's what he said."

"So, you started seeing each other?" Ryan rose from the sofa. "Like really seeing each other? Like boyfriends and everything?"

"Yeah. We've been together ever since that night, and it's been incredible. I've never been happier."

Ryan dropped his gaze and took a deep breath. "You haven't been sleeping with him, have you?" He crossed his arms. "Because that really wouldn't be fair to Erica."

"No, we've been taking things slow." Joel turned to look at Ryan. "I don't know what happened. I thought we had something, Ethan and I. But then this Karl shows up and everything we've been building together just evaporated."

Ryan took Joel by the shoulders and caught his gaze. "Joel, listen to me. I'm sorry he did this to you, but Ethan has obviously moved on with Karl. Whatever was happening between the two of you is over. You're a married man with a baby on the way. You need to stay focused on Erica and the baby from now on, all right? You need to forget about Ethan and move on with your life."

"Yeah, I know. I just needed to hear someone else say it." Joel smiled at Ryan and turned back to look out the window. He pushed up his sleeve and stared at the stars on his arm—there were fifteen now. Ethan had added more the day before to express his growing feelings.

Joel groaned as he felt the weight on his heart shifting around uncomfortably, and wrapped his arms tightly across his chest to keep his breathing even. He closed his eyes and forced himself to adjust his outlook for a second time, and place Erica and the baby firmly back in his mind.

He pulled his wedding ring out of his pocket and pushed it back on his finger.

It was close to midnight by the time Joel made his way back home. After leaving Ryan's, he had walked around the neighborhood aimlessly for the entire day, trying to figure out what had happened between him and Ethan.

His mind had wandered back through all the time he'd spent with Ethan recently, and the depth of emotion he'd felt while in his company. He couldn't imagine feeling that way about anyone else ever again. He'd dropped down onto a bench at one of the bus stops and erupted into tears as he clung desperately to the post of the enclosure, certain he would never feel as connected to another person as what he had with Ethan. When he'd finally managed to pull himself off the bench, he had headed to the beach parking lot to freeze his ass off, attempting to numb the pain, or to die of hypothermia, he didn't care which. Being unsuccessful on both counts, he had made his way over to the church on the other side of the main road.

The sight of the gravestones in the churchyard had forced him to think about his life and the lives of the people in his life. He had perused through the graveyard reading all the names and had tried to come up with stories about them, based on their age at death, and the headstones of the loved ones around them. It had brought home the fact that life was short and the people he cared about wouldn't be around forever. Resigned and at peace with his decision, he'd headed for home with visions of the baby in his mind.

When Joel arrived at his house, the front door was locked, and the only keys he could find in his coat pocket were the ones to Ethan's house. He studied them carefully and was about to pitch them over the hedge when Erica opened the door. Not wanting her to see them, he stuffed them back in his pocket and followed her inside. After making the rounds to speak to each of his parents, Joel followed Erica into the bedroom and flopped down on the bed.

"I wasn't expecting to see you home so early tonight," Erica said. "Did you and Ethan have another fight?" She smiled, then her eyes narrowed when she saw Joel's reaction.

An even wider smile crossed her face.

"You did," she said. "You did have a fight."

"It wasn't a fight. It was a misunderstanding." Joel rolled onto his stomach and tucked a pillow under his head. "A huge one."

"So, does this mean you won't be hanging out with him anymore?" Erica tucked in beside Joel and kissed him on the cheek. "Because it would be nice to have a full-time husband."

"I'm all yours. Ethan and I are done."

"I can't say I'm sorry to hear that." Erica climbed off the bed and pulled a nightie out of her drawer. "What happened?"

"I don't want to talk about it."

Joel pulled his shirt off over his head and threw it onto the chair before undoing his belt and squirming out of his pants. He fell onto the bed, yanked his socks off, and climbed beneath the covers to wait for Erica. He watched her remove her makeup and brush her hair out, and smiled with a brief moment of contentment as she turned toward him, and he caught the profile of her stomach.

Erica snuggled her back into Joel's chest and shivered as the warmth of his body took the chill off. She ran her hand along his arm and smiled as he squirmed behind her, but as her fingers ran over the inner surface of his arm, Joel flinched.

"Did you get Ethan to add more stars?" Erica asked.

"No. He added them."

"That's what I asked." Erica turned toward Joel, confused.

"It's not the same thing." Joel tucked his face down and tried unsuccessfully to hold back the tears. "The stars have to be with Ethan before he can add them. I don't ask for them. They're created within him, and then he adds to the stars on my arm."

"What the fuck kind of drugs has Ethan been feeding you?" Erica rolled over and took Joel's face in her hands.

"Funny thing that. I've never actually seen Ethan taking any drugs." Joel laughed softly and let Erica wipe the tears off his face.

"This fight has really upset you, hasn't it?" Erica sighed and continued wiping away the tears that were spilling down Joel's cheeks. "Sweetheart, I'm sorry. I can't stand him, but he obviously means a lot to you." She ran her fingers through Joel's hair and kissed him softly on the lips. "Can't you patch things up with him?"

"No. Not something like this." Joel took a deep breath and tried to calm his mind. He looked into Erica's eyes and searched them for the softness he was craving—but it wasn't there. There was only one person that could comfort him with their eyes.

He closed his own and kissed Erica, wrapping his arms around her, hoping the feel of her warm and familiar body would clear away any thoughts of Ethan, but it only made him feel more desperate.

He wanted to be holding Ethan …not Erica.

The hallways were packed full of people all trying to secure a coveted spot in a multi-purpose room that was only designed to seat twenty percent of the student body. Joel and his friends had arrived as quickly as they could, but their progress was being impeded by a traffic jam of people at the entrance.

"What the hell is the problem?" Ryan jumped up and down attempting to see over the heads of the people in front of him.

"I think I can probably guess." Joel squeezed through a couple of people, but still couldn't see anything. A few people finally started moving and streamed off to one side or the other. As the blockage cleared, Joel could see what had caused the delay. Ethan and five of his friends had taken over a bank of tables in the very center of the multi-purpose room, and Ethan was stretched out flat on one of the tables with his legs crossed at the ankles, smoking a cigarette. He was keeping an eye on the door, and when Joel pushed his way into the room, Ethan spun himself up into a sitting position.

Joel stood and stared at Ethan for a second, but recognizing that Ethan was waiting for him, and his delay was causing other people to have less time to eat their lunch, he told Ryan he would catch up with him later, and motioned for Ethan to follow him down one of the long corridors just off to one side.

"What do you want?" Joel asked bluntly.

"I want to talk to you." Ethan finished his cigarette and crushed it out on the floor. "You've been avoiding me for days. You're not answering my calls or my texts. You've stopped coming to my house. And when I go by your place …Erica tells me you're not there, even when I know you are." His thumbnail was poised near his mouth, but he thought better of it and crossed his arms instead. "I know you're mad at me, but—"

"Mad at you?" Joel took off for a short distance down the hall and then came storming back. "Ethan, I am more than mad at you! You ripped my entire fucking existence apart!"

Realizing he'd been yelling, Joel lowered his voice and turned his back on the people now staring at them. "You never told me about Karl," he continued. "You never told me there was even a possibility of a Karl returning. And suddenly he's moving back in with you." He crossed his arms and pushed Ethan's discarded cigarette butt around with his foot. "I know we've been taking things slow, and I'm obviously still with Erica, but I had no idea that meant you'd be fucking around with other guys. That really hurt. Walking in and seeing him there."

"Babe, I never meant to hurt you."

"Then you shouldn't have let him move back in with you."

"Look, Karl is gone. We split up." Ethan searched Joel's eyes looking for forgiveness. "For good this time. I promise."

"And that's supposed to fix things?" Joel grabbed Ethan's sleeve and pulled him further down the corridor toward the exterior door at the end. "I thought there was something special happening between us." He tugged on the bottom of Ethan's jacket for a second and then let go. "Something that was causing me to reconsider how I saw myself living my life. And with whom."

"Babe …"

"Stop!" Joel ran his hand up through his hair, gripping it tightly in his fingers, and then lowered his voice again. "You've got to stop calling me that. I am not your *babe*. Not anymore. I thought we were building something amazing together, but obviously, someone like Karl can come along and take precedence over me without a second thought. I'm sorry, Ethan. We're done."

Ethan dropped his gaze, unable to speak, and wiped his thumb across his cheek and sighed deeply.

When he looked up, Joel's heart twisted as he watched tears forming in Ethan's eyes.

"Jeez, Ethan." Joel looked back over his shoulder to make sure no one was eavesdropping on them. "If I thought you were serious about us, that would be one thing, but I can't be messing around in some casual affair with you. I've got Erica and the baby to think of."

"I know you do. I'm sorry."

"Sorry for what? Damn it, Ethan!" Joel pushed the door to outside open and pulled Ethan out through it. "What exactly are you sorry for? Because I can think of a few things."

"I'm sorry for starting what I did. It was my fault, that day at your house. I shouldn't have touched you."

"That's what you're sorry about? That you shouldn't have touched me?" Joel pushed Ethan hard against the wall. "I wanted you to touch me. That was *not* your fault. The way I feel about you now. The way I desperately want to be with you more than anything I have ever wanted in my entire life. That …is *not* your fault."

Joel dropped his head into his hands and turned away in tears. "Fuck, I can't believe this is happening."

Ethan leaned against the wall and watched Joel pacing back and forth in front of him deep in thought. His eyes tracked Joel's face, looking for any sign of the decision Joel was going to make ...but he couldn't contain the fear building in his heart any longer and decided to step forward as Joel made another pass.

He gripped Joel by the shoulders and brought him to a stop.

"You don't need to figure this out right now," Ethan said, and ran both his hands down Joel's arms, and briefly pulled on his fingers before letting go. "Please. Don't decide this right now."

Joel pushed up his sleeve, exposing the stars. "I let you put these stars on my arm because they were a permanent reminder of what we had together." He shook his head and paused as his breath caught. "Except I have no idea what the fuck that was we had."

He brusquely wiped some tears from his cheeks and pulled his sleeve back down. "I'm married, and I have a child on the way. I know those things for sure about my life. Whatever it was that was happening between us ...I don't know what that was, or where it was going. But it obviously meant more to me than it did to you. I have to forget about you. Again. And this is the final time, Ethan. I need to move on and get my life back."

Joel turned and attempted to head back toward the school, fighting to keep his legs moving, but the tears coating his face were making it difficult to see, and he could barely breathe; his lungs were sticky with grief. He gripped his chest, as his body shook with each painful step that took him further away from the one person that had ever made him feel whole, and he stumbled, his heart crushing in on itself, along with his hopes of making some type of life with Ethan.

He righted himself and kept moving.

Clutching at his own chest, Ethan tried to call out to Joel, but his breath snagged, sharp, and brutal, and he only managed a wordless sob as he sunk down into the dirt— Joel wasn't stopping.

"Please! God, no!" Ethan finally cried out, not caring if anyone heard him. "Joel, please! Please don't leave me!"

He collapsed and wrapped his hands over his head, rocking himself gently to try to soothe the pain ripping through his body.

Joel slowed his retreat and covered his mouth to contain his response upon hearing the sound of anguish behind him. He looked back over his shoulder and felt his soul twisting in agony at what he saw. Gasping desperately, he almost collapsed, and then nearly slipped in his haste to reach Ethan.

Ethan stumbled to his feet, pulled Joel into his arms, and gripped him tightly to his body as he continued to sob. He buried his face in Joel's hair and inhaled the scent of him, but then he pulled back, scrubbed some tears from his own cheeks, and held Joel's face in his hands, looking deep into his eyes.

"I'd be lost without you," Ethan said. "Please don't leave me."

"But you keep tearing me up inside." Joel gripped Ethan's hands and held them firmly in his. "I don't know what to do."

"Just give me a chance to explain."

"I don't know. I don't think I can take any more of this."

"Please. I'll tell you everything. I promise."

Joel nodded his head, and Ethan took Joel's hand and led him further away from the school toward a treed area near the back of the property where they stopped for a second, so they could each catch their breath, and then Ethan began.

"Karl has never been my boyfriend."

"Great. Then who the fuck is he?"

"He's someone I work for, Joel. My driver's license—it's not fake. I really am twenty-one." Ethan held up his hand as Joel made to interject. "What you saw in my kitchen with Karl. That's a standard cover for the two of us. I just fell into it without thinking, and then after I did, I had to stick with it, or he would've suspected something."

"I don't understand. A cover?"

"Joel, I've been working with Karl and your police liaison officer to suss out kids dealing drugs in your school." Ethan held his hand up again. "And occasionally, I work with the police doing surveillance on known drug dealers." He stopped and watched Joel's expression. "That's why I got arrested just before Valentine's Day. They had to keep me locked up for a few days to make it look good."

"You're a narc?" Joel reached over, snatched the cigarette package from Ethan's coat pocket, and motioned for the lighter. He needed the calming effect he'd witnessed when Ethan lit up. He figured this was as good a time as any to start smoking.

He coughed after he took the first draw, prompting Ethan to move closer to him and begin rubbing his back.

"Why didn't you tell me?" Joel asked.

"I couldn't," Ethan replied. "I was working undercover."

"Then what makes it all right for you to tell me now?"

"It's not. This is extremely reckless on my part, but I can't lose you. I can't have you thinking that what's been happening between us meant nothing to me, because it did. It has meant everything to me."

Ethan turned Joel toward him and stroked his face.

"I don't want you thinking there's a Karl out there somewhere that could take your place, because there isn't. You're *it* for me."

He watched the confusion in Joel's eyes as he sorted through everything he'd been told.

"Are you a police officer?" Joel threw the cigarette down, crushed it out, and crossed his arms.

"No, I work for Karl on a contract basis."

"All those drugs I saw you buying at school?"

"I was just building a case."

"You don't use drugs?"

"Occasionally, I have to, to maintain my cover, but I haven't touched drugs recreationally since I was probably sixteen."

Joel motioned for Ethan to follow him a bit further into the forested area, away from where anyone from the school would be hanging around. "What do you mean I'm *it* for you?"

"I don't want to be with anyone else." Ethan rubbed his eyes and looked shyly in Joel's direction. "Those first stars represented the beginning of something much deeper than casual affection."

"Are you in love with me?"

"Jeez, Joel." Ethan lit up a cigarette, passed it to Joel, and lit another for himself. "Put me on the spot, or what?"

"I need to know what it is we're talking about here." Joel stopped walking and turned to face Ethan. "I've never felt more connected to anyone in my entire life, and you know I'm willing to give up everything for you. But I need to know you're there with me wanting the same thing. And I don't want to keep hiding from everyone anymore. I want us to be a proper couple."

"I'm there with you," Ethan replied. "I want the same thing, but we *can't* let anyone know about us."

"Not this again." Joel turned away from Ethan in frustration "Why not? And don't say you can't tell me, or I'm walking."

"Joel, it's because of your age. Nothing else. You're only seventeen, and I'm technically in a position of authority at the school."

"So what?"

"Babe, you're a minor. I could be arrested for what we've done together. The program that Karl runs is difficult enough to sell to the parent-teacher associations without one of its members being charged with sexual exploitation."

"That's ridiculous. We've barely touched each other, and besides, I turn eighteen in June. That's less than three months away." Joel slid down the trunk of the tree he'd been standing under and settled himself on the ground beneath it.

"I don't make the laws," Ethan said. "But that's why I put so many restrictions on what we were doing together."

"So, we really do have to keep our relationship a secret." Joel crushed out the cigarette and brushed his hand on his pants.

"Just until a month or so after your birthday." Ethan sat down beside Joel. "Then I'll be right there with you. Telling everyone what's up with us. That we're together as a couple."

"This is going to get fucking complicated." Joel sighed and lay his hand on Ethan's leg. It was unlikely that anyone from the school would be out this far and he needed the calm that came from being close to Ethan. He breathed easier as Ethan took his hand.

"Because of Erica?" Ethan asked.

"Mostly, yeah. Having to lie to her for another three or four months is going to be heartbreaking. She's a bitch sometimes, but she doesn't deserve to be treated the way I've been treating her."

"I know. Everything we've been doing behind her back doesn't sit well with me either." Ethan paused, unsure. "Maybe we should wait until you turn eighteen before we start seeing each other more seriously. Then we won't have to run around hiding."

"No way. This past couple of days has been agonizing. I'm completely lost without you. You're like my other half."

Ethan looked over at Joel and dropped his gaze. "You really feel that way about me?"

"Yeah, of course, I do." Joel squeezed Ethan's hand and brought it to his lips. "I wouldn't be doing this otherwise."

Ethan took a deep breath and shook his head in amazement. "And you're really going to leave Erica for me?"

"Ethan, I offered to leave her back in December, remember?"

"I look back on that, and I feel like such an idiot. We could've been together all this time. Instead, you're married to Erica." Ethan shook his head. "I completely fucked up."

"We're together now. That's all that matters." Joel squeezed Ethan's hand. "So. The house? Your dad? All the things you told me about yourself and your life? All that personal stuff we talked about? Was it all part of your cover?"

Ethan settled in against the tree, breathing easier now that he knew he hadn't lost Joel. "No, every personal thing I shared with you is true. The house. It really is my dad's house. He lives in Britain, but he's always wanted a place here. This latest assignment of mine gave him a perfect excuse to buy something. Chances of him actually coming out and using it are pretty slim though."

"What made you decide to be a narc?"

Ethan switched hands, wrapped his other arm around Joel's shoulder, and pulled him closer.

"When I was five," Ethan began, "my mom was coming home from a fundraiser, on her own, because my dad wasn't able to attend." He paused as his mind faltered, not wanting to remember. "She innocently ended up in the middle of a botched drug deal that night."

He stopped and rested the side of his face on Joel's head.

"According to the coroner, both she and her driver never felt a thing. The spray of bullets killed them instantly."

"God, that's horrible." Joel gripped ahold of Ethan's coat, pulling him closer. "I'm so sorry, Ethan."

"It turned out to be a bunch of kids, no older than you." Ethan shifted back so he could see Joel's face. "That's why I joined Karl's program. Our focus is on finding kids in the schools that are dealing, so we can get them help before they get themselves in too deep, and become a statistic. This program is really important to me. I'm doing it for my mom."

"That's so amazing." Joel tucked himself back into Ethan's side. "You're amazing. I knew you weren't a druggie."

Ethan laughed and hugged Joel closer. "The program is the reason I kept changing my mind about us. It felt as though I had to choose between you and my mom."

"I'm sorry. I had no idea I was forcing you to make such a difficult decision." Joel brushed his thumb across Ethan's hand. "But you did finally decide …how?"

"I had a few long talks with my dad, and he insisted that the greatest way to honor my mom's life would be to find happiness with someone."

"Your dad sounds like a smart guy."

"He has his moments."

"When did you start working for Karl?"

"When I turned eighteen. I've pulled in a good fifty plus guys and more than a few girls. No one ever suspects that the psychotic British guy with all the piercings and tattoos is actually a narc."

"It's a pretty good cover. You had me partially fooled, and I thought I knew you really well." Joel leaned his head against Ethan's shoulder and rubbed his cheek against the smooth leather.

"You do know me really well." Ethan kissed Joel on the head. "From the first day we met, you saw through all my crap."

"No, the first day we met, I thought you were a psychopath. It wasn't until the second day that I changed my mind."

Ethan laughed and ruffled Joel's hair, then suddenly sat up, and peered off into the distance.

"What is it?" Joel asked nervously.

"Nothing. I thought I saw someone. But it's just the wind blowing those branches around."

"This is crazy. I'm really looking forward to finally coming out together." Joel gripped Ethan's hand and looked up into his eyes. "I want everyone to know how amazing I think you are."

Ethan brought his mouth down close to Joel's and stroked his palm along Joel's face. "You're the one that's amazing. And you were right. I'm deeply and hopelessly in love with you."

He kissed Joel softly then ran his thumb across Joel's lips.

"Damn, Ethan." Joel slid his hand up into Ethan's hair and moved to take his mouth, but Ethan stopped him.

"We can't be doing that where anyone might see us. You got one inappropriate kiss during what seemed like an appropriate moment." Ethan grinned down at Joel. "It's important that I don't compromise the program any more than I have already." He let go of Joel and lit up a cigarette. "All it would take is for someone to catch us and start talking, and then one of the teachers or the parents in the association might overhear. Next thing you know, I'm being arrested, and the program is dead."

"I definitely don't want you getting arrested. A pushover like you would never survive a day in prison." Joel laughed as he shoved Ethan with his shoulder. "We should probably head back to the school anyway. Lunch is almost over, and my friends are going to be wondering what happened to me." He winked at Ethan as he rose to his feet. "These stars on my arm just took on a whole new meaning for me." He reached for Ethan and helped him to his feet.

"I'm going to need to add more," Ethan said.

"You can add as many as you like …but I need you to start filling some of them in …for how I feel about you."

Joel smiled brightly as Ethan's eyes changed.

God, I love you, so much." Ethan leaned down and took Joel's mouth, gentle but urgent, leaving Ethan's heart beating rapidly as he pulled away.

"I thought you said no kissing in public," Joel teased.

"You're so beautiful when you smile like that. I couldn't help myself." Ethan studied Joel's face. "You're coming to my house tonight, aren't you?"

"Fuck that. Can we go there now?"

"I can't. I have a meeting with the principal this afternoon, and then I'm doing a presentation for another *Youth at Risk* group. I'll be home by eight though. Can you meet me there?"

"That depends." Joel tapped his own lips with his finger. "I don't see anyone else around, and I'm going to need some serious convincing." His eyes completely lit up with excitement when Ethan moved in on him and attacked his mouth.

Joel was running a bit late. Erica had brought home a stack of wallpaper books and paint chips from an interior design store, and after what was already a late dinner, she'd brought them all out and wanted to discuss them. Joel was attempting to participate, not wanting to let on just how *not* interested he was, and that he really wanted to be somewhere else, but the events of that afternoon in the forest with Ethan were making it impossible for him to concentrate.

He felt a warm flush come over him as he played the scene over in his mind, and smiled.

Ethan was in love with him.

"Joel?" Erica interrupted.

"Sorry, what?" answered Joel.

"Do you think we should go with the yellow?"

Joel shifted in his seat and checked around the room, looking for his dad. "Isn't yellow more of a kitchen color?"

"It can be," Carol said, "but it's also a good choice if you don't know the sex of the baby."

"I really don't think the baby will care," Joel said, and then sighed with relief as he spotted his dad heading in from the garage.

"Sorry to interrupt, ladies," Arthur said. "But could I steal Joel for a few minutes? I need a hand in the garage."

"But we were just about to start talking borders," Joel said as he jumped up from his seat, and followed his dad out to the garage. "I owe you with my life, Arthur. Thank you."

"Someday I'll collect on that, but since I have you out here now, could you give me a hand with this lawnmower blade?"

"Actually, I was supposed to be at Ethan's like two hours ago. We have a lot of homework to finish tonight."

"You haven't been over to his place in a few days." Arthur leaned against the workbench and crossed his arms. "Erica said you two had a fight. Did you manage to work everything out?"

"Yeah, it was a huge misunderstanding. Bad communication. But it's all good now."

"All right, good." Arthur patted Joel affectionately on the back. "He's a good kid, that Ethan. More than I ever could've expected. I'd hate for you to fall out with him."

"Sure thing, Arthur." Joel placed his hand on his dad's shoulder, stunned by the sudden accolades for Ethan's character. He knew his dad liked Ethan enough to tolerate him, but he'd never expressed any admiration for him before.

"Well, off you go then," Arthur said. "I'll cover for you."

Joel turned and dashed out of the garage, up the driveway, and into Ethan's house. It was completely silent, and Edgar wasn't lurking at the front door for a change. He looked in the kitchen and through to the den, but Ethan wasn't there, so he continued down to the smoking lounge at the end of the hall.

Ethan was stretched out on the sofa, enjoying the warmth of a roaring fire and a brandy. Joel had texted him earlier to tell him he was being held captive, but that he would be over as soon as he could, so Ethan had settled in to wait for him.

He glanced over toward the doorway when he heard Joel enter the room, but didn't bother to get up.

"Hiya, babe," he said. "You finally managed to escape."

"I barely made it out alive." Joel lifted Ethan's feet out of the way, so he could sit down, and then put them back on his lap. "My dad had to come to my rescue."

"Baby stuff again?"

"Yeah. Decorating the nursery." Joel smiled and punched Ethan in the arm when he started laughing at him, at which point Ethan grabbed Joel's hand and delicately kissed each of his knuckles.

When Ethan looked up, he burst out laughing. Joel had a seriously mischievous glint in his eyes.

"Oh, boy," Ethan said. "What's with that look?"

"I was thinking."

"Mm …really? And what were you thinking?"

"I was thinking, now that I know the truth about you, and that you're in love with me." Joel dropped his gaze, smiled coyly, and shrieked when Ethan jabbed him with his foot.

"I was thinking …," Joel said again, and then paused teasingly.

"What?" Ethan let his tongue drag across the top of Joel's hand, and then he looked up. "Tell me what you were thinking."

Joel gasped and tried to maintain his composure as Ethan took one of his fingers into his mouth and sucked on it while moaning softly and playing it with his tongue.

"I was thinking," Joel said, breathing heavier now, "that I don't want to take things slow with you anymore."

Ethan let Joel's finger drop and then licked the next one over, lingering over the taste of it.

"What did you have in mind?" he asked.

"I don't know. But I need more from you."

"Well, I've been sitting here on my own for hours thinking about you. And I'm going to need more from you as well." Ethan sat up, set his glass down on the coffee table, and took Joel's cigarette off him and crushed it out. "So much more."

Ethan motioned for Joel to come closer, then grabbed him, flipped him to the other end of the sofa, shoved him down, and attacked his mouth. The move was rough and calculated and had caught Joel entirely off guard, but once he felt Ethan's mouth on his, he became focused on the sensations coursing through his body, the aggressive nature of Ethan's grip on him soon forgotten.

A soft moan escaped Joel's throat as he savored the burning heat of Ethan's hunger. He'd been dreaming of this for so long. The feel of Ethan's hot, moist breath, and the hard metal of Ethan's piercing, caressing his skin. His hips bucked in response, and he clutched at Ethan's clothes, wanting them gone.

Ethan chuckled against Joel's lips. "No," he whispered then grabbed ahold of Joel's wrists, forcefully pinning Joel's hands above his head.

Joel managed a soft, "Ethan, please...," before Ethan descended on him again, working his mouth along Joel's neck to his shoulder, biting and sucking, driving Joel to struggle beneath Ethan's weight.

Then Joel's eyes flew open, his heart thundering out of control, as Ethan's hand shot down and found its way in behind his belt, into the front of his pants, sending a rush of fireworks up through his body.

Joel rode through the emotion and need building within him, reveling in Ethan's heavy caress, and let his body respond with ever-increasing urgency. He shifted slightly, trying to give Ethan greater access as he felt himself reaching the limit of his endurance. But then Ethan stopped and withdrew his hand, and slowed everything down, contenting himself by licking long lines along Joel's collarbone and up the center of Joel's throat to his chin.

Ethan lifted his body away from Joel, brought his lips down softly on Joel's mouth, and pulled himself off the sofa.

"Fuck, Ethan. Did I do something wrong?" Joel pulled himself up and swung his feet back onto the floor.

"No, but I was definitely on my way to doing something wrong." Ethan sat back down beside him. "What we've been doing up until now was nice, but I've wanted to kiss you like that for so long." He nudged Joel with his shoulder. "It felt really good."

"It felt good enough to do it again." Joel reached up, turned Ethan's face toward him, and ran his fingers along the rings in his lip and down the surface of the piercings on his chin. "But this time ...finish what you started." He shifted uncomfortably. "I'm dying over here."

Ethan grinned at him. "Sorry, but that felt good enough to keep it going all night. And that's exactly what we can't be doing." He placed his finger on Joel's lips so he could finish what he was saying. "Your dad showed up at the parent-teacher meeting last week." He lit up a cigarette and passed it to Joel. "He was a bit shocked to see me there."

"He never said anything to me." Joel thought back to his dad's comment about Ethan in the garage, and now it made sense.

"You're a student. You're not supposed to know who I am." Ethan leaned in and let Joel hold the cigarette to his lips. He inhaled slowly and then let his eyes follow Joel's fingers back to his own lips, and shivered as his body responded. "If he found out we were fucking around with each other, he would definitely report me, and because aside from the fact that you're only seventeen and you're married, I don't get the feeling your dad is very same-sex friendly."

"You've got that right," Joel replied. "You have no idea."

Ethan watched Joel grab the ashtray and crush out the cigarette.

"If I was to end up in court," he said. "I'd still be looking at exploitation charges. I want to be able to say, truthfully, that I never had sex with you before you were eighteen."

"All right." Joel pulled himself up and straddled Ethan's hips, and started rocking and rubbing his body against Ethan's. "But what constitutes sex exactly?"

"You're going to cause me grief, aren't you?"

"Mm...hm." Joel leaned in and took Ethan's mouth, savoring the taste of his lips and his tongue, and basking in the desire it was invoking in him. He sighed in response when Ethan's hands went up under his shirt and started caressing his skin, sending his emotions ebbing and flowing like the movement of his hips.

Staring into Ethan's eyes, he stopped abruptly. They'd taken on a fluidity and fire that was sending a burn straight through to his core.

Joel couldn't take his eyes off them.

"Hey, don't stop," Ethan said, redirecting Joel's attention. "It's a bit unconventional, but it feels amazing." He ran his hands up Joel's chest and pulled his shirt off over his head, letting his hands drift back down along Joel's throat. Joel dropped his head back and continued rocking as Ethan's tongue circled his nipple. He held Ethan's head against his chest and moaned softly as Ethan's mouth pulled more aggressively at it.

"God, that feels good," Joel said as he reached down and started to undo Ethan's belt, but Ethan grabbed his hand.

"Babe, don't. This is going to be difficult enough to stretch out until you're eighteen. Let's slow things down and enjoy each other without adding any dangerous elements for the time being."

He laughed when Joel groaned.

"Do what you want with the rest of me," Ethan said. "But the pants stay on. And so do yours."

"We'll see about that."

Joel winked, then removed Ethan's shirt, and ran his hands over the rings in his nipples. Curious, he shuffled down and took one carefully into his mouth. As he played with it, Ethan ran his hands down Joel's bare back and smacked him hard on the ass—causing Joel to pull sharply on the ring.

Ethan groaned in satisfaction, adding a husky laugh when Joel looked up at him. "Big difference between most girls and me is I'm not particularly breakable, and I enjoy a bit of …power."

Joel's eyes flashed with excitement.

"I take it that's not a problem," Ethan said, somewhat surprised.

Joel winked, slid further down Ethan's body, grabbed onto Ethan's hips, and hauled him off the sofa onto the hard marble floor. He straddled Ethan again, but this time took his mouth more aggressively, probing and pushing with his tongue, and biting roughly at Ethan's lips. Enjoying the rush of adrenaline coursing through his body, Joel ran his hand up into Ethan's hair, grabbed a handful, and pulled Ethan's head back, exposing his throat.

His pulse raced wildly as Ethan groaned and cursed at him, encouraging, and enticing him further.

"You like that, do you?" Joel pulled harder, eliciting a throaty groan from Ethan. Emboldened, he indulged in the taste of Ethan's throat, hovering momentarily over the rapid thrumming of Ethan's increasing pulse while his other hand swept across his chest. Joel was attempting to stay in control, but the sound that erupted from Ethan's chest when he pinched and pulled at his nipple forced Joel to lick a hungry path down the center of Ethan's body, much sooner than he'd intended. He reluctantly passed over the belt buckle and used his mouth to tease Ethan mercilessly through the fabric of his jeans instead. He increased the intensity when Ethan arched up beneath him and grabbed a handful of his hair, forcing him closer.

Ethan could feel himself losing the battle to keep things calm between him and Joel. He hadn't expected Joel to pursue him quite so aggressively, and it was taking every ounce of self-control he had not to surrender and give Joel what he was seeking. He reminded himself that dropping his restraint could potentially lead to significant jail time, but that particular consequence seemed of little deterrence at the moment. He groaned at the injustice of his situation and gathered up the remainder of his strength.

Joel's mind shuddered helplessly as it tried to cope with the crushing response of his body as his attempts to weaken Ethan's resolve continued to fail. He was breathing heavily and trying half-heartedly to calm himself when he finally gave up, lay his head down on Ethan's stomach, and used his hand to stroke Ethan through his jeans, mesmerized by the effect he'd had on him.

"Babe, when I was waiting for you in the multi today," Ethan said. "I had no idea the day was going to end like this."

"Mm …me either." Joel stopped stroking Ethan and slipped down between his legs. He looked up the length of Ethan's body and into Ethan's eyes, and slowly kissed and licked the front of his jeans, before laying a path up to Ethan's lips. "I could stay here all night doing this. Maybe you should just surrender now."

He crawled on top of Ethan and began tasting his lips again.

Ethan wrapped his arms around Joel, pressing his body closer, and felt his control begin to slip when Joel started thrusting his hips against him. He cradled Joel's face and pulled him away. "You're comfortable with all this, aren't you?" He brushed the hair from Joel's eyes so he could watch them. "You seem more than fine to me, but I thought I'd be a gentleman and ask."

"Do you mean because you're a guy?"

"Yeah. I remember being a bit tentative at first. But then my introduction was a completely different situation."

"Why? What happened?"

"That is a story for another time. Right now, I want to know about you."

"I wasn't really giving it much thought." Joel tapped on the ring in the center of Ethan's lip. "I have all these overwhelming feelings for your intellectual body, and I feel like your physical body is simply a tangible and touchable extension of that."

"You might feel that way now because we've got all of our clothes on for the most part, but you're here because of me, specifically …not because you're typically attracted to guys, right?"

"I wouldn't say that exactly."

"You're not here because of me?"

"No. I'm just here for your body." Joel grinned and wiggled with excitement. "I've had a hankering for dick that just wouldn't go away. And I thought …hey—he'll do."

"Very funny." Ethan stroked Joel's face and watched his expression change. "Joel, if you ever feel uncomfortable with anything we're doing, you have to tell me, all right?"

"Yeah, sure." Joel dropped into a kiss and began grinding his hips rhythmically against Ethan's, his desire swelling as he felt Ethan's response pressed up against him. He grabbed at Ethan's hips and forced him closer to his body.

"So, I take it you're comfortable," Ethan said.

"Fuck yeah."

"Mm …I'm loving you more every minute." Ethan pulled Joel back onto his mouth, but then stopped, and turned his head toward the door. He'd heard Erica's voice coming from the foyer.

"Shit, it's Erica." Joel pushed off, struggling to his feet, and dashed over Ethan to the sofa, where he hoped to find his shirt, but he couldn't see it. He looked back over at Ethan and laughed.

"Are you all right down there?" he asked.

"No, you've incapacitated me," Ethan said. "The only way I'm getting off this floor any time soon is if I take these pants off."

"Then you're out of luck. Pants stay on. Remember." Joel pulled his shirt out from between two cushions and put it on, then unzipped his pants and made an attempt to adjust himself as best as possible.

"It's your own fault for wearing such tight jeans," he added.

"I'll remember to wear my sweatpants next time."

"Good idea. Those will be much easier to get off." Joel winked at Ethan, and then tugged his shirt down over the front of his pants and checked behind him. He could hear Erica going through some of the other rooms down the hall, calling his name.

"She's getting closer," he said, and dropped down onto his knees beside Ethan, giving him a long slow kiss. "I have to go, but I'll text you later and make sure you've fully recovered." He smiled and kissed Ethan again before standing up.

"Babe, before you go. Next time you come over. Lock the front door." Ethan rolled over onto his side and grabbed his cigarettes off the coffee table. "I don't like unexpected visitors." He smirked as he lit one up and waved Joel out of the room.

Erica was halfway down the hall when Joel left the lounge.

"Joel, what are you doing over here?" she asked. "You told me that you and Ethan weren't friends anymore."

"We worked things out at school today."

"Well, that's good I guess." Erica hooked her arm through Joel's and tucked her face into his neck. "Have you been smoking?"

Joel opened the pack of cigarettes he'd lifted from Ethan's coffee table and lit one. "Yes, I have." He pushed the lighter back into the pack and blew the smoke away from her.

"Joel. I don't like you smoking."

"Erica. I'm giving up a lot for you. Don't start with me."

Erica glared at him but didn't continue. "Your mom and I picked out the paint. Can you buy it tomorrow after school?"

"Sure, no problem." Joel threw the cigarette down outside his front door, crushed it out, and kissed Erica on the forehead.

He was about to turn away when she traced her finger down the front of his shirt, trying to get his attention.

"I was reading that when it comes closer to my due date, sex helps start labor," Erica said. "I thought we could practice."

"Practice?" Joel pulled away from her and crossed his arms. "Um ...no. Not tonight." He led the way inside the house and down to the bedroom, where he immediately stripped off and climbed into bed. "I think those cigarettes have given me a headache."

"Did you want me to get you some aspirin?"

"No, don't put yourself out." Joel motioned for her. "Climb into bed. It's late." He wrapped his arms around her as she backed into his chest. "When do the natural childbirth classes start?"

"Tomorrow night. They're going to start with a birth video." Erica smiled when she felt Joel cringe.

"Can I miss tomorrow?"

"No. Just be thankful you don't have to give birth."

"True. There are definite advantages to being a guy." Joel smiled to himself, remembering the feel of Ethan's hard body beneath him, and the urgent need he'd felt to rip Ethan's clothes off and devour him. His gut tightened in anticipation as he felt his body respond to the memory, and then a shiver of panic ran up his spine when he realized Erica would've felt his response against her.

"It feels like you've changed your mind," Erica said and reached back for him.

"Damn it, Erica!" Joel pulled away and rolled over. "I told you not tonight!" He closed his eyes and listened to Erica breathing behind him, the cold reality of his situation seeping in. He wrapped his arms around his body as his mind struggled to quell the intense waves of guilt lapping at his consciousness. He held tight and fought to contain an overwhelming urge to cry out.

"What is it, Joel?" Erica asked as she touched Joel's arm.

Joel rolled back to face her and smiled. "It's nothing. I'm just stressed out. There's a lot going on right now."

"We're in this together. You can talk to me."

"I'll be all right. It's just a bit overwhelming." Joel touched Erica's beautifully delicate face, and his breath caught as he remembered all the good times they'd had together. He immediately dropped his gaze.

"You're an amazing person," he said.

"So are you."

"No, I'm not ...I'm really not." Joel lifted his eyes and tucked a stray strand of hair behind Erica's ear. "No matter what happens, Erica, I want you to remember that this child of ours is the most precious thing in my life." His attention fell to the sheets again, and he sighed, his heart heavy, and let a few tears escape.

"I know that." Erica touched his hand and tried to get him to make eye contact, but he wouldn't look up. "Joel, what's wrong?"

Joel shook his head and closed his eyes. "It's nothing. I think I'm just really tired. It's been a long day." He relaxed as he heard Erica breathe her acceptance and settle in and then rolled onto his back, staring up at the ceiling of the darkened room.

He tried to justify continuing his relationship with Ethan based on the reality he'd never been in love with Erica in the first place and would soon be leaving her—but it was pointless.

A stream of fresh tears broke free and coated his face as he conceded that Erica didn't deserve a husband who ran around behind her back ...cheating on her, especially while she was carrying his child, and that Ethan was taking on too much of a risk by continuing to see him before he turned eighteen.

Joel shivered, sending a tingle of numbness through to his extremities, and wrenching his core, as he made the agonizing decision to call things off with Ethan—for now.

He struggled out of bed, gathered up his clothes, and headed next door.

Chapter Fourteen

The loud hammering on the door was becoming too much to ignore. Ethan pried himself out of bed and threw on his kimono before making his way downstairs. As he stood in the front foyer, he listened to the hammering, wondering who the hell could be at his door at three in the morning. He shook his head and peered out through the small window near the top of the door.

His eyebrows rose slightly when he saw it was Joel.

They had seen very little of each other since Joel had decided to put their relationship on hold. Ethan remembered how Joel had shown up at his house months back, kissed him, and dropped the heartbreaking decision at his feet. But before Joel had turned to go that night, he'd held Ethan and whispered words that Ethan carried close to his heart—Joel had asked him to *please* wait for him.

The baby had been born a few days after the May twelfth due date, three weeks ago, and since then Ethan's cell phone had been inundated with pictures of baby Sam. He had tried to sound enthusiastic about the baby whenever Joel spoke of him, and he knew that a new baby was prone to occupy the waking thoughts of any new parent, but Joel's growing enthusiasm about parenthood was beginning to concern him.

He looked out through the window again and watched Joel's escalating agitation. He took a deep breath and opened the door.

"Finally! What took you so long?" Joel pushed past him and headed for the lounge. "Why is your door locked?"

"I wasn't expecting visitors. And you have a key." Ethan closed the door and followed him. By the time he arrived, Joel had already poured himself a drink and was stretching out on the sofa.

"It is so quiet here. You have no idea," Joel said.

"Is the baby crying a lot?" Ethan poured himself a drink and tried to determine the reason for tonight's late night visit. Usually, when Joel showed up like this, it was just for a quick drink, and then he would take off back home without a single acknowledgment of their separation. But tonight Joel had arrived much later than usual, and he seemed particularly preoccupied.

"Babies don't cry," Joel continued. "They shriek mercilessly until your ears bleed. I swear I haven't slept in three days." He threw back the remains of his drink and tucked a cushion behind his head.

"I was sleeping just fine until two minutes ago," Ethan commented. "You do realize it's three in the morning, right?" He sat on the footstool in front of the sofa and crunched on the ice from his glass.

"I'm sorry, but I really needed to see you. It couldn't wait until tomorrow." Joel rolled onto his side and propped his head upon his hand, and carefully studied Ethan's face.

"What's up?" Ethan asked.

Joel sat up and motioned for Ethan to come sit beside him. "I've been doing a lot of thinking recently." He reached for the pack of cigarettes on the coffee table, lit one up, and passed it to Ethan.

Ethan tentatively took a drag, and as he exhaled, he watched the smoke drift lazily toward Joel's face. "What have you been thinking about?" His breath faltered when Joel took the cigarette back and crushed it out before he'd even finished it. It looked like Joel was about to open a serious discussion with him, and he suddenly felt as if he was going to be sick. His greatest fear was that Joel would decide he was content with his life, now that the baby had arrived.

"I've been thinking about this," Joel said and pulled Ethan toward him and brought their mouths together, seeking out the metal ball he knew he would find there. He shivered as his tongue rolled over it and felt Ethan pulling him closer. He let his body relax as Ethan pushed him over, and moaned with contentment as the weight of Ethan's body pinned him to the sofa.

Joel's hands caressed their way up along Ethan's body and back down again while his pulse surged, wanting more. He reached further and gathered the loose fabric of the kimono, pulling it up to Ethan's waist, then became distracted, turning his head away from Ethan's mouth when the feel of Ethan's bare ass beneath his fingers started a fire within him that had him quivering with desire.

Ethan laughed softly and pulled away. "That's what you've been thinking about?"

Joel grinned at him. "It's been keeping me awake more than the baby has."

"Are you going to be able to sleep now?" Ethan smiled and brushed his thumb across Joel's lower lip, and then removed himself, and took a seat at the far end of the sofa.

"Sleep is not really on my mind at the moment."

"What is on your mind?" Ethan asked as he lay back in the cushions, and placed his arms delicately above his head.

"The same thing that's been keeping me awake for months." Joel licked his lips and ran his hands up Ethan's legs as he moved closer. "That is if you still want me." He stopped and waited, and his breath erupted in short exhalations as Ethan slid the kimono open to expose his inner thigh.

Dragging his legs apart further, Ethan tucked a hand into his kimono, letting it run over the smooth surface of his chest, caressing his nipple and playing with the ring.

"Babe, I love you," he said. "I still want you. I'll never stop wanting you. But are you sure this is what you want?"

Joel reached forward and let his hand drift over the silk of Ethan's kimono, and smiled with anticipation as he stroked his hand all the way down the front of the garment until he reached the knot in the tie that held it closed. His fingers worked the knot loose, and he pulled the kimono open, taking the time to smooth out the material on either side of Ethan's body as he gazed down at him.

He repositioned himself, laid his hands on Ethan's stomach, and paused for a second.

"I did what I felt was the right thing for Erica at the time, but now that the baby's been born, I need to do what's right for me." Joel brushed his hands across Ethan's stomach and looked up into his eyes. "And what's right for me, is being with you. I want to be with you more than anything else."

Ethan looked down at his body, lying exposed. "And here tonight. With me. Like this. This is part of what you want?"

"Mm ...hm." Joel leaned over and kissed Ethan's lips, and then started running a trail with his mouth across Ethan's chest and down the center of his body. As he reached the soft hollow between Ethan's hipbones, he stopped and raised his eyes. "This is definitely what I want." He laughed softly when the only response he got from Ethan was a deep groan.

Overwhelming emotion had Ethan's head swimming as he tried to process what had just happened. He covered his face and howled loudly in exhilaration, making Joel laugh and climb back up to kiss him. He took Joel's mouth ardently, and then let Joel drift out of his hands to work his way back down his body.

As Joel descended, Ethan exhaled and licked his lips until Joel's warm tongue slid up the outside of his cock and over the tip. He was going to warn Joel to watch his teeth on the piercings but found it wasn't necessary. Joel was exploring each piercing in detail with his fingers, and then his tongue. Ethan clenched his teeth and inhaled sharply as Joel persisted in pulling at the ring at his tip with his mouth. Joel stopped and caught his eye.

"Do you like that?" Joel asked.

"Fuck, yeah."

"Mm …good to know." Joel pulled at the ring one more time and then used his hand to stroke Ethan as he dipped down further, forcing Ethan's knees up, and taking the time to taste and enjoy everything he was encountering.

"Jeez, Joel." Ethan clutched at Joel's hair, but then let go, not wanting him to stop. He sunk into the cushions, only moving when Joel prompted him to, allowing him to explore at will. His body tensed in anticipation as Joel started running his tongue in long slow lines back up his shaft, and then moaned in exhilaration as Joel's warm mouth finally took him in.

Joel pulled at him longingly and finished what he'd set out to do, savoring the absolute rush he felt when Ethan's body shuddered to completion. He ran his finger lazily through the fluid on Ethan's stomach and then placed it in his mouth, and watched Ethan's eyes widen as he sucked on it contentedly.

"Holy fuck, babe," Ethan said in disbelief. "Are you sure you haven't done this before?"

"Uh …no. I've thought about it a lot though."

"Really? You've thought about doing this?"

Joel grinned at Ethan and winked, and then drew a swirl across Ethan's stomach and placed his finger back in his mouth.

Ethan continued to watch him, his heart rate accelerating rapidly as Joel removed his finger and slowly ran his tongue across his stomach, tasting more of what he'd sampled.

Joel lifted his head to look at Ethan and licked his lips.

"Ever since that party of yours," Joel said. "When I saw that guy going into your bedroom, and heard what you were doing with him …I haven't been able to stop thinking about you, and what it would be like to take you into my mouth, make you incredibly hard, and have you fuck me all night."

"Jeez, Joel. I had no idea you were looking at me that way."

"It was quite the shocking revelation for me, and I wasn't prepared to act on it, of course, but then we started getting closer, and I began having all these feelings for you. I got really scared."

"What were you afraid of?"

Joel dropped his gaze and laughed. "I was afraid that you wouldn't be interested in someone like me, and that making a move on you would drive you away." He looked back up and caught Ethan's eyes. "Losing you as a friend would've torn me up."

"Babe, I wish you'd said something. And why on earth would you think I wouldn't be interested in you?"

"I don't know. I didn't think I was your type." Joel dropped his finger back onto Ethan's stomach and started drawing small circles, and then repositioned himself to take Ethan's softening cock back into his mouth. He sucked on him gently, savoring the last few drops and then released him. "I guess I was wrong."

"You couldn't have been more wrong. You're perfect."

Joel climbed off Ethan and dropped down into the corner of the sofa. "Are you sure we have to wait? We've pretty much crossed the line already tonight."

"We can wait. It's only a few more days until your birthday." Ethan sat up and loosely covered himself with the kimono. "You know, I was really scared too."

"That I wouldn't be interested in you?"

"That you wouldn't come back to me." Ethan lowered his head, clinging to the realization that Joel *had* come back.

"Ethan, there were so many times I wanted to abandon everything and run over here, but I couldn't do that until I knew Erica and Sam were going to be all right."

"I know." Ethan sighed, wanting to change the subject to something else. "It's interesting. What you were saying earlier." He reached for his cigarettes and lit one. "I hadn't really considered that you'd want to bottom."

"Why is that?"

"It isn't for everyone, and from everything you've told me about yours and Erica's relationship, you seem like a fairly comfortable top to me."

"You like it, don't you?" Joel smirked. "It sure sounded like you liked it when that guy was fucking you ...Harder! Harder!"

Ethan leaned forward and smacked Joel in the head.

"Yeah, I actually prefer it," Ethan said, "but I'm versatile, so we'll go with whatever works best for you." He passed the cigarette to Joel and chewed lightly on his thumbnail. "We don't have to do anything, you know? I know plenty of guys that don't go in for any of it." He caught Joel's gaze.

"If you don't like it, we'll find something else. Or nothing. It doesn't matter."

"I'm not much of a *nothing* guy." Joel enjoyed the cigarette for a few seconds before passing it back, and then reclined into the cushions and closed his eyes. "Ethan?"

"Yeah, babe."

"I think I might be gay."

Ethan snorted loudly, making Joel sit up and open his eyes. "What could possibly have given you that idea?"

"I'm serious," replied Joel.

"I'm sorry. Go ahead. Why do you think that?"

"Well, it could just be that you're fucking hot, but the thought of getting my hands on you turns me on something fierce."

"Mm …I'm flattered." Ethan handed the cigarette back to Joel, so he could lift Joel's feet into his lap where he started rubbing them. "Are you still interested in having sex with Erica?"

"God, no. I haven't touched her in ages." Joel wiggled his toes and stretched his feet out as Ethan worked on them. "Does that mean I'm gay?" He struggled momentarily when Ethan playfully ran his finger up the bottom of his foot.

Ethan just smiled and went back to massaging Joel's feet.

"Ethan?" Joel prompted.

"I'm thinking. Give me a second." Ethan pursed his lips and paused, deep in thought. "I don't think there's any set criteria in determining whether or not you're queer."

"That's not very helpful."

Ethan creased up briefly and then started in on Joel's feet again.

"But if you're attracted to guys," he said. "And you feel more inclined to pursue an intimate and meaningful relationship with a guy. And that there, that's the important bit. A meaningful relationship. Then it might be something you should consider. If labels are important to you." He ran his hands further up Joel's legs. "Labels can be a dangerous thing though. That's why I don't go around telling people I'm queer."

"I don't fully understand why you do that."

"First of all, it's none of anyone's business who I choose to fuck, love, and spend my life with. Secondly, people tend to have preconceived notions about what a gay man should look like, and how they should behave. And when someone doesn't fit their criteria, like me, then that someone becomes an unknown entity and people start feeling threatened. And that's when things can become dangerous. Even for someone like me."

"But let's say labels are important to me," Joel replied. "And I'm not saying that they are. How do I know for sure?"

"Joel, you're killing me."

"This is important to me, Ethan."

"All right, I'm sorry. I haven't thought about this stuff in ages." Ethan scrubbed his face, thinking. "Aside from the attraction and the relationship aspect …I believe that a person needs to think about how they want to present themselves to the world, and that doesn't necessarily mean in a public, screaming at the sky, kind of way."

"So, taking on the label is something I decide based on how I see myself living my life?" Joel tapped his chin, deep in thought. "The truth of what I understand about myself and how I want to relate to others, and how I want others to relate to me."

"That works."

"I'll have to give it more thought."

"I wouldn't expect anything less from you." Ethan lifted Joel's foot up and kissed his toes, making Joel squeal.

Joel caught his breath. "I want you to pierce something."

Ethan pulled himself off the sofa, tied the kimono closed, and reached for his cigarettes, tucking them neatly in his pocket along with his lighter. "Why would you want me to do that?"

"Because it'll connect us visually. And emotionally. I know how important piercing and tattooing is to you, and I want to share that part of your life with you."

"You're too good to be true sometimes." Ethan motioned for Joel to follow him down the hall to the studio, and then flicked on the light and grabbed a towel off one of the shelving units. He used it to wipe his stomach clean then dropped it in the laundry, and directed Joel into the chair.

"So, what am I piercing?" he asked.

Joel sat quietly and breathed through the pain as Ethan worked. The plan was to come back every few days until he had everything he wanted, or more precisely, everything he wanted to start with.

He opened his eyes as he felt Ethan move away.

"Are you done?" he asked.

"Yeah, here." Ethan handed him a mirror and watched as Joel examined the two eyebrow piercings and the circular barbell hanging from his septum.

"I love it."

"Erica is going to freak when she sees you."

"I don't care." Joel handed the mirror back and pulled his shirt off over his head, exposing his chest. "These will hurt the worst?"

"Possibly. Everyone is different. Rings or barbells?"

"Um …rings, I guess."

The pain of the nipple piercings definitely cleared Joel's head as the surge of endorphins flooded his system. He laid his head back after Ethan finished and took a minute to catch his breath and collect his thoughts. "That was definitely an experience."

Ethan pulled his gloves off and threw them in the garbage. "You look awful cute." He playfully flicked one of Joel's nipple rings. "Aftercare instructions. Here." He handed Joel a few pamphlets and then lingered, running his hand down Joel's chest and across his stomach. He closed his eyes and cleared his throat before removing his hand. "I'm going to say goodnight now."

Joel reached down and undid the buttons of his jeans while keeping steady eye contact with Ethan. He lifted Ethan's hand and tucked it into the front of his pants. "But it's almost morning, and I need help getting up." He snorted when Ethan laughed aloud and then grabbed Ethan's kimono to pull him closer.

"You're a fuckin' lunatic, babe." Ethan kissed Joel with full-on aggression, grabbed hold of Joel's jeans, and hauled them off his hips.

Joel struggled out of the piercing chair and attempted to redo the buttons of his jeans, but gave up. He leaned against the door and yawned. "I'll come by sometime later tonight."

Ethan crossed his arms in thought and rubbed his chin. "Are you sure you want a pink heart on your ass?"

"Yes, I do. You said you wouldn't question what I wanted."

"I'm not questioning it. I think it's adorable. But I'm wondering if your wife is going to figure out what we're up to."

"No, she'll just think I've cracked up." Joel laughed and made a crazy person face at Ethan and reached out for him.

Ethan pulled Joel into his arms and did his best to support him.

"You need to get some sleep," he said.

"I'd sleep better if I was with you."

"Not yet, babe." Ethan brushed his hand through Joel's hair and held his head to his chest. "I love you, so much. But you have to be patient. We'll be together soon, all right?"

Joel scratched at his face and stepped away. He gripped the handle of the door and reluctantly turned it. "Say it again."

Ethan smiled at Joel and wrapped his arms tight around his own body, not wanting to see him go. "I love you."

Joel hummed happily, as he closed the door after himself, then slowly made his way back to his house. He let himself into the sound of silence and breathed a sigh of relief.

The sun was starting to come up, providing him with just enough light to find his way over to the bed. He pulled his pants off and threw them on a chair, and contemplated leaving his shirt on, but it was already irritating the piercings, so he pulled it off.

He carefully climbed into bed, so as not to wake Erica, but she immediately stirred.

"Where have you been?" Erica rolled over and tucked into Joel's shoulder. "I was starting to worry."

"I was just blowing off a little steam at Ethan's." Joel looked at Erica, laid his head down on his pillow, and licked his lips; he could still taste Ethan on them. This was so, so wrong.

He tried to get comfortable, but his breath literally left his body when Erica ran her hand across his stomach.

Then all the air appeared to leave the room at the exact moment she made contact with one of the rings.

"What the hell is this?" Erica rolled over and flicked the lights on. "Blowing off steam! This is blowing off steam?" She looked at Joel's chest and then moved up to his face. "Oh, for fuck's sake, Joel! What the hell were you two up to? Were you drinking?"

She touched his eyebrows and then lifted up the ring hanging from his nose. "These have to go. Especially this one. You look like a bloody water buffalo."

"I'm not getting rid of them, and Ethan and I have planned out a lot more over the next few weeks."

"So, all of a sudden, you're hanging out with Ethan again?"

"I told you I was only taking a break from him until the baby was born. You needed me, and I wanted to be there for you."

"I still need you."

"It's not the same, and you know it."

Erica threw the covers off and pulled herself out of bed. "Fine, but you look ridiculous. You look like Ethan."

"I happen to like the way Ethan looks."

"Well, maybe you should've married him instead."

Erica chucked a pillow at Joel's head and stormed off to the bathroom to get a shower.

Joel tucked the pillow behind his head and closed his eyes. She had no idea just how much truth was in that statement.

Ethan was tidying up the dinner dishes when Joel arrived in his kitchen that evening and stepped up behind him at the sink. He shivered as Joel's arms wrapped around his waist. And the gentle kisses Joel began laying across his back set his heart beating so fast he could barely pull his mind together.

"It's not often I see you doing dishes," Joel said as he ran his hands up under Ethan's shirt and across his chest. He pulled Ethan closer and began to breathe heavily as he caressed him.

Ethan leaned into Joel, shuddering as Joel pushed up behind him and started to thrust his hips, making his own need surge.

"Fuck, Joel, you need to slow it down." Ethan reached back for Joel and dropped his head back against Joel's shoulder. "I had to cook for Sophie tonight."

"Did you now?" Joel reached down across Ethan's hip and gripped the front of his jeans, caressing and pulling him tighter to his body. "And why would you have to do that?"

Ethan stopped Joel's probing hand and smiled. "Apparently, we made a mess ...on the sofa."

Joel snorted loudly. "No way!"

"Sometimes, I feel like I'm ten again." Ethan smirked and tossed his towel onto the counter. "I figured I owed her dinner at least."

"You should've called me. I could've helped." Joel bit playfully at Ethan's shoulder blade and then moved his hand to grab at Ethan's ass. "How was the rest of your day?"

"I couldn't sleep. I kept thinking about you." Ethan turned to face Joel and kissed him softly, holding him tight.

"Then let me stay with you tonight."

"Joel, I know it's hard to believe, but I'm really trying to draw a line for myself." He brushed his fingers over Joel's lips. "But the things I'd like to do to you ..."

"Tell me—" Joel grabbed Ethan's hand and led him over to the den, pulling him down onto the sofa beside him. "I want you to tell me exactly what you're going to do to me."

Ethan smiled deviously, leaned in close to Joel's ear, and whispered things that had Joel struggling to sit still. He held

Joel in place and continued telling him all the places he would like to explore, and what he'd like to be doing there.

He sighed, content, when Joel quivered with desire and finished by kissing him on the ear.

"So," Ethan said, "is it a date on your eighteenth birthday?" He released Joel and stood up, and laughed uproariously as Joel fell over on the sofa and rolled onto the floor.

"Oh, my god! Kill me now." Joel stretched himself out on the floor, and closed his eyes, willing his heart rate to calm down. "Just give me a minute. I'll meet you in the studio."

Ethan made his way down the hall and stepped into the studio. He sat down on the edge of the table and dropped his head into his hands, and waited for his own heart rate to return to normal.

Joel wasn't making it easy to resist him. The thought of ravaging Joel's body was all he could think about ...but not yet.

Resigned, Ethan got up and busied himself over at the counter putting together the supplies they would need for tonight's session. In addition to the tattoo, they would potentially be doing a tongue piercing, depending on how Joel was feeling about it.

He was assembling the last of his equipment when Joel let himself into the room.

"Hiya, babe. All better?" Ethan asked Joel.

"I don't know how much longer I can do this."

"Two more days, that's it." Ethan laid a towel down on the table and slipped on a pair of gloves. "Maybe this isn't the best place to be tattooing tonight, given its prominent role in my story."

"I thought you were a professional—" Joel undid the buttons of his pants and let them fall to the floor, leaving himself nude from the waist down. He was still sporting a reasonably firm erection.

"Fuckin' hell," Ethan whispered under his breath, then motioned for Joel to lay face down on the table. "Don't you wear underwear when you leave the house?"

"Generally, yes. But tonight …just for you—no."

"Couldn't you have waited a few more minutes until you were back to normal at least? You almost stopped my fuckin' heart."

"I was anxious to get started." Joel smiled to himself as he rested his head down on his hands and waited for Ethan to start. Taunting and teasing Ethan was proving to be more fun than he'd anticipated.

Ethan laid his hand on Joel's ass to begin the tattoo, but paused for a second, and then set the gun down. He stood, leaned over, and kissed the base of Joel's spine—and lingered.

Feeling defeated, he pushed Joel's shirt up and continued a line with his lips all the way up to Joel's neck, and then collapsed on top of him, breathing heavy, as he fought to regain his composure.

"How are you doing back there?" Joel laughed. "I was kind of hoping to get a tattoo tonight. But if you'd rather take a nap on me, that's all right too."

"You ambushed me. I'm getting to it." Ethan ran his mouth back down along Joel's spine, and then bit lightly at his ass before sitting back in his chair. "All right, one pink heart coming right up."

Ethan worked most of the heart freehand and had just begun to fill in the color when Joel stopped him with a surprising request. He finished the tattoo, grabbed his black light, and turned the lights off to show Joel the result. As long as Erica didn't invest in a black light for the bedroom any time soon, she would never know that it said *Joel + Ethan* in the big pink heart on her husband's ass.

"That is so cool," Joel said.

"It's pretty cute all right." Ethan pulled his gloves off and kissed the skin just above the tattoo. "You're a bit of a romantic in your own bizarre and twisted way."

"Only for you, baby." Joel rolled onto his side, took Ethan's hand, and ran it up along his thigh, over his waist, and across his chest. Then he sunk onto his back and cringed, swearing, as the fresh tattoo hit the table.

"Yeah," Ethan said. "You might want to stay off your ass for a bit." He helped Joel roll back onto his stomach and reached over to turn one small light back on. "Close your eyes and relax."

Ethan lifted Joel's shirt off, tossed it to one side, and swept down Joel's legs to remove his socks. He stood, staring at Joel's naked body for a second, trying to take in all the little curves and indents. He blinked and closed his eyes, exhaling through his nose. This was an impossible situation. He didn't officially work for the school and doubted anyone would actually call him on it, legally speaking, but the program would end up being scrapped.

He brushed his hand across Joel's ass. Surely, he could control his impulses for two more days; he wasn't some kind of sex addict. But he loved Joel so much. Making love to him was all he'd been thinking about since Joel had shown up at his door last night.

"Ethan?"

"Yeah, sorry. I was thinking." Ethan started at Joel's shoulders, using his hands to relax the muscles there, and slowly worked his way down Joel's entire body, being careful not to brush across the tattoo.

Joel moaned in exhilaration as Ethan moved along, his muscles being soothed beyond anything he'd ever experienced before. He sighed in resignation when Ethan's hands completed their trip all the way down his body to his feet.

"That felt amazing." Joel opened his eyes and was about to get up when Ethan pressed him back down. He waited out the long pause and listened to Ethan's breathing, then shivered as Ethan's tongue licked a long line from his shoulders all the way down to his ass.

As Ethan's warm tongue graced the skin between his thighs, Joel's heart began to beat out of control, realizing what was happening. Then Ethan's hands assisted in its quest, separating the tight rounds of his ass. His breath escaped in short, shallow gasps, and his mind swam unsuccessfully to provide him with any experience that could match what he was feeling.

"Fuck ...Ethan ...don't stop," escaped his lips.

Joel was only coming to terms with those sensations when he hesitantly pulled himself up onto his knees at

Ethan's urging. His body quaking with uncertainty, anticipating what was about to happen. He dropped his head forward in shock and couldn't contain the sounds erupting from deep within him. The overwhelming surge of energy elicited by the actions of Ethan's probing tongue coursed through his body and had him grasping desperately to the edge of the table.

Ethan finally relented and playfully bit Joel's ass.

"How are you doing?" he asked.

"Honestly? I had no idea it would be so sensitive back there."

"Mm ...so, if I was to do this—" Ethan sucked on one of his fingers and slowly slipped it in, in place of his tongue.

Joel gasped and clenched, almost pulling away.

"Fucking hell ...," he whispered.

"Joel, do you want me to stop? Is this too much for you?"

"No. Fuck, no." Joel exhaled and held his breath. Then dropped his head and braced himself as Ethan continued the pressure, and began a slow, steady rhythm. He groaned as intense feelings of need began building within him, and was relieved when Ethan reached through and started stroking his cock, but just about fell off the table when Ethan added another finger. The feelings built quickly after that and within minutes, he was collapsing onto the table in complete and shattering fulfillment. He lay still for a second, trying to catch his breath, and sighed with contentment when Ethan whispered in his ear.

"How are you doing now?" asked Ethan.

"That felt fucking amazing."

"For a second there, I thought I'd crossed the line."

"I'd like to see you try."

"Mm …now that's an interesting bit of information."

Joel shrieked and snorted, squirming when Ethan ran a finger down his spine and then left him to wash his hands.

He wasn't sure what to do with himself after that, so he stretched out on the table. He was still in shock from the depth of the sensations he'd experienced pulsing through his body. Hearing Ethan come back into the room, Joel turned his head to look at him.

"Is it always like that?" he asked.

Ethan grinned at Joel, grabbed a fresh towel off the rack, and passed it to him. "That was nothing. Judging by how readily you responded to that, I think you'll find your experiences with me are going to be intense. And I'm not saying that to brag. Although I've been told I'm pretty damn skilled."

Joel reached out and grabbed one of Ethan's nipples through his shirt, pulling him down to kiss him. "That sounds a lot like bragging."

He held fast and studied Ethan's face, motioning for him to stick his tongue out. Ethan tried not to laugh as Joel fingered the piercing in it. "I want you to do my tongue."

"Are you going to be able to sit still on that fresh tattoo of yours, because if I'm not extremely careful about placement, I can cause a lot of bleeding, maybe even nerve damage?"

"No, I'm good," Joel said, and rolled off the table, using the towel to clean up before swinging into the piercing chair.

"All right, I'm not going to complain. It'll certainly add a positive aspect to your future tongue action on me." Ethan winked when Joel smiled at him. "Now, this is going to hurt, but you need to stay perfectly still. And I mean it. You can't move."

"Got it. No moving."

Ethan gathered up his equipment and threw on a fresh pair of gloves. He worked as quickly as he could, and Joel only flinched a tiny bit, so within seconds he'd finished.

"So ...how does ...oh, fuck," Joel said.

"Just take it easy with what you're eating over the next couple of days. The barbell I put in should be sufficient for any swelling. If you think anything weird is happening, come see me."

Ethan kissed Joel, and shivered exquisitely with desire, thinking of where his lips and tongue had been just moments before.

"You were very brave, my sweet babe," he said.

Joel laughed to himself and drew Ethan into his arms. He kissed his cheek, and then went to collect his clothes and put them back on.

Winking at Ethan, Joel indicated with his hands that he would text him later, then let himself out, and headed for home.

Erica was still up when Joel arrived back.

"Hey, where were you?" she asked. "Were you at Ethan's again?" She rocked Sam as she moved toward him. "I thought I asked you not to go over there again tonight."

Joel just shook his head, not wanting to speak, and wishing he hadn't headed home so soon.

He visibly cringed when a look of realization crossed Erica's face.

"Why Joel?" Erica asked. "Why are you doing this to yourself?"

"I'm sorry." Joel swallowed slowly. His tongue wasn't hurting nearly as much as it had been a few minutes ago. "I was just having a bit of fun with Ethan."

"That is not normal fun, Joel."

"Well, that's good. Because Ethan and I aren't normal guys." Joel followed Erica into Sam's bedroom and stood by while she continued rocking him to sleep. "We enjoy doing our own thing."

"I don't understand it. What is it about Ethan that fascinates you so much?" Erica turned to face Joel after she lay Sam down in his crib, and led him from the room. "You become a different person whenever you hang out with him."

"I become myself when I hang out with him."

"Rubbish. This isn't you. This is you trying to be like him." Erica climbed into bed and pulled the covers up over her shoulders. "And I don't like Ethan, so that's not going to work in your favor."

Joel climbed into bed beside Erica and closed his eyes, his stomach twisting as he listened to her complaining endlessly about Ethan and his bad influence on him, detailing the changes in Joel's behavior every time he hung out with Ethan.

Then she suggested it might be beneficial to limit his exposure to Ethan, in the interest of their son's development.

Shuddering silently, Joel fought to stop the pain, but his desperation was undeniable. He couldn't do this. He couldn't sleep in a bed with Erica any longer.

He moved away when Erica pushed back to tuck in against him.

"I'm not tired," Joel said placing his hand on her back. "I think I'm going to sleep on the sofa, so I don't keep you awake."

"Can you check on Sam later?"

"Sure." Joel pulled away further when Erica turned to face him. The thought of her wanting to kiss him made his stomach churn.

"I'm going for a run in the morning," he said. "Give me a call if you wake up and I'm not here, and you need help with Sam."

Erica smiled at him and patted his face affectionately.

"I'll see you in the morning," she said. "Love you."

"Yeah, I'll see you later."

Joel scurried out of bed and pulled his clothes back on. But before he left the room, he stopped in the doorway and looked back at Erica.

He didn't belong here anymore.

Joel breathed a sigh of relief as he closed the front door behind him, then he leaned against it, lit up a cigarette, and analyzed the emotional justification for what he was contemplating, and how it would affect all of their lives.

He walked over to Ethan's house and just stood outside the front door for a few minutes, brushing his hand hesitantly along the door handle. He'd never been so nervous about anything in his entire life.

Taking a deep breath, he let himself in using the key Ethan had given him, and slipped his shoes off, locked the door, and quietly climbed the stairs to Ethan's bedroom.

Pushing the bedroom door open, Joel slowed, listening to the sound of Ethan sleeping.

This was definitely where he wanted to be.

He closed the door behind him, and made his way over to the bed where he crushed out his cigarette and watched Ethan's tranquil form taking in and expelling one breath after another with such serenity, it made his heart ache.

Joel undressed, pulled the covers back, and climbed in as carefully as he could. He wanted to spend as much time as possible nestled up against Ethan before he woke up and potentially threw him out.

He rolled onto his side and shuffled over so his head was tucked into Ethan's shoulder, and then he draped his arm across Ethan's chest. The feel of Ethan's warm body against his and the sound of him breathing beside him brought Joel the sense of peace he'd been seeking when he left his house.

He held his breath when Ethan shifted and tried to roll over.

"Joel?" Ethan sat straight up and looked down at Joel staring sheepishly up at him. "What are you doing here?"

"I couldn't sleep. My wife snores."

"Hm …" Ethan gave Joel a skeptical look. "She's not going to come looking for you, is she?"

"I locked the door."

Ethan smiled at him and lay back down on his pillow. He settled in and pulled Joel into his arms. "You shouldn't be here."

"This is exactly where I should be."

Ethan turned Joel's face up to his and kissed him, then pulled him closer, soaking in the feeling of Joel's bare skin pressed up against his. "God, you feel so good."

Joel tucked his head into Ethan's chest and fought to control his emotions, but his body began to shake, despite his efforts.

"Hey," Ethan said. "What's wrong?"

"I can't stand living like this anymore. With you over here and me next door. I need to be with you." Joel's body heaved as he tried to catch his breath. "I know we talked about waiting until a month after my birthday, but I can't do it, Ethan. I can't. I love you too much. I don't want to be without you for another minute."

Ethan felt his heart race and soar as Joel uttered the declaration of love he'd been longing to hear. He pulled Joel closer and clung to him.

"I love you too, babe. We'll figure something out. I promise."

Joel tucked himself tight against Ethan's chest, breathing in the comforting scent of his skin, and brushed his hand across Ethan's stomach, settled in, and contentedly drifted off to sleep, knowing that the man he loved, who loved him as well, was going to be there for him.

Because he had no intention of ever leaving his side again.

Joel's phone started ringing incessantly, and after what seemed like the tenth consecutive call, he finally decided to roll over and check who it was. He looked at the display and saw it was his sister, Jocelyn, which was weird because she never phoned him.

"Where the hell are you?" Jocelyn asked when he answered it.

"I'm sleeping." Joel looked around and realized he was still at Ethan's. He'd intended on setting the alarm on his phone so he could get back to the house to grab some of his things before Erica woke up, but he'd fallen asleep in Ethan's arms before he'd even had a chance to consider it.

"You're not in your bed," Jocelyn said with a hint of righteousness in her voice. "Whose bed are you in exactly?"

"Who says I'm in anyone's bed." Joel rolled over and pushed Ethan with his foot.

"What?" Ethan grunted, completely disoriented.

"Who was that?" Jocelyn asked. "That sounded like Ethan."

"That's because it was Ethan." Joel switched the phone to his other ear. "I crashed at his place last night …just a second." He held the phone out to check the time.

"Why did you kick me?" Ethan asked and rubbed his eyes.

"Because it's time to get up." Joel brought the phone back to his ear. "Is Erica looking for me?"

"She thinks you're out running for some reason."

"What time is it?" Ethan climbed out of bed and headed to the bathroom. "Are we going to be late for school?"

"No, we're good for time," Joel replied. "Just grab a shower, and I'll get Sophie started on some breakfast." He turned his attention back to Jocelyn. "Sorry …Ethan is not a morning person. I had to get him moving."

"I heard you and Erica arguing last night."

"Is that why you're calling me?"

"Yeah, I was afraid you'd taken off to some girl's house."

"No, I'm just at Ethan's." Joel walked into the bathroom and started looking for a spare toothbrush. Sophie always kept a supply of extra personal items in each bathroom.

"Are you coming home to get ready for school?"

"No, I'll grab a shower here." Joel found the toothbrushes and selected one along with a fresh razor and some shaving foam. "Could you tell Erica I'll meet her at school?"

"Hey, are you having a shower?" Ethan asked from inside the shower stall. He turned off the water and opened the door.

"I'll be there in a second," Joel said, and then turned his attention back to Jocelyn. "Can you let her know?"

"Yeah, sure," Jocelyn replied.

Then she flipped her phone closed and sat down on the end of her bed. Something Joel had said wasn't sitting well with her. She'd had her suspicions for a while, but her brother had just inadvertently confirmed them when he'd answered Ethan about the shower—that he would *be there in a second*, presumably to join him.

Ethan leaned against the lockers, spitting little paper balls through a straw at what few people were walking the halls during class time while Joel attempted to dig his chemistry textbook out from underneath a pile of other books. They'd spent a long time in the shower together and had arrived at school extremely late, so they'd decided to sit out first block. The bell for the first break was about to ring, but they still had a few minutes.

"Do you need any help?" Ethan asked as he stuffed the straw into his pocket and crouched down beside Joel. He looked up, caught Joel's eye, and winked at him. "Last night was amazing, babe."

Joel checked over his shoulder. "Which part was amazing? The falling asleep together part? The waking up together part? Or the part where I told you I loved you?"

"Definitely the waking up part. I like a good kick in the ass in the morning." Ethan laughed and slid onto the floor. "No, seriously." He stroked Joel's arm then lit up a cigarette. "When you told me you loved me. That was the most amazing part."

"I know it was a long time coming, but I wanted to be sure before I said anything. I really do love you. A lot."

"Babe, you couldn't have made me happier."

"We'll just have to see about that." Joel sat down beside Ethan and took the cigarette from him. "I'm feeling pretty content right now. And then that bell is going to ring. And this lovely feeling is going to go away. And I'm going to be forced back to reality."

"I think we could have some fun before that happens." Ethan pulled out another cigarette for himself, lit it, and stuck his legs straight out into the hallway as the bell rang. His legs were so long, it was going to make it difficult for anyone to get around him.

Joel laughed and took another drag off his cigarette, and as people spilled out of the classrooms, they immediately spotted Ethan and tried to find another way to meet up with their friends that didn't involve stepping over his legs. A few people, however, stopped and stared for a minute when they spotted Joel sitting beside him. When Joel had left school on Friday afternoon, he'd been wearing cream-colored chino pants, a pale yellow button-down shirt, and loafers. Now, he was sprawled out in the hallway, smoking a cigarette, dressed all in black, his eyes rimmed in black eyeliner, and most shocking, sporting a multitude of piercings.

Max had met up with Ryan in the hallway, headed toward Joel's locker to check if Joel's stuff was there because he hadn't shown up in the first block of chemistry. They were wondering what had happened to him, especially since Erica hadn't seen him either, and he wasn't answering his phone or any of the texts they'd been sending him. They rounded the last corner and came to a jarring stop.

"What the fuck?" Max said. "Is that Joel?"

"Yeah," Ryan replied, his response drawn out in disbelief.

"Could you stay back here for a minute," he said to Max, "while I talk to him? And if you see Erica, try to keep her away."

"Why? What's going on?"

"I'm not sure, yet. Just stay here."

Ryan strode down the hall and sank onto the floor beside Joel.

"I was going to ask what you did this weekend," he said, "but I think I can probably guess."

"Yeah, Ethan and I were goofing around," said Joel.

"By sticking holes in your face."

"Pretty much. My tongue too." Joel stuck his tongue out for Ryan to see. "And my nipples. And I got a tattoo on my ass."

"That's great, Joel. I'm sensing an Ethan Cooke 'Borg'esque weekend …but did that need to include his clothing and makeup?"

"I stayed with Ethan last night, so I raided his closet this morning. Some of his stuff actually fits me."

"You stayed *with* Ethan last night?" Ryan scrubbed his face with his hand. "So, you guys are back together." He shook his head. "Why am I not surprised."

Joel crushed out his cigarette on the floor and looked over at Ethan, who nodded at him. "We're going to take off for a little bit."

"What do you mean, take off?" Ryan asked.

"Joel's birthday is tomorrow," Ethan said. "So, we're going to head out for the rest of the week and spend some time together celebrating. Without the confines of our current situation."

"I'm going to tell Erica that I'm attending a prospective, environmental student conference in Vancouver," Joel said as he looked up and down the hall, watching for her. The bell had rung, signaling the end of break, and he could see Max standing halfway down the hall, looking very confused, but staying put.

"We need you to back up Joel's story," said Ethan.

"You want me to lie to Erica?" Ryan crossed his arms and exhaled in frustration. "Why are you doing this Joel?" He looked down the hall at Max and waved him away, indicating he would text him later.

Max reluctantly wandered off to class.

"Because I want to be with him," Joel said as he gazed in Ethan's direction. "We had a long talk in the shower this morning, and we've decided to move forward a bit earlier than planned." He looked up at Ryan. "When we get back, I'll be asking Erica for a divorce, and then Ethan and I will be coming out as a couple. We just need some time to clear our heads and prepare for that."

"You're actually going to throw away your marriage …for Ethan?" Ryan looked at Joel, who nodded at him. He crashed his head back against the lockers and tried to collect his thoughts. "I don't get it. You've been with Erica for years."

"I know. But it never felt right. I never had that absolute gut-wrenching passion for her. Not like what I have for Ethan." Joel laughed when Ryan looked at him funny. "Not just physically. Emotionally. I'm in love with him so bad, it hurts."

"You're in love with him?" Ryan dropped his head and laughed.

"What's so funny?" asked Ethan.

"I'm sorry," Ryan replied. "I was thinking about all those boyfriend jokes we used to throw at Joel because the two of you fought so much. I guess they were lovers' quarrels after all."

"Yeah," Ethan said. "We had our share of disagreements and break-ups, but not anymore. We're all good now."

"Are you sure this is what you want, Joel?" asked Ryan.

"Yeah, Ethan and I are in this forever, aren't we?" Joel turned to Ethan and watched his eyes take on a different kind of softness.

"God, yeah." Ethan tucked his knees up and held the heels of his hands to his eyes to stop the tears. He turned his head to look at Joel and laughed. "I love you ...so much."

"I love you more," Joel said, and then smiled as Ethan's eyes changed yet again. He winked at him, dropped his gaze shyly, and turned back to Ryan. "Will you help us out?"

Chapter Fifteen

It was late evening by the time they pulled off the gravel road they'd been traveling on for almost an hour. It was off-season in the mountains, so they hadn't passed many cars on the way in, which was fortunate because the road was barely wide enough for the truck that Ethan had rented for the trip.

The entrance was marked by a short distance of log fencing and a large sign suspended from two trees. Joel directed Ethan to park the truck off to one side in front of a large chalet built entirely from logs, and then proceeded to jump out of the vehicle.

"I'll come with you to check-in," Joel said. "Mr. Cartwright and I go way back. My family has been coming here every summer since I was eight." He stopped and took a deep breath." Isn't that smell amazing …the fresh air and the trees mixed with just a little bit of wood smoke?"

"It's peaceful, that's for sure." Ethan followed Joel up the steps and into the office where an older gentleman pulled himself off a chair in the back room and stepped up to the counter, immediately recognizing Joel.

"Joel Carrigan," he said as he peered at Joel. "Look at you all grown up. We missed seeing your family last summer."

"Hey, Mr. Cartwright," replied Joel. "That was my fault. I wasn't too thrilled with the idea of a family vacation."

"Well, you're here now. And who is this you have with you?" Mr. Cartwright adjusted his glasses, then jumped back when Ethan approached the desk. He'd been so focused on Joel that he hadn't really noticed Ethan standing in the shadows by the door.

"This is my friend, Ethan Cooke," Joel said. "He'll be putting the cabin on his card." He took the credit card from Ethan and handed it over. "He's from London, England. I thought he'd enjoy a taste of Canadian wilderness. And what better place than here."

"Right. What better place indeed?" Mr. Cartwright said as he opened the registration book and turned it toward Joel. "I just need you to sign in, and then I'll meet you down at your cabin." He scanned the registration. "You've requested the Elk Cabin. Beautiful view of the lake this time of year." He ran the credit card through and waited for Joel to finish, and then closed the book.

"We'll meet you down there," Joel said, and led Ethan back to the truck, and climbed into the passenger seat. "We have to head down this road over here." He pointed out to Ethan what looked like a sheer drop off amongst a clump of large trees.

"That looks really steep," Ethan said as he maneuvered the truck around some trees and headed down the hill.

"That's why I wanted a four-wheel drive vehicle. All it would take is a bit of rain, and we'd be trapped down here for days." Joel practically stood up and peered over the dash, directing Ethan around huge potholes in the long dirt road.

Safely arriving at the bottom, Joel pointed the way along the edge of the small lake to a clearing close to their cabin.

"I'm going to let you drive this beast next time," Ethan said. "It doesn't handle anything like my car." He jumped out and followed Joel around a clump of young trees.

The Elk cabin was tucked into the tree line and appeared to have sprung forth from it, with its stone path and roughly hewn log exterior. It was situated in such a way as to catch the morning sun on its front porch, as it came up over the lake.

Ethan ran his hands along the smooth surface of the logs as they made their way up the front steps, marveling at their warmth as if they still contained life somehow. He stopped short as Mr. Cartwright hurried past him to open the door.

"All right," Mr. Cartwright said as he stepped into the main room and turned to face them. "You've got your fridge and stove over there." He pointed to one side of the room where a tiny sink, stove, and fridge lined one wall underneath a large window. "You've got your woodstove over there." He pointed to the other side of the room where a wood stove was already blazing. "It's still gets pretty cold here in the mountains at night, and that fire is your only source of heat, so keep it well stoked. Joel, do you remember where the wood is stored?"

"Across the field," Joel replied. "I know where it is."

"Good. Now there's one bedroom on this floor with a double. You boys will have to flip for it. And then the other beds are in the loft area up this ladder."

"Same rules as usual?" asked Joel, trying to appear completely nonchalant, while in reality, his heart was racing with anticipation.

"The rules are on the back of the front door there, but since you have a family staying next door, I will emphasize a couple of them. No noise after eleven at night or before seven in the morning, and no parties …I don't want to be called down here, because you boys have drunken girls running around half naked in your cabin."

"We're just here for the peace and quiet," Joel said as he checked the temperature of the fridge.

"And no smoking inside," Mr. Cartwright said. He'd just noticed the cigarette tucked behind Ethan's ear. "I'll leave you to unpack. Give me a holler if you need anything." Then he quickly exited the cabin and closed the door.

"So, what do you think?" Joel asked Ethan.

"It's really romantic." Ethan squatted down in front of the fire and held his hands up to the heat. "All the earthy smells and the woodstove …it's got a primal appeal."

He stood and turned back around to face Joel.

Joel grinned at him.

"I call dibs on the double bed!" Joel shouted as he made a leap for the bedroom, but didn't quite manage to make it before Ethan pounced through and onto the bed ahead of him.

Joel immediately dropped down on top of Ethan and attacked his mouth.

Ethan basked in Joel's ardent need, and then reluctantly rolled him onto his back, and sat up on the edge of the bed and stretched out his shoulders. "Before we get all cozy, my survival skills are telling me we need to bring our stuff in and get dinner started."

"Ever practical, aren't you?" Joel replied.

"No, I'm trying to stick to my word, and lounging around in bed with you is not going help me do that.

"Fine." Joel shuffled over and lifted himself off the bed. "If you want to bring the food in first, I'll start cooking while you put everything else away." He kissed Ethan on the head, affectionately, and headed out to the main room.

Picking out what to bring for food had been a challenge. Joel knew there were no microwaves in the cabins, and the ovens weren't reliable, so the best option was something that could be cooked stovetop, or on the barbeque that was provided with each cabin. Since it was their first night and it was already late, Joel had decided to make spaghetti. It didn't take long to boil the noodles and heat up the prepared sauce. He'd even put together some makeshift garlic bread with toast and garlic spread by the time Ethan brought in the last of their stuff.

"Looks good, babe," Ethan said as he took a seat at the table. He waited for Joel to sit down and then reached for his hand. "This is nice, sitting down with you like this."

"It is, and if I can manage not to poison us both this week, we'll be golden." Joel winked at him, and then pushed the parmesan cheese his way. "Maybe after dinner, we can take a walk."

Ethan lifted Joel's hand and brought it to his lips. "I would love to go for a walk with you. It's been driving me crazy, not being able to do everyday couple stuff with you."

"Well, we've got all week together." Joel squeezed Ethan's hand. "Let's make the most of it before our lives get crazy."

Ethan studied Joel's face, then released his hand, and dumped a heap of parmesan cheese on his spaghetti. He took the first forkful and watched Joel for a second, trying to gauge his apprehension.

"What are you thinking about?" Joel asked.

Ethan smiled and replied. "I can't believe we're going to go a whole week without alcohol."

"I brought a case of beer."

Joel smirked as Ethan rolled his eyes.

"You better make it up to me." Ethan reached under the table and grabbed Joel's leg, and then ran his hand up and down it.

"I'm planning on it." Joel stopped eating and propped his head on his hand. "I was going to tell you …I finished thinking."

"About what?"

"Labels." Ripping a piece of bread in two, Joel used one side to clean up the sauce on his plate.

Ethan sat back in his chair and studied Joel, trying to figure out where this conversation was going to go.

"And what did you decide?" he asked.

"That I want to interact with the world as a gay man." Joel pushed up out of his chair and brought his plate over to the sink. "I thought about the things we talked about, and then I thought about what's happening between us." He turned back to face Ethan and leaned against the counter. "It would be a strange thing indeed if I were in love with, sleeping with, and spending my life with another man and not label myself as gay, don't you think?"

"That's a very clever deduction, Watson." Ethan grinned at Joel and then lifted his own plate over to the sink. "But not necessarily concise. Tell me …if we were to break up for some reason…"

"Like hell! After what we've been through to be together?"

"Theoretically then," Ethan replied. "If we were to break up, and you were looking to start a new relationship, would you be shopping in the girl store or the boy store?"

"You know how much I hate shopping." Joel grinned. "But if I did find myself in that situation, I wouldn't even be window shopping at the girl store unless there was a really hot guy with an amazing ass working there."

He laughed as Ethan shoved him affectionately.

"All right, my adorable, gay boyfriend." Ethan gazed down at Joel and felt his heart surge. "I believe I was promised a walk."

Joel grabbed their coats and tossed Ethan his. He pushed some more wood into the woodstove and damped it down before following Ethan outside. "The cabin should be nice and toasty by the time we get back."

"I'm glad you know what you're doing with the fire," Ethan said as he reached for Joel's hand. "If it were left up to me, we'd probably freeze to death."

"We'll make a Canadian boy out of you yet," Joel said. "Let's head up toward the main lodge and then follow the road back around past the other cabins. I want to show you where my family usually stays."

He squeezed Ethan's hand.

"And we need to stay close to the buildings at this time of night anyway," he added.

"Why, anyway?" Ethan stopped mid-stride and looked down at Joel. "Babe, please tell me there are no wild animals out here."

"We're in the middle of the fucking forest. Of course, there are wild animals out here." Joel shoved Ethan playfully and gripped his hand tighter. "Don't worry. I'll protect you from the big bad cougars and bears. Actually, it's the deer you have to look out for. Those things can be vicious."

"How the hell would you know if something was sneaking up on us? I can't even see my fuckin' feet. It's pitch-black out here."

Joel pulled sharply on Ethan's hand. "Ethan, stop …look up."

He smiled when he heard Ethan sigh with amazement.

"I've never seen so many stars." Ethan pulled Joel in front of him, pressing Joel's back to his chest, and wrapped his arms around him.

"That is exactly how many stars would be required to express my love for you," he said. "Infinite."

"I don't think my arm is big enough."

"That is the most spectacular thing I've ever seen." Ethan's arms hugged Joel closer to him and kissed the back of Joel's head, as he continued to stare up into the skies.

Joel jumped when he heard gravel crunching behind them, but then relaxed when he realized the light from a flashlight was accompanying it. He pulled Ethan's arms tighter around his body and turned to see who was approaching.

"Hey, Mr. Cartwright," he said.

"I thought I heard voices out here." Mr. Cartwright stepped up beside them and looked up at the stars. "It's a beautiful clear night, isn't it, boys?"

"It's absolutely amazing," Ethan replied. "We don't get to see stars like this back in London."

"There's too much light pollution in a city that size," Mr. Cartwright said. "You need to be out where it's pure to enjoy nature's wonders." He stopped and rubbed his nose. "Joel? You didn't tell me you boys were together."

"Why?" Joel asked hesitantly. "Is that a problem?"

"Heavens, no," Mr. Cartwright said, and then laughed and patted Joel on the head. "I would've told you there's another gay couple staying here. Just up the road there. You can see their bonfire through the trees."

"We weren't really looking to socialize," Ethan said.

"Don't be silly," Mr. Cartwright replied. "They're in their early twenties. Nice couple of boys. I was just heading up there to say goodnight to them before I turned in for the evening."

Then he started walking and motioned for them to follow.

"It's pointless arguing with him," Joel said to Ethan. "He's like a bulldog when he latches on to an idea."

Ethan sighed, gripped Joel's hand, and trudged up the hill after Mr. Cartwright. They turned down a short road that opened up onto a small bonfire area with an assortment of benches and stumps to sit on. On the far side of the fire sat the *nice couple of boys*.

Ethan took a deep breath as Mr. Cartwright began the introductions.

"And this is the nice young couple I was telling you boys about," Mr. Cartwright said. "This is Bruce."

Bruce nodded and then the other man spoke.

"And I'm Seth."

Ethan discreetly rolled his eyes as the two men stood up. They fit the gay stereotype perfectly and were doing their best to play it up.

He doubted those were even their real names.

"Hey," Joel said. "I'm Joel, and this is my boyfriend, Ethan."

He bumped Ethan with his hip in hopes of getting him to behave and sighed in relief when Ethan shook both their hands.

Bruce grabbed a couple of stumps and rolled them over so Joel and Ethan would have somewhere to sit.

"I'm off," Mr. Cartwright said as he headed out onto the road. "I'll see all you boys tomorrow."

"Night, Mr. Cartwright," Joel said.

"Can I get either of you a drink?" Seth asked as he studied the two men in front of him, and tried to figure out their story.

"No, we're trying to—" Joel replied, but was interrupted by Ethan scrambling to his feet. "What's wrong?"

"I thought I saw something in the bushes," answered Ethan.

"Ethan, relax," Joel said. "If we stay near the fire, we won't get eaten by anything, I promise."

Ethan sat back down but didn't take his eyes off the bushes at the edge of the bonfire. "Is it all right if I have a beer?"

"Sure thing," Seth said as he rifled through the cooler behind him.

He stopped when Bruce tapped him on the shoulder.

"He wasn't asking you," Bruce said in a whisper.

Seth swung back around so he could watch the interaction between the most unlikely couple he'd ever laid eyes on.

"Sure, you can have a beer," Joel said. "As long as you're all right with having to pee in the potentially occupied bushes." He reached for Ethan's hand and bumped him softly with his shoulder.

"No fuckin' way," Ethan said as he wrapped his arm around Joel's shoulders. "I'm likely to get one of my fuckin' piercings stuck on a twig or something. I'd be like a sitting duck."

He laughed, picturing it.

"Can you imagine?" he added, snorting.

"Yes, it was a sad day in news today," Joel announced while trying to keep a straight face. "Ethan Cooke was left to fend for himself in the Canadian wilderness last night after accidentally being tethered to a bush by his dick. His only weapons for survival against the wild animals ...a lighter, a spike from his jacket, and a couple of fags." He gasped and snorted, and then burst out laughing.

Bruce and Seth just stared at them.

"You're a fuckin' lunatic, babe," Ethan said as he held him closer. "One of the many reasons I love you."

"I love you too." Joel kissed Ethan with intense longing, and then wiped the moisture from his lips.

"So," Seth said. "How long have you two been together?"

"Just five months, sort of," Joel said. "We've been friends since last summer though." He tucked his hands up between his knees and tried to look interested. "What about you two?"

"We're actually here for our anniversary," Bruce replied enthusiastically. "We've been married two years now."

"Hey, congratulations," Joel said.

Seth sat back and crossed his arms, and stared at Ethan. "I'm sure I've seen you before somewhere."

"Do you spend a lot of time in Vancouver?" Ethan asked.

"Yeah, that's where we live," Bruce replied. "Do you frequent the clubs?" He paused and shook his finger at Ethan. "That's where we've seen you. You don't exactly blend in."

"I used to work the clubs," Ethan said, and then grinned as he realized that was going to sound salacious.

"Excuse me?" Seth said and laughed.

"For the police," Ethan added. "There were a couple of guys I used to keep an eye on for the drug squad."

"You're older than you look," Seth said. "I could've sworn you were both in high school."

"Well …on that note," Joel said as he rose to his feet and held his hands out to Ethan. "It's way past my bedtime, and I'm tired." He looked over at Bruce and Seth. "Maybe we'll see you guys around tomorrow. I'm thinking of torturing Ethan by making him go fishing. It'll be fun to watch." He winked at them, and then laced his arm through Ethan's, and led him away.

"Have a good night," Bruce said as he watched them head away from the bonfire. He turned to Seth. "Do you remember when we were like that?"

Seth grinned. "Yeah. We're not going to see them for days."

The road back was dark, only lit by the moonlight, and the wind had picked up, making the bushes rustle. Ethan was doing his best not to jump every time he heard a noise, but being unfamiliar with the potential threats, the sounds were making him uneasy.

"How are we going to get back without being attacked by something?" Ethan asked as gripped Joel's arm nervously.

"By doing what I did as a kid. Running really, really fast and making lots of noise." Joel released Ethan and took off running, whooping loudly, and almost made it back to their cabin ahead of Ethan, but as he was about to take the steps,

Joel was swept off his feet and carried the rest of the way up.

Ethan fumbled with the door, and then carried Joel straight through to the bedroom and tossed him on the bed. He slipped off his own boots and then worked the knots loose on Joel's.

Joel lay quietly and only shifted when necessary as Ethan undressed him. Once Ethan had removed the last of his clothes, Joel pulled back the covers and climbed in, watching as Ethan stripped off his own clothing, and noting that the firelight from the woodstove was illuminating the bedroom through the open doorway, casting a golden hue on Ethan's bare skin.

Joel lay back and soaked in the ambiance of the moment …the sound of the crackling fire, the smell of warmed wood, and the sight of the one person in the world that he loved more than any other.

"I think I know what bliss feels like," Joel said.

"You're feeling that too, are you?" Ethan lay down beside Joel and delicately ran his fingers down the side of Joel's face, and then his neck, and all the way down to his shoulder.

Joel shivered at Ethan's touch.

"Are you nervous, at all?" Ethan asked.

Joel pulled Ethan over for a kiss and felt his heart skipping beats in anticipation. "Not really. Not with you." He hummed when Ethan kissed him more ardently. Then Ethan released him and gazed down the length of Joel's body as he slowly removed the covers.

"You're so incredibly beautiful," Ethan said as his fingers ran down Joel's chest and around each of his nipples, and then down the center of his stomach. He encased Joel's cock and started stroking him gently, then shifted himself down the bed and began licking long slow lines across Joel's stomach, his senses surging as the taste of Joel's skin consumed him, urging him to continue along the curve of Joel's hip and down his inner thigh.

His desire ignited with ferocity when he heard Joel calling his name.

Joel closed his eyes and soaked in the sensation of Ethan's hot breath floating across him, each stroke of Ethan's tongue or touch of his lips sending exhilarating rushes of tension through to his core.

He laid his hand firmly on Ethan's as it made its way up to his chest, and then directed it across his body, brushing his skin.

Joel arched up dramatically as Ethan delicately sucked and licked at his cock without actually taking him in, teasing his body into waves of absolutely unrelenting passion.

Ethan lifted his head and smiled. "Do you like that?"

Joel opened his eyes to speak but was immediately silenced by the fire burning in Ethan's eyes. He hadn't fully realized the depth of Ethan's desire for him until that moment. His chest began to rise and fall rapidly as he considered what this night was going to bring to their relationship. He refocused and let his body take over again.

"Yeah, it feels fucking amazing," he replied. "Don't stop."

"Mm …but I was about to do this."

Joel's breath caught, and he clung aggressively to the sheets as Ethan's powerful mouth took him in, and pulled at him longingly.

He shifted his body, and used his hips to thrust himself closer, then rolled Ethan onto his back, and straddled Ethan's chest, gripping the headboard as drove his cock back into Ethan's mouth.

Ethan's mind raced with excitement at Joel's sudden change in position; something he hadn't expected. He could feel Joel's body quivering with uncertainty as he took him in deeper. He caught Joel's eyes challenging him to continue. He wanted Joel to reach the very edge of his restraint before he released him.

As Joel began calling out to him, Ethan dropped Joel from his mouth, wrapped a hand around Joel's neck and pulled him down, letting the individual tastes of their mouths become one.

Then he rolled Joel over onto his back and reached for his phone. He looked at it and grinned. "Happy Birthday, babe."

Joel ran his hand down Ethan's arm and grinned back at him. "I can't believe we made it to my birthday."

"Barely—" Ethan hung over the edge of the bed and grabbed his bag. He rooted around for a second and then lifted a large box of condoms onto the bed, making Joel shriek with laughter.

"Did you get those from the warehouse store?" Joel asked.

"I figured we'd have a busy week. And I like to play safe."

Ethan grinned at Joel again and gave him a quick kiss. He ripped open a package, removed the condom and placed it in his mouth, and then winked at Joel and shuffled back down the bed.

Joel's face creased up in confusion. He looked down to see what Ethan was doing, and then cursed softly with lust filled elation as Ethan carefully rolled the condom into place with his mouth.

The condom in place, Joel shuddered and clawed frantically at Ethan, bringing him back up to his mouth, and dove into the warm depth he found there. He eventually tore himself away, gasping for breath and clinging to Ethan's face.

"Where the fuck did you learn to do that?" he asked.

"You liked that, did you?" Ethan pulled himself up and straddled Joel's hips. "Just one of my many skills."

"Can't wait to see the rest of them." Joel ran his hands up Ethan's thighs to his chest and back down again, taking in the sight of Ethan towering over him. It was a sight he knew he could spend a lifetime looking at. He watched Ethan arch up, then his eyes widened and his breath quickened as Ethan reached back and slowly guided him in. His gut tightened with exhilaration when Ethan completed his descent, dropped his head back, and swore loudly.

Joel smiled playfully. "Are you all right?"

Ethan whooped loudly and shook out his hair, making Joel's eyebrows shoot up in surprise. Ethan circled his hands back around and cradled Joel's face, kissing him aggressively, and then reached forward to grab hold of the headboard.

"I've never been more all right," Ethan replied.

Joel kept his hands on Ethan's hips and followed the motion of Ethan moving up and down on top of him until he felt his own need increasing rapidly as the movement of their bodies became far more intense than what Joel had dreamed possible.

He moved his hands around to Ethan's ass, and encouraged him to rise and fall more rapidly, but as he did his gaze dropped and he looked down his chest to his stomach, and watched the movement of Ethan's hardened cock swaying seductively above him, and felt his desire swell. He brought a hand back around and started stroking Ethan aggressively, causing Ethan to ride him even harder.

Joel caught Ethan's gaze and joined him in his voluminous stream of guttural, ecstasy induced sound.

Ethan's entire core was trembling as Joel moved within him. It had been far too long since he'd been with anyone, and he'd missed the rush of emotion that came from having someone possess you so completely. And the fact it was Joel was prompting an unprecedented euphoria to take over his entire being.

He dropped his head back again and rode through the swelling tide building in him as Joel stroked him, and erupted vocally with intense sound from deep within.

The increasing tempo coming from Joel had him tipping his head forward and opening his eyes. He studied Joel's face to see where he was at, and a fire immediately burst to life within him as he sensed Joel was cresting.

He swiftly dropped his restraint and completed in unison with him.

Quaking with fulfillment, Joel released a rough exhalation, breathing through the emotion that was pulsing throughout his body in an attempt to control it. But was unable to do so.

He sighed as a few tears ran down his cheeks, and then laughed, embarrassed, when Ethan leaned forward and delicately licked them off his face.

Ethan sat back up and brushed his thumbs across Joel's cheeks.

"Why are you crying?" he asked.

"I'm just a bit emotional," Joel replied. "I've been craving that intense closeness with you for a long time. And ever since I realized I was in love with you, that longing has been tearing me apart. I desperately needed to become one with you."

Ethan lifted his body up and pulled himself off Joel's cock, making Joel cringe. He stretched out at Joel's side and let his gaze wander across Joel's face. "What could I have possibly done to deserve you? You are the most gorgeous and sentimental creature I've ever set eyes on."

He stroked Joel's face, smiling when Joel rolled over to face him.

"You're not so bad yourself." Joel grinned and affectionately touched the tip of Ethan's nose.

"In your eyes maybe."

"Isn't that all that matters?" Joel kissed Ethan and then ran his fingers across Ethan's lips. "You're perfect in my eyes."

"God, I love you." Ethan reached down, removed Joel's condom, and tossed it onto the floor. "Want to have another go?"

"Mm …a man after my own heart," Joel said, and then laughed and shrieked as Ethan dove under the covers.

Erica had been phoning and texting Joel all morning, but he wasn't responding to her. She had been in the counseling office trying to organize her applications for university and had mentioned that Joel was taking part in the conference in Vancouver for perspective environmental students entering university.

The counselor had told her she'd never heard of it.

She'd made her way to Ryan's locker to wait for the bell to ring for lunch, and waved him down when she saw him coming down the hall. Then dropped her hands on her hips when it looked like he was going to ignore her and turn back down the hall.

Her face creased up with concern as Ryan approached her.

"Hey, Erica," Ryan said, keeping his head down in an attempt to *not* make eye contact as he fiddled with the lock on his locker.

"Where is Joel really?" Erica asked. "I was just at the counselor's office, and there is no conference in Vancouver."

"Erica, please," Ryan replied. "This has got nothing to do with me. You need to speak to Joel." The lock finally relenting, he pulled open his locker, threw his books in, and slammed it shut.

"That's what I've been trying to do, but he's not answering my calls or my texts." Erica crossed her arms and glared at Ryan. "Give me your phone."

"What? No. Come on, Erica." Ryan pulled away from her when she grabbed at his sleeve.

Erica smiled as she saw Max approaching. "Max, my phone has died. Can I borrow yours?"

"Sure," Max said as he handed it to her, and shrugged at Ryan, who was furiously shaking his head *no* at him. "What?"

Erica leaned against Ryan's locker and smirked when Joel finally picked up. "So, you are screening your calls."

"No," Joel said. "I forgot to charge my phone last night. I just pulled it off the charger a few minutes ago."

"How's the conference?"

"Kind of a non-event really."

"Clever."

"What is it, Erica? How's Sam?"

"He's doing great. He's at daycare. Exactly where he's supposed to be. Exactly where I would expect to find him."

Joel held his hand over the phone and lowered it for a second. He turned to Ethan. "She knows I'm not in Vancouver," he whispered, then lifted the phone back to his ear. "Erica?"

"Joel, where are you?"

"I just needed a break. I'll be back on Saturday night."

"A break from what ...me?" Erica sniffed and wiped at the stream of tears that had suddenly appeared, prompting Ryan to punch Max hard in the arm, then smack him in the back of the head.

"How the hell was I supposed to know?" Max asked. "You guys never tell me anything. What's going on?"

"Was I not shaking my head hard enough for your liking?" Ryan replied as he hauled Max down the hall. He walked him around the corner and pushed him against the wall, and waited until the small group of students behind them moved on. "Joel isn't in Vancouver."

"Duh. I figured that out. Where is he?"

"He's staying in one of those cabins his family usually goes to every summer." Ryan scrubbed his face and ran his hand around the back of his neck. "Look, Joel has been seeing someone, and he's up there with them for the rest of the week. When he gets back, he's going to be asking Erica for a divorce. That's all I can tell you."

"He's divorcing Erica? But they're like the perfect couple."

"Joel doesn't think so."

"Do you know who he's with?"

"Yes, I know who he's with." Ryan stuffed his hands in his pockets and exhaled loudly. "Fuck it. You're going to find out anyway. But you have to keep it to yourself. There are potential legal implications if you spill. Do you understand?"

"I would never betray Joel. You know that."

"Yeah, but this might be a difficult one. You'll be walking around with a shocked expression for days. I know I did."

"Jeez, Ryan." Max looked at him anxiously. "You're freaking me out. Who the fuck is it?"

"Max. Who is the one person, other than Erica, that Joel spends all of his time with?" Ryan stepped back when Max coughed, almost choking, then doubled over holding his stomach.

"And he guessed it in one," Ryan said.

Max breathed in deep, trying to quell his nausea.

"Are you fucking serious?" he said. "Ethan?"

"I told you it was shocking."

Max slowly straightened up and gripped the wall behind him for support. "He's divorcing Erica, so he can be with Ethan?" He looked up and searched Ryan's eyes. "That's not possible. They're just friends." He shook his head. "They must be fucking with you."

"I'm afraid not." Ryan leaned against the wall beside Max. "I've known about him and Ethan for a while now."

"Seriously? How long has this been going on?"

"They've had a thing going on since December. But it didn't get serious until February ...and now apparently ...they're in love."

"They're in love?" Max sunk down onto the ground and tucked his knees up. He looked over at Ryan as he took a seat beside him. "What the hell does Joel see in a guy like Ethan? Fuck, what the hell does he see in any guy? Joel isn't gay. Is he?"

"Last I heard, he hadn't come to a decision on that yet. He says physiologically he's gay, but he's not sure about adopting the label."

Ryan shook his head as Max looked at him funny. "Don't ask. I have no idea how his mind works."

"What about Ethan?"

"Apparently, he came out years ago."

"So, Joel is spending the entire week locked away in a cabin with Ethan freakin' Cooke." Max suddenly gripped his stomach again. "Fuck! That means they're—" He ran his hands up through his hair. "Jeez, Ryan. Joel's letting that psychopath fuck him. How could you let this happen?"

"Ethan's not a psychopath. He's actually a really nice, fairly normal guy …once you get to know him. Long story, but his little act at school here, was just that—acting. Joel loves him like you wouldn't believe, and I think Ethan is genuinely in love with Joel."

"I'm so confused right now." Max dropped his head and wrapped his arms around his body. "I did *not* see this coming."

Ryan patted Max on the back, then turned when he heard Erica calling for him from down the hall.

She walked up to them and held Max's phone out to Ryan.

"He wants to talk to you," she said.

Ryan took it cautiously. "Hey, Joel."

"I want to apologize for putting you in the middle of this," Joel said. "She suspects I'm with someone, but for obvious reasons, I haven't confirmed anything. But I think you should fill Max in."

"Just did."

"How did he take it?"

"He almost threw up. Twice." Ryan smiled when he heard Joel laughing at the other end. He stepped away from Max and deliberately walked out of Erica's earshot.

"Happy birthday, by the way," he said.

"Thanks, Ryan. Just have to say. Best birthday ever."

"So the holiday is going well?"

"It's incredible. Ethan is fucking amazing."

Ryan laughed aloud when he heard Joel shrieking as Ethan wrestled the phone out of his hands.

"Hey, Ryan?" Ethan said.

"Yes, Ethan."

"Joel and I just finished lunch, and we've gone back to bed. He needs to hang up now—bye."

Ryan ended the call and just shook his head. He had to admit they sounded happy, and he'd never seen Joel look at Erica the way he looked at Ethan. He sighed aloud and turned around—straight into Erica. She'd been standing right behind him.

Tucking himself in closer to Ethan, Joel breathed in the scent of Ethan's skin while pulling the covers up higher over their shoulders, trying to glean some warmth off him. They had let the fire die down, and now that the sun was setting, the cabin was getting really cold.

He shivered against Ethan and nudged him with his elbow.

"Don't be poking me if you're cold," Ethan said. "I know nothing about woodstoves."

"Oh, fine." Joel threw back the covers, grabbed Ethan's shirt off of a hook on the wall, and pulled it on over his head. He scurried into the bathroom first and grabbed the garbage can, and brought it back to the bedroom, setting it near the bed.

"I'll stoke the fire," Joel said, then smirked. "You're on condom duty. The floor looks like a really sad slug festival."

"Maybe I should learn how to stoke the fire for next time," Ethan replied and then groaned as he realized how cold it was in the room.

He cleaned up the mess they'd made of the floor, then grabbed a clean shirt from his bag, and took up a seat near the fire.

"It's pretty easy," Joel said. "Fire needs two things to survive. Fuel and oxygen."

"I'm sorry, babe, but I can't concentrate on what you're saying with your bare ass hanging out the bottom of that shirt."

Joel wiggled his ass playfully, and then crouched down and began stabbing at the embers in the bottom of the woodstove. He reached for some new wood and placed it in, pushing it back with the poker. He blew on it for a minute, but gave up and grabbed a couple of sheets of newspaper, crumpled them into balls and pushed them into the fire. He closed the door over just enough to cause air to rush in and ignite the paper, and then closed it up.

"That should do it," he said. "What do you want me to attempt for dinner?" He stepped back, straddled Ethan's lap, and wrapped his arms around Ethan's neck, delirious with contentment.

"I'll cook tonight," Ethan replied. "I'm craving curry, and that is one thing I definitely know how to make." He kissed Joel's chin and looked toward the kitchen. "Are you hungry?"

"Mm…hm." Joel turned Ethan's face back toward him and set about devouring his mouth.

The sun was streaming into the bedroom through the blinds that had been mistakenly left open. Joel protected his eyes, rolled over, and felt his heart soar as his gaze landed on Ethan's sleeping form. He had half expected that the events, which had unfolded on his birthday, had been a dream. He tucked himself in against Ethan's side and kissed him softly on the shoulder, waking him up.

"Good morning." Ethan shifted onto his side and kissed Joel on the lips. "How are you feeling?"

"Wonderful."

"Mm, …that's so nice to hear." Ethan pulled Joel closer to his body and ran his hand across Joel's hip.

"I love waking up next to you," Joel said. "I don't ever want to wake up without you again."

"You won't, babe. We're together now."

Ethan rolled back and let Joel nestle in against him. "Hey, have you ever done any art classes?"

"No. Art classes aren't exactly a prerequisite for the field I'm going into at university." Joel rolled onto his stomach and licked a long line with his tongue all the way along Ethan's bicep, and then kissed it. "Why?"

"I was hoping to teach you some tattooing skills." Ethan squirmed as Joel pushed his arm up and started licking the underside, pulling at the hairs there, but then was overtaken by need, as his body reacted to the intimate nature of Joel's attention.

Joel finished savoring the skin under Ethan's arm and moved across to his chest, licking wide swaths, and flicking playfully at the ring in his nipple. He stopped, his curiosity distracting him.

"Why would you want to teach me how to tattoo?" he asked.

"So, you can eventually do some work on my harder to reach places." Ethan smiled as a grin spread across Joel's face.

"What places would those be?" Joel laughed, and then ducked under the covers. "I'll see if I can find them."

Ethan clenched his teeth as Joel's tongue started tickling him. "Babe, what are you doing down there?" He squirmed, sinking his ass deeper into the mattress. "Fuckin' hell, you're unstoppable."

Tipping his head back, Ethan enjoyed the short duration of the ride until Joel threw back the covers, and climbed out from beneath them. "Why did you stop?" he asked as Joel laid his head down on his chest and softly stroked at his arm with his fingers.

"I want to try it …" Joel paused. "Bottoming for you."

"I thought we agreed to wait. To give you more time to think about it." Ethan brushed the hair from Joel's eyes. "It's a big step letting someone take you like that."

"Ethan, I love you so much that it's overwhelming sometimes. I want to share everything with you. Mind and body."

Joel laid a gentle kiss on Ethan's chest and then moved up to whisper in his ear. He licked at it carefully first, and then kissed it, breathing heavily. "I desperately want to feel you moving in me."

Cupping Joel's face, Ethan brought him in close so he could savor Joel's mouth, letting his body soak in the passion that was being caressed into an overwhelming desire, as Joel rubbed his body against him. His senses spiked as Joel shifted his position, causing Ethan's mind to explode with possible scenarios—but then he reminded himself that he needed to take things slow with Joel, and reluctantly sunk into the relaxed pace Joel was setting for them.

Joel continued to explore the sensations created by Ethan's mouth and then by the slender curve of his neck. He ran his lips down Ethan's body and across the soft, warm skin of his stomach, inhaling the intoxicating scent of him. He eased his hands up under Ethan's hips and lifted him closer, as he surrounded Ethan's cock completely, pulling at him gently until Ethan's body was ready.

Ethan climbed away from Joel, grabbed a condom and some lube from the bedside table, and lay flat out beside him.

"We'll try it this way to start," he said. "You'll have all the control. So, if you find it hurts too much, and you want to pull away, you can." Ethan removed the ring from his tip and deftly rolled the condom into place. "We'll do it without the *Prince* for now."

"But ...I don't want to sit on top of you like that." Joel turned to face Ethan, determined. "I like having you looking down on me." He brushed his fingers across Ethan's lips. "I trust you not to hurt me."

"Are you sure?"

"Ethan, please."

Ethan nodded his head and perched himself above Joel's body, and just breathed deeply for a minute, reveling in the exhilarating emotion coursing through his body, and then lowered himself down onto Joel, and lovingly took his mouth.

Joel positioned himself as Ethan slid off his body and dropped down between his legs. He shifted nervously, but then consciously took a deep breath to relax as Ethan's gentle touch reminded him of how much he was loved. He felt immense contentment with his decision as Ethan crawled back up his body, hitching his legs up onto his shoulders on the way up to give him a kiss.

"I'll be as gentle as I can, all right?" Ethan said.

Joel nodded, then clung desperately to Ethan, wanting him close so he could seek comfort in Ethan's eyes, as he crossed the line into something, that less than one year ago, he never could've imagined he'd be doing. But then, he never could've imagined someone would come along and change his life so completely as what Ethan had.

The fire was finally starting to take the chill off the moist evening air. It had begun raining in the late afternoon, cutting short Joel's futile and ultimately hilarious attempt to show Ethan how to row a boat and use a fishing rod. They'd taken to the cabin, cooked an early dinner, and were now set up at the table with a game of Scrabble—and Joel was losing miserably.

"I knew I should've brought a dictionary," Joel said. "I have no idea what that word is."

"You don't know what perspicacious means, and yet that's exactly what you are. Interesting."

"Fuck, you're not going to tell me are you?" Joel shuffled his letter tiles around, then crossed his arms. "How did you even manage to get a word that long?"

"I'll let you masticate on that one further."

"All right, smarty pants." Smiling at Ethan, Joel reached for his beer, finishing it off. "You win. Again."

Ethan jumped up and took a bow, and proceeded to put the game away. "Babe, I have something I want to talk to you about. But let's sit on the porch and have a smoke. I'll grab some blankets." He placed the lid on the game box and headed over to the bedroom.

"Sure, I'll meet you out there." Joel looked over his shoulder as he stepped out onto the porch. It wasn't like Ethan to announce he wanted to talk about something. He pulled the can they were using as an ashtray out from under one of the chairs and set it on the armrest, and lit up a cigarette. He leaned against a post and looked out at the rain; it was peaceful in its own way.

He turned when he heard Ethan close the door.

"Come sit," Ethan said, then waited for Joel to sit down before passing him a blanket. He settled into his own chair and lit up a cigarette. He took a few draws before looking over at Joel.

"This is our last night here," Ethan continued. "So, I'm wondering what's going to happen when we go home tomorrow."

"Well, I want us to go home as a couple."

"How do you want to handle that?"

Joel lifted his cell phone from his pocket and stroked it with his thumb. "I need to phone Erica and tell her I'm not coming home to my parents' house for starters." He looked up at Ethan. "But I don't want to get into everything over the phone. She deserves to be told in person."

Ethan nodded his head and stared down at the rain hitting the ground just off the front of the porch, scrubbing his face with his hand, then set in on chewing his thumbnail.

Joel set his phone on the ground and leaned toward Ethan.

"Was there something else you wanted to talk about?" he asked. "You're tweaking out a little."

"Um …yeah." Ethan crushed out his cigarette, reached for Joel's hand, and raised his eyes. "Joel, would it be safe to assume that we've decided to become life partners?"

Joel laughed and squeezed Ethan's hand in reassurance. "Yes, that would be a safe assumption." He studied Ethan's face momentarily. "Is that what you wanted to ask me?"

"No. Well ...sort of." Ethan ran his hand across his mouth. "I was just wondering—" He paused and sighed with anxiety.

Joel leaned on the arm of his chair, brought Ethan's hand to his lips, and left it there while continuing to study Ethan's face.

"What is it?" he asked.

"What about marriage?" Ethan replied rapidly as a swath of fluid motion took over his eyes, and tears began to form at the edges. "I know it's still early days with us," he continued. "But would it be safe to assume that we might get married someday?" He looked out toward the rain again. "Because I really want to ..."

He listened to his heart beating steadily against his chest, and then lifted his eyes to meet Joel's again, and felt his heart surge.

"Absolutely," Joel said. "That would definitely be within the realms of safe assumptions."

"Really?" Ethan grinned at him. "You would marry me?"

"Without hesitation. You mean everything to me."

Ethan exhaled pure relief and used the heels of his hand to wipe the tears off his cheeks. He laughed in relief as Joel reached over and briskly rubbed his leg.

"That wasn't so hard, was it?" Joel teased.

"Fuckin' nerve-racking is what it was."

Joel sat back in his chair and blew air noisily up at his hair.

"Speaking of which," he said. "This is going to be brutal." He lifted his phone, hesitated, and then dialed Erica's phone.

A shiver of remorse crawled up his spine as he waited.

Erica picked up after the second ring. "Joel?"

"Hey, Erica. We need to talk."

"What's going on?" Erica said, and then sucked in a sob. "Ryan won't tell me anything, and I can't ask Ethan, because he's out of town. And Max. Max has turned into a babbling idiot. And your sister. I don't know what's gotten into her. She's locked herself in her room and won't speak to me." Erica waited out the silence, but there was no response. "They all know already, don't they?" She covered her mouth. "Joel, are you leaving me?"

Joel rose to his feet and pulled Ethan's hand tight to his chest as he moved to sit in Ethan's lap.

"Erica," he said. "We rushed into getting married because you were pregnant and our parents were pushing us, saying it was the right thing to do. But it was the wrong thing to do, and I should've put a stop to it." He stopped and brushed off a spattering of tears from his cheek. "I'm sorry I put you through this. You deserve so much better. You have no idea how horrible I feel."

"Don't you love me?"

"I thought I did." Joel leaned against Ethan's shoulder and relaxed as he felt Ethan's arm wrap around him.

"Is there someone else?" Erica asked.

Joel sighed deeply. "Yeah, there's someone else." He took a long draw off the cigarette Ethan offered him, and then passed it back. "There has been for a while. I'm sorry."

"Who is she? Do I know her?"

"Erica, we'll talk more when I get back. I'll tell you then."

"Is she there with you now?" Erica's breath caught, and she leaned against the doorframe of Sam's room for support. "Is that why you went away? To be with her?"

"Something like that. Look. We'll talk later."

"So, what's going to happen to us?"

"I won't be coming back to the house tomorrow." Joel took a deep breath and felt the tightness in his chest start to relinquish its hold slightly. "I'll be moving out right away."

Erica wrapped her arm around her waist and tried to contain her confusion. She wasn't entirely sure of where her emotions were sitting at that moment. She was rapidly switching between anger, sadness, and surprisingly— immense relief.

Her relationship with Joel had always been a bit strange, but since she had moved in with him, she'd seen a side of Joel she wasn't entirely comfortable with, and the truth was, she was glad he'd decided to move on. "Where are you going to be living?"

"I'm going to move in with Ethan," Joel replied, then shivered at the stirring sound of those words.

"All right, that makes sense. If you're next door, you'll be able to see Sam every day." Erica slid down onto the floor beside Sam's crib. "I'll …um …I have to go. Sam needs his bath. I want to talk about this some more. When will I see you?"

"I'll come over on Sunday." Joel sighed and wiped the stream of tears from his face. "I'm so sorry, Erica."

Ethan and Joel had just finished hauling the last of their gear into the house when the doorbell rang. Ethan set the box of leftover food on the counter for Sophie to put away, dropped into the sofa in the den, and waited for Edgar to announce whoever it was.

Joel sat down beside him and lit up a cigarette.

"Do you think it's my parents?" he asked.

"That would be my guess," Ethan replied. "They probably saw you move your car into my driveway." He looked over his shoulder and caught a glimpse of whom Edgar was leading down to the lounge. "Yeah, it's your parents."

"What should I do?" Joel jumped to his feet and fidgeted with the cigarette. "Should I head down to the lounge?"

"Not until Edgar comes to get you. Protocol dictates you wait. You don't want him thinking he's not doing his job properly by—"

Ethan crushed out his cigarette as Edgar came into the den.

"A Mister and Missus Carrigan to see Master Carrigan, Sir," Edgar said and bowed.

"Thank you, Edgar." Ethan waited until Edgar left the room, then directed his attention back to Joel. "Do you want me to come with you to talk to them?"

"No, I won't be telling them much. I want to talk to Erica first before I start coming out to people about us.

"I'll wait for you upstairs then." Ethan pulled himself off the sofa, wrapped his arms around Joel's waist, and bit affectionately at his chin. "If you need me. I'm here, all right?"

"I know you are. You'll always be." Joel kissed Ethan and squeezed his hand, then headed down the hall to the lounge where he stood outside for a second, collecting his thoughts before stepping into the room.

The conversation with his parents rapidly deteriorated. His dad wouldn't stop yelling at him, and his mom wouldn't stop crying. He'd only been in there with them for less than thirty minutes, and he'd already downed at least three drinks. He felt as if his chest was going to explode from the stress. They couldn't understand what had changed between him and Erica in such a short space of time, and he couldn't tell them yet, which was making it impossible for him to come across with any credibility whatsoever.

Joel supported himself on the bar and lit up a cigarette.

"I'm not going back," he said for what felt like the millionth time. "I don't want to be with Erica anymore."

"Whether or not you want to be with her," Arthur said, "you're married, and you have a responsibility to your wife, and especially to that son of yours."

"I'm not planning on shirking my responsibilities," Joel replied. "I just can't live with her anymore."

"You've only been married for five months, and you have a newborn baby in the house," Arthur continued. "That is a stressful environment for anyone. But it doesn't give you an excuse to run away and hide out in the bush with your buddy, and then decide you don't want to come home." He shot to his feet, paced the room, and then came up in Joel's face. "I want you to head back to the house, right now!" He poked Joel hard in the chest. "Your childish protest is over. I won't stand for it anymore! You have a family, and it's time for you to stand up and be a man."

"I've never felt like more of a man." Joel shoved Arthur away from him. "This past week my soul was revived. Every morning when I woke up, I thought to myself …this is what it feels like to be truly alive and at peace with oneself."

Joel turned when he heard the lounge door open, whereby Ethan peered in, then stepped into the room.

"Hiya," Ethan said quietly, not sure if he should be interrupting. "I've been hearing a lot of loud voices coming up the stairs, and just wanted to make sure everything was all right down here."

He glanced over at Joel and could see that he was completely wound up. "Are you all right, Joel?" he asked.

"Never been better," Joel replied sarcastically, and then threw back the remains of his drink, and dragged his arm across his mouth.

"Is there anything I can do to help?" Ethan asked.

"Yes," Arthur said. "You can tell my son to smarten up and stop being such a coward when it comes to his responsibilities."

"A coward?" Ethan replied. "Joel is the most courageous person I know. He stopped long enough to listen to his heart and followed what it desired. It took a lot of courage for him to do that."

"What on earth are you talking about?" Arthur asked in frustration. "You and Joel both. Always spouting your *airy-fairy* crap that has no bearing on the real world. In the real world, Joel is married and has a baby that he needs to provide for."

"And I will," Joel stated. "My hands are pretty much tied until I graduate. But that was always the case. You promised to support Erica and me until I finished university."

"And we will, sweetheart," Carol said. "Come home, and we'll set you up in the guest room. You can have your own space until you and Erica work things out."

"We're not going to work things out." Joel fell into the big chair by the bar and dropped his head into his hands.

"You just need time to get used to living with each other," Carol said. "All couples have the same problem."

"All couples do not have the same problem as us," Joel replied.

Ethan looked at Joel nervously. He could see where this conversation was going to end up.

"Maybe you can discuss this again tomorrow," Ethan suggested. "Let everyone calm down a bit."

"We'll discuss it now. Back at home," Arthur demanded. "Joel, you're coming home with us."

Joel leaped up from his seat and positioned himself directly in front of Arthur. "For the last fucking time! I'm not going back to your fucking house and making nice with Erica!" He crossed his arms and glared at Arthur. "I don't want to be with her *ever* again."

"Don't you speak to me like that," Arthur said.

"Please come home," Carol interrupted as she dabbed at new tears streaming down her face. "Tomorrow is a new day. Maybe you just had a bad day today."

Joel groaned in frustration. "I didn't just have a bad day."

"We could arrange for you and Erica to attend counseling," Carol continued. "My sister's friend's niece was having marriage problems, and they found counseling very helpful."

Joel spun around, walked back over to the bar, and began pouring himself another drink, but Ethan stopped him by placing a hand on his arm. "Joel, I think you've had enough for tonight."

Ethan set his hand on Joel's back and started rubbing small circles to calm him down. "What do you want to do? I'm behind you no matter what you decide."

Joel turned to face Ethan and then looked at his parents staring at him, waiting for his next response. "I want to do what I've wanted to do since December. I want to stop hiding. I want to be myself." He turned away and went to sit down.

Ethan took a seat on the coffee table in front of Arthur and Carol and leaned forward with his elbows resting on his knees.

"What is it, Ethan?" Carol said. "What's wrong with our son?"

"Joel has been going through a difficult transition these past few months," Ethan said. "I'm doing my best to be supportive of his decision to make a change in his life, and so is Ryan."

"What the hell are you on about?" Arthur demanded.

"I'm gay, Arthur," Joel stated emphatically. "It took me a while to actualize the extent to which I've been fooling myself, but now it's pretty undeniable." He wandered over and sat down beside Ethan.

"I'm sorry, Carol," he continued. "I know this isn't what you wanted for me." He reached forward and took her hands. "I haven't told Erica yet, so please keep this to yourself for now. But that's why I can't stay with her any longer. It's not fair to either one of us."

"But you and Erica. You had a baby together," Carol said. "How can you be gay …when you had a baby?"

"It was just sex, Carol," Joel said. "Erica and I have never connected on an emotional level."

"Ethan," Arthur said. "You must have some experience with teens exhibiting this type of behavior. Surely you can talk to Joel and make him understand that this isn't a choice he wants to make." He turned to Joel. "Son, you don't want to be gay. Like your mom said. We'll arrange some counseling and get to the bottom of this."

"All right!" Ethan interjected. "Now *I'm* getting pissed off."

He jumped to his feet and went to stand by the window.

"Arthur, how can you be so fuckin' archaic?" he said finally, then turned back to face him. "Being gay is not a choice or a behavior that needs to be modified, or counseled."

"We just think he'd be happier if he weren't gay," Carol said.

Ethan laughed aloud and headed for the bar. He poured himself a double and threw it back, then refilled his glass.

"You have no idea how soul destroying it is to live a lie," he said. "Joel was damn lucky to uncover the truth of who he is early in life because now he has the opportunity to experience a lifetime of peace with his inner self."

"There you go again with all your fantasy crap," Arthur replied.

"It's not fantasy crap!" Ethan shouted. "I get to experience that kind of peace every day of my life." He took a long drink. "Not that it's a secret, because I came out years ago, but I'm positive at this point that neither one of you has any idea that I'm queer."

"Ethan," Carol said. "Don't be silly. You don't look gay."

"My head is going to officially explode," Joel said and rose to join Ethan. "I'm tired ...I'm going to bed." He cupped Ethan's face lovingly in his hands and kissed him slowly on the lips.

"I'll see you up there," he said to Ethan, and then turned back to his parents, who were looking at him in shock. "I'll have Edgar see you out." Then he left the room.

Erica was surprised to hear someone knocking on the door so early in the morning. She'd been awake all night thinking about her relationship with Joel, and where it had all gone wrong, but she hadn't expected to be getting an explanation from him so soon.

Arthur and Carol had gone over to Ethan's the night before to talk to Joel, and had come home completely distraught. Carol had looked at her and burst into tears, and Arthur had just turned away from her.

They had both refused to tell her anything.

She opened the door and was annoyed to see Ethan standing on the doorstep beside Joel.

"Why didn't you just come in?" she asked Joel.

"I don't live here anymore," Joel replied. "And I'm pretty sure Arthur and Carol have disowned me by now."

"Don't be ridiculous. They would never disown you." Erica looked over at Ethan. "Why did you have to bring *him* along?"

"Erica, please," Joel said. "I like having Ethan with me."

"Yes, I know." Erica let her eyes wander over the outfit Joel was wearing and sighed with exasperation. "But he's obviously a bad influence on you. Look at you. I don't think you should move in with him." She led the way into the living room, but Joel directed her toward the bedroom instead so they would have some privacy.

"You could always stay at Ryan's instead," she added.

Joel motioned for Ethan to wait out in the hall for a minute.

"I don't want to stay at Ryan's," he said to Erica, then sat down on the edge of the bed and waited for Erica to sit down beside him. "Look, I'm here to explain why I'm leaving you."

Erica sniffed and shrugged her shoulders.

"You've already told me," she said. "There's someone else."

"It's more complicated than that." Joel reached for her hands. "Erica, I'm not sure how to tell you this."

"Great. Who is she? I know you've been seeing her for a while now. It was only a couple of weeks after we got married that you started taking off every night—coming in late …and telling me you'd been at Ethan's. It was all lies, wasn't it?"

"No, I wasn't lying." Joel took a deep breath. "I really was at Ethan's." He shifted nervously. "That's who I've been seeing. That's why I'm moving in with him …not Ryan. Ethan's my boyfriend. And he has been, for quite a while now."

Erica's shoulders slumped forward, and she dropped her face into her hands and burst out laughing. "Ethan's your boyfriend? That's so disturbing, it's not even funny." She lifted her head and glared at him. "You're seeing one of my friends, aren't you? Is it Angela?"

"No! I'm not making this up, Erica."

"What? So, now you're gay too." Erica snorted in disbelief. "Of course you are. You want to be just like him, don't you?"

"No …I just want to be *with* him."

"That's ridiculous. We've been together for years. How could you not know you were gay?"

"I wasn't oblivious to the possibility. But I hadn't met anyone that made me want to take that leap until Ethan came along."

"You fucking bastard!"

Erica slapped Joel hard across the face as she realized he wasn't lying to her. A brief image of her husband with

Ethan flashed through her mind, and she felt like she was going to throw up.

"How could you?" she continued to shout. "You cheated on me ...with Ethan?" She covered her face as she felt a wave of nausea rising.

"I'm sorry, Erica." Joel shifted around when he heard Ethan step into the doorway. "But ever since that first day Ethan and I started hanging out with each other, we just clicked."

"Clicking with him is one thing. Fucking him is another." Erica turned away from Joel. "I'm going to be sick."

Erica's eyes flicked up as she caught movement by the door, and she stopped to study Ethan's face. His features were dark and without emotion, and he was staring back at her with absolute indifference. She watched as his gaze shifted to Joel, and his entire expression changed. She sat back and looked at Joel's response to him, and was shocked by what she saw.

"Are you in love with him?" Erica asked Joel.

"Yeah. Very much so." Joel dropped his gaze to the floor, not embarrassed, just uncomfortable with Erica's reaction.

Ethan looked over his shoulder when he heard Sam start crying.

"Babe," he said to Joel. "I'll get Sam up and started. I have baby morning routines down to a science."

"Don't you dare touch him!" Erica made to leap up and stop Ethan, but Joel grabbed her arm and kept her in place.

"Ethan won't hurt him," Joel said "He's had a lot of experience with kids. If anything, Sam will be the one to find something to pull on and cause Ethan significant amounts of pain."

Erica yanked her arm away and crossed them in resignation. She studied Joel's face, looking for a trace of the boy she'd fallen in love with, her high school sweetheart. But even if she were to remove all the piercings and makeup from Joel's face, she knew she wouldn't be looking at the same person. Something had changed in his eyes and the way they viewed the world. The Joel she knew was gone.

She rose to her feet and walked over toward the door, so she could hear into Sam's room. She thought about Joel's refusal to have sex with her for the past few months, and now it made sense.

"When did this start?" Erica asked Joel. "When did you start seeing him?"

"Erica, it doesn't matter."

"Joel. When did this start?"

Joel reluctantly got to his feet and approached her. "We started talking about seeing each other back in December."

"December?" Erica wrapped her arms around her stomach and began pacing the room. She thought back to winter break when Joel had been so upset about Ethan leaving the ski chalet that he'd refused to participate in anything for the rest of the week.

"The hickeys?" she inquired, already knowing the answer.

Joel dropped his gaze and nodded his head.

"Fuck, I can't believe this," Erica said. "Why did you marry me? Why didn't you just run off with him?"

"Because you were pregnant," Joel replied. "I thought it was the right thing to do. And Ethan had called things off between us. It looked like it was never going to happen between Ethan and me—"

"So, I was your second best choice?"

"It wasn't like that."

"What was it like? Did you ever really love me?"

"Jeez, Erica. I don't know that I can even answer that anymore. I thought I loved you, but now, with Ethan …my feelings are so much more intense."

Erica recalled the night at the end of January when Joel had gone dancing with Ethan in Vancouver. The clothes and makeup he'd been wearing the next morning—she hadn't even questioned it.

Then she remembered the night at the beginning of March when Joel had arrived home and broken down in tears after a big fight with Ethan—and she felt sick. He'd made love to her that night, and she remembered how desperate his need to possess her had been.

He hadn't been thinking about her at all.

"When did you start sleeping with him?" Erica asked.

"That's none of your business."

"It is *so* my business!" Erica ran at Joel and shoved him hard in the chest. "When Joel? When did you start fucking each other?"

"I never touched you after Ethan and I became intimate with each other. I promise."

"Jeez, Joel." Erica crouched down on the ground and covered her mouth with her hands. "How can you stand touching him?"

"I love him, Erica. You don't see what I see."

Erica closed her eyes, recalling the night last week when Joel had come home with his nipples pierced, and wondered what else they'd been up to that night. She couldn't wrap her head around how Joel could be in love with someone so repulsive.

She covered her face as she remembered something else.

The following night, after the nipple piercings, when Joel had climbed into bed, she'd caught a glimpse of what looked like a pink heart on his ass, but she hadn't commented.

She felt so stupid for not noticing the clues Joel had been so obviously laying down.

"Hey, babe?" Ethan poked his head in the door with Sam cradled gently in his arms. "I've cleaned him up and put a new sleeper on him, but I think your boy here is hungry." Then he smiled at Sam, cooing at him. "He's doing his best to remove my thumbnail."

He motioned for Erica to stay where she was when he saw her moving toward him.

"I'll feed him," he said. "I'm just letting you know where I'm taking him."

Erica, outraged at the suggestion, stepped up in Ethan's face, practically spitting her words. "And what would a sick fuck like you know about feeding babies?"

"More than you could possibly imagine," Ethan replied, barely managing to keep the word *bitch* off the end of his sentence.

He turned down the hallway and made his way into the kitchen. It was empty, and he hoped it would stay that way. He wasn't in the mood to run into Arthur and Carol. Jocelyn had nipped next door earlier that morning and given them both a hug and her support, but he wasn't expecting a change in attitude or a similar reception from Joel's parents.

He pulled open the fridge and sorted through the baby bottles that were already made up. He picked one of the smaller ones and set it on the counter.

"Ethan, do you need a hand?" Carol stepped through the patio door and into the kitchen and headed for the kettle that Ethan was trying to fill with one hand.

Ethan let her take the kettle and grabbed a container to set the bottle in.

"You look like you've done this before," Carol said.

"There are always a lot of babies back home." Ethan looked over at Carol anxiously, not sure why she was acting so normal around him. "My mom's sister had a lot of kids. And they, in turn, had far too many, so I inevitably end up babysitting."

He grabbed the boiled kettle and filled up the container.

"Do you ever think about moving back home now that you're almost finished with work?" Carol asked him. "I'm sure your family misses you."

Ethan shifted Sam in his arms and pulled the bottle out of the water. He expertly tested it and went to sit in the family room.

Tucking Sam into the crook of his arm, Ethan settled in, smiling as Sam found the bottle and hungrily went after it.

"My family is here now," he replied. "Joel is my family."

Carol sighed and looked away, and fussed with her skirt.

"Ethan," she said. "I think you're a lovely boy and you've always been welcome in our home, but I can't have you interfering with my son's family, and ultimately with his happiness." She sat down across from Ethan and looked him in the eye. "He's in there right now speaking with Erica. And I'm sure they'll work things out."

"There's nothing to work out. Your son is gay."

"We don't know that for sure. He wasn't gay before he met you. Perhaps you influenced him." Carol clasped her hands together in her lap. "Once he stops associating with you, he'll realize it was all a mistake. And he'll carry on like a *normal* person."

Ethan laughed and shook his head with incredulous shock. "I think if you talk to Joel, you'll find that deep down he's known he was gay for a long time."

"I'm his mother. I would've noticed something like that."

"It's pointless arguing about this." Ethan set the bottle down on the coffee table and tossed the cloth he'd carried in with him, over his shoulder. He carefully lifted Sam up onto it and started rubbing Sam's back as he bounced him up and down. Ethan smiled and kissed Sam's head when Sam let out a satisfying burp.

"They're not discussing getting back together," Ethan said as he stood up to look out the window.

"You're awfully sure of yourself, aren't you?" Carol replied. "What makes you think he'd choose you over his wife and child?"

"Because I know your son's heart as intimately as my own."

"That's ridiculous. You'll see."

"Carol, stop." Joel walked into the room and headed for her, wrapping his mother up in his arms. "I'm in love with Ethan. And I want to spend the rest of my life with him. Not Erica."

"But, Joel. Your family."

"Will keep living here for now, if that's all right with you." Joel went to stand beside Ethan, and took Sam from Ethan's arms and covered Sam's face in kisses. "I want to be able to see Sam as much as possible."

"But what about Erica?" Carol asked.

"We're getting a divorce. It was a mistake to marry her when I really wanted to be with someone else." Joel wrapped his arm around Ethan's waist and pulled him close. "This guy here is who I was meant to be with." He kissed Ethan on the shoulder and tucked his head against him, and gazed up into Ethan's face, then redirected his attention back over at his mother. "I really hope you can accept this and be happy for us someday."

All heads turned as the patio door flew open and crashed into the wall. Arthur stepped into the room and slammed the door shut behind him, rattling all the dishes in the kitchen cupboard.

"That's it," Arthur said. "I don't want to see you two in my house ever again. I won't have my grandson growing up around people like you." He reached for Sam, but Joel sidestepped him and handed Sam back to Ethan.

"People like us? Seriously?" Joel said as he placed himself in front of Ethan. "You don't want your grandson growing up in an environment filled with love and acceptance?"

He grunted in exasperation and decided against continuing the argument. His parents were going to think and act the way they wanted, regardless of anything he said to them.

He turned back to Ethan.

"Erica has asked me to hang with Sam on Tuesday and Wednesday nights when she's at work," Joel said to Ethan. "And all day Saturday, so she can have a break. But since we're no longer welcome over here, …we'll have to set up a nursery at our house."

"No problem," Ethan said. "I'll get working on that right away, so the room is ready for Tuesday night. Sophie is going to be thrilled. She loves babies." He held Sam up in front of his face and kissed him. "Uncle Ethan is a big fat liar. Auntie Sophie is going to blow a gasket when she sees baby stuff coming into the house."

Ethan grinned at Joel.

"And that makes me ever so happy," he added.

"Absolutely not. Ethan's house isn't a good environment for a child," Carol said. "He'll end up having nightmares."

Joel ignored his mother's statement and took Sam back off Ethan, and started rocking him to sleep

"There's my sweet boy," he cooed.

"We're going to need a car seat as well," Ethan said, "just in case we want to take Sam to the park or something on Saturday. Of course, then we'll need a stroller and a diaper bag."

"All right," Joel said to Ethan. "You seem to know more about this than I do, so I'm leaving you in charge of everything while I get caught up with the school work I missed this past week. If I don't start soon, I'm never going to get it all done."

"Yeah, sure. Here …" Ethan took Sam's sleepy form into his arms and followed Joel to the front door. "I'll put Sam back in his crib. I have to scope out his room to make sure I don't miss anything we need to buy as well."

Joel moved in close to Ethan—and was overcome by the feeling of protection they were providing for Sam as they cradled him between their bodies. He held Ethan's face and kissed him slowly and softly, then lowered his head to Ethan's shoulder when he heard his parents' sharp intake of breath. He kissed Ethan again, then reluctantly let go of his face, and ran his hands down Ethan's arms.

"No skulls or crosses," Joel said and smiled teasingly. "And I don't want to see anything black unless it's backed up by some cheerier colors. And not just red and purple."

"Got it," Ethan replied. "No gothic baby stuff."

"Mm …" Joel kissed Ethan and then laid a kiss on Sam's head. "I love you guys."

Ethan brushed a thumb across Joel's cheek. "We love you too."

Chapter Sixteen

Joel had never been on a plane before, and the thought of being on one for over fourteen hours was not sitting well with him. But it was the only way he was going to be able to meet Ethan's rather large extended family. They'd initially planned on going to Britain in July, but Ethan's work with the *Youth at Risk* program had kept him busy with his final paperwork until the middle of August. His contract with Karl wasn't scheduled to complete until the end of August, but Karl had let Ethan out early as an engagement present.

Ethan had officially asked Joel to marry him on the last day of high school, as a marker, representing the new chapter he was starting in his life. When Joel had accepted, Ethan had phoned his dad to tell him the news, and his dad had insisted on holding a separate ceremony in Britain for all of Ethan's relatives.

They'd just finished checking their bags, and Ethan was leading Joel, who was clutching fiercely to his arm, across the airport toward the security gate in the international terminal.

"You're sure we're not going to set the metal detectors off?" Joel asked again as he looked along the line to where the security officers were checking people. They didn't seem overly friendly.

"I've never had a problem before." Ethan removed Joel's hand from his sleeve and gripped it tight in his own. "It'll be fine."

Ethan glanced around at the other people in the security area. He was used to people staring at him, but it had freaked Joel out when they'd first arrived at the airport. Joel wasn't used to the stares and nasty comments that had become a regular part of his own life.

They'd had a busy summer so far, but had kept mostly to themselves, with Ethan spending many hours a day designing and applying the intricately detailed pieces of art onto Joel's body, along with an expanding display of piercings.

One of the benefits of spending so much time at home was they'd discovered Joel had a natural aptitude for art that he'd never explored until Ethan had handed him a design idea to sketch up for one of his clients. It had fueled a desire in Joel to continue, and he was now apprenticing under Ethan to become a tattoo artist.

The decision had further alienated his parents, but Ethan was ecstatic and had been so impressed with some of Joel's latest designs that he'd let him start a series of work on the most visible canvas he had, beginning at his jawline.

"I'll go through first, all right?" Ethan said as he looked into Joel's eyes and pried their hands apart. He waved off the security officer that was motioning for him to hurry up. "Don't stress about it. You'll be fine." He kissed Joel's lips, then the top of Joel's head before turning and heading through the metal detector.

Ethan had been right. They hadn't set off the metal detectors, and shortly after arriving at the gate, the first class passengers had been asked to board. Joel was pleased to see there were very few seats in first class, and that their seats were at the back, so they wouldn't have people staring at them. He still couldn't believe the fuss they'd caused by simply walking through the airport terminal together, hand in hand. It had momentarily frightened him, but after the first couple of hateful words had been thrown at them, it had occurred to him that these people didn't deserve the power he was giving them to affect his happiness, and he'd decided to ignore them.

"So, what do you think of flying so far?" Ethan asked.

"I think the people in the terminal were scarier than the actual plane itself." Joel finished his drink and motioned for the attendant to bring him another one. "I'm so glad we're up here, and not stuffed in the back with all those other people."

"That's one of the benefits of first class. A little privacy." Ethan flicked a button and his seat reclined back into a bed. "And this is another." He settled a face mask over his eyes and shut the lights off over his head.

"I think I might join you." Joel looked at the arm of his seat and tried to figure out which one would recline it. As he was fidgeting with the different options, a young Japanese woman walked up the aisle but slowed as she reached their seats.

"Ethan?" she inquired, not sure if it was him under the mask.

Ethan pulled the mask off and turned the lights back on.

"Kyoko!" He jumped up out of his seat and stepped over Joel and into the aisle. He swept her up in his arms and covered her face in kisses. "I can't believe it. Are you headed home?"

"Yeah," Kyoko replied. "I got a break from my charity work, so I thought I'd go see the parents. What about you?"

Ethan stepped back over Joel and reached down to grab Joel's hand. "Kyoko, this is Joel. We're actually headed to my dad's for a commitment ceremony ...our commitment ceremony."

"Oh my god!" Kyoto shrieked with such volume and excitement that it caused more than a few people to turn their heads.

"Oh my god," she said much quieter behind cupped hands, and then climbed over Joel, headed for Ethan's seat.

Ethan scooted her over and brought the seat back up, then motioned for her to sit on his lap, where she immediately curled up.

"We're going to be legally married in Canada," Ethan said. "But we can't do that right away, so my dad has arranged a little ceremony."

"Your dad. A little ceremony. What planet have you been living on?" Kyoko said. "How come I didn't get an invite?"

"He probably sent it to your parents—enough said."

"True that." Kyoko smiled brightly at Joel and then held out her hands to take his. "It's a pleasure to meet you, Joel.

Ethan and I practically grew up together. You're a lucky guy to have found him. He's one of the most genuine and loving people I know."

Joel blushed and gripped her hands tighter. "I feel pretty lucky to even know him. But getting to call him mine, that's more than luck—that's providence."

"Oh my god," Kyoko said. "You're absolutely adorable." She turned and grabbed Ethan's face and kissed him on the forehead. "I love him. Where did you two meet?"

"He's my next door neighbor," Ethan replied.

"Well, that was convenient." Kyoko leaned into Ethan's chest and looked at Joel. "How come you can't get married right away?"

"Joel is already married," Ethan said. "We have to wait until his divorce goes through."

"Uh, …that sucks," Kyoko replied, and then studied Joel. "You look awful young to be moving on to your second marriage. Was the last guy abusive or something?"

"No." Joel looked to Ethan for guidance, not knowing how much he should be telling her.

"Joel married his girlfriend from high school when she got pregnant," Ethan said. "It turned out to be a mistake."

"Did she have the baby?" Kyoko leaned forward expectantly.

"Yeah, we had a boy," Joel replied.

"Do you have pictures?" Kyoko squirmed off Ethan's lap and perched at the edge of Joel's seat. She clapped her hands together as Joel pulled out his phone and brought up the pictures of Sam.

She paged through them slowly, taking in the details of each photo, including who was in them.

"These are recent, aren't they?" she asked.

"Yeah, Sam is only a few months old," said Ethan as he peered over Kyoko's shoulder at the pictures. He reached in and clicked through them until he found his favorite. It was one of him and Joel holding a screaming Sam, and they were making full, tongue out, crazy man expressions in response.

"Oh my god. That is priceless," Kyoko said as she held her hand to her mouth. She passed the phone back to Joel and settled herself back in Ethan's lap.

Ethan shifted and sighed.

"How are things with you and Lucien?" he asked.

"Same as always. The man is a bore." Kyoko sat up and threw her hand to her chest. "God, I'm sorry, Ethan. I wasn't thinking."

"It's all right. I've moved on. It's all good." Ethan ducked his eyes and caught Joel's concerned expression, and reached out for his hand. "I'll tell you the whole story later, babe."

"Yeah, sure," Joel replied.

"Speaking of Lucien," said Kyoko. "He's traveling with me, so I need to get back to him. He's probably wondering what's become of me." She kissed Ethan on the forehead.

"I'll tell him to leave you alone," she added.

"Thanks. I'll see you at the ceremony?"

"I wouldn't miss it. Text me the details."

Kyoko brushed her hand along Ethan's face and then turned to Joel. She gave Joel a kiss on each cheek and whispered to him once again that he was a lucky man and that he was to take good care of Ethan, and then she was off down the aisle.

Ethan took a deep breath and reclined his seat, and motioned for Joel to come join him. Then he reached up and flicked the light off as Joel attempted to get comfortable on the seat with him.

"So, there's more to the Lucien story," Joel said.

"Much more." Ethan laid a kiss on Joel's cheek. "Kyoko is the girl I dated in high school ...and for a few years after that. We were in Paris together when we met Lucien. It was her crazy idea to bring him back to our hotel room after a night of clubbing. She was always looking for something new and exciting to try. The three of us ended up in bed together, but I'd never been with a guy before, and I hadn't considered that having sex with him was going to be part of the deal." He tucked his face in tighter to Joel's. "It took me by surprise when he started doing stuff to me."

"He didn't rape you, did he?"

"Fuck, I don't know? I suppose he did. I was too drunk to stop him."

Ethan turned and grabbed some nicotine gum from his coat, and handed one to Joel, then popped a piece into his own mouth.

"I remember waking up the next morning beside him," he continued. "We were alone. Kyoko had gone out to run some errands. Lucien apologized for not realizing I was a virgin, and he kissed me like I'd never been kissed before, and then he made love to me."

He sighed deeply. "I know it was just fucking, but it felt like more than that, and I found myself swimming in a torrent of self-realization."

"That you liked guys better?"

"It wasn't just a case of *better*. One of the reasons Kyoko was always on the lookout for new stuff was because I wasn't into sex, at all. But with Lucien ...completely different story."

"So, how did she end up with Lucien?"

"The three of us spent every night together for the next month. During the early part of the day, Kyoko would usually head out to check out some museum or another, and Lucien and I would be left to amuse ourselves. Sometimes we would go out, but most of the time we would stay in bed. We had some really nice times together, talking and making love. So much so, I fell in love with him." He sighed again, the memory of those days washing over him.

"What I didn't realize," he said after a long pause, "was that he and Kyoko had made a real connection. They were in love with each other. When I told Lucien, I loved him. He laughed."

"What?"

"He was surprised that I hadn't picked up on what was happening between him and Kyoko, and even more surprised that I hadn't realized that what was happening between us was just sex."

"How can anyone be that oblivious?"

"Thanks a lot, Joel. I know I'm stupid."

"Not you. Lucien." Joel shifted to relieve the pressure of the seat handle poking into his back. "How could he spend a month of mornings fucking you and not realize you had feelings for him? That's absolute bullshit. You have some of the most expressive eyes I've ever seen. You wear your emotions in them as clearly as if you'd tattooed your feelings across your forehead."

"Maybe you're the only one that can see that."

Joel gazed into Ethan's eyes for a second. "That's possible." He reached back, grabbed the pillow off his seat, and stuffed it behind his back. "But I still think the man is an idiot." Whereby Ethan laughed and kissed Joel soundly on the lips.

"Mm …his loss," Joel said. "Ethan, I love you, but I can't sleep here in this seat with you." He pulled himself off Ethan and fell into his own seat, then grabbed his pillow back, and tucked it behind his head. "I want to be able to feel my legs when we land."

"We've only got another—" Ethan checked his phone. "Eight hours to go. Try to get some sleep. When we get to my house, all hell is going to break loose."

"Yeah, about that. Exactly how many people are in your family?"

"I lost count." Ethan turned to face Joel. "Get some sleep."

The sound of the plane's engines eventually lulled Joel to sleep, and he dreamed about Ethan's family and what they would be like. Ethan had told him how fun and accepting they were, and that made him feel better. He was trying to picture what Ethan's dad would be like when he was awoken by someone leaning over him.

"Excuse me?" Joel said as he looked up at the man hovering over him. It had to be Lucien. He had the whole upper-class French thing going on, with his expensive clothes, cologne, and *pompeux* attitude.

Joel crossed his arms across his chest.

Lucien was a tall, muscular guy with dark hair, and Joel hated to admit it, but he was absolutely gorgeous.

"Pardon," Lucien said. "Je veux parler a Ethan." He looked down at Joel and waited for a response. "N'etes-vous pas au Canada?"

"Oui. But I'm from British Columbia, Canada," Joel replied indignantly. "And even though I can understand most of what you're saying, you'd have better luck getting a beaver to speak French."

He waited, then sighed in exasperation, and reached over and poked Ethan awake. "Lucien wants to talk to you."

Ethan rubbed his eyes and bolted straight up.

Joel, could you change seats with me, please?" he asked, then waited for Joel to pass behind him so he could sink into Joel's seat.

He leaned back and looked up at Lucien—he hadn't changed much.

"Que veux-tu?" he asked.

Joel tucked his arms across his chest again, prepared to translate as much of the conversation as he could. He was off to a good start. Even a kid from the west coast knew Ethan had asked, *What do you want*?

"Kyoko m'a demande de ne pas vous deranger," Lucien said.

Joel dropped his head back onto the headrest and sighed deeply. Other than Kyoko's name, he had no idea what Lucien had just said.

He grunted to himself.

So much for four years of high school French.

"Alors. Pourquoi vous avez fait?" Ethan shifted forward in his seat and threw his hands up. "Laissez moi et mon fiancé seul."

Joel sat up. He'd recognized two things. *Alor* was an exclamation, and the word *fiancé* was universal.

He smiled to himself and leaned back in his seat. Ethan had called him his fiancé. He glanced over. Lucien was staring at him.

"Il est juste un enfant," Lucien said.

"Hey, now hold on a second," Joel said. "I understood that. I am not a child." He was ready to jump up out of his seat but immediately calmed down when Ethan grabbed his hand.

"Tu me manques," Lucien said to Ethan.

"You miss me?" Ethan stood up suddenly. "You've got to be fuckin' kidding me!" He shoved Lucien hard almost knocking him over. "Vous etes un malade batard!"

He scanned the cabin, trying to spot Kyoko, but had to give up when two attendants rushed over and asked him to be seated.

Ethan waved them away as he sat down and Lucien wandered off.

The rest of the flight was uneventful, and once they landed, Kyoko and Lucien managed to stay ahead of them, which was fine by Ethan.

He could talk to Kyoko at the ceremony about her choice of boyfriend.

Ethan had explained to Joel that they were going to be staying at his dad's country house in North Yorkshire because it had the most garden space to hold the ceremony in and enough rooms for any overnight visitors that might be attending. But while in the car, he went on to add that they were going to be making a detour first.

Joel attempted to see where they were going, but couldn't see anything through the darkened glass of the limousine. He played with a few switches and finally found the one to lower the window, and pulled himself up to get a better look.

He sedately watched the countryside passing by, but then got right up on his knees as they entered the village.

Ethan laughed and pulled on the back of Joel's pants.

"Don't fall out," he said as he pulled harder until Joel fell backward into his lap, whereupon he stroked Joel's face and took his mouth urgently while his hands began searching Joel's body, looking for a way into his clothing. They had been cooped up on the plane for a long time, and he found himself seriously craving the taste of Joel's mouth and the feel of his skin.

He moaned in disappointment as he felt the car pull over.

"Bollocks," he exclaimed.

"What's wrong?" Joel asked as he tried to sit up again.

"This village is way too small for my liking. I'll have to ask the driver to drive around in circles next time we go out."

"Where are we?"

"The shop where I got my very first tattoo."

"Seriously? That is so cool." Joel climbed out of the car behind Ethan and followed him to the door of the studio. "What are we getting done?"

"See, this is why I love you. You're a doer, not a watcher."

"And here I thought you just loved me for my ass." Joel smacked Ethan's on the way past and went to look around the eclectic space. He walked over to one of the counters and started to flip through some photos of tattoos and piercings that had been done at the studio. The artwork was impressive enough that he decided to take a look around to see what was being worked on.

Ethan stood at one of the counters and pretended to look through some jewelry. He was actually watching Joel wander through the studio, and his heart swelled with pride at the fact Joel was perfectly at ease in an environment that was so familiar and cherished in his own life.

Joel approached a table where quite an intense piece of art was being added to a man's chest and decided to watch for a minute, admiring the skill of the artist's hand.

"That's really incredible," he said.

The artist stopped working and sat back to look at Joel. "I haven't seen you in here before. Who does your work?"

He rolled his chair closer and motioned for Joel to show him his arm where Ethan had recently completed an intricate piece.

"My boyfriend does everything."

"Really? And is your boyfriend here with you?" He set his gun down and looked around the studio, then laughed aloud, shaking his immense frame, and slammed his hands together when he found who he was looking for. "Would you look at what the fuckin' cat drug in!" Leaping up, he ran over to where Ethan was standing. "Ethan fuckin' Cooke!"

Ethan turned, and a grin spread across his face. "Luke. How the fuck are you?" He reached out and grasped Luke's hand.

"I've been keepin' busy working for a livin'." Luke clapped Ethan roughly on the back. "How goes the life of a prince?"

"Fuck you. I've been working for Karl."

"Right. Right. It's a good program that." Luke looked back to where Joel was standing talking to some of the other artists. "I recognized your hand on that boy's work."

"I've done everything on him." Deciding to play it cool, Ethan pulled a cigarette out and lit it. "Tattoos and piercings."

"He says you're his boyfriend."

"Does he now?" Ethan turned his head and blew the smoke out as he laughed. "Would that be a problem?"

"Jeez, Ethan. I didn't know you were in to boys." Luke looked back over at Joel. "How old is he anyway?"

"He's old enough to know what he wants." Ethan stuffed his hand into his pocket and leaned against the counter. "I'd like you to sketch up a couple of simple designs for us."

"Sure thing. What are you looking for?" Luke reached behind the counter, grabbed a pencil and pad of paper, and handed them to Ethan.

Ethan drew out the basic design with a quick hand and handed it to Luke.

"Wedding rings?" Luke asked in surprise.

"Mm …my dad's throwing us a commitment ceremony of sorts while we're here, and then we're going to get married properly in a year or so." Ethan crushed out the cigarette and looked at Luke. "It seemed appropriate for our wedding rings to be tattooed. And I wanted them done in your shop for sentimental reasons."

"You're going to marry him?" Luke looked at Joel, and then back to Ethan. "I don't understand."

Ethan laughed and lit up another cigarette. "What don't you understand?" He checked his pack and upon finding it empty, threw it into a garbage can. "I'm in love with the little bugger, and I want exclusive rights to his sweet little ass."

Luke was silent.

"This is a great studio," Joel said as he nudged up against Ethan.

"Only the best get to apprentice here," Ethan replied. "And if they're really exceptional, they get to train under Luke here."

"Yeah. Hey, I'm Joel." Joel shook Luke's hand. "I'm going to assume by the introduction that Ethan apprenticed with you."

"Our Ethan has a tendency to be modest," Luke said, and crossed his arms and looked Joel over properly. He wasn't a typical example of the clientele he would normally see with that much work done. Joel looked like someone Ethan had pulled straight off a surfer beach in California somewhere and then spent the next few months doing modifications. Ethan had done an excellent job making everything mesh, and the overall effect was stunning. But Joel's blond hair and tanned skin were in such startling contrast to Ethan's dark gothic look, that it was somewhat disconcerting.

"You've had that problem with him too, eh?" Joel said.

Luke laughed heartily. "You Canadians really say, *eh*?"

"Not where I come from. But I pulled that one out of the hat just for you, eh." Joel laughed and snorted. "Sorry, I couldn't resist. It won't happen again, eh."

"Moving on ..." Ethan slid over, wrapped his arm around Joel, and took the drawings back off Luke. He passed them to Joel and waited for his response.

"These are the tattoos you want done today?" Joel asked, and then crossed his arms, and closed his eyes.

"Is that all right?" Ethan said. "It's kind of permanent." His heart starting collapsing as he sensed Joel was hesitating.

"I love them. They're perfect, Ethan," Joel said finally as he opened his eyes. "And I'll be more than thrilled to get them done on one condition." He paused. "After what you told me on the plane today …I can't help but feel that the pink heart on your stomach needs a serious modification done to it first. And I won't be using that secret glow in the dark ink. I want a gun full of black ink."

Ethan let out a sigh of relief. "Do what you want with the heart. Just don't ever give me a heart attack like that again." He lit up a cigarette from a new pack and passed it to Joel. "Luke, do you mind if we use the equipment? I think the rings will have more meaning if we do each other's."

"Sure thing, Ethan," Luke said. "You can use your old station at the back there. I'll get these drawn up for you right away. Give me a shout if you need anything."

Ethan nodded as Joel shoved him toward his old table at the back, and slid up onto it, and stretched out, grinning as he watched Joel chewing on his lip as he sorted through some scripts before drawing up his pattern. He closed his eyes and steadied his breathing as Joel set it.

Joel was naturally quick and steady, and was soon finished modifying the pink heart that had originally been intended for Lucien. It now contained the words *Ethan loves Joel forever*.

Ethan pulled himself off the table, stood in front of the mirror, and tried to read it. He smiled as he deciphered it.

"Your pink heart," he said to Joel, "is going to be next with the black ink."

"Definitely. But not today," Joel replied as he retrieved the patterns Luke had done up for them. "Let's get these rings done."

He reached for Ethan and kissed him, then held out his hand and wiggled his fingers until Ethan burst out laughing.

The studio was long past closed by the time they finished, and it was already getting dark. Ethan had phoned his dad earlier to let him know there was going to be a delayed in their arrival, and that they wouldn't be there in time for supper.

Joel flicked on one of the interior lights in the limousine soon after they got in, and held his hand up to better examine the ring Ethan had designed for him. It was an intricate series of braided knots skillfully intertwined with Ethan's name, and on the underside, he'd left an open space to put their wedding date in.

The one he had done for Ethan wasn't nearly as complex, because his skill level just wasn't there yet, but Ethan had designed something that was elegant and just as meaningful.

He flicked the light off as he felt the car turn into a driveway.

Ethan's father David had been pacing the floor of the lounge for hours in anticipation of his son's arrival. He hadn't seen Ethan in almost three years and a reunion was long overdue.

Plus, the circumstances surrounding the reunion were particularly joyous, and he couldn't wait to begin the visit.

After the whole incident with Lucien, David had been very concerned about Ethan. He was such a loving person, just like his mother, and that personality trait had caused him pain. When he'd heard that Ethan had found someone new, he'd been excited to hear the news until Ethan had begun filling him in on the details of their relationship and the potential legal issues. His heart had sunk and he had lost countless night's sleep over it, not wanting his son to get hurt again. Now, he was finally going to meet the boy that Ethan had been willing to risk so much for.

He raced out through the front door when he heard the car pull up outside, and watched Ethan get out first; he looked much older than the last time he had seen him, and David was a little surprised to see how far he'd progressed with the piercings on his face, and that he had started adding facial tattoos as well.

David watched anxiously as Ethan reached into the car and helped Joel out. The first thing he saw was a shock of sun bleached hair, followed by a tanned arm with a swarm of colorful tattoos. He peered across the top of the car and his heart soared when he saw Ethan gazing down at his fiancé, the love for him obvious. Then Ethan's eyes smiled as Joel reached up, held his face, and brought him down for a kiss. That was all he needed to see.

He liked the boy already.

Ethan glanced up and caught sight of his dad waiting for them, and started waving furiously. He grabbed Joel by the arm and ran with him toward the front door.

"Dad!" Ethan leaped into David's arms and swung him around. He set him down and squeezed him tight, causing his dad to cough.

"Ethan, my boy." David patted Ethan firmly on the back. "You're going to kill your old man." He sighed as Ethan let him go.

"Dad, this is Joel." Ethan hugged Joel to him.

"Mr. Cooke." Joel smiled as he held his hand out.

"Mr. Cooke was my father. Call me David, or better yet, call me Dad." He pulled Joel into his arms, held him briefly, and then kissed the top of his head. He stepped back, cupping Joel's face, and studied him. He should've expected that Joel would have the same type of facial piercings as his son, but he'd been under the impression Joel hadn't been into all that before he'd met Ethan. If that was the case, they'd been busy working on him. He was an attractive young man under it all, which pleased him, because, after Lucien, Ethan had, according to his friends, gone through a phase of dating the most hideous natured and vile looking men ever.

"All right. Dad it is," Joel replied.

"Excellent," David said. "Well, let's go inside and get you boys something to eat." He held the door open as they stepped inside, then followed up behind them. "How was the flight?"

"Interesting," Ethan said. "Kyoko was on the plane, and we had a good visit. She's coming to the ceremony."

"That's wonderful," David said. "Her parents aren't coming of course. I'll never understand some people ...love is love." He bustled into the kitchen and pulled open the fridge. "Nancy was here earlier. She's sorry to have missed you two, but she'll be around all week. Apparently, she had

Joel pegged as your soul mate from the moment she met him."

"I wish she would've told us," Joel said. "It would've saved us a lot of grief …and time." He took the covered plate David handed him and passed it to Ethan.

"Seriously, Joel, you would've thought she was insane," Ethan said as he took the next plate from Joel.

"Why do you say that?" David asked.

"Joel had a girlfriend. And he'd only just met me days before that …plus I'm a guy." Ethan removed one of the plates from the microwave and set the next one in.

"I would've listened if she'd said something." Joel grabbed the fork David handed him and went to sit at the large island running the length of the massive kitchen.

"Why's that?" David asked as he leaned on the counter across from him. "Why would you have listened?"

"Because I thought your son was hot." Joel grinned as Ethan spun around with a shocked expression on his face.

"You did not," Ethan said.

"Yeah, I did. That first day in the pool when you stepped out of the water in front of me …when I saw that *cupido* tattoo gracing the top of your ass like that …I felt stuff." Joel pushed his food around on the plate and took another mouthful.

"You little bugger." Ethan shook his head and took a seat beside him. "Why didn't you say anything?"

"First off. I didn't know you were gay. And I'd never had such a strong reaction to a guy before. So the whole thing freaked me out. That's why I took off to my house so quick after we got out of the pool." He set his fork down and supported his head in his hand. "And then I went back to your house that night looking for pain meds." He laughed and shook his head. "When you carried me home, I thought for sure I was going to pass out. Being that close to you, combined with the pain meds made me a bit heady. Hell, I almost pulled you down on top of me on the lounge chair. I think if Erica hadn't been there, I might have."

"I wish you had," Ethan said. "Seeing you all relaxed and goofy like that ...I wanted to kiss you so bad."

"So you were attracted to me from the beginning after all," Joel replied. "Now the truth comes out." He shoved Ethan affectionately with his elbow.

"Yeah, but I'd resigned myself to strictly being a friend. And it was working out well." Ethan stroked the hair above Joel's ear. "I was happy to even have you in my life."

"Same." Joel rested his head on Ethan's shoulder. "But then by December, I couldn't stand it anymore. I wanted us to be so much more than friends."

Ethan turned and kissed Joel's head. "I'm glad you listened to your heart." He looked up at his dad. "Joel actually made the first move. It was bloody subtle though." He hugged Joel to him. "When I kissed the back of his neck, I wasn't sure what was going to happen. He could've just as easily turned around and hit me."

"I would never hit you." Joel smirked and winked at Ethan, whereby Ethan poked him roughly in the ribs, making him gasp.

"Well you managed to work it out—you're together now," David said. "That's all that matters."

Joel took Ethan's hand to his lips and kissed it. "It is, isn't it?" A flush ran up Ethan's face as Joel smiled at him.

"David ...Dad, I'm sorry, but I can't eat any more," Joel said. "I'm exhausted. I just want to crawl into bed, if that's all right."

"Of course, Joel. It was a long flight," David replied, and then turned to Ethan. "I've got your old room set up. You two go ahead. I'll tidy up down here." He beamed at them. "I'm so excited for both of you. I'll see you in the morning."

Ethan took Joel's hand and led him back out through the foyer and toward the massive staircase they'd passed on the way in. "My room is up this way." He guided Joel up the long set of stairs and turned toward an even longer hallway. "We used to spend every summer at this house. I think my dad still does for the most part."

"He must be lonely here all by himself."

"You're forgetting about the massive family. Trust me. He probably wishes he had more time to himself."

They approached a set of double doors, and Ethan pushed one side open and directed Joel to enter. The room was beautifully decorated with a classic, English country motif that Joel found to be a bit stuffy for his liking, but the sight of the massive bed had him reconsidering.

He wandered over to the chair beside it and began peeling off his clothes, but halfway through he became too tired to continue, and decided to sit down.

Ethan undressed and walked around to Joel's side of the bed to see what was slowing him down.

"Are you all right?" he asked,

"I'm really exhausted. I don't think my body likes flying."

Ethan bent down to remove Joel's shoes and socks, and had him stand up so he could take his pants off, then pulled back the covers, tucking Joel in after Joel managed to climb up into the voluminous bedding.

Joel pulled the covers up over his shoulders, barely able to keep his eyes open. He could hear the familiar sound of Ethan sitting up having his evening smoke, and decided to make his way over to that side of the bed, so he could cuddle into him.

He completed his final shuffle and laid his head on Ethan's stomach, being careful not to bump the new tattoo, and started to drift off, only stirring when Ethan lifted him away, so he could lay down. He tucked his head onto Ethan's chest and yawned.

Ethan looked down at Joel and laughed quietly when he heard him yawn. He kissed the top of Joel's head and hugged him tighter, and then closed his eyes, ready to pass out from exhaustion.

He was surprised when he felt Joel kiss his chest.

"I thought you were asleep already," he said.

"I'm feeling a little insecure."

"About what?"

"Why you're with someone like me when you can get guys like Lucien." Joel sat up so he could see Ethan's face.

"You mean stuck-up, arrogant, conceited assholes."

"Exactly," Joel replied, and then laughed.

"I'd much rather spend my life with a courageous, insightful, and passionate man. Especially one that I'm in love with."

"Mm ...I feel better now." Joel rolled back in to the pillows. "Good night." He turned the rest of the way over and backed himself up against Ethan's body. He smiled when he felt Ethan's mouth moving across his shoulder, and then moaned softly with contentment when Ethan's hand ran up his chest and over his throat, tipping him back far enough so he could take his mouth.

"I'd like to make you feel even better." Ethan kissed Joel again and hugged him close. "I've been meaning to ask you something."

"What is it?"

"You know I haven't been with anyone else since October."

"I know."

Ethan stroked nervously at Joel's hair and kissed his shoulder. "I had myself tested recently, and I'm definitely clean."

"You want to fuck bareback?"

"We're going to be married, and I have no intention of sleeping with anyone else. You're *it* for me."

"What about me? I haven't been tested for anything."

"Weren't you and Erica each other's first and only?"

"Yeah, we were." Joel thought back to the night they had lost their virginity together, and how ridiculously awkward it had been. He laughed at the memory. "Jeez, that seems like a lifetime ago."

"Chances are you're fine. I'm willing to risk it." Ethan kissed the back of Joel's neck. "So, what do you think?"

He held his breath as he waited.

"You're *it* for me too." Joel reached back and wrapped his arm around Ethan's neck, and brought him back to his mouth.

"No more condoms," Joel said after he released Ethan.

"Brilliant. Can we start tonight?"

Joel just laughed in response, fully expecting that to be Ethan's response.

Ethan climbed out of bed, wandered into the bathroom, and rooted through one of his bags until he found the small bottle of lube he was looking for. He jumped back into bed and dispensed some into his hand, and began stroking his cock.

"Do you want me to take the Prince Albert out?"

"No, leave it in. I like the feel of it." Joel pushed back against Ethan's hand, welcoming the intrusion, and was lulled into submission by his gentle touch within him.

"If it's too uncomfortable for you, I'll take it out."

Joel sighed as his body came alive.

"I'm sure it'll be fine," he said, then reached back for Ethan's hand, stopping him. "That's enough. I'm more than ready."

Ethan sucked at a small patch of skin on the back of Joel's neck as he caressed Joel's body, breathing heavier as he sensed Joel's increasing need. He reached down, slipping himself in, and then held Joel tight to him. "Are you all right?"

"It feels really good. Totally different."

Ethan tucked his face into Joel's neck and started a series of slow steady thrusts, keeping his hand on Joel's stomach to hold him firmly in place.

"Ethan—," Joel said, and then gasped sharply.

"Yeah, babe? What's wrong?"

"Nothing." Joel arched his back. "Can you leave it in when you cum? I want you to fill me."

"I can most definitely do that." Ethan bit at Joel's shoulder and pressed him closer to his body, thrusting deeper.

The feeling of Ethan moving inside him was adding a sense of delirium to Joel's exhaustion, and the loud rapturous noises Ethan was making were soon causing him to respond in kind.

Ethan tucked his head even closer into the nape of Joel's neck, so he could feel the vibrations being produced by Joel's sounds of passion. He increased the force and pace until the stars flashing behind his eyes carried him through to ecstasy. He gripped Joel possessively to him as he felt his body release, shuddered in exhilaration as he sensed Joel cresting in unison.

He slowed everything down, enjoying the intense closeness he was feeling with Joel at that moment.

Joel rolled over to face Ethan, took Ethan's face in his hands, then ran his fingers across Ethan's lips, and gazed into his eyes.

"Now, I really am yours," he said, then shuffled down and curled up against Ethan's chest. He was asleep within minutes.

People were scheduled to start arriving just after lunch. The ceremony wasn't for another two days, but Ethan's relatives were anxious to meet the man that was not only brave enough to venture into Ethan's world but had decided to stay in it with him.

According to his family, Ethan had always been an unusual child with very little aptitude for making friends. In preschool, he often had to be separated from the other children and disciplined for what his teachers described as *aggressive outbursts with a tendency to display outrageous and bawdy facial expressions*. His father had discounted it, theorizing it was due to losing his mother.

In primary school, Ethan had developed a habit of trying to frighten the other children in his class by simply staring at them. Even the teachers had been freaked out by it, and he had spent a lot of time in the detention room on his own, doing his schoolwork.

Once he began attending high school, Ethan had begun wearing long black clothes and combat boots, and found that his staring game was intensified by adding black eyeliner to his eyes. During his final two years at high school, he had acquired some fake identification, and that's when the piercings and tattoos had started. Add in the chain smoking, leather, chains and spikes—and you had the persona Ethan felt most comfortable wearing. It was this dark, sullen person that his relatives were expecting to see when they arrived at David's house, and they presumed his fiancé wouldn't be much different.

Joel grabbed his bright floral swim shorts out of his bag and pulled them on, then checked out the window, and shrugged with disappointment. August in Britain was not the same as August back home. But he didn't want to have his tan fade for the sake of a few degrees. He knocked on the bathroom door and poked his head in.

"I'm going out on the patio for some sun," he said to Ethan.

"Have fun finding it," Ethan replied in jest.

"It looks all right out there." Joel went back to the bedroom to grab his SPF 8 sunblock, decided against it, and found his tanning oil instead. He threw his flip-flops and sunglasses on, tucked his cigarettes into his shorts, then headed down the stairs. He was turning the last corner on the way to the patio when he ran into David, who was making his way from the kitchen with a coffee.

"You look like you're on your way to the seaside," David said.

"I'm not going any further than the back patio." Joel smiled. "Between the tanning and the cigarettes, I'm not likely to see fifty."

"I hope you're wrong about that. How did you sleep?"

"That bed is amazing. It's like a massive feather pillow. Ethan had to find me and dig me out this morning."

"There's nothing like an old fashioned country mattress. Is Ethan coming down soon?"

"He's in the shower right now, and would normally go back to bed afterward …but if he smells coffee, he'll find a way to slither down here. Just give him a good kick in the ass if he doesn't get up."

Joel paused.

"I'll see you in a bit ...Dad," he added.

"Enjoy the sun." David clapped Joel on the arm affectionately and let him continue on his way to the patio.

Joel dusted off one of the lounge chairs and threw down the towel he'd draped around his neck. He settled in and lit up a cigarette. He had to move the lounge a few times in an attempt to block the cool breezes blowing across him, but eventually had himself situated perfectly, whereupon he went back to sleep.

He was awoken by the sound of whispering voices.

"Do you think that's him?" a woman's voice asked.

"Who else could it be?" another woman answered.

"He looks like one of those American surfer dudes."

"That can't be him," yet another woman commented.

"It has to be. Who else would do all of *that* to their body? He's a lovely looking boy though, isn't he?"

Joel was listening to the comments and trying not to let on that he was awake. He had his eyes open, but the lenses on his glasses weren't letting them see that.

"What are we looking at?" a man's voice asked.

"It's Ethan's fiancé, Granddad."

"She's awfully bold lying out here with no top on."

"His fiancé is a boy, Granddad. Remember I told you that."

"All this newfangled stuff ...in my day, boys married girls." He puffed heavily. "And why is his face covered in earrings?"

Joel couldn't contain himself any longer. He rolled onto his side and laughed as he reached for his cigarettes and took his glasses off.

"I was wondering how long it was going to take for you to crack." A girl about the same age as Ethan and with very similar coloring grinned at him and extended her hand. "I'm Emily and this is my mother Millicent, my sisters Eunice and Alison, and the comedic relief this afternoon is Granddad Philip."

"Nice to meet you all." Joel stood up and shook hands with each one of them, not knowing what the protocol was. "I'm Joel ...as you've already guessed." He looked at each of them and then turned to Millicent. "You're Ethan's mom Margaret's sister?"

"Yes, that's right," Millicent said.

"Eunice, Alison and Emily ...you're Ethan's first cousins along with your sister Sarah, and your brothers William and Daniel?"

"Very good, but can you name all the grandbabies?" Philip asked as he slapped his thigh and laughed. "Don't worry if you can't. I lost track years ago."

"Dad, that's horrible," Millicent said and turned back to speak with Joel. "So, tell me, where is that nephew of mine?"

Joel peered over Millicent's shoulder toward the door into the house and could see Ethan struggling to pass through the room, surrounded by children.

"Aunt Millie!" Ethan shouted. "I somehow managed to get myself roped into baby duty. Someone heard that Joel had a bairn. And now I'm suddenly an expert."

"Don't give me that," Aunt Millie replied. "You've been caring for them babies since you were eight years old."

"I know. I was just looking for a little sympathy." Ethan made it through the door with a baby in each arm and stepped out to give his Aunt Millie as kiss on the cheek. He looked around and his eyebrows shot up at the sight of Emily. "What the—"

"Don't even say it, Ethan," Emily said.

"What happened? I thought we were partners in crime." Ethan turned to face Joel. "This girl here used to be like my twin." He circled around Emily, perusing her. "The new hair color isn't too hideous, and the fitted clothes make your ass look hot, but I'm not sure I like the absence of metal." He grinned at her and passed the babies to Joel, then swept her up in his arms.

"You look beautiful," he said. "It suits you." He planted a noisy kiss on her cheek and then set her down. "What precipitated the change?"

"I met a guy," Emily said. "He's a banker—"

"Emma, no!" Ethan took a fake arrow to the heart and fell onto the ground, pretending to writhe in pain. "Not a banker…. God, anything, but that." He rolled onto his side when there was no response.

Emily was no longer standing alone, and Ethan immediately jumped to his feet. "And you must be him." Ethan held out his hand to the stiff man at his cousin's side. "Ethan Cooke. Pleasure."

"William Bradford." Reluctantly taking Ethan's hand, William shook it brusquely, making Ethan roll his eyes at Emily.

"William and I are engaged," Emily said as she held out her hand to show off her engagement ring.

"Congratulations," Ethan said as he examined the ring. "Joel and I tattooed our wedding rings on each other yesterday." He grinned and leered obstinately at William, who chose to look away.

"Oh, let me see," Emily said as she grabbed Ethan's hand. "It's got Joel's name in it and everything. That is *so* beautiful."

She motioned for Joel to step closer and show her his ring.

Joel did a bit of baby juggling, eventually passing one of them back to Ethan before showing Emily the ring.

"Mine's a bit more intricate," he said. "Ethan has a lot more experience than me. I only started tattooing this summer."

"You actually tattooed each other's rings?" Emily asked enthusiastically. "That is so romantic." She smacked William hard across the chest. "Isn't that romantic, William?"

William just looked at her funny.

"You're such a stuffy old thing," she said.

"Both my parents are bankers," Joel said, attempting to draw William into a conversation.

"They must be so proud," William replied dryly, then turned back toward the house.

"Don't mind him," Aunt Millie said as she approached. "He was born with an aristocratic stick up his ass, and has yet to find the right tool to pry it out with."

Both Ethan and Joel burst out laughing with the same thought in mind. Emily tried to pretend she hadn't caught on, and did her best to hold it together as tears began streaming down her face.

Aunt Millie looked at the three of them and walked away.

"God, Ethan, I've missed you and your filthy mind," Emily said as she motioned for someone to take the babies. "William is a bit of a bore sometimes. But he has his moments."

"Speaking of bores, I saw Kyoko on the plane," Ethan said.

"Since when has Kyoko ever been a bore?" Emily replied.

"She's not. But she thinks Lucien is."

"No. Was he there too?"

"Yeah, we had a brief conversation where he told me he missed me. Can you believe that?"

Emily thanked one of the many people lingering around for taking the babies off their hands, and then led the way across the grass toward an enclosed strolling garden. She found a seat that would fit the three of them and sat down.

"Did you tell Kyoko?" Emily said.

"No, she's coming to the ceremony. I'll tell her then," Ethan replied as he wrapped his arm around Joel. "I must be the luckiest guy in the world to have found someone so amazing."

"That makes two of us," Joel said, and then kissed Ethan on the cheek. "You don't think Lucien will come to the ceremony, do you? It seemed like he really wanted to talk to you."

"I don't honestly care," Ethan said. "I'm going to be looking at you the entire time, trying to measure the depth of my love for you."

Then he held Joel's face and kissed him with such incredible intensity, it removed the incident with Lucien from his mind.

"I'm going to cry," Emily said as she held her hands delicately over her mouth. "You two are adorable." She dropped her hands in her lap and laughed. They weren't paying any attention to her.

Not wanting to interrupt their moment, Emily walked over to the hedge surrounding the garden, and lingered, watching them for a minute. There was so much passion and love there.

Emily sighed deeply and went to look for William.

"I'm so tired." Joel stretched out on a sofa in the reception room at the rear of the house and tried to get comfortable, but he had one baby asleep on his chest and another tucked into the crook of his arm with a bottle. "No wonder you're such an expert when it comes to dealing with Sam. Where are these babies' mothers?"

Ethan had a two year old seated on his lap that insisted on touching his facial piercings and trying to pull on them. He gently held the little girl's hands in his and looked into her eyes. "Don't touch. That's owwie for Uncle Ethan." But she just giggled at him and went back to pulling on things.

"As a guy in my family," Ethan said to Joel. "The deal is that during family gatherings you walk in and grab a baby—or two. You make sure the baby is safe, happy, and free of spit up or smelly diapers. And when the mother wants her baby back, she'll come looking for him or her, at which point you are free to pick up another baby ...or as is my special privilege today, a toddler."

"God, I need a cigarette." Joel checked the baby with the bottle, and seeing that he was finished, set him up on his chest beside the other one, where he promptly spit up all over Joel's shirt.

"That's just perfect," he said. "But I suppose it matches the other five spit up stains I have." He reached over to the coffee table, grabbed a clean flannel cloth, and set it under the baby's head, so he wasn't lying in his own spit up at least.

I'm soaked, and it's making me itchy," he added.

"Here—" Ethan struggled to his feet and lifted his charge onto his hip. "We've been doing this long enough. I think we should be off the clock now." He grinned and rubbed his chin. "In fact, I think we should go find William. I'm sure he hasn't done any babysitting yet. And he is going to be part of the family after all."

Joel pulled himself off the sofa and tucked a baby into each arm, and followed Ethan to find William. They didn't have to go far before they tracked William down, and it didn't take long for Ethan to convince William that it was in his best interest to take the kids off their hands, if he wanted to keep his kneecaps intact. Unfortunately, the look of fear on William's face was cut short by an intervention by Emily—a devious act which Ethan swore he would avenge.

Ethan grinned at Emily as she removed the children from their care, then led Joel back through into the kitchen, and handed him a case of beer, a carton of cigarettes, and a bottle of rum.

"Are we having a party?" Joel asked.

"Party for two. I don't intend on emerging from that bedroom until the day of the ceremony."

"Won't we need food?"

"On it. I'll put a call in to Nancy. She can push food under the door." Ethan lit up a cigarette and fanned the smoke around. "Fuck, my dad will kill me if he finds out I'm smoking in the house."

Ducking past Joel, Ethan grabbed a box of pastries and some nacho chips, then pushed Joel out through the door.

"Hurry, before someone catches us —," he said, then took off up the stairs and motioned for Joel to hustle.

"Won't your dad wonder what happened to us?"

Joel stepped into the bedroom, used his foot to close the door, stepping out of the way as Ethan locked it.

Ethan set the food down on a big desk and pulled out his phone. "I'm sending Emily a text right now, telling her to tell my dad that we're taking an early honeymoon in my room." He read the text that came back from Emily and laughed. "And she says I have a filthy mind?" He smirked and typed something back.

Joel opened a beer and headed for the bathroom. He had a lot of baby spit up that needed to be washed off.

"This is a nice deep tub," he said. "Do you want to have a bath with me?" Joel leaned over, dropped the plug into place, and started running the water. He checked the temperature before he grabbed a couple of towels off the shelf and set them down beside the tub.

"Hey, before you get in," Ethan said. "I need to check something."

He directed Joel to get undressed and sit on the edge of the tub.

"I'm going to take this one out for now," he said as he unscrewed Joel's Prince Albert piercing and removed it.

"I thought you weren't supposed to do that."

"You're all healed now. I'm going to replace it with a different ring." Ethan scanned over all the other intimate piercings he had done on Joel. "Everything looks good. You're set to go."

"Meaning?"

"It means you can pitch for a few sets."

"Awesome. That'll make you happy."

"You know I don't mind either way." Ethan stood and started pulling his clothes off, but stopped to look for something.

"Yeah ...right." Joel looked at Ethan skeptically and shook his head. "What are you looking for?"

"We need to throw something onto the bottom of the bath. I don't want to scratch the porcelain with these guiche rings."

In the end, Ethan decided to use a towel, throwing it into the water and standing on it until it flattened out.

He sat down on it and waited for Joel to join him.

"I thought you were going to put a new ring in for me." Joel stepped into the tub and settled his back against Ethan's chest, then grabbed a washcloth and went to work cleaning the baby spit up from his skin.

"I'll do that later." Ethan brushed his fingers along Joel's shoulders. "I had an idea, which led to me wanting to sequester us."

He motioned for the cloth and soaped it up, then gently washed Joel's shoulders.

"What was your idea?" Joel took the washcloth back off Ethan and wrung it out before setting it on the tub edge. He turned over so he was facing Ethan, snorting in surprise, as he slid down the front of Ethan's body and almost ended up under the water.

"Apparently, new swimming lessons for you." Ethan laughed. "What happened to treading water?"

"Completely useless in soapy situations." Joel grabbed onto Ethan as he righted himself, and exhaled, laughing when he was back sitting safely. "Sorry …your idea?"

"Once we're safely out of the water …I was hoping you'd make me yours as well." Ethan stroked his hands down Joel's arms. "It's important to me too. The trust and the possession."

"In that case, why are we still in the tub?" Joel stood and stepped carefully out of the tub, and held his hands out for Ethan to take. "I'm clean enough …to get dirty with you."

Joel led Ethan into the bedroom, soaking the carpet along the way, and pulled Ethan's mouth down to meet his. He reveled momentarily in the familiar taste, and then shoved Ethan onto his knees at his feet, demanding his submission.

Ethan obeyed, crawling closer and licked Joel's cock into his mouth, working feverishly to encourage it.

Joel raked his hands through Ethan's hair and gripped onto it as he set Ethan's pace, and then grabbed a deeper handful and pulled Ethan back to his feet, causing Ethan to cry out as Joel yanked his head back, exposing his throat.

He ran his tongue along Ethan's throat as he ground against Ethan's thigh, sending his desire raging. Then shoving Ethan toward the edge of the bed, Joel forced Ethan to bend over, pinning his head to the bed, and then didn't waste a second pushing into Ethan, rough and aggressive, and began riding him, hard.

Wanting to hear more noise coming from Ethan, Joel reached forward and twisted Ethan's hair around his hand and hauled Ethan's head back until his spine curved up just the way he liked to see it—with the wings making a nice arc.

He smacked Ethan hard on the ass and started a stream of forceful jagged thrusts.

Ethan groaned as Joel rode him, overwhelmed by the power being forced upon him. He cried out Joel's name, pleading with him to hit him again, and fuck him harder.

Joel smiled to himself, hoping no one was anywhere near their bedroom. Anyone listening in would wonder what he was doing to torture Ethan, but he'd learned early on that Ethan liked it rough when he was being fucked, and he was only too happy to oblige.

The sounds Ethan made were such a turn on that Joel often found it difficult to keep it going for very long.

He took a deep breath and tried to pace himself.

Joel reached down toward the end of the bed, grabbed a bag of nacho chips, and settled back against his pillow beside Ethan.

He waited until Ethan lifted a handful of chips for himself then passed him back his beer.

"I seriously need a nap," Joel said. "You've completely worn me out. We've been at it for hours."

"Did you want to trade off for a while?"

Joel shuffled himself down further in the bed. "No, I'm going to throw back a few more beers. And then I'm going to sleep."

"Sounds like a marvelous plan, except we have to make an appearance at dinner, or my dad will have our heads."

"I figured the early, extended honeymoon was too good to be true. What time do we have to be down there?"

"Not until seven thirty." Ethan reached for his phone and checked the time. "It's only six now." He scanned through his text messages and answered a few.

"Anything exciting?"

"Yeah, Kyoko just sent me one." Ethan sat up straighter to read it. "Apparently, she's downstairs. Lucien broke up with her." He turned and looked at Joel. "Fuck, I hope it wasn't because of me."

His face creased with concern, Ethan typed a response and slid his phone closed.

"So, what's happening?" Joel asked.

"She's on her way up." Ethan climbed out of bed, unlocked the bedroom door, and opened it a crack to look down the hall.

"Aren't you going to put some clothes on?"

"Nah, she's seen it all before." Ethan stepped back and opened the door all the way, as Kyoko ran into the room.

Kyoko launched herself into Ethan's arms as soon as he had the door closed again. She was sobbing uncontrollably as she clung helplessly to Ethan's neck, attempting to calm herself down.

"Ethan, I'm so sorry to intrude on the two of you like this," she said. "But I didn't know who else to turn to."

"No, hey. That's all right. We were taking a break anyway."

Ethan took Kyoko's hand, led her over to the bed, and helped her up onto the end. "I'll get you a drink."

He walked back across the room, lifted a glass off the dresser, and poured her a double. He smiled and cocked an eyebrow at her on the way back to the bed when he caught her grinning at him.

"What happened to your ass, crop man?" Kyoko asked and took the glass from him. "Your boy here is rather enthusiastic."

"A little crop rash never hurt anyone," Ethan said and winked.

"Yeah, I got a bit carried away," Joel said. "It's been a while."

He shifted over when Ethan climbed back into bed and was surprised when Kyoko crawled up in between them.

"Oh, no, you don't," Ethan said to her. "Climb over. You're on the outside. I don't want you getting any ideas with my fiancé." He shifted over as Kyoko climbed over him, but ended up grabbing her when she deliberately fell onto his body. He kissed her and smacked her ass to get her to move.

"Off," Ethan said as he helped Kyoko complete her trip to the other side of him. "Joel, you have to watch this one. She's crafty."

Joel grabbed Ethan's arm and tugged him closer.

"So, are you guys looking for a girly third?" Kyoko asked. "We still have over an hour before dinner is served."

"Not interested, Kyoko," Ethan replied.

"Come on, Ethan," Kyoko continued. "It'll be like old times."

"And look what happened last time," Joel said.

Kyoko sighed deeply and let a few tears run down her cheeks. She tucked the pillow under her head and relaxed into the bed.

"I know, Joel," she said. "I was just looking for a distraction from my current romantic disaster." Kyoko looked at Ethan. "This is your fault, you know?"

"Kyoko," Ethan said. "I did nothing to encourage him, trust me. I don't know what the hell is going through his head."

"I know exactly what's going through his head," Kyoko replied. "He's been fine all these years, but I knew as soon as he saw you again, all his feelings for you would overwhelm him."

"What the fuck are you talking about?" Ethan demanded.

"Ethan, baby," Kyoko replied. "Lucien comes from a very prominent family in France. No matter what his feelings were, he never would've been permitted to have a gay lover."

Joel kissed Ethan's shoulder nervously.

"So, what are you saying?" Joel asked.

"Lucien has never really loved me," Kyoko said. "Not the way he loved Ethan." She lifted her eyes to study Ethan's face. "Not the way he still loves you. I'm sorry he never told you the truth about his feelings, but he thought it would be kinder to break it off clean."

"Kinder? How could he do that to me? He should've told me—" Ethan's breath caught and he paused. "He could've told me he loved me—but that we couldn't be together. At least I would've known the truth." He pulled his knees up and brusquely wiped away the tears streaming down his face. "Fuck, I suffered, Kyoko. I cried for months over him. I tried to kill myself …twice."

He grasped Joel's hand in his own and brought it to his lips.

"I thought I'd never find love like that again," he added.

Joel rested his head against Ethan's shoulder and squeezed his hand reassuringly. "I think you should go talk to him."

"Why? I don't want to see him," Ethan said.

"Ethan, you need to hear this from him," Joel replied. "It's the only way you're going to know for sure that he really felt that way—that he really feels that way."

"What difference does it make? I'm with you now."

"The difference is that you're always going to have that doubt hanging over your head, wondering if he really loved you. The pain he caused you will always be a part of who you are, but so should the love he felt for you. You deserve that."

"God, I love you so much, babe." Ethan pulled Joel to him, buried his face in Joel's hair, and kissed him.

Joel reached over and grabbed Ethan's phone, then handed it to him. "Get his number off Kyoko. Phone him. Meet up with him. Please, do it for me. I want you whole and unencumbered when I take you as my husband."

David stood up at the head of the table and tapped his glass to get everyone's attention. He cleared his throat and smiled over at his son and his fiancé.

"Thank you all for coming tonight," David began. "We are gathered here tonight, as a family, to celebrate the love between two very special people." He paused. "My son, Ethan hasn't had it easy. He lost his mother at a very young age and never fully recovered, in my opinion, because he inherited the same generous and fragile spirit she once embodied. But then he met Joel." He beamed over at Joel. "And I have witnessed an amazing transformation in Ethan—from the sullen, suffering, and broken man he once was, into this joyful and confident man you see before you today."

David raised his glass and waited for the rest of the table to rise with glasses in hand. "To Joel, who had the courage and the insight to see beyond the walls my son had built for himself. And to Ethan, for recognizing his true worth through the eyes of this man that loves him." He smiled and drank as the rest of the family agreed with his sentiment and toasted the couple.

Ethan pushed his chair back, stood, and cleared his throat.

"I want to thank you all for being here to support Joel and me," he said and took a deep breath to calm himself. "My dad is right. It hasn't been easy for me over the years, but not necessarily for the reasons he outlined. The world is slowly becoming a more tolerant place for those in love, and for that, I'm hopeful. But it is still a difficult path for a gay man to walk in this society." He looked down at Joel and motioned for him to stand up. "But my dad was entirely right about Joel's courage. He could've coasted through life without drawing prejudice, but he chose to follow his heart instead …and miraculously his heart felt I was worthy of its love." He pulled Joel to him as Joel began to tear up. "I love you, Joel."

Joel sighed, trying to catch his breath, as he tried to fan the tears from escaping "I don't know what to say. This is all too much." He exhaled deeply and composed himself. "I'm overwhelmed by the love and warmth of this family. My new family." He smiled over at David. "As some of you may know my own family doesn't support my relationship with Ethan. In fact, they refuse to accept that I'm gay. They honestly believe I'll outgrow it." He paused as a few people laughed, and then he smiled. "What they don't understand is that Ethan and I are connected on a spiritual level of profound proportions that has nothing to do with gender. And since the first day we met—" He grinned over at Ethan. "All right, the second day. He's inspired me to live each day with the honesty and integrity that my soul deserves, and for that I will be forever grateful to, and madly in love with him."

Ethan grinned widely as the table began tapping their glasses, and grabbed Joel, dipping him away from the table, to lay a sloppy kiss on him, to the cheers of his family. It was mushy, but it felt good having his family excited for him and Joel.

David clapped his hands loudly to get everyone's attention back. "As you all know, we will be holding a very special ceremony here on Saturday for Ethan and Joel, but Ethan has made some special arrangements for some very special people."

Joel eyed Ethan quizzically, then burst out laughing when he heard someone whooping loudly from the foyer.

"No fucking way," he said. "You didn't!"

"Yeah, I flew them out for you," Ethan said as he struggled away from the table so he could pulled Joel's seat out for him. "Jocelyn wanted to come too, but your parents wouldn't let her. I'm sorry. She sends her love though." He followed Joel into the foyer, where they were met by an exuberant Ryan and Max.

"Hey, congratulations you tattooed freaks," Ryan said as he pounded Joel affectionately on the back.

Max reached out and shook both their hands, then clapped his hands together gleefully. "So, when's the bachelor party?"

"Tonight works," Ethan replied. "I might be able to scare up a few of my old buddies, but if not, we could bring William."

He cocked an eyebrow at Joel, making Joel snort and collapse in on himself, laughing hysterically.

"Who the fuck is William?" Max asked.

"Only the most obnoxious toff you'll ever come across," Joel replied as he gasped for breath. "Damn. Here he comes."

William walked straight past them.

"Yikes," Matt said.

"Yup." Joel nodded.

"So, have you guys put your stuff up in your rooms yet?" Ethan inquired after William had left the foyer.

"Yeah. Once we finally found them. This place is fucking huge," Ryan said. "How many bedrooms does it have?"

"I don't know. Twenty or so, I think," Ethan answered, then headed back toward the dining room. "I'm going to thank everyone and tell my dad we're going out for the night."

"What about Lucien?" Joel asked. "Aren't you supposed to meet him in half an hour?"

"Maybe he could come with us," Ryan said, and then crunched up his face when a look of pain crossed Ethan's face. "Did I say the wrong thing? Who is Lucien?"

"No," Ethan said. "It's all right. I just need to talk to him alone." He kissed Joel on the cheek. "I'll head over to his hotel now. Take the guys to the *Lion's Head* pub in town. I'll meet you there."

"All right," Joel replied quietly. "I love you."

"I love you too." Ethan kissed Joel again. "I'll see you in a bit."

Joel watched Ethan walk out the front door, then lowered his head, his heart was racing out of control. He reminded himself that he had to trust in the love they shared together.

"Who's Lucien?" Max asked, concerned about Joel's sudden change in demeanor.

"He's Ethan's first love," Joel said, and turned to face his friends. "For years he thought Lucien had just used him, but today he found out Lucien has been in love with him all along."

"Why is he going to see him?" Ryan asked.

"He needs to hear Lucien tell him he loves him," Joel answered. "And then he needs to choose between us."

"Joel?" Ryan said. "Why are you letting him do this?"

"Because I love him." Joel rubbed at his eyes, then sighed. "He's still in love with Lucien though. I can see it in his eyes."

"And you're just letting him go to him?" Max exclaimed.

"I have to."

"I'll never understand the way your mind works," Ryan said.

"It'll be all right, whatever he decides. As long as he's happy." Joel patted each of his friends on the shoulder. "I'm going to tell his dad we're heading out."

Ethan stood outside Lucien's hotel room door and just stared at the shiny number on its surface. He thought about what Kyoko had told him, and wondered if she had said anything to Lucien about their conversation. When he'd texted Lucien earlier in the day, he'd just stated that they needed to talk.

He rubbed his hand across his face, wondering if it had been a mistake agreeing to meet him in his hotel room rather than the lounge downstairs. He had conceded to Lucien's suggestion because he wanted Lucien to feel he could be completely honest with him, and he didn't think a busy lounge was the appropriate place for that to happen. In a village as small as this, a man professing his love to another would draw attention.

Knocking lightly, Ethan waited, and his heart skipped a beat when Lucien opened the door and smiled shyly at him.

"Bonjour, mon amour," Lucien said.

Ethan sighed and shook his head. "Lucien …don't."

He followed Lucien into the room and shut the door behind him.

"Don't what?" Lucien turned to face Ethan and trapped him against the wall. "Don't do this." He held Ethan's face and passionately attacked his mouth, drawing Ethan in to the familiarity and longing. "Or this, mon cheri." His hand circled around Ethan's body and pulled him against his hips, and then he deepened the kiss.

Ethan closed his eyes, his knees becoming weak beneath him, and moaned softly as Lucien kissed a path along his jaw line to his ear.

His heart shivered in ecstasy as Lucien whispered that he loved him—and that he'd always loved him.

Ethan tried to keep Joel fixed in his mind, but was finding it increasingly difficult to resist the man he'd never forgotten; a man he now knew loved him after all — a man he'd been willing to take his life for.

"Or this," Ethan said, stripping his shirt off over his head before pushing Lucien toward the bed.

Joel sat and stared at the walls of the pub and tortured himself occasionally by looking over toward the door. They had been there for hours and the bell had been rung for last call.

"Joel, I'm really sorry," Ryan said as he placed his arm around Joel's shoulders. "I don't think he's coming."

"No —" Joel shook his head emphatically. "No, he wouldn't do this to me." His hand hovered over his mouth as the realization that Ethan might not be coming washed over him. "No …no …no …he wouldn't leave me like this." He pushed Ryan away roughly. "Not like this …no …he wouldn't. Ethan loves me."

"Let's head back to the house." Ryan tucked his hand under Joel's elbow to help him up. "Max and I will grab your stuff and we'll find a hotel room for the night. Then we'll get you out of here on the first plane tomorrow."

"No, he'll come for me." Joel struggled out of Ryan's grasp and crossed his arms. "I'm going to wait here for him."

"They're closing up, Joel," Max said. "He's not coming."

"Shut the fuck up, Max," Joel said as tears began coating his cheeks. "He'll come for me. I just need to wait for him."

"Joel ..." Ryan touched Joel's shoulder, but removed his hand when he realized it was pointless. He felt completely helpless as he witnessed the heart being ripped from his friend's chest.

Joel slumped over in the corner of the booth and held his hand out so he could study the wedding ring Ethan had tattooed there. Then he pulled up the sleeve of his shirt to let his gaze wander over the stars that stretched from his wrist all the way up past his shoulder. They'd run out of room on his left arm and were working their way across the upper part of his back, with the intention of continuing down the other arm, interspersing stars with the other designs.

"He really loved me," Joel said as he pulled his phone from his pocket and stared at it. He'd promised himself he wouldn't phone Ethan—but he needed to hear his voice. It was the only thing that could comfort him right now. Even if that voice was telling him he wasn't coming back to him. He just needed to hear it one last time, and then he'd go. He brushed the tears from his cheeks and waited for Ethan to pick up.

"Hiya, Joel," Ethan said after far too many rings.

"Hey, Ethan." Joel shuddered. "The pub is closing."

"I know. I'm so sorry."

Joel fell over on the seat of the booth and wrapped his arms over his head as he listened to Ethan breathing on the other end. Then he had the distinct sensation of his insides collapsing when he heard Ethan hang up. Curling himself into a ball, he began wailing in anguish, regretting the day he'd ever laid eyes on Ethan.

Max leaped up to comfort Joel but immediately ended up stepping out of the way when Ethan raced up to the booth, fell in beside Joel, and covered him protectively.

"Shh …hey," Ethan whispered as he stroked Joel's hair. "Everything is all right. I'm here." He gripped Joel's chin to lift his face, but Joel refused. "Fuck, I'm sorry. I should've called you."

"He's been going out of his head waiting for you," Ryan said as he placed his hand on Joel's back and tried to soothe the tears that were still flowing. "He thought you'd abandoned him."

"I'm so sorry, Joel," Ethan said. "I wasn't thinking. Things got a bit intense with Lucien. I lost track of time—"

"Things got intense?" Joel lifted his head and sniffed loudly. "What kind of intense? Did you sleep with him?"

"Could we have a minute, guys?" Ethan looked at Ryan and Max and then waited for them to leave.

"What happened, Ethan?" Joel asked.

"I met Lucien in his hotel room. We kissed—and he told me he loved me. And I *almost* slept with him." Ethan brushed his thumb across Joel's cheek and wiped the last of the tears away.

"What stopped you?"

"My love for you." Ethan kissed Joel's head and closed his eyes. "When Lucien pushed me onto the bed and started hauling my pants off—" He held Joel tighter as he felt him cringe. "I want to be honest with you about what happened."

"I know." Joel shivered. "Go ahead."

"I looked down and saw the pink heart on my stomach, and I read the words you'd placed in it, *Ethan loves Joel forever*, and the love I'd been holding on to for Lucien, for all those years, just evaporated, and I realized what I'd felt for him was nothing in comparison to what I feel for you."

"So, if you didn't sleep with him, what was so intense that it took you forever to get here?"

Ethan laughed. "Poor Lucien had to sit through a very long telling of my love affair with you." He stroked Joel's face and tried to read his expression. "What can I say? We laughed. We cried. It took forever. Joel…, please tell me you forgive me."

"Of course I forgive you. I know how much Lucien meant to you. It must've been overwhelming to hear him say he loved you."

"It was. But not as overwhelming as the day you first told me you loved me. It just took a second for me to realize that."

"So, everything is good between the two of you?"

Ethan looked over his shoulder and motioned for Lucien, who'd been standing by the door, to join them. "He has something he wants to share with you. He insisted. I'll translate for you."

Lucien approached the table and bowed his head to Joel, and then began to speak. He spoke of the depth of love Ethan had expressed in his telling of their love affair, and how he'd been moved to let his feelings for Ethan go, so Ethan's spirit would be unencumbered to pair with Joel's in what he felt was a predestined intertwining of two souls that would survive the ravages of time for all eternity.

"I love you, Ethan," Joel said after Lucien was finished. "I want to spend the rest of my life with you, and only you. But if you ever give me a heart attack like that again ..."

Ethan brushed his lips against Joel's and basked in the soft warmth of Joel's breath as it fused with his own. "Never," he said between their shared inhalations. "Those stars on your arm reflect the stars in my heart for you. You're my forever love." He caressed his fingers along the curve of Joel's throat and kissed him.

About the Author

Leigh Jarrett is a queer, quirky, and passionate author of LGBTQ Romantic Fiction. Lover of antique stores, the smell of lye and oil as it turns to soap, and the awe-inspiring majesty of the ancient Douglas firs of Vancouver Island's Cathedral Grove.

In her hometown of Kelowna, BC, Leigh can be found nestled up with her fabulously supportive wife, her trusty laptop, and their persistent treat seeker, Miss Mimi-dog.

Please consider joining Leigh's mailing list:
http://eepurl.com/xuhej

To connect with Leigh Jarrett:
Email: leigh@leighjarrett.com
Website: www.leighjarrett.com
You can also find Leigh on Facebook and Twitter

SIMPLY MARVELLOUS

TEKLA SERIES

Annie Luka has always been home-schooled, but she's convinced her mother to let her attend public school for her graduating year. When it is learned that Annie Luka is actually Attila Luka, a beautiful cross-gender guy struggling with his identity, it tears a small group of friends apart. Only when they all reunite years later is the full extent of Attila's deception revealed, bringing some of the group closer together, and pushing others further apart.

What transpires over the next few years after the reunion leaves Attila wondering if he'll ever find true love.

TWO NIGHTS A WEEK

TEKLA SERIES

Chad Parker, the privileged son of a wealthy hotelier, has made the decision to transfer to Tekla Senior High for his graduating year. Events during the summer have made it far too dangerous for him to remain at his old school.

But on the very first day, he meets Derek Steeple, and finds himself in precisely the same situation, except this time, the consequences of his actions will forever change the lives of those he loves.

Other Books by Leigh Jarrett

Drakkar Coven Series

Callum of Drakkar Coven

Oleander, Son of Drakkar

Alexander, Prince of the North (Coming soon!)

Shadows On My Soul

Possession Pointe

Healing Hands of E'lan